CW00863485

CIA
£2.49
(

Copyright © Claire Smith 2015

The right of Claire Smith to be identified as the author of this work has been asserted in accordance with the Copyright, Designs and Patents Act 1988.

For Lisa
For dedication as a sister above and beyond the call of
duty.

C. xxx

CROSSED STEELE

(STORM SERIES #2)

CLAIRE SMITH

~CHAPTER ONE~

"Tell me you have a plan to get us out of this mess Bruce?" Senator Raymond Cabot demanded, nursing a large balloon of cognac as he paced the plush office belonging to Bruce Harrison, majority shareholder and CEO of the multi-billion dollar Harrison Oil Corporation.

"Which particular mess would that be Ray?" Bruce raised an eyebrow at the soon to be ex-senator. "The Abigail Storm mess or the Gabon mess?"

"Well, as they're related then both I guess although I was really just thinking about the situation that Storm bitch has caused."

"To be fair Senator, I think Aaron Steele should probably bare most of the blame for causing your current situation. If he hadn't been so perverse in his ways everything would have more than likely gone to plan."

"What do you mean 'my situation', surely you mean *our* situation?" Senator Cabot glared at Harrison.

"Not at all Ray, I mean what I say. Sure Ms Storm's article has forced me to change my plans, which is inconvenient and somewhat annoying but hardly the end of the world, but it hasn't caused any further disruption to my life."

"You're not even angry with her?" Cabot could not believe what he was hearing. Harrison's reputation as a ruthless businessman seemed, at this moment, to be unwarranted.

"Angry? No, she was a good reporter in the making, she got wind of a story and she pursued it. No Ray, I'm not angry with her, I am however, way past angry with Aaron Steele!" Harrison hissed through clenched teeth, even the mention of the man's name caused him heartburn these days. "If he hadn't been such a sexual deviant it's likely everything about my exceptionally well thought out and carefully executed plan would still be on track."

"But she's the one who wrote the damn article, even if it was him who first went public with it! Now my presidential ambitions are down the toilet, I'm having to stand down as a senator and to cap it all even Eden..." He stopped abruptly as he realised what he had been about to say and to whom.

"Eden what Raymond?" Bruce regarded the senator coldly. "What were you about to say about my daughter?"

"I...er...nothing." Cabot stared resolutely into his brandy wishing he had kept his mouth shut.

"Oh, don't be so coy Ray, save your denials for the House! I've known all along about your affair with Eden." He chuckled as Cabot's cheeks flushed and a wary look spread across the senator's face.

"What...what do you mean?"

"She told me when it started. I encouraged her to keep seeing you in fact. Had you ever proved reluctant to keep to our agreement she would have been perfect leverage. As it was, we hadn't needed her so far, but had you achieved the Presidency who knows what might have come up in the future." He added with an obviously sarcastic but benevolent smile, "All irrelevant now though, the only way you're ever going to see the inside of the White House again is if you buy a ticket for the public tour."

As far as Bruce Harrison was concerned Senator Raymond Cabot was now more of a liability than an asset with his presidential aspirations now wholly and completely destroyed. As President of the USA and as such, arguably, leader of the free world he would have been an invaluable person to know and an even more useful puppet to be used as Bruce saw fit. That possibility was now well and truly out of reach.

However, so far Harrison had avoided too much public scrutiny in the wake of the Abigail Storm story and he wanted, or rather, needed to keep it that way. Fortunately the Senator too could not afford deeper investigations and so the allegations of his affair with his daughter-in-law had not been too vehemently denied prior to the announcement of his withdrawal from public life. A public split now between the Senator and one of his most ardent supporters might look to the outside world as an admission that Ms Storm's speculations may have actually carried some weight. As it was, Harrison's publicly known involvement was not criminal in any way, merely supportive of a potential presidential candidate. Should anyone, the FBI for example, care to dig deeper he was sure his planning and involvement thus far in Gabon, a small resources rich sub-Saharan state in West Africa, together with his plans to get his pet President to lie to both Congress and the Senate to further his business interests, would land him and the

Senator in some very hot water, despite any and all attempts he had made to cover his tracks.

For the time being therefore he and Raymond remained friends, publicly at least and conversely their joint business venture in Gabon was still as live as it was secret.

Privately however, he was finding it increasingly difficult to tolerate the egotistical son of a bitch.

"Anyway, it's unimportant now.   If Eden has dropped you she has probably realised the affair can now only hurt her socially if you are no longer headed for the Presidency. Can't say I blame her." He concluded with finality.

"I thought she cared about me..." Cabot whined, a sullen, dejected look on his face.

Harrison chuckled and shook his head, he knew his daughter well and she was as socially astute as it was possible to be. The only reason she had an affair with Cabot was because it gave her greater social standing than that provided by already being married to his son.   To be the President's daughter-in-law was prestigious but to be his mistress as well would have sent her influential status into the stratosphere.   She would have been courted by every rich and powerful man in Washington and beyond, just to get her to mention them when they needed something from Mr President himself. She would have been in a position to persuade her lover to make or break people according to her will. The absolute hypocrisy of Washington society never ceased to amaze him. Had Cabot gained the Presidency everyone would have known about him and Eden, obviously nobody would ever have said anything out loud and any suspicions her husband harboured would have been vehemently denied, but Michael's rise through the ranks in the law firm would have been meteoric. In direct contrast, even just the unsupported and totally unproven hint of impropriety as a presidential candidate had completely ended Raymond's political career.

Now, he was just an over the hill politician with nowhere to go but down. He had been good looking in his prime but at sixty two he was almost completely grey and his growing paunch was evidence of too many long political lunches and not enough time in the gym.

Eden's only hope now, she had confided to her father only a few days before, was to encourage Michael, her husband and Raymond Cabot's eldest son, into politics and see if he had the potential to succeed where his father had failed. Being First Lady may take some years to achieve but socially it was the jackpot.

"Enough." Harrison held up a hand to stop Cabot from continuing his self-pitying whine. "We have important things to discuss."

"You're a hard man Bruce." Cabot grumbled, shifting in his seat, "I guess that's where Eden gets it from."

"I'm a businessman Ray and sometimes business gets tough. Now, all the agitation we stirred up in Gabon is having the desired effect. Civil unrest is brewing daily, however, now that we are not going to be able to send the peacekeeping troops in and therefore take charge of the situation, we're going to have to change plans and change them fast." He paused while he judged Cabot's reaction, but as ever he apparently failed to grasp the problem. "Raymond, a civil war in Gabon was only advantageous to us if we had boots on the ground, and, more importantly, control of those boots on the ground! Even if Obama was to send in the troops, unlikely now as I doubt Gabon would ask for US help without nudges from us, we would have no control of them." He paused again, this time gratified to see at least some spark of understanding in Cabot's eyes. "Therefore, it's now better for us if the unrest is managed locally until we can regroup and rethink our strategy. I'm wondering whether directing the unrest at our competitors might have the desired effect."

"How so?" Cabot had roused himself from the self-pity induced by the memories of Eden and leaned forward indicating his attention was piqued.

"If we can arrange it so that the unrest and civil disobedience looks like it originates from projects managed by Sullivan Industries we could manoeuver ourselves into a position whereby we could offer to step in and take over these 'problem' projects, with Gabonese Government approval, and restore order."

Cabot began to grin, "Legitimate control of the oil fields and vastly more lucrative other natural resources?"

"Absolutely!"

"Sullivan won't take it lying down though." Added Cabot who was now deep in thought. "In fact, it would take something seriously critical to get the Gabonese government to agree to oust him, I mean, he may be making millions..."

"Billions I should think." Corrected Harrison.

"...OK, billions, but he's also doing the country a lot of good. He'd be difficult to unseat is all I'm saying." Cabot stared at Harrison as if to weight his point.

"I agree, although Gabon's President is more easily swayed by money than by local economic benefits." Harrison swirled the last of his brandy around in his glass as he spoke. "And Sullivan will definitely seek to dampen things down, especially if he gets wind of us waiting to step in."

"Perhaps we need to divert his attention elsewhere then." Cabot suggested quietly.

"How so?"

"Well...there's always the girl." Replied Cabot with a half raised eyebrow and a hint of a smirk around the corners of his mouth.

"The girl?" Harrison was momentarily confused but quickly realised Cabot's expression could mean only one thing, "You mean the Storm girl?" He was intrigued, "Go on."

"It would appear Sullivan has a thing for the lovely Ms Storm. Apparently, so rumour has it, it was him and his sidekick who pulled her away from Steele's perverted clutches."

"Really? There's no mention of him in the pre-trial reporting." Harrison was sceptical.

"No, but the witness they have under wraps who can allegedly corroborate her story of kidnap and such, as he claims to have rescued her from the apartment himself is, I am lead to believe, Frank Molloy." Cabot stated with a wry smile. Both he and Harrison knew if Frank was involved then Sullivan could not have been far away.

"If he's 'under wraps' as you put it, how do we know this is true?"

"I got it from the investigating officer in charge, obviously strictly hush hush."

"Interesting." Agreed Harrison. "I wonder what connection he has to her."

"No idea but I doubt it's purely altruistic, I mean, he didn't just happen to find out she needed help now did he? He's not clairvoyant or anything, they were on different continents for Christ's sake. Therefore, he must have had somebody looking out for her and the only reason I can think of for him doing that for some lowly wedding reporter is because she means something to him." He concluded adding, "It doesn't even matter what she is to him, just that fact she means something is enough to use her." Cabot delivered his conclusion with an air of finality, hoping Harrison agreed with his deductions.

"You're probably right there Ray, certainly it would suggest some significant connection but unfortunately we can't do anything to Abigail Storm." Harrison replied with a rueful smile, "We'd be suspect numbers one and two if anything happened to her now Steele's behind bars."

"Hmmm..." Cabot mused, "Shame Steele won't be free anytime soon."

"You can forget Steele too, he hasn't even got a lawyer at the moment, nobody wants to touch the case, and if he has to defend himself, well, you and I both know how much he'll suck at that! The man is as much of a liability to himself as he was to those women. I wouldn't be surprised if, when he's found guilty on all charges, the judge just locks him up and throws away the key."

"Still...it's a shame though." Cabot repeated. "I'm quite sure if he was free he'd go after the lovely Ms Storm, providing us with just the distraction we need. Oh well, no mileage there, we'll just have to think of something else." He raised his glass in salute to Harrison before draining the last of its contents. "I suggest you instruct our agitators in Africa to make calming noises for a while until we come up with another way to distract Mr Sullivan and his lackey. No point letting them get all flustered until we're ready to act." He added as he stood to leave, retrieving his coat from the stand as he spoke. "I'll be in touch in the next few days, or sooner if I have any other great ideas about distracting our friend."

Harrison watched as the soon to be ex-Senator Raymond Cabot strode purposefully from his office, knowing he had just been given an instruction but undecided whether to be furious or impressed with the diplomacy of the command.

Shrugging to work out the kinks in his shoulders he shook his head at the audacity of ex-senator Cabot then, he reached for the telephone and placed a call, wondering as he did so whether the plan his mind was busy forming was indeed possible without any attention falling on himself.

~CHAPTER TWO~

"I'm sorry Mr Harrison, no matter how much money you are willing to throw at this, what you are asking for is impossible." An impeccably dressed, clean shaven man in his forties addressed the CEO from his seat across the coffee table. Between them a tray of coffees and biscuits remained untouched.

"Mr Marchant, or, may I call you James?" Bruce Harrison paused to see James Marchant nod deferentially. "I am told you are one of the best in the business, hence your exorbitant hourly rate, and yet you tell me you can't do what I ask?"

"Actually Bruce, I assume I may call you Bruce? I'm telling you it's not possible, hence, nobody can do it." James did not pause for permission to be casual.

James Marchant was a lawyer of some considerable standing. His law firm had represented many very rich and some very famous clients over the years and had, in his humble opinion, performed many miraculous feats, both in court and out, to secure those clients' acquittals from charges many had apparently been guilty of. As a defence lawyer his job was to exploit the grey areas in the prosecution's case. After all, reasonable doubt was all he needed to force a jury to acquit. In this case however, the one or two grey areas he could use were spectacularly eclipsed by the other areas which were very definitely very, very black.

"But, there must be a way to get him out." Bruce demanded forcefully, then seeing the mild shock on James Marchant's face he added. "He's a very good friend of mine you see, I hate the fact he's locked up in that place." He had no real desire to lie to the lawyer in front of him but felt some subterfuge was necessary in case he ever had to defend this action.

If at some point in the future he was vilified for being a friend of the monster who was Aaron Steele, he felt it would be far less harmful to his liberty than the knowledge he had helped secure this man's release for exactly the purpose a freed Aaron Steele would serve.

"Let's look at the facts as we know them shall we Bruce." James said patiently, "I could muddy the waters enough to get all the rape charges to appear false, he may have depraved sexual tendencies but all the women consented etc etc. The kidnapping charge should be fairly easy to discredit as Ms Storm has absolutely no recollection of the events and the only witness to the alleged kidnapping is Frank Molloy who, I am positive is hiding something and who I am sure I can unsettle on the stand. So we are left with two other charges. With the alleged first victim, Ms Foster, again the rape, anal sex etc can be presented as having been with her consent however, when Mr Steele subsequently tried unsuccessfully to catheterise her and permanently damaged both her urethra and her uterus, instead of taking her to the ER when he had torn her rectum during said anal sex, are undisputable medical facts. In short, there is nothing I can say to justify these actions.

So at the very least Mr Steele will be found guilty on this charge."

"You said two charges were left?"

"Yes, the attempted murder of Ms Storm in her hospital bed. As far as evidence goes it's all fairly damning, Steele was found on the floor of her room, covered in her blood, next to a scalpel with his fingerprints on whilst Ms Storm had been tied up and Ms Winters had been drugged. I'm certain Steele would be found guilty of at least assault in this case, it's possible I could muddy the waters as to his intent so attempted murder may not stick." Marchant delivered his assessment with the confidence of a man who knew his job well.

"Would it have to be a custodial sentence? Is there any possibility it could be suspended?" Bruce asked even though he felt he already knew the answer.

"Given the severity of the injuries to Ms Foster and the fact that the judge will be less inclined to agree with the jury's verdicts on all the other charges I think you can expect Mr Steele to receive the maximum sentence allowable." James confirmed what he could tell Harrison already knew.

"Which is?"

"Anything from 10 years to life."

"Shit!" Harrison exclaimed.

"Personally, Mr Harrison, having read the charges and evidence in this case, and having met the man at your request, I'd be inclined to chalk up your 'friendship' to bad experience and walk away. I'd say he is guilty on all counts and deserves to go to prison for a very long time."

"But you will still represent him?"

"As long as he wants me to represent him and you continue to pay my fees I will do my job Mr Harrison and I will do it to the best of my abilities. My suggestion would be for him to plea bargain with the prosecutor's office, if I can do a deal with them and get him to plead guilty to just the charges we definitely can't win then it's possible he may get the minimum sentence of ten years, it's also possible then to get him into a minimum, or at least medium, security facility, certainly a more comfortable way to spend his incarceration."

"Well, thank you for your candour James, for the record I will continue to pay your fees and I concur, a plea bargain may be the best way forward but I'll leave it to you to try to persuade your client." He stood, indicating the meeting was over, "One last thing, as I mentioned on the telephone, Mr Steele is a proud man, he would not accept such help as I am offering by paying you, I would therefore be grateful if he was never aware of this fact."

"As you are paying the bills then technically you are also the client Mr Harrison, client confidentiality is therefore yours. I will keep you informed." The two men shook hands as James Marchant headed out the way he had entered some half hour earlier.

Closing the door after the retreating lawyer Bruce returned to the chair behind his desk, he was deep in thought. It had already taken ten years of his life to get to the position he was in. He had spent a good deal of time and money grooming Senator Cabot for the presidency, only to be thwarted at the last minute by Aaron Steele's sexual perversions and an unknown reporter called Abigail Storm. His buyers were expecting initial deliveries within the next twelve months, there was no way they would wait ten years until Aaron Steele was out of prison in order to run interference for Harrison Oil Corporation in Gabon.

Ten years ago when he had started this venture he had known he could not unseat Sullivan Industries by legitimate means. No amount of negotiating with the Gabonese Government was going to win him the drilling and mining contracts he needed. So he had backed Senator Cabot for the Presidency. It may have been an audacious plan but right up until a few weeks ago it had been working like a dream. The Senator had been inches away from securing the republican vote for his candidacy to run for President in next years' elections.

Only Aaron Steele's greed and sickening sexual perversions together with the audacity and ingenuity of a lowly wedding reporter had blown all his plans sky high. Instead of getting himself in a position within the news media world where he could help Senator Cabot's presidential campaign, Aaron Steele had landed himself in prison, tarnishing the reputation of the Senator irreparably in the process and effectively ending both the Senator's political career and Harrison's well laid plans.

With the President of the USA in his pocket he could have demanded any drilling rights he wanted, even taken them by force if necessary but now he was going to have to get them by other means.

Abigail Storm was an unfortunate pawn in this game, ordinarily he would have felt sorry for her, especially after reading what Aaron Steele had done to her but, if she was somehow connected to Sullivan, better still if she were connected in a romantic way, then she was the obvious choice as a target to distract Sullivan while Harrison got what he needed from Gabon.

But with Steele not getting out of prison any time soon he was going to have to be careful how he orchestrated any plan which involved Ms Storm, as he had pointed out to Ray Cabot, they would be first on the list of suspects if anything untoward happened to her. Even cast iron alibis would do no good, investigators would merely assume he or Cabot had paid others to do their dirty work and they would be correct in their assumption. He doubted it would take any decent FBI agent too long to make the necessary connections.

As he pondered the problem a glimmer of an idea started to form in his overactive imagination.

"*What if...?*" He thought as he reached for the intercom button. "Felicity?" He said, calling his secretary from the office beyond his door.

"Yes Mr Harrison?" Came the immediate if disembodied reply through his telephone console.

"Get me Burt Tomasino from BTM Securities please Felicity." Bruce said with the makings of a smile starting to play around the corners of his mouth.

"On the telephone Mr Harrison?"

"No, I want to see him in person, try and get him here sometime today please, rearrange anything you need to." Bruce answered, severing the connection.

He sat back in his chair and smiled, the perfect solution now a fully formed idea if not quite yet a distinct possibility.

~CHAPTER THREE~

Abigail Storm, known to her friends as Abi, was sitting on the floor surrounded by packing boxes. It had been three months since she had left Boston, three months since that ridiculous suicide attempt had landed her in a hospital bed where she had been helpless against Aaron Steele's endeavour to first rape her then kill her. If it hadn't been for John, sneaking around like the milk tray man, who nobody but she believed was there anyway, the outcome would have been so very different.

She looked down at the letter in her left hand and then at the cheque in her right hand, still not quite believing what she was seeing. Not only had John sent her a cheque for some £148,500 which, he claimed was the profit he had made after selling her grandmother's house to pay off her parents' debt to him, he had said sending it was a matter of conscience.

"But gangsters don't have consciences." She said aloud despite being alone, turning the letter over to read his words again. "For that matter, gangsters don't fly across the Atlantic to rescue women they hardly know, twice!" She couldn't help but chuckle at the thought as she re-read the last paragraph of his letter,

"Have dinner with me at least?   Maybe I can persuade you I'm not the monster you think I am..."

But that had been a fortnight ago, she reflected as she put the finishing touches to her hair and make-up. Now she was actually going to have dinner with a man of whom her last fully cognitive memory was of having her parents, possibly justifiably, tied up and herself, unjustifiably in her opinion, in fear of her life. She discounted the dim recollection she may or may not have had from her hospital bed as even if it had been him, she had hardly been in any fit state to judge his intentions towards her, despite her vague recollection of him blowing her a kiss as he left her room.

Therefore, it had been with considerable trepidation that she had accepted his invitation to dinner. Regardless of his gangster status she felt she at least owed him this, he had rescued her from the apartment where Aaron had her tied up and drugged after he had stolen her story about Senator Cabot and his daughter-in-law. She knew for a fact John and Frank had saved her life that night so, gangster or not, John had earned dinner with her, if only to give her chance to thank him.

A tentative knock at the door told her the car, sent by John at his absolute insistence, had arrived. She threw a cashmere wrap over her simple blue and purple wiggle dress, hoping she was neither under or over dressed, and headed for the door.

She was pleasantly surprised to find her driver for the night was Frank. She had spoken to him briefly in Boston when he had offered himself as a witness to her ordeal at the hands of Aaron Steele. She had found him quite endearing at the time in a slightly scary gangster's sidekick sort of way, even though she had been in a dark and difficult place herself.

"Good Evening Frank." She smiled at him as she stepped out of the house, turning to lock the door behind her.

"Evening Miss Storm." Frank replied quietly, he was obviously surprised she remembered his name. He had thought their meeting too brief and her too distraught for her to have such recollection. Offering her his arm he walked her down the drive to the waiting car.

"Thank you Frank." Abi said as she climbed into the car.

"Welcome, Miss Storm." Frank replied with a smile and a bob of his head.

"It's just Abi, Frank, Miss Storm makes me feel like a teacher or something." She said with a giggle.

"Won't be right Miss." Frank shook his head but said nothing further as he closed the door behind her and wandered round to the driver's door.

Frank did not speak again on the short trip into Manchester's Chinatown where Abi was to meet John. For her part Abi tried to reconcile the thug and gangsters sidekick she knew Frank must be with the courteous and deferential driver she had now met twice.

As she descended the steps into the small but cosy looking Chinese restaurant she immediately saw John at a table near the back. As soon as he saw her he jumped to his feet and pulled out a chair for her to sit on. The waiter took her wrap and poured the ready chilled champagne John had obviously pre-arranged.

"Good evening Abigail." John said with a smile, "Or, may I call you Abi? I hear that's what you prefer."

"Good evening." She replied trying hard to swallow the butterflies threatening to jump out of her stomach and into her throat. "Abi is fine, thank you."

"Do I really make you this nervous Abi?" John enquired with a slightly wicked grin. Apparently he could read her thoughts Abi was somewhat dismayed to learn. She had thought she was managing to hide the tumultuous feelings inside her. She had no idea whether to be terrified, excited or just plain embarrassed knowing the states this man had already seen her in. She decided to ignore the question and tried to divert his attention elsewhere.

"I told Frank he could call me Abi too," she began, "But he said for some reason it wouldn't be right."

"Ahh, yes, that's Frank for you. He's called me Boss since the day we met, when I was ten years old. Won't call me anything else despite the fact we've been friends from that day to this."

"That reminds me." She said, daring to look straight at him for the first time. "What would he call you if not 'Boss'?"

"Oh, I was hoping you might have forgotten I half promised to tell you my real name." He said with what looked to Abi to be a slight but definite blush.

"How could I forget? I need to know what to call you?" Abi replied so very logically he had to chuckle.

"OK, first of all, you can call me John. It kind of is and isn't my real name but it is the name I use, well, professionally at least." He said enigmatically.

Abi wasn't going to let him off that lightly, "Go on." She prompted.

"No laughing!" He said, wagging a warning finger at her.

"*As if I'd dare!*" She thought, but managed to make "Wouldn't dream of it." Come out of her mouth instead.

"My full name, the one you will find on my passport is…" he looked up at her as if willing her to tell him it didn't matter. When she made no such move he took a deep breath and said. "Sean Padraig Seamus O'Sullivan the fifth!"

Unfortunately Abi had taken that moment to sample the champagne and very nearly choked on the bubbles as she rapidly stifled a laugh, she clamped a hand over her mouth while she regained her composure.

"I guess you're Irish Mancunian then?" She managed eventually, after she was sure the giggle in her throat had gone back down.

"I told you not to laugh." He replied, as seriously as he could under the circumstances.

"I'm not laughing." Abi declared, although she knew the giggle was still dancing in her eyes, she could see it reflected in his. "No wonder you prefer to use 'John' then."

"Well, John is English for Sean, so John is my name, in English at least."

"And 'the fifth'? There are more of you then?"

"There have been, no longer though, my father died last year. He was Sean Padraig Seamus O'Sullivan the fourth. And my grandfather…"

"The third?" Abi interrupted with a smile, her nerves starting to dissipate a little.

"Exactly!" He grinned.

"And the second and first?" She asked with raised eyebrows "Great and Great, great grandfathers by any chance?"

"So now you want my whole family history do you?" He said trying to look stern and affronted. He failed, his eyes danced with mirth.

"Well, you did say you were going to prove to me you are not a monster, your family history would seem like a good place to start." She said, hoping she wasn't overstepping the mark, her instincts still told her this man was a gangster, even if her eyes were telling her he was fun, personable and sexy as hell.

"OK then, let's order and I can tell you the entire O'Sullivan family saga, as much as I know it, while we eat."

He held the menu open for her to see, "I suggest the banquet, unless there's anything on there you dislike?"

A quick scan down the banquet menu told Abi she loved almost every dish, apart from the couple she had never tried, although, there was so much of it she was starting to wish she'd worn a more forgiving dress, she was not going to be able to move after that lot. She hoped he had a good appetite.

"The banquet looks lovely." She smiled back at him. "Before we start, may I call you Sean? Or would you prefer I called you John?"

"I'd very much like you to call me Sean." He said quietly, his eyes smiling deeply at her.

After he had ordered and refilled her champagne, he loosened his tie, rested his chin on his hands and began to speak.

"In 1847, two years after the start of the Great Irish Famine, Mary O'Sullivan, a farmer's wife from somewhere near Cork, put her last remaining child on a boat headed for Boston, America. He was fifteen years old and the youngest of the eleven children Mary and

Padraig O'Sullivan had produced. The rest of the family had died of starvation and it seemed she was determined to give her last remaining son a chance. How she paid for his passage is unknown, she had nothing in the way of money and few possessions, but, somehow she managed to get Sean passage on the USS Jamestown's return to Boston." He paused to look up at Abi, she was enthralled, he had to force himself to tear his eyes away from hers and continue. "So, Sean Padraig Seamus O'Sullivan arrived in Boston at the tender age of fifteen with no money, no family and probably just the clothes on his back. Petty crime was the only way for such a lad to survive but survive he did, probably by running errands for the established crime families. Anyway, our Sean was something of a fighter it seemed and by 1859, twelve years after his arrival, he was head of a very successful extortion operation, making considerable sums of money and married to a delightful young lady by the name of Elizabeth." Sean paused while the waiters reorganised the table to make room for the first of their banquet courses. Abi took the opportunity to study him more closely, whilst he was distracted with the waiters and the food.

Sitting down she couldn't tell how tall he was but she had a vague recollection of him probably being a little over 6 feet. He had dark, thick, slightly unruly looking hair, greying elegantly at the temples. She guessed, despite the grey, he was probably not yet forty, although maybe not too far off. He was what is commonly termed as ruggedly handsome, clean shaven, impeccably dressed and with the most spectacular blue grey eyes Abi had ever come across. He exuded a calm confidence which Abi found both soothing and exciting in equal measures.

"Did I pass?" His question broke into her thoughts.

"Pass?" She repeated as innocently as she could manage.

"Your inspection." He stated, looking directly into her eyes.

Abi blushed scarlet, there was nothing she could say to that statement, she bit her bottom lip hard and stared pointedly at her plate.

"Don't worry." He chuckled, "You passed mine too!" He said offering her a pancake for her duck. "So, where was I?"

"Sean the first married Elizabeth." Abi prompted, glad he had changed the subject.

"Ah yes. 1859, Sean, now rich and his new wife Elizabeth made the journey back to Cork looking for his mother. He found the graves he had helped dig for his ten brothers and sisters and for his father but there was no trace of his mother. No records of her death could be found and nobody knew if she had moved elsewhere. When he left Cork for the last time he left money with a lawyer with instructions to find her but nothing ever came of it."

"How very sad. For her to never know she made the right decision to send her son away." Abi tried to imagine her pain but it was too great to envisage.

"Anyway, back in Boston the O'Sullivan's produced a son, Sean Padraig Seamus O'Sullivan the second, in 1861. Sean the third was born in 1903, Sean the forth, my father, in 1937 and then me Sean the fifth in 1976. So there you have it, how I come to be the fifth in line for the very Irish name!"

Abi chuckled, "But, you're Mancunian! As Mancunian as I am, granted your name couldn't get any more Irish if it tried but if you're Boston Irish how come you don't sound American?"

"Ah, well, Sean the second, back in the early 1900's had three sons, Sean, Ronan and Malachi. The eldest, Sean the third, was something of a rebel and decided, as all three couldn't inherit the family business he would emigrate from Boston to England, Manchester to be exact, and start a new business. So, by the time of the Second World War the three brothers were all running different parts of the family empire. Sean was head of the crime syndicate in Manchester, Ronan head of the Boston Crime business and youngest brother Malachi, having had nothing else to do, started a legitimate business in oil, coal, property, finance and anything else he could get a foot into. Although these legitimate businesses were probably all started on the back of the organised crime, once established they were very successful."

"And Sean the third is your grandfather?"

"Exactly!"

"OK, so that explains why you are Mancunian not Bostonian, but, forgive me for pointing it out, so far all you have proved is you are, as I suspected, a gangster, from a long line of gangsters. Or are you suggesting that as you inherited the '*gangsterness*' it doesn't really count?" She raised an eyebrow as she said it, hoping she came across as sarcastic but not too challenging.

"Gangsterness?" Sean was laughing now. "Is that even a word?"

"I don't think so." Abi couldn't help but laugh with him. "But you know what I mean."

"I do know what you mean Abi, but I haven't finished my story yet. I'm really not *gangsterish* at all, I promise you." He held up a hand to stop her as she made to interrupt, "If you can have gangsterness I can have gangsterish!"

Abi nodded her acquiescence. "Do go on then." She added, sipping champagne before delving into the new course of crab and sweetcorn soup which had just arrived.

"As I was saying, by the time World War Two started there were three brothers running three businesses. Unfortunately, all three brothers, having been born in the first decade of the century, were called up to fight in the war. Ronan and Malachi were killed leaving only Sean to take over the reins of all three businesses after the war was over. Sean the Second had managed them during the war but he was now in his eighties and couldn't go on much longer. Sean the Third had a wife and child in Manchester so had no desire to move back to Boston, so he sold off the organised crime to other families who controlled other areas of the city and he moved the legitimate business headquarters to Manchester. He also brought Sean the Second over but his age, the upheaval and the deaths of two of his sons had taken its toll and he barely lasted a year." Sean paused while yet another course arrived and the soup was cleared away.

"What happened to the organised crime business already in Manchester?" Abi asked as she sampled the Yeung Chow fried rice and the chicken satay.

"Oh, he had that too. For many years he ran them both, grooming Sean the Fourth, my father, to take over after him, in fact it wasn't until I was born and my mother insisted I was never to be involved in the criminal side of things that the two businesses where completely separated. I was sent to the best schools including

Harvard after getting a degree in business finance over here."

"What did you study at Harvard?" Abi couldn't help but interrupt.

"Law!" he answered with a slight grimace. "Anyway, the point is, since I finished my degrees I have been in charge of the legitimate side of the family businesses."

"Sullivan Industries?" A light bulb went off in Abi's head.

"What do you know about Sullivan Industries?" He asked slightly shocked she had even heard of it.

"Nothing really, I just remembered the name had come up when I was researching Harrison Oil Corporation for my story, something about them being competitors in a little African place called Gabon?" She stated, dredging the memory back from somewhere in the archives of her mind.

"I'm impressed!" Sean seemed genuinely surprised. "But, in answer to your question, yes, Sullivan Industries is mine."

"And the organised crime?" Abi still was not convinced.

"Was run by my father until he passed away last year!"

"And now it's yours?"

"No, and now it's sold, for a very large sum of money, and before you ask, no I didn't keep it, I donated it anonymously to several drug rehabs and homeless charities around Manchester."

"If you were just going to give the money away why sell it at all. Why not just close it down?" Abi asked implying that surely one less extortion, drugs and prostitution operation would have been a better option.

"You don't just walk away from organised crime Abi, not if you want to live to see your retirement. It had to pass to someone else, very carefully planned and controlled."

Abi was now deep in thought, was it possible? Could he really have only been involved in the legitimate side of things, and did it matter or was she just being pedantic? He was still from a long line of family gangsters, then a thought occurred to her, she looked up and was about to speak when he stopped her.

"You want an explanation for when we last met?" He asked although it was really more of a statement.

"You mean, the last time we met and I was conscious?" She replied with a slightly embarrassed smile.

"Yes, I guess so!" He chuckled. "Well, at that time my father had been diagnosed with cancer and was undergoing chemotherapy. That kind of business will not wait for its leader to recover so I had to step in while he was incapacitated. I ran the business for three months, unfortunately it was during that three months that the problem with your parents' thievery was brought to my attention by an informant from another family. Had I been able to keep it in house it could have waited until my father returned but I had to be seen to be in charge so I had to act. And, I must say, although I regret the experience must have been somewhat terrifying for you, I am glad it was me that day and not my father." He looked her directly in the eye and she could see his meaning without him having to utter another word. He was telling her that his father would not have taken the deal she had offered. She and her parents would have died that day.

"I'm glad too." She whispered, the full extent of the alternate possibilities hitting her hard. "So I guess you're telling me you're not a gangster but you can help out if they're short-handed?" she added quietly as she tried to unravel her thoughts to form the next question she needed to ask.

"That probably about covers it yes." He replied with a small chuckle, hoping to ease her tension a little. "But, enough." He said reaching across the table to lay his hand over hers. The effect was almost electric and Abi had to concentrate hard not to yank her hand away. "There are many things we should probably talk about but not tonight. We need a change of subject I think." He winked at her as she raised her eyes from the tablecloth, "How's Ginny?"

Abi wasn't sure whether to be grateful or annoyed, there were indeed many things they needed to talk about but she was unsure if she had the stomach for any more reflection tonight. Although, if she didn't at least get to thank him this evening it would mean she had to see him again. Guessing that was just what he wanted she tried to steer the conversation back in the direction it had been going.

"But, I need to thank..."

He stopped her with a look, it was a look unlike any she had ever seen. It was neither angry nor reproachful but it very definitely told her to stop. It also sent shivers up and down her spine, or was that because his hand was still covering hers?

"How is Ginny?" He repeated slightly more forcefully than before.

"She's very well." Abi resigned herself to the fact she was going to have to agree to see him again, a thought which didn't displease her as much as it should have. "She has been seeing quite a lot of Sam, he's been over once or twice and he came to stay for Christmas." She informed him.

"Sam?" He had obviously forgotten.

"The doctor, Sam O'Connor, from Boston?" she prompted, immediately seeing enlightenment in his face.

"Oh, how interesting, the doctor and Miss Winters, well, I never would have put those two together. Is it serious?"

"I think so." She confirmed, trying to sound upbeat about it. There was no need to tell him how worried she was that Ginny and Sam might indeed be very serious and her best friend could therefore end up moving to America.

"Would they live here or over there?" He asked seeming to read her mind yet again.

"She hasn't mentioned it yet and I don't like to ask, I wouldn't want to influence her decision." Abi replied, hoping he couldn't tell how terrified she really was about being separated from her best friend again. After all it had hardly gone well the last time.

"If you'll let me Abi I would very much like to be your friend too, maybe then you won't be so worried about losing Ginny, and if she does decide to go to Boston, she will only be a short flight away." His eyes were so sincere as he spoke Abi could not help the tears welling up in hers. Even she hadn't realised how much she needed to feel more secure without relying so heavily on Ginny. She tried to swallow the emotion threatening to engulf her, wondering if he actually knew how long she had dreamed of someone like him who may be able to genuinely care about her. Her negative side was pulling her away though, telling her she still could not trust him, even if he had very nearly successfully proved to her he was no gangster. "I guess that battle will rage inside you until I prove to you that you can trust me." He added gently, squeezing her hand beneath his, "I hope you'll let me stick around to try?"

~CHAPTER FOUR~

Aaron paced restlessly up and down the longest aspect of his unbearably small cell. At 10 feet by 7 feet it felt to him as if he were living in a cupboard and his pacing consisted of far more turning than actually walking.

He was both apprehensive and encouraged as it appeared that today he was finally going to meet with a lawyer willing to take his case. Since his previous lawyer had rather unceremoniously severed relations with him after his arraignment hearing he had been struggling to find a replacement.

His initial thought had been to represent himself but when the paperwork had started to arrive he had quickly decided that route was a non-starter. And so his case was just being further and further delayed by the fact he had no legal representation. He had been here, kicking his heels on remand, for several weeks now and still no trial date could be set nor further applications for bail lodged.

Despite what had happened at his arraignment when bail had been refused on the grounds that he was potentially dangerous and posed a real threat to the prosecution witnesses, Aaron was still convinced he would be exonerated at trial. When the facts were examined he believed a jury would have to conclude that all he had done was have sex with these four stupid women, who were now allowing themselves to be used by the prosecution to discredit him and therefore deny him his rightful and destined status in life. He was equally convinced that Bruce Harrison and Raymond Cabot were behind the entire case against him and that with the right lawyer he could prove they had paid these women to invent their stories of rape and battery.

Just because the boring missionary position, deemed normal in matters of sex, didn't interest him, hardly made him a criminal or even some sort of deviant. It merely made him a proper man, capable of fulfilling his own sexual needs instead of being kow-towed by a politically correct society.

The sooner he could get into court and explain this to a jury the happier he would be and the sooner accurate stories about him could be sold to the press, instead of the lies they had printed so far, making him as rich and famous as he had always deserved to be.

Eventually his short fat jailer arrived to escort him to his meeting with James Marchant, the hotshot lawyer who he had first met the previous week when he had requested an opportunity to try to persuade Aaron to appoint him. At that first meeting Aaron had declared his innocence and given the lawyer permission to request the trial papers from the court. In the intervening few days Aaron had made enquiries as best he could and found out that Marchant was indeed a very successful defence lawyer. Today Aaron was to find out whether James Marchant intended to take his case.

His tubby jailer led him into the interview room and Aaron was surprised to find James Marchant seated at a table with an empty chair on its opposite side and no sign of the seemingly obligatory screen/telephone affair Aaron had expected to find.

"How did you manage this?" He enquired with genuine wonder.

"I had to surrender my briefcase, my wallet, my watch, my tie & tie pin, my belt, my shoelaces, my mobile phone and all my pens so unless you can figure out how to escape or do someone harm with my underpants I have nothing you may find useful!" The lawyer stated, seemingly without mirth, as he gestured for Aaron to sit.

"Wow, I hope it was worth it?" Aaron added as he sat.

"I find clients are more comfortable without the Plexiglas, and a comfortable client is much easier to work with." Marchant said by way of justification. "I have however, been allowed to keep my digital voice recorder," he added indicating the slim black object Aaron had as yet failed to notice sitting between them on the table. "I trust you have no objection?"

"Well, I guess it'd be tough to take notes without a pen." Aaron tried again to be humorous and this time he did at least manage to get Marchant to smile thinly.

"Quite so Mr Steele." Marchant agreed. "Now, since our last meeting I have reviewed all the trial documents and have concluded I am in a position to take this case should you ask me to represent you." He looked pointedly at Aaron as he finished speaking.

"Oh, yes, yes please." Aaron replied, hoping that was all he needed to say.

"You don't wish to know what this is all going to cost you Mr Steele?" Marchant raised an eyebrow at Aaron as he spoke.

"I...I thought you said last week it would be pro-bono?" Aaron was nonplussed for a moment, he distinctly remembered the lawyer yapping on about it being good for his professional reputation to be seen to take on high profile pro-bono cases from time to time.

"Oh...er, yes that's quite correct Mr Steele, I apologise, that was indeed the offer I made." Marchant hurriedly tried to correct his mistake, hoping Aaron hadn't made any unfortunate connections. To have a third party pay for his fees was not in itself uncommon, but to have the client know nothing of the arrangement was highly unusual. "So many cases on at the moment, I temporarily forgot you were my pro-bono." He added, studying Aaron's eyes as he spoke to see if any suspicion lurked there. He was pleased to see it didn't. "Moving on." He turned to face Aaron directly. "Mr Steele, I have been through the prosecution's case and I can confirm your defence about having had these women's consent to various sexual acts will, in my hands, plant reasonable doubt in the minds of the jurors and I am sure therefore, I can get you acquitted of all rape charges."

Aaron beamed, at last someone who spoke sense, of course he'd had their consent, it wasn't as if he'd picked them up on the street, all four of them had been his girlfriend at the time each alleged he had raped them. "I'm glad we agree." He nodded with satisfaction. "Go on."

"Second, the kidnapping and drugging charges, again regardless of the photographic evidence which does prove a crime was committed, without Ms Storm actually being able to place you at the scene I am confident I can create enough doubt for the jury to believe the crime could have been committed by anyone. Without forensic evidence from the scene the prosecution will be hard pressed to even place you in the apartment and as Ms Storm was unconscious by her own admission for the entire week the alleged crime took place, I am confident I can also get you acquitted of these charges." He paused to look into Aaron's eyes and was satisfied to see smug acquiescence lulling his client into a relaxed and trusting state.

"So, we are left with the charges of attempted murder against Abigail Storm in her hospital bed and assault against Anna Foster." He paused to see if Aaron was following.

"The catheter thing?" Aaron asked with a somewhat bored tone to his voice. "I was trying to help!" He said defiantly.

"Yes, the catheter thing." Marchant took a deep breath. "The fact that you have already admitted to attempting to catheterise Ms Foster, regardless of your claim to be trying to help." He held up a hand to prevent Aaron from interrupting. "This makes this charge much harder to defend. The prosecution will argue that if the initial damage done to Ms Foster had been an accidental consequence of rather too robust sexual activity, albeit with her consent, your attempt to cover up the consequences of your actions is still regarded as assault. Had you taken her straight to hospital it would simply have been your word against hers as to consent issues. The damage you did is a fully documented medical fact and it is also irreparable. Miss Foster can no longer have children because of your actions."

"So, what are you saying?" Aaron was less relaxed suddenly and stared intently at the lawyer.

"I am saying I cannot guarantee an acquittal on this charge. Unfortunately, if the jury find you guilty on this charge it will also affect their decisions regarding the rape charges, meaning that whatever reasonable doubt I have planted could be eroded by a guilty verdict here. Do you understand what I'm saying?"

"Yes I think so." Aaron answered, his mind still processing how one little catheter could cause such problems. "What about the attempted murder charge?" He asked instead.

"Again, a difficult one to defend. As far as the facts go, you were found unconscious on the floor of her hospital room. Miss Winters was found on the bathroom floor sedated and she will swear it was you who sedated her. Miss Storm was found half tied to her bed and full of bleeding holes made, it is alleged, by a scalpel, said instrument was found on the floor only a foot from your hand and, upon forensic examination, was discovered to have your fingerprints all over it. Added to that you were covered in Miss Storm's blood so I am sure there can be little doubt a jury will believe it was you who inflicted Miss Storm's injuries. Your suggestion at the time that in her depressed state Miss Storm had inflicted these wounds on herself and you had tried to stop her will not fly because of the sedation of Miss Winters and the fact that Ms Storm was found with her wrists bound to the bed." Again he held up a hand to silence Aaron, "I think however, we can get this charge reduced to assault by claiming you were not in your right mind because of the stress Miss Storm and her co-plaintiffs had caused you. We could argue you went to see her to plead your case and knowing Miss Winters wouldn't let you anywhere near her, had, in a moment of poor judgement decided to sedate Miss Winters. We could then further argue that your initially calm discussion with Miss Storm had failed to persuade her of her erroneous charges against you and the resulting rage had temporarily rendered you incompetent to answer for your own actions." He looked at Aaron pointedly.

"Do you think that will fly?" Asked Aaron dubiously.

"Not with a jury I don't." Marchant replied quietly, hoping Steele was at least more intelligent than he appeared to be.

"So what's the point then? Why don't I just stick to the story I've already told the police?"

"The changed story you told later, about the unidentified man?"

"Yes. He was in the process of doing the crime when I arrived, I pulled him off, he rendered me unconscious and I don't know where he went after that. What's wrong with that defence?"

"Apart from it being wholly at odds with your first claim about Ms Storm inflicting her own injuries, nobody fitting the description you gave was found within the hospital and nobody else's fingerprints were found in the room and Miss Winters will swear absolutely she looked up, into a mirror in the bathroom and saw you standing right behind her with a large syringe in your hand. Together with the fact that Ms Storm was conscious throughout the attack and has confirmed it was you who attacked her, and does not place an unidentified man in the room at any time, the evidence supports the prosecution's version of events and does not support yours. Your defence will not fly." Marchant concluded.

"So what now then? Are you saying you can't get me off?" Aaron was becoming angry, how could it be possible that his sexual preferences were even to be questioned let alone potentially land him in prison?

"I am saying that as the charges stand, I cannot guarantee anything apart from that you will, most certainly, be found guilty on at least two charges. Assault against Miss Foster and Attempted Murder or assault against Miss Storm. As I say, guilty verdicts on these two charges will also possibly affect the jury's decision on the other charges whether or not I have previously managed to implant reasonable doubt in their minds."

"How long would that put me in prison for?"

"Life!" Marchant was blunt, he needed his next statement to be seen as offering some hope despite it being exactly the opposite of what Aaron expected of him.

"What kind of hotshot lawyer are you?" Aaron exploded from the chair, almost sending the table and the digital recorder crashing to the floor.

"Calm down Mr Steele, I said, *'as the charges stand'*, and, I would be confident in saying there isn't a lawyer in this country who could get you acquitted of all charges as they stand." Replied Marchant without even a hint of agitation.

"What do you mean by that? As they stand?" Aaron was curious despite his anger.

"If we can lessen the charges I can lessen the jail time, I could also get you softer jail time but it will require your cooperation." Marchant stated looking directly into Aaron's eyes and hoping the sadistic fool wasn't completely deranged, he really didn't want to have to go into court and defend this man, his reputation would be in shreds.

"Explain." Aaron demanded as he sat down again, regaining a little of his composure despite his bubbling anger.

"If I go to the prosecution with the defence I just outlined and suggested we would be willing to plea bargain, I would bet heavily that they would accept. The bargain I propose would be for you to plead guilty to assault against Miss Foster and to a lesser charge of assault against Miss Storm in her hospital bed. All other charges to be dropped saving all those ladies the need to testify in court. Saving the prosecution from a projected court battle which at best will have a very murky outcome. And saving you and I from having to defend any of your actions thus denying the judge time to decide he hates you." Marchant knew he was playing on Steele's own paranoia here but whatever got the job done.

"What good would that do?" Aaron was beginning to sulk, this meeting wasn't going at all as he had planned it.

"It will get you ten years in minimum or medium security prison instead of potentially life in a maximum security facility."

"Would I have to do the whole ten years?" Aaron was cold with rage but the few rational parts of his brain were still functioning and he realised this was probably his best option under the circumstances. Although he knew he was simply a man with a proper man's needs and desires, he was also rational enough to realise that the largely supressed wider society looked upon him with envy and so would seek to crush him wherever possible. As his fate lay with just such people he would have to accept, for now, that he was powerless to change his situation. That said, as long as he wasn't in prison for the rest of his life he could seek retribution at a later date.

"That would depend on you, good behaviour, remorse, a sense of humility will all put you in line for early parole. I'm sorry but I can't say how early, it's impossible to tell."

"And you're sure." Aaron's pout was real, his whole demeanour was that of a small boy told he couldn't have what he wanted for Christmas.

James Marchant regarded his client with coldly dispassionate eyes and marvelled at how a man so obviously evil could pretend to be anything resembling normal. He sincerely hoped he lived up to his bullying belligerent personality when in prison and didn't fool the parole board into releasing him earlier than his full term.

"Am I sure I can do the deal with the prosecution or am I sure you'll get out in less than ten years?"

"Both." Aaron was still pouting.

"I am confident I can get a deal done with the prosecutor's office, especially after all the noise I have started to make about you not being able to get a fair trial due to the coverage in the media. How long you subsequently spend in jail will depend entirely on your behaviour, I will have nothing to do with it." Marchant replied honestly, willing Steele to accept the deal.

"OK, do it then." Aaron agreed, standing and heading for the door before he succumbed to his urge to do some damage to the unfortunate lawyer. The seeds of hatred he had already germinated for Abigail Storm now flourishing into full grown weeds enmeshing themselves into his mind.

"Very well Mr Steele." Marchant said to Steele's retreating form, "I will be back when I have something to report. For what it's worth..." He waited for Steele to turn to look at him, "...under the circumstances I think you are doing the right thing."

Steele did not answer, merely banged his fist against the door for his jailer to let him out.

~CHAPTER FIVE~

Staring blankly at the wall opposite, sitting on the cot which the Massachusetts State Prison Service laughingly called a bed, Aaron seethed with resentment and disappointment. He'd had high hopes for the hotshot lawyer but now it seemed he had to resign himself to going to prison.

On some level he understood the need for society to conform to what it perceived as *normal*, but he wholly resented being forced to be the same as all the other deadbeats he saw around him. He found it difficult to accept that his sexual preferences could put him in prison. He had no doubt in his mind that the women who were now accusing him of rape and other crimes had, at the time, enjoyed his attentions. Each of them had been his girlfriend during the period in question and even when they had protested about anal sex or whatever he was offering them, he had known it was merely social protocol talking.

They had enjoyed the power he had over them as much as he had enjoyed his dominance and they had wanted him to be brutal and manly with his strength both in mind and body. He refused to accept any notion other than Abigail Storm had forced them to support her complaint and he was convinced she was only persisting in this venture to get back at him for stealing her stupid story. As if he couldn't have done such a story himself? If only he'd killed her when he had first had the chance, if only he hadn't been so soft as to just keep her sedated in that apartment.

"Yes," he thought bitterly and not for the first time, "*It's all her fault. If she hadn't got out of that apartment the world would still be mine. I would still be the journalist who brought down a presidential candidate, I would still be being wooed by TV and other print media, I could've had my pick of jobs and made the kind of money I am entitled to.*"

His mind wandered back to that Saturday morning in July 2012. His flight from Washington had landed at 3.30am, two full days earlier than Abi had been expecting him to be home. By 5am he was letting himself into her flat, he had decided to finish things with her. After four weeks without her in Washington, having enjoyed the delights of an assortment of escorts, most of whom had enthusiastically participated in whatever sexual antics he had dreamed up, Aaron had decided it was time to end things with Abigail. She had proved time and again she was unwilling to service his needs even though he knew she would enjoy it. She was selfish and petulant and all too often he was having to lock her into her apartment overnight to ensure she was pliable and non-combative when he returned. It never ceased to amaze and arouse him to see her so subservient after a night locked in on her own. He would miss that particular delight if he finished with her but, he reasoned, he could always just turn up from time to time and surprise her.

Finding paperwork, photographs, her laptop and flash drive strewn around the living room he almost marched straight into her bedroom to drag her from her bed and tell her to clean the place up. She was well aware she needed to keep the place tidy and clean at all times unless she wanted to upset him and therefore reap the consequences.

However, the headline on the topmost page sitting in the printer tray caught his eye and he was drawn across the room towards it instead, his thoughts of chastising Abigail momentarily forgotten. As he read through the sheaf of paperwork his excitement began to rise, it seemed Abi had somehow stumbled across a news story of epic proportions. If it were true, it would end the political life of the man tipped to be the next President of the United States, who also happened to be one of the thorns in Aaron Steele's side, together with his biggest campaign contributor, Bruce Harrison. Whilst he read Aaron rifled through the other paperwork strewn about and found Abi's notes from the various meetings she'd had, detailing beautifully where the information had come from and how she had made the connections to which she referred. Her laptop corroborated her story further and Aaron, who was never one to pass up a chance of making himself look good, was just in the process of working out how to take this story from her without her getting all sulky and childish on him when he heard a noise from behind him.

He turned to find a sleepy Abigail standing in the doorway, her expression was a mixture of surprise and confusion. Obviously she hadn't expected to see him here today, and her still sluggish mind was having trouble reconciling what she saw with what it thought it knew.

He reacted before she had chance to process any more of the scene before her. Stepping rapidly across the room he grabbed her by the hair making sure he caught her completely off guard, and hissed at her.

"You've been a busy little bitch haven't you!" It was a statement not a question, and Abi fought for control of her groggy senses in an effort to formulate a response which would not incur his further anger, but she need not have bothered, he continued, "How dare you disobey me? I told you to stay here and wait for me to return not go gallivanting off round the country!"

Before Abigail had any chance to react Aaron hit her hard in the side of her head with his bunched fist. An unsuspecting Abi was rendered unconscious immediately and Aaron half dragged and half carried her into the bedroom. After roughly laying her on the bed he rummaged through her closet for several scarves. Finding what he was looking for he used two to tie both her wrists and her ankles to the bed frame, then he used a third to securely gag her in case she regained consciousness and tried to scream for help, all the while he was calculating what to do next.

Remembering Anna Foster several years earlier Aaron soon decided what he was going to do with Abigail.

Anna had been a disaster and it was her fault Bruce Harrison and Senator Cabot had such a hold over him. How was he supposed to have known that misplacing a catheter by puncturing the urethra would lead to her near death and subsequent inability to have children? He had just been trying to help her after all.

Anyway, this time would be different, now he had the internet and could look up training videos to make sure he placed the catheter just right. He knew he could get everything he needed from Walmart, apart from the sedatives but he had a supplier for them already. After making sure Abigail was secure and could not raise the alarm if she came round before he returned, he hurried out to get the supplies he needed.

Several hours later Aaron was pleased with his day's work. Abigail was tied securely to her bed with a drip in her arm and a properly placed and working catheter draining her urine into a bag placed under her bed. The drip contained all the necessary components to keep her alive but unconscious until Aaron decided on a permanent solution to the problem she now represented. All he had to do was come back every six hours to change the drip bag, empty the catheter bag and add more sedative to her drip feed.

Although Aaron had no idea how long he could keep her like this he was unconcerned. He had no doubt he would come up with a permanent solution soon and until then he neither knew nor cared how much damage her current condition might do to her.

He rounded up all her paperwork, her laptop and her flash-drive and after making sure there was no more evidence of the story anywhere in the apartment he headed for home to upload the story and her notes and photographs to his own computer before he sent it in to the Boston Globe for publication in his name. This story was going to catapult him into the fame and fortune he so deserved.

But all this had happened over six months ago now, and much had changed since that Saturday in July. Quite how Abigail had escaped from the apartment Aaron realised he may never know now that he was unlikely to be going to trial. A plea bargain, if Marchant could pull it off, would negate the need for a trial and he wouldn't get to hear how somebody had managed to find her and spirit not only her but all her belongings away into thin air, leaving a completely empty apartment for Aaron to walk into one Monday morning after having had her there for over a week.

He had often wondered whether Harrison and Cabot had been responsible for Abigail's release but could not quite work out what they would stand to gain from such action. Apart from giving them more ammunition against him, it served no purpose for them to rescue Abigail. According to the trial papers the man who had actually entered the apartment was going to appear as an anonymous witness but Aaron was at a loss as to who would carry so much clout as to be able to secure anonymity for a witness in such a way.

Aaron was no expert on the law but as far as he could gather anonymity in court was not granted often, or without good reason. Which all brought him back round to the Senator having had something to do with it. It was a conundrum he would, it seemed, have plenty of time to consider, although, by the time he was released both Cabot and Harrison had better be watching their backs, whatever he did or did not find out about their involvement in this mess, he was going after them when he was released.

If it hadn't been for them using him like some kind of puppet and sending him off to Washington for that month he would have been there all the time Abi was trying to research the story, he would have been able to get it from her just by ensuring she hadn't got too big for her own station and believed she could do it herself. By the time he had finished with her, had he had the time, she would have gladly let him go to publication in his own name after he had convinced her no-one would believe she was capable of delivering such an item without having stolen it from someone far cleverer, and more experienced, such as him.

Her lack of self-confidence and her resultant total inability to assert herself was the main reason he had chosen her as his girlfriend in the first place. Women like her needed a strong man to guide and teach them otherwise where would the world get to. It had been a shame the relationship had ended when it did, there had been a great deal more she had needed to learn but as far as Aaron was concerned it was her loss. He was well aware he could have eventually turned her into someone worthy of his time but she was a reluctant student and an ungrateful hostess.

As it now turned out she was also a major pain in the backside. Obviously she had help, but had she not escaped and then started to cause such a ruckus, his life would have carried on moving through the higher echelons of first Boston society followed by Washington and the world, of this Aaron had no doubt.

One day she would pay, and pay dearly for her errors. It looked like he would have plenty of time to dream up ways of reminding her how much better than her he was and how small and insignificant her contribution to the world had always and would always be. The dream would sustain him during the long years of incarceration ahead.

~CHAPTER SIX~

"Bastard!" Abigail slammed down the telephone she had been apparently quite calmly talking into only moments before and proceeded to stamp around the kitchen, throwing unsuspecting dirty pots, cups and assorted cutlery into the wide open mouth of the dishwasher. "Slimy, conniving bastard!"

"Steady there." Ginny intervened, catching a china cup just before it was smashed to smithereens in the bowels of the machine. "If you need to throw things, go outside, there are plenty of logs which need stacking in the wood pile, you can hurl them as hard as you like, don't come back until you've calmed down." She shoved Abigail out into the back garden as she spoke, firmly locking the door behind her. All she knew at this point was that Abigail had been talking to her American lawyer, Mr Calhoon, Ginny surmised the news wasn't good.

Sometime later, a sheepish and cold-looking Abigail tapped contritely on her own back door. Ginny had been watching her closely from the window and had noted the change from frustration and anger to sadness and dismay. She unlocked the door, she had already made coffee and she placed a seaming mug in Abigail's hand as she guided her to the kitchen table to sit down.

"I ran out of logs!" Abigail stated as she stared blankly into the swirling coffee mug.

"Well, it was a job needed doing anyway, I can't believe you hadn't already moved them after Sam spent so long chopping them for you last week." Ginny knew better than to press Abi for answers, she would always tell her what had happened in her own time, although she had a feeling she wasn't going to have to wait long this time.

"He coped a plea." Abi sighed, looking up at her friend for the first time, the hint of tears in her deep blue eyes.

"Who..." Ginny was momentarily confused until the obvious clicked into place. "Steele?" She added incredulously, knowing it had to be but not really believing he would ever have done such a thing. She sat down heavily opposite her friend, unsure how to proceed. She knew Abi had not been looking forward to the trial, in fact she had been terrified of it but she also knew Abi had been psyching herself into it, in the same way the other three women involved had been.

"I knew that bloody lawyer was up to something." Abi continued, almost as if she were talking to herself. "All that noise he was making about Aaron not getting a fair trial because of all the adverse publicity he'd already had, I knew it was going somewhere, I just couldn't figure out where."

"How do you mean?" Ginny asked, it had never occurred to her the lawyer was doing anything other than trying to ensure his client an unbiased hearing, as was surely his job. "As far as I can see he may well have had a point, there was an awful lot of bad press for

Aaron before and after he was arrested, I could see it being difficult to get twelve jurors who hadn't already decided he was a monster."

"Possibly, but that doesn't mean the trial would be unfair, as long as the jurors were honest and willing to do the job they were tasked to do, there's no reason to assume they couldn't try him fairly. If that wasn't possible hardly any case would come to trial if there had been any whiff of it in the press beforehand." Abi stated flatly, staring reproachfully at her friend. "You have to at least be able to believe twelve jurors on any trial are capable of weighing up the actual evidence and making a decision, otherwise the whole justice system would fall flat on its face."

"OK, good point well made." Ginny smiled, trying to lift Abi's mood even just a little. "So what was the lawyer up to then?" She added.

"Calhoon agrees, Marchant has made such a song and dance about the possibility of an unfair trial that the prosecution just know, if the trial went ahead and Steele was convicted, the defence would immediately launch an appeal on these grounds. However, the possibility of a trial elsewhere was also a problem as the Steele story had gone almost global, following the Presidential candidate exposé which he first claimed was his and was subsequently found to be mine." Abi paused to sip her coffee, a look of resigned despair settling onto her face. "Effectively Mr Marchant put the prosecution up against the ropes then offered them a way out."

"How so?" Ginny was genuinely intrigued now.

"He offered them a plea bargain. If they reduced the charges to assault, Aaron would plead guilty."

"So no trial?"

"No trial." Abi confirmed with a sigh.

"Isn't that a good thing then?" Ginny asked gently.

"No, it's not!" Abi replied defiantly, her eyes suddenly blazing with anger. "It means he'll get ten years instead of life for a start and no doubt he'll be eligible for parole long before he serves ten years. It also means those poor girls who I promised would be able to lay their ghosts to rest now won't get to. They won't have their day in court, they won't get justice and they won't get the satisfaction of watching that monster take his last ever breaths as a free man. It means, sometime in the not too distant future all four of us will have to spend our lives wondering if that bastard is going to come after us for bringing this case in the first place." Abi was shouting now, she was so angry she was having a hard time preventing herself from hurling what was left of her coffee at the far wall of her kitchen.

Ginny sensed the danger and gently prised the cup from Abi's white knuckled hand.

"You can't think like that Abigail." She said seriously but gently, she had no desire to further upset her friend. "You have to look at the positive side of the situation. He's going to prison, albeit not for as long as he should but I doubt he'll have a nice time there, when he gets out he'll have a criminal record so he won't be living anything like the kind of life he's used to. He's hardly going to be employed by any media group ever again, given what he did to you. You won't have to go to trial now, which is no bad thing, I know you were terrified of the whole thing. And, yes..." she held up a hand to stop Abi from interrupting. "...I know how cathartic you were hoping the process would be, but, there's no guarantee that's what would have happened, it could just as easily have traumatised you all over again."

"Well, we'll never know now will we." Abi said quietly with tears in her eyes.

"No, we won't." Agreed Ginny. "But, we can find the catharsis you need elsewhere, whereas had you been further traumatised who knows where we'd have been. I for one am glad it's happened this way." She added, realising for the first time as she said it she had been dreading the trial almost as much as Abi even if it were for entirely different reasons.

"And what about Anna, Polly and Elaina? What about the promises I made to them about laying their Aaron Steele ghosts to rest?" Abi asked tearfully.

"You didn't ask them to do anything Abigail..." Ginny had her stern motherly voice on now, she knew it was the best one to use with Abi in such circumstances. "...they came to you. When you were lying in that hospital bed they chose to come and offer their help and their experiences at his hands. You didn't ask them or force them. Now I'm sure they'll be as disappointed as you are that they won't get to look him in the eye and call him a monster but, the same applies to them as it does to you. The trial would have been awful, you would all have had to relive stuff you should never have had to go through once let alone repeatedly. So, ultimately, they will have to work out another way to deal with their ghosts. Maybe the fact that the four of you are now friends and can possibly talk to each other about things will help, who knows." She shrugged as she tried to encourage Abi to look on the positives of the situation. "Regardless, none of this is your fault. You are not responsible for the other three, they are entirely responsible for themselves. And, I guarantee, none of them will blame you for this." She concluded, staring deep into her friend's eyes to try to convey her heartfelt belief in her own words.

"So why do I feel like it's my fault?"

"Because you always feel things are your fault." Replied Ginny with a grin, she knew she was winning.

"And why do I do that?"

"Because you were taught to take the blame regardless of the crime. You were taught it was always your fault, whatever you did and unfortunately, things so deeply ingrained in childhood are extremely difficult to unlearn. I know it's tough to be you right now Abi but you are making progress. A year ago you wouldn't have believed a word of that but you do now, I can tell by your eyes."

"So if I believe it why do I still feel like I do."

"I takes time babe, but as long as you know it's true you just have to keep telling yourself, when in any situation, to look logically at the facts and determine for yourself whether it really is your fault or not. I guess you have to believe it's OK for things not to be your fault. And that's why you need to see a psychiatrist."

Abi sighed deeply. "We back to that old record again then Gin?"

"I understand your reluctance Abi I really do, but I can't get you any further forward, my 'A' level psychology just isn't enough. You need a professional." Ginny answered, reaching for and squeezing her friend's hand, whilst pushing her half-finished coffee back to within her reach. "You know Sam offered to vet a few for you next time he's here, maybe you should let him. You don't actually have to go to see anybody, just let him find somebody suitable so we know who to call when you're ready?" She added hopefully. This was a subject they had visited many times but Abi seemed more scared of talking to a psychiatrist than she was about living with her demons. It wasn't that she didn't think she needed a psychiatrist, she was the first to admit it would probably do her a lot of good. But, by her own admission she had major trust issues, and talking about herself, even to a trained professional, was, to Abi, opening herself up to trusting another human being. It was this which stood in her way, this obstacle she had so far been unable to get around.

"When is Sam coming over then?" Abi asked, as brightly as she could manage.

Ginny was well aware Abi was trying to sidestep the subject but she had no intention of letting her. "Next week, so shall I tell him to go ahead?"

"Just to find a suitable candidate?"

"Absolutely." Ginny held her breath, this was further than she'd ever got before.

"Somebody I might relate to?"

"That's right. You don't have to see him or her, just identify someone possible."

"OK."

Ginny was elated. "Sam will be thrilled, he's been so worried about you."

"I didn't say I'd see anybody!" Abi was instantly guarded.

"I know, I know..." Ginny placated her quickly. "...but this is a step further than you've been willing to go so far and Sam will be delighted. It a step in the right direction." She asserted fondly, patting her friend's outstretched hand.

"Why's Sam worried about me anyway?" Abi asked with genuine puzzlement. She still found it difficult to believe anyone could care about her just for being her, without requiring something of her in return.

"He cares about you that's why." Ginny replied, a far off look in her eyes.

"You care about him too don't you?" Abi teased, indicating her crisis moment was over.

"He's adorable Abi, I'm so grateful you found him for me."

"I think you'll probably have to thank Sean for that one too." Abi laughed. "I was unconscious if you remember."

Ginny giggled, she loved it when Abi was able to joke about her traumas. Sam said it meant she was learning to live with them.

"You weren't unconscious when you very bravely decided to go back to Boston to confront Aaron Steele!" Ginny asserted proudly, "And that's when you introduced me to Sam, the first time I met him I was too distraught at the state you were in to notice him properly."

"Sorry..." Abi began,

"Don't you dare!" Ginny stopped her in her tracks with a command and a stern look. It was all Abi needed. Sometimes Ginny was grateful Abi had such god-awful parents, it had caused her all manner of harm but the one thing she could always use was Abi's deep seated desire to be good. Psychologically Ginny knew the damage was far reaching and severe, but superficially it enabled her to stop Abi from wallowing in self-loathing every time she felt she had let someone down or put someone out.

"It's serious with Sam then? This'll be the fifth time he's been over in less than four months." Abi almost didn't dare ask. She was delighted her friend had found someone she was so obviously in love with and she couldn't think of a nicer man than Sam for Ginny to be with. But neither could she get away from the fact that Sam lived in Boston and Ginny lived in Cheshire. So far Sam had been over to see Ginny several times but Abi knew, if they were as serious about each other as they seemed, it was only a matter of time before the question of which side of the world they were going to live on together came up. Abi prayed they decided to make a home here in England but she couldn't convey her hope to Ginny for fear of influencing her friend. Ultimately she hoped Ginny and Sam would be happy whatever they decided and she would just have to deal with it if it turned out they were happy to live on the other side of the vast Atlantic Ocean.

"Yes it's serious with Sam." Ginny mused, a grin spreading across her face and lighting up her eyes. "He's amazing, I know I've only really known him four months but I can talk to him about anything, it's like I've known him all my life. He says he has something important to ask me next week." She confided with a conspiratorial wink at Abi. "I hope it's not what I think it is."

"Why what do you think it is?" Abi asked with her heart in her mouth, she hoped Ginny wasn't about to say Sam was going to ask her to move to America.

"I think he might be going to propose."

Unfortunately Abi had chosen to try to hide her trepidation by taking a swig of her now nearly cold coffee and Ginny's matter of fact statement caught her so off guard she instantly and very messily spat the entire mouthful all over the table in front of her.

Ginny laughed riotously as she sprang to her feet to get a cloth for the still almost choking Abi.

"I guess I'd better not react like that if he does propose." She chuckled as Abi mopped up and composed herself at the same time.

"Sorry..." She said sincerely, "...I was surprised that's all." She trailed off, unsure if she was making her faux pas worse.

"Well, I can't say I won't be surprised, I mean, we haven't been together very long, but those are the sort of noises he's making, and it's obviously a big question or he wouldn't have felt the need to forewarn me would he?" She raised any enquiring eyebrow at her friend.

"Will you accept?" Abi asked beaming the best smile she could manage at Ginny to try to reassure her she would be fine whatever Ginny decided. She knew her friend well enough to know her welfare would factor into Ginny's decision, even when it really shouldn't.

"I don't know Abi, I mean, yes, I'd love to marry him. He's definitely the man for me, it's just, well, I'm not sure I want to live in America." She shrugged as she spoke, looking up at Abi, "...and before you go off on one, no it's not just because I would be scared of leaving you on your own, I genuinely don't know if I want to live in America."

"Wouldn't he move here?" Abi asked tentatively, the possibility of Sam moving to England would be her dream come true. Ginny could marry the man of her dreams and she would still have her best friend and pillar of support. She held her breath.

"I don't know, we've never seriously talked about it. I mean, we've discussed things we'd like to do in the future, you know, places we'd both like to visit, ambitions we both have in our jobs, kids n'stuff. But we've never actually discussed which country we'd live in. I know it's mad, but we really haven't and I'm wondering if the reason we've not talked about it is because, subconsciously we both know we don't want to move."

"Wow, that's nearly as bonkers as me!" Abi said laughing with mirth she didn't really feel. "Maybe you should wait to see what he asks you next week before you go off at a tangent. He may just ask you to go on holiday with him or something!"

"I guess." Ginny agreed, laughing at herself.

"And maybe you should broach the subject of who is expecting who to move? It'd be good for you to know if he's flexible or not." Abi added, trying to make it sound like it was for Ginny's benefit not just her own.

~CHAPTER SEVEN~

"A toast." Sean raised his glass to the assembled diners. "To Sam and Ginny, congratulations on your engagement!"

"Here, here." Added Abi, smiling gratefully at Sean. Seconds earlier Sam had announced that Ginny had accepted his marriage proposal and Abi had been momentarily lost for words. Whilst being delighted Ginny was so obviously happy, she was instantly aware that the decision as to where the happy couple would live had either been made or would be so imminently. Sean's toast had diverted attention from her and given her the moment she needed to compose herself.

"So where will you live?" Sean decided to cut right to the chase, he was well aware the question was like the *Sword of Damocles* hanging over Abigail's head. "Have you given it any thought yet?" He added as innocently as he could, trying to avoid Abigail's disapproving stare.

"I know individually, both Ginny and I have given it a great deal of thought, Sean. However, we haven't actually concluded anything together as yet." Said Sam with a chuckle, glancing at Ginny for confirmation. He had only actually met Sean once before, in quite trying circumstances, and was finding it a little surreal to find himself sitting in an expensive restaurant now having dinner with him as if they were old friends. "Is that what this dinner is for?" He knew he could be walking on thin ice but he didn't like being cornered.

"No of course not." Abi stated at once, "I told you already, Sean had said he would like to meet Ginny and when I told him you would also be here this weekend he said it would be nice to see you again too, so here we are." She glared at Sam, who, had he not already been kicked under the table by a now furious Ginny would readily have taken her chastisement.

"I apologise of course." He nodded deferentially to Sean who, he was relieved to see, was supressing a chuckle.

"No apology required." Sean replied, raising his glass in Sam's direction. "And, by way of explanation, I asked Abigail to organise this dinner for two reasons, the first was so that I could thank you both personally for your help last summer when I effectively forced both of you to look after Abi when that bastard Steele had left her for dead." He paused to let his words sink in and to banish the image of Abigail tied to that bed from his mind.

"There's no need to thank us." Ginny replied for both of them. "I for one am just relived you found her and brought her home." She nodded her approval in Sean's direction, all the while not taking her eyes off Abi. She knew her friend would find this utterly embarrassing. "And the second reason?" She added, raising an eyebrow at Sean, who, despite Abi's excellent descriptions, possessed the most penetrating and alarmingly sexy grey-blue gaze for which she had been wholly unprepared.

Sean grinned wickedly, "It was the only way I could persuade Abi to go out on a second date with me."

Sam chuckled, whilst Abi almost spat her wine onto the tablecloth. "That's wicked." Sam said raising his glass to Sean in a venerable salute.

"I didn't know we'd had a first date." Abi had regained her composure and was looking at Sean with a mixture of alarm and mirth.

"So, what was dinner last week?" Sean replied.

"That was just for me to thank you for rescuing me, and to thank you for letting me buy the house from you, and to thank you for sending me the rest of the money from my grandmother's house." Abi trailed off, unable to hold Sean's sensual gaze any longer.

"But, if I remember correctly, you did none of those things." Sean was taunting her now and she blushed scarlet at the thought.

Ginny sensed Sam itching to intervene and she silently and discreetly reached for his hand, a gentle squeeze telling him to keep quiet. She had thought to interrupt Sean herself but the look in his eyes had told her to let him carry on. He was pushing Abigail beyond her comfort zone but Ginny could see that he was doing it with as much tenderness and care as possible. He was making her stand up for herself, if only momentarily, in order to boost her confidence. His eyes told Ginny he would do anything for Abi and suddenly she understood exactly why he had engineered this dinner. He was letting her know she didn't need to worry about Abi if she chose to move to America, he would be here for her no matter what.

"Only because you wouldn't let me." Abi finally found her voice, although she dared not look at Sean as she challenged him.

Ginny thought her heart would burst with pride, ordinarily Abi's reaction would have been to apologise for her own perceived failings. But she answered him back. This meant two things to Ginny, the first was that she was safe with the knowledge that Sean would step in whenever she was unable to be there for Abigail, and the second, probable more important was that, whether Abi was aware of it or not at this point, she was willing to trust Sean. It may take some time, certainly before she was ready to admit that to herself, but it was a step Ginny had never seen Abigail take before.

"Very true, Abigail!" Sean exclaimed, patting her hand gently as it lay on the table between them. He waited for her to look up at him before winking at her and carrying on. "So, as that conversation would be wholly inappropriate for tonight you'll just have to agree to see me again."

Abi couldn't help but smile. The notion that this man was a gangster was receding into the back of her mind and the thoughtful if slightly wicked man she saw before her was beginning to have a physical effect on her. She had no idea why his presence should make her bolder than she really was, but whenever she was with him she found she was much more readily able to voice her own opinion.

"Was that an invitation?" She answered, still lost in his eyes, hearing her own voice as if it was coming from someone else.

By way of reply Sean merely lifted her hand from the table and brought it gently to his lips, all the time his eyes never left hers. Abi was mesmerized, wholly out of her depth and just starting to feel the panic set in when Ginny came to her rescue.

"Let's eat." She announced loudly, causing both Abi and Sean to look in her direction and breaking the spell Sean had almost had Abi under. As Sean looked over to her Ginny's expression conveyed both her gratitude and therefore her understanding of Sean's feelings towards Abi but it also held a warning and Sean was in no doubt about how angry Ginny would be if he pushed Abi too far too fast.

"So, as a final word on the subject for tonight." He looked at both Ginny and Sam in turn. "All I want to say is that if any financial obstacles present themselves whilst you are deciding which country to live in I would be happy to help. I will not say anything further at this point as I know Abi would be horrified to think I was trying to influence you either way. But, please let me know if there is anything I can do for you. I owe you both as far as I am concerned and it would be my pleasure to help. Now, as you so eloquently put it Miss Winters, let's eat." And with that he summoned the never too far away waiter.

~CHAPTER EIGHT~

Abi slowly realised the incessant ringing of her mobile was not in fact part of the very strange dream she had been having but her actual phone ringing beside her bed.

She groped groggily for the offending article and had pressed answer before her half-closed eyes had registered who was calling.

"Surely you're not still in bed?" Came the altogether too cheerful sound of Sean's voice. Glancing over at her alarm clock Abi eventually managed to decipher that the time was 11.30 and judging by the light streaming through the gap in her curtains she deduced it was 11.30am. Memories of large quantities of champagne at dinner the night before suddenly came flooding back to Abi and she realised why she felt so awful.

"I thought champagne wasn't supposed to make you feel like this." She grumbled, not really registering she was actually speaking out loud.

"I think it kind of depends how much you drink." Came the slightly amused reply.

"I said that out loud didn't I?" She was horrified at her error, even though it sounded as if Sean was unconcerned.

"Very much so!" He confirmed with another chuckle. "As a cure I recommend two paracetamol, breakfast and a shower." He added. "In that order."

"Yes Sir." She mumbled as she dragged her reluctant body out of bed and padded through to the bathroom to see if there were any paracetamol to be had. Disappointingly the box was empty. "No paracetamol in the house." She grumbled. "Just have to go back to bed then." She headed back towards her bedroom.

"Just open the front door Abi, I have paracetamol, I have homemade coffee and I have croissants for breakfast."

Abi was about to protest that she was in her pyjamas when she realised Sean had already seen her in far worse states, and she really could use some paracetamol. After hesitating for another few seconds she turned on her heel, grabbed her dressing gown from the back of her bedroom door and headed down the stairs. "OK, I'm coming." She mumbled into the phone before hanging up and slipping it into her pocket.

Even the watery January sunshine was more than Abi's eyes could stand so she let Sean in with her eyes firmly closed.

Taking his opportunity Sean quickly leant in and kissed her gently on the cheek before striding past her and into the kitchen before she had chance to either comment or protest.

Having hurriedly closed the front door behind him she stood with her back to the kitchen resting her throbbing head on the cool glass of the door, her foggy mind trying to process what had just happened. On the one hand, he hadn't really done any harm but, on the other hand, he had taken a liberty and she felt maybe she should say something.

"That was a bit cheeky, even if you have brought breakfast." She said as she wandered into the kitchen and found him searching for plates to put the croissants on.

His smirk was brief but she didn't miss it.

"What's funny?" She demanded.

"It's not funny at all." He replied immediately becoming serious. "I was just pleased you felt able to chastise me. You are perfectly correct, it was very cheeky of me and I apologise unreservedly." He gestured for her to sit as he spoke and as his words penetrated her brain Abi couldn't help but feel a slight pride in her actions. Not so long ago she would just have worried herself half to death over such an incident, unable to dismiss the notion that it was her fault somehow, that she had unwittingly given her consent. Ginny's insistence that she analyse events to determine whether or not the fault was hers did seem to work. She was pleased, not least because Sean was apparently pleased with her too.

"So I guess I can't grumble at you getting me up too early but I'm still puzzled that you're here." She said as she accepted the offered paracetamol and the large mug of coffee with them. "Did we arrange this last night?" Abi was sure she hadn't been so drunk that she wouldn't remember arranging to meet Sean but stranger things had happened to her.

"No, don't worry, you haven't forgotten anything. You had plenty enough champagne to give you a thick head but you were perfectly in control of your senses. I just decided this morning that I wanted to surprise you and, I have a bit of a proposition to put to you." Sean smiled as he sipped his coffee, even as dishevelled and hung-over as she was he found her totally captivating. Her lack of self-confidence was really the only thing preventing her from allowing her indomitable spirit to shine. The fact was, successive people she had trusted had completely eroded her self-esteem, until she truly believed she was worth nothing. Sean had long since decided that even if it took him the rest of his life he was going to make her believe in herself. He was going to teach her to see herself through his eyes not through the eyes of the bullies she had so far encountered.

"Not sure I'm dressed for a proposition." The caffeine was starting to work and Abi's sense of humour was returning.

"Eat your croissants, my proposition can wait until you're feeling more human."

Abi and Sean made idle chatter as they ate the fabulously fluffy hot croissants and Abi was already feeling much better by the time she left Sean clearing away the dirty plates so she could go in the shower. It seemed each time she met him something about him surprised her. Here he was, a seriously rich man and yet he seemed perfectly happy to load her dishwasher for her. Her idea of how rich people lived their lives was obviously born more out of TV programmes and books than reality but she imagined all such people would insist on being waited on wherever they were. The normal down to earth things she did every day somehow seemed monumental when he did them.

Now showered and dressed and feeling much more like herself she wandered back into the kitchen to find Sean sitting at her kitchen table reading a newspaper. He put it to one side as soon as she entered the room.

"Sorry but I couldn't find your coffee machine." He began indicating the absence of such a gadget with a sweep of his arm. "So I couldn't make more coffee."

Abi giggled, well maybe he was a rich bloke after all. "I don't have a coffee machine." She said between chuckles. "I have a kettle and a jar of Gold Blend though if you're interested?"

"Gold Blend? Is that instant?" He asked looking surprisingly alarmed.

Abi could contain herself no longer and threw her head back and laughed, when she managed to contain her mirth she replied. "It's instant yes, however, it's very nice. Would you like some?"

She couldn't tell if he was pretending to be horrified or if in fact he had never had to drink instant coffee before, she suspected the latter, given that his family had been very wealthy long before he was born. Well, this would certainly be a new experience for him. She decided she'd better make it quite strong, he was unlikely to be sold on it if she gave him her usual weak and extra milky variety.

Moments later she was seated opposite him at her own kitchen table, two steaming mugs of coffee between them and he was eyeing his suspiciously. The whole situation was so surreal to her she felt she had no choice but to just go with it and see how it went. She was intrigued as to what a proposition from such a man could entail and hoped fervently it was nothing to do with relationships or sex. She most definitely wasn't ready to go down that particular road any time soon, if ever again after the mess Aaron Steele had left her in. She watched as he took a tentative sip of his coffee and giggled inwardly as she saw the look of horror and distaste he tried so desperately to hide from her.

"If you really think it's that bad don't drink it." She advised. "I won't be offended in the slightest. In fact, if you'd prefer I can probably find a tea bag somewhere. Ginny likes tea every now and then so there's probably a box in the cupboard." She offered helpfully.

"Er...no thanks...this is fine." He said stoically, even though his face said something entirely different. "I take it you don't drink tea then?" He added as he tortured himself with another sip of coffee.

"Never." Abu confirmed, and Sean was left in no doubt she would not comment further just as he understood tea held some memory for her which was not favourable. Quite how tea could offend her was beyond him at this time but it was something else he hoped he would be able to find out from her as their friendship progressed. He was well aware the only way he was going to get to know her at this point in her life was as a friend. Anything further than that would have to wait, he was a patient man.

"There's a *Costa's* just down the road you know, if you'd rather have real coffee?" Abi offered, unable to watch him suffer any longer.

"What a fantastic idea." He stood immediately and reached for his jacket. "Get your coat, we'll got to *Costa's*." He agreed with a very relieved smile.

As Abi went upstairs to her bedroom to find her handbag and shoes she could hear him talking on the phone but by the time she re-joined him in the hallway he had finished and she had been unable to make out anything he had said.

"Is it close enough to walk or shall we take the car?" He asked as he held the front door open for her to go through.

"It's not far, we could take the car but it's difficult to park." She replied gazing at the beautiful sleek Aston Martin DB9 sitting quietly in her driveway.

"Let's walk then." He decided for them, offering her his arm like all good gentlemen should.

From anybody else Abi would have though he was mocking her but she felt, not for the first time, Sean was sincere in everything he did. So she linked her arm through his and they set off together to walk the half mile or so to the nearest *Costa's* coffee shop.

When finally they were seated with coffee acceptable to Sean's palate which Abi had managed, with not inconsiderable argument, to pay for, Sean finally decided to tell her about the proposal to which he had alluded earlier.

"So, now that you don't have to go back to Boston for the trial what do you intend to do with yourself? Have you had any thoughts?" He began.

"How do you know about that?" Abi had only found out herself the previous week and was not sure if it was common knowledge yet as Aaron was still waiting to be sentenced.

"Frank told me." He smiled gently at her. Even her instant suspicion could not faze him it seemed. Anyone else might have been angry at her apparent accusation but Sean merely let it bounce off him. "Calhoon had to let him know he wouldn't be required to testify." He added in case she needed further explanation.

"Sorry." She said, looking into her coffee cup guiltily.

"Don't be." He replied, and when she looked up at him obviously surprised at his calmness he merely smiled reassuringly at her.

"So...have you had any thoughts?" He repeated, dragging her back to the conversation they had started.

"Not really." She answered with a smile, "I'd just about got my head round not having to go to trial really. It wasn't something I had been looking forward to but getting myself psyched up for it had taken up more of my time than I realised." She admitted.

"I can imagine." He waited patiently for her to continue.

"I suppose I'll have to think about getting a job at some point in the not too distant future. I've got enough money to keep me for a year or two I suppose so there's no mad rush but after that I'm going to need some sort of income."

"In journalism?" He prompted.

"Yeah...coz that went really well last time!" She half smiled, half grimaced.

"It was the company which was rotten, not the quality of your work." He reminded her gently. "You could have fallen foul of the likes of Aaron Steele in any industry you had chosen, unfortunately he isn't unique. Don't let that bastard put you off doing something you are obviously very good at."

"Hmmm...I suppose. Although I'm really not sure journalism as such is for me. I know I investigated and wrote a great story but it was more by good luck than good management that I stumbled across the story in the first place. I think to be a successful journalist of that ilk you need a far bigger ruthless streak than I possess, or ever want to possess if I'm honest." She stared into the middle distance as she spoke and Sean could see there was an idea tugging at her from somewhere. "I think I'd still like to write though, just perhaps not as an investigative journalist."

"What about a book?" Sean suggested with a grin, he couldn't help being delighted that without his help the conversation was going in the direction he had thought he was going to have to very cleverly steer it.

Abi noted his grin and wondered what it signified but the idea of writing a book, for the moment at least, occupied her thoughts more significantly. "A book could be good. I mean, if I don't actually have to go out to work right now, it would seem a good time to try." She concluded and was further perplexed to see Sean's grin grow wider. "Why are you grinning?" She demanded.

"That's exactly what I hoped you'd say." He said, obviously pleased with himself.

"Why?"

"Because I have the perfect subject for you to write a book about."

"Really? What?" Abi was intrigued, she wondered vaguely if she ought to be annoyed that he had apparently already decided a possible future for her but dismissed the thought almost before it was fully formed. He had after all merely made a suggestion, she had taken it on board and agreed it was a good idea. That was what friends did, they helped you make decisions and it was becoming increasingly apparent, gangster or not, Sean Sullivan was becoming her friend.

"Well, building on the story you have already started, with the Senator and the oil billionaire, I can give you more information about what really motivated them. Now, you could choose to turn that information into a follow up to your original story, or, you could change a few names and places and invent some extra plot lines and make it into a novel." Sean had obviously given the subject some thought before putting the idea to Abi and she was impressed with his efforts.

"You know why Harrison and Cabot were manipulating Steele?" She asked with obvious disbelief.

"I do." He confirmed with a wicked grin.

"Was I right about the hold Harrison has over Cabot? Was it about a relationship with his daughter-in-law?"

"Yes and no." He replied enigmatically, pausing until the look on Abi's face turned murderous. "Senator Cabot was indeed having an affair with Eden, his daughter-in-law and no doubt had he become president Harrison would have used it against him whenever necessary. However, it was pure greed which had him working with Harrison so far. The oldest reason in the book, money, lots and lots of money."

"So I was half right?" Abi was delighted, her lack of proof of the affair had always bothered her.

"Everything you wrote was right Abi, it just wasn't the entire story. You did a damn fine job, I hope you are very proud of yourself." He added with obvious admiration in his voice.

"Thank you." She answered sheepishly, accepting praise was a rarity for Abi and she found it difficult to do.

"So, to my proposition." He shifted in his seat so he was directly facing her. "Certain of my business interests directly compete with Harrison's. In particular the oil and gas exploration arm of Sullivan Industries..."

"The one I found reference to when I was investigating Harrison's oil business?" Abi interrupted.

"That one." Sean nodded his agreement. "Anyway, I am proposing you shadow me whilst I work so I can explain the way the industry works, and the connections to Harrison, and what he's really after in Africa."

"Like research? For the book?" Abi hoped she understood him correctly.

"Exactly!" He agreed.

"And what's in it for you?" Abi's suspicions surfaced again, her belief that nobody would do something purely for someone else's benefit was deeply ingrained, and although the knowledge saddened Sean, he was also grateful as it meant her self-preservation instincts were working well.

"I get to spend time with you and hopefully I will be able to convince you I'm not a gangster. I want to get to know you better because you fascinate me and I would dearly love to be able to call you a friend..." He held up a hand to prevent her from speaking until he was finished. "I swear I will never *expect* anything more than friendship from you. I know how rough a hand life has dealt you so far and I would very much like to be able to help you to get over at least some of your traumas so you can look to the future without fear."

"You practiced that?"

"Only the last bit!" He confessed sheepishly, "I wanted you to understand I was sincere and not some weird creep coming on to you."

"You succeeded." Abi said with a smile. "I'd love to follow you around for a while and see if I can get a book, or even a new friend, out of it." She added offering him her hand to seal the deal.

~CHAPTER NINE~

"So Burt, do you have a plan? Steele gets sentenced tomorrow. The lawyers think he'll get ten years, at least the recommendation from the prosecutor's office will be ten years minimum security, it's part of the plea bargain he made. You've had a few weeks now to think about my request, what have you got?" Bruce Harrison was behind his leather topped mahogany desk staring at Burt Tomasino over his morning coffee.

"Ok, Mr Harrison, just so we're clear. You want me to arrange for Aaron Steele to escape from federal prison, be provided with false paperwork, a considerable quantity of money and certain information and help him to flee the country?" Burt stared back at the oil billionaire.

"In a nutshell."

"OK, you do know how many laws this would be breaking right?"

"Many I should think, I really don't care as it isn't going to be traceable to either myself or you. Is it?"

"I'm sure I've covered our backs Mr Harrison, financially it's easy, you pay my company plenty already, we can just lose the extra in amongst the legitimate bills. False paperwork is no problem, my contact is as solid as they come and even if he gets a tug from the feds he won't squeal, he'd be out of business pretty damn quick if he did. Until we know which prison he's getting sent to we can't source a man on the inside assuming we need one, or find a con to befriend Steele, I do however have a guy ready to take the instructions into whoever we pick. He's one of my best men, he's played a chaplain before, getting messages and other stuff to guys on the inside. So, yes Mr Harrison, I'd say we're as ready as we can be until we know which prison we're dealing with." He concluded with a satisfied nod.

"This is the last time we meet about this, no calls, no texts, no emails. If you need money send an urgent invoice for my attention, reference it BH/JS/op13 and I'll have it passed and paid within 24 hours. If for some reason I need to get a message to you I'll do it through Raymond Cabot, he won't know what it means so don't ask him, you'll just have to work it out for yourself. You know what the ultimate objective is so make it happen, I don't need any other details. Are we clear?" Harrison stood and headed towards the door, indicating the meeting was over.

"Very clear Mr Harrison, I'll see to it." And Burt Tomasino nodded politely to his client as he left.

Harrison returned to his seat but this time swivelled his chair round to look out at the view. From his palatial office on the thirty-third floor of Frost Bank Tower in Downtown Austin, Texas, he had a great view of the Colorado River and the Town Lake Metropolitan Park complete with its Stevie Ray Vaughan statue beyond.

His plan was embarrassingly simple. Get Aaron Steele out of prison, equip him with the necessary paperwork and money and send him out of the country after Abigail Storm. John Sullivan obviously had a thing for Ms Storm and the more trouble Steele could cause for her the less attention Mr Sullivan would be paying to his business interests, especially those in West Central Africa in a small, resources rich country called Gabon.

Without his presidential puppet Harrison had no choice but to try to get the drilling rights he needed by other means. His buyers were expecting first deliveries by the end of the year so he had no time to waste on probably useless negotiations. The Gabonese Government thought the sun shone out of John Sullivan's corporate backside and there was little Harrison could do legally to get them to change allegiance to his company.

All he had to do now was wait until he heard Steele had escaped before he gave the order for his assets on the ground in Gabon to start causing the kind of unrest guaranteed to both attract the attention of the Gabonese government and be easily traced back to Sullivan himself. Gabonese police were certainly nothing like the FBI or even the Texas State law enforcement. They could be led in any direction with just a few crumbs of evidence scattered in their path. Which was exactly what Harrison intended to do, and of course, he would be right there ready and waiting when Sullivan was forcibly ejected from Gabon. And if Steele did his job correctly, Sullivan wouldn't even see it coming as he'd be far too busy trying to protect his little Abigail.

~CHAPTER TEN~

"So what you in for then?" The weasely-looking Hispanic man who had been watching Aaron for the past two days finally decided to speak to him.

"What's it to you?" Aaron replied rudely, he had no desire to interact with any of the lowlifes in this hovel he now found himself. Medium security it may have been but it was definitely minimal comfort and totally devoid of aesthetics.

"Just askin'." Came the slightly bored sounding yet persistent reply.

"Don't."

"Why not? You ashamed? Or...I get it...you're one of them innocent types...they got it all wrong...wasn't me...I was framed...yada, yada, yada." He nudged Aaron in the shoulder as he spoke, a wide grin on his face.

"Actually..." Aaron began but the weasel interrupted.

"Don't go there man, it'll eat you up. My advice, keep your head down and your nose clean and get out of here as soon as possible. Me, I'm doing five for breaking and entering with intent to commit a felony." He added with more grinning.

"What the hell does that mean?" Aaron was intrigued even though he found the little man annoying.

"It means I broke into a house and stole a heap of stuff."

"What for?"

"What you mean what for? Cause I wanted to is what for! You dumb or som'ink?"

"I mean, why didn't you just buy whatever it was you wanted? Why risk ending up in this place by stealing it?"

"Coz I couldn't afford to buy stuff, obviously!"

"Didn't you have a job?"

"Course I had a job, but my girl she needs all that money coz she's gonna have a baby and all that." He shrugged as he spoke and Aaron hoped that would be an end to it and the little man would go away. He was disappointed.

"So, what did ya say you were in for?" The weasel started again.

"For fuck's sake, don't you get the hint?" Aaron hissed as he shoved away from the wall he'd been leaning on and started to walk away.

"What hint's that then?" The little weasel was right beside Aaron and looked as if he intended to stay there.

"Jesus Christ." Aaron stopped and turned to face his tormentor. "I'm doing ten for assault! Carry on and I may practice on you." He added and started to walk away again.

"Names José 'case you're interested." Little weasel called after Aaron's retreating figure.

"I'm not." Aaron called back without looking round.

"This is going to be fun." José muttered to himself as he dug his hands further into his pockets to try to keep them warm, wondering what tack he could use next to get Steele to talk to him.

As far as he was concerned this job was a dream. He hadn't been able to believe his luck when the chaplain had come to see him shortly after he had arrived here and told him there was a job he could be perfect for if he was interested.

As the chaplain had explained that the job, if done right, would make him enough money to go back to Mexico and live with his wife and child without financial worries, he was very definitely interested. Even when the chaplain had gone on to explain that if the job went wrong he would either be dead or in prison for a great deal longer than the five years he had just started, he was still interested.

So, this morning when Father Delgado had arrived he had received his first instructions. He was to get close to Aaron Steele, an arrogant bastard who would no doubt think he was better than everybody else, well the chaplain hadn't been wrong there, and then start to encourage Steele to voice his anger and resentment with a woman called Abigail Storm. Apparently the chaplain and whoever was paying him wanted Steele wound up like a coiled spring with thoughts of vengeance and justice against this woman, whoever she was, and they wanted it done in three days. José was good at winding people up, he could play the dumb chancer with his eyes shut. He had wondered what was going to happen when he got Steele wound up good and tight but the chaplain had assured him he wasn't going to have to fight Steele or anything like that. He was small and fast on his feet but violence wasn't his thing, he preferred to use his speed to put as much distance between himself and whatever fights were going down.

Apparently Father Delgado would be back in three days so José had no time to lose.

For the next twenty four hours he dogged Aaron's every footstep, apart from lockdown, he spent every waking minute badgering the man to tell him who he'd assaulted and why. Eventually Aaron lost his temper and turned on José, pinning him to the nearest wall with his fist balled into the front of José's overalls.

"What the fuck do you want? You annoying little man." Aaron hissed into José's face, his own face contorted with rage. "Why won't you leave me alone?"

José managed to keep his cool, despite the fact that his heart was hammering to get out of his chest.

"Everyone needs a friend in here, and you don't look as weird as the rest of them." José managed through gritted teeth.

"What do you mean?" Aaron demanded, showing no signs of letting José go.

"Look man, I don't mean no harm." José tried a placating tone whilst he tried to prise Aaron's fingers open to extract himself. "Shit happens in here, you need someone watching your back. I don't really want any of them other weirdos watching my back so I picked you. Nothing else to it."

"You picked me?" Aaron seemed to be trying to process this information and the sudden look on his face indicated he had taken two and two and come up with about nine and a half. "Don't you fucking dare you little creep, I am definitely not going *there*!"

It took José a moment but he suddenly realised where *there* was. "Oh my God! I'm not going there either! Jesus, is that what you thought I was? Fuck

you, maybe you are just as weird as the rest of them."
José managed to finally wriggle out of Aaron's grip. "I
just thought we could maybe help each other survive
this place, I mean, two sets of eyes and ears are more
likely to see trouble coming before it's right at the door."

Aaron decided this wouldn't be a prudent
moment to point out that however many sets of ears you
had none of them would *see* anything. He had however,
already been approached in the shower and was ready to
concede that someone watching his back at such a
moment would definitely be preferable. "OK." He said
with a sigh. "That could work."

"Glad we sorted that out finally." José replied
cheerily extending his hand for Aaron to shake. "My
name is José, pleased to meet you."

"Aaron Steele, likewise." Aaron replied without
even the hint of a smile.

"Really?" José's look of astonishment would have
won him awards in any other circumstance, "You're the
journalist guy? The one in all the papers a couple of
months back? Wow, I really am pleased to meet you.
Didn't you stop that two-faced Senator from running for
president?" José knew he was going to have to lay it on
thickly now as he'd already wasted a day of the three he
had getting this arrogant prick to talk to him.

"Yeah, that was me." Aaron confirmed with a
small, slightly condescending shrug.

"How the hell d'ya end up in here then? I
thought you was some kinda star?" José could see his
wide eyed celebrity worship was beginning to work on
Aaron, he watched as Steele visibly puffed himself up
before answering.

"Bitch of an ex-girlfriend couldn't stand how
famous I'd become and went to the police with a pack of

lies." Aaron had no qualms about his version of events, he very much doubted José could even read and he didn't appear to remember many of the details of the events as they had unfolded judging by his inane questions. Aaron had chosen to be completely honest with José, the reason he was in here was actually Abigail's fault, notwithstanding the fact that the story had been hers, he wouldn't be here if she had just left it at that, got her apology from the Globe and gone home.

"Women." José breathed, "Can't live with 'em, can't live without 'em."

"Oh, I'm very sure I can live without this one thank you very much." Aaron interjected with feeling.

"So, go on then, tell me what she did?"

By this time the pair had wandered back to Aaron's cell and for the next two hours José sat on the bed whilst Aaron paced up and down the cell recounting the events which had brought him and Abigail together. Obviously he was telling the Aaron Steele version of events but José didn't care. He remembered every word of the newspaper stories at the time, including the ones about what this monster had done to four women, but for his purposes the truth was irrelevant, what mattered was what Aaron Steele believed and José did his utmost to support the notion that Abigail was to blame for everything.

By the time he left the cell Aaron was beaming, finally he had found a kindred spirit, someone who totally agreed with him. He had known all along Abigail was the one in the wrong not him. Finally he had confirmation from another proper man that his actions when it came to his sexual preferences were worthy of anyone professing to be a real man, unafraid to follow his natural manly urges, and she had only complained and incited the others to complain because politically correct society dictated how everyone was supposed to behave, even though nobody actually wanted to. His only crime, it seemed to him, was to have enough courage to act like the real man he undoubtedly was.

~CHAPTER ELEVEN~

Two days later José was back in Aaron's cell, a wide grin on his face. He had spent most of the previous forty eight hours encouraging Aaron's sense of persecution at the hands of Abigail Storm. It hadn't been hard, the man was the most egotistical, self-centred, self-important pig of a man José had ever met. Right about now Aaron Steele would have walked through walls if he thought Abigail Storm was on the other side.

Somewhere in the back of José's mind it had occurred to him he should be worried about his role in this scenario. He had never met Miss Storm and therefore had no real opinion of her save being grateful to have been offered this chance to make serious money out of her situation, certainly he felt no animosity towards her. He consoled himself with the fact that Aaron was stupid and arrogant and highly unlikely to be smart enough or resourceful enough to pull off any of the nasty eventualities he had bragged about to José. He was vaguely aware that should some catastrophe befall Miss Storm he should and would feel very guilty for having played a part, albeit a detached part, in helping Steele on his way. However, when back in Mexico he knew he would have to actively seek out such news and vowed it was something he never wanted to know and would therefore never look for.

It had also occurred to him that whoever was bankrolling this (so far his only contact had been with the Padre and he either did not know who the money man was or wasn't telling, which suited José just fine), had to have some serious money and influence. The less he knew the better, although, he was streetwise enough to know that even his lack of knowledge would not guarantee him his safety. To leave anyone alive with the knowledge that Aaron Steele had serious financial and influential help for his escape would be unwise as far as the anonymous backers were concerned, any trail for the FBI to follow would surely be eliminated as much as possible.

It was why he had chosen Guadalajara as the venue for the payoff, and insisted the Padre was the courier. There they could meet very publically and then José could melt away into the crowds and eventually back to his home. He had no idea whether his real name was known to the Padre's associates, but as he had never used it here in the US he could only hope it was unknown to them and that they thought José Menendez was his real name. It could take years for them to track all the José Menendez's in Mexico, there had to be thousands of them.

José had not seen Aaron so far this morning as he had been getting his further instructions from Father Delgado, and as far as he was concerned the news could not have been better.

"What you got to grin about, that girl of yours been visiting?" Aaron asked as he couldn't fail to notice José's beaming smile.

"Nah, better than that my friend." Replied José and he plonked himself down on Aaron's bed. "Much, much better!"

"So who was it then?"

"My padre!" José was going to make Aaron work for every morsel of information today, he knew it would make Aaron angry but, it was an angry, unfocused and reckless Aaron he needed if he hoped to succeed in his new task.

"Why the fuck would your Padre make you grin so stupidly?" Aaron demanded, barely concealing his exasperation. Whilst having José around to massage his ego was one thing, the little man was still as irritating as hell.

"He's my cousin." José added still grinning.

"So?"

"The guard on this wing on the night shift is also my cousin."

"Great, so you have lots of cousins, so what?"

"He can get us out!" José let the statement hang in the air between them.

"What? So we can wander round the prison in the dark? What the fuck would we want to do that for?" Aaron was either being deliberately dense or he really was so angry he could not see the wood for the trees.

"No man...*out* out!" José looked hard at Aaron, willing him to finally get the message.

"Why the hell would he want to do that? He'll get fired for sure, and anyway, who said anything about us getting out?" Aaron would dearly have loved to get out of this place but the possibility of escape had never entered his head and he was going to need time to process the thought.

"Well, I'm going and I'm going tonight." José had no intention of giving Aaron any time to think about it. "My girl's gonna have a baby and I'm stuck in here for five years, no thanks, I got the chance to get out and get back to Mexico and my girl, I'm gonna take it, even if you's too chicken to, case you have to live up to all that *'when I get out I'm gonna...'* shit you been spoutin'." José sat back and waited for the explosion. He wasn't disappointed.

Aaron, now red with rage, took two long strides across the room and grabbed José by the front of his overalls.

"It's NOT shit!" He hissed. "I meant every word, that bitch will pay for what she's done to me!"

"Just not yet huh?" José was taunting him now, he knew all Aaron needed was another little shove.

"Now is fine with me!" Said Aaron through gritted teeth as he threw José back onto the bed. "Just fine!"

"See, I knew you wasn't full of shit really." José smiled at Aaron, straightening his attire as he hauled himself up from the bed. "Be ready, we'll come get you." He added as he strolled from Aaron's cell.

"What time?" Aaron asked José's retreating form.

"How the fuck do I know? My cousin comes for me, I come for you. Just be ready." He shook his head disapprovingly and rolled his eyes heavenward, it was all well and good taking on the job of getting this idiot incensed enough to want to escape but the man was a liability. José had to hope he could manage to neutralise Aaron's stupidity long enough to get them both to the docks in Boston where they would be catching separate ships, José possibly to Panama, although with a transit time of four weeks or more he was considering whether going overland to Mexico would be better, and Aaron to who knew where. José didn't care where Aaron headed after he got him to Boston docks as long as he never had to see the arrogant prick again.

Strolling back to his own cell José hoped, not for the first time, that the Padre wasn't playing him. Doing a job without at least some of the money upfront might be considered foolhardy but José had little choice, the Padre could hardly bring the money here, nor would it be wise to try to smuggle it into Mexico when he got there. If he were caught crossing the border into Mexico he would simply be an illegal immigrant coming home, he doubted there would be too much outcry. Certainly the American side of the border would just be glad to be rid of him, his real name was unknown to the American authorities, as was his home address so even if the border guards knew of an escaped convict from Old Colony Correctional Centre, Bridgewater, Massachusetts, they were unlikely to realise he was who they were looking for. The plan as it stood was for him to meet the Padre in Guadalajara where he would be paid and although it meant he had to do this whole operation on trust he knew it was the only way he could get the money undetected into Mexico.

The $50,000 he had been promised if he got Aaron to Boston docks filled with the murderous intent to go after Abigail Storm would keep his wife and young sons very well indeed for a very long time back in Guaymas, Mexico, a village on the east coast of the Gulf of California. He would no longer have to steal to get money to send home. He could be at home with his family and do something locally, maybe boat trips for tourists or fishing or something. The thought made him smile broadly, if he had to kiss Aaron Steele's obnoxious backside all the way to Boston docks it would be worth every second.

~CHAPTER TWELVE~

Aaron's heart did a backflip as he heard the tell-tale hiss click of his cell door being unlocked. He lay as still as possible, fully dressed under the covers. Despite expecting José he was not going to move until he was sure it was not just some random inspection.

"You coming?" A hissed whisper from outside the door convinced Aaron it was time to go. He leapt out of bed and hastily rearranged the pillows so a cursory glance might convince a passing guard there was a body in the bed. His heart hammering wildly he slid over to the door and peeked nervously out of the small crack where José had opened it.

"Come on!" José's whisper was low but urgent. "We haven't got all night."

Aaron took a deep breath and stepped out onto the landing, it was silent except for the occasional muffled snore coming from various other cells. He followed José along the dimly lit corridor towards the door at the end which he knew led to the stairwell. The guard station at the end of the landing was deserted and the door to the stairwell was ajar.

José and Aaron slipped silently into the stairwell, closing the door gently behind them, Aaron heard it re-lock.

"Now where?" He whispered to the back of José's head.

"Down." José didn't even look round, just started purposefully down the stairs. Aaron could do nothing else but follow.

At the bottom of the stairs was the recreation room, a large expanse dotted with sofas, a pool table, ping pong tables, bookcases and other recreational equipment. Aaron knew this room had CCTV cameras at every angle. On the few occasions he had been in there and an altercation had occurred, armed guards had materialised in seconds to subdue the perpetrators and not one inmate was ever questioned about what had happened, the guards already knew.

"What about the cameras?" He whispered urgently to José who had his hand on the mysteriously unlocked door.

"It's 2.30am, only one guard is monitoring the CCTV at the moment, seeing as all inmates are in bed asleep, guess who?" José grinned as he yanked open the door and stepped through.

"Who?" Aaron was not at his best at this hour and the abject terror he was experiencing was not helping his cognitive prowess.

"My fucking Cousin! You numbskull, who the fuck do you think is unlocking all these doors?" José was reminded yet again of the risk he was taking escorting this idiot anywhere, especially on the run.

"What, he's just going to let us stroll out of here?" Aaron was as surprised at the thought as he was impressed.

"Not quite. It gets a bit more complicated in a minute but just shut up and follow me for now, we don't have much time." José jogged across the rec room to the opposite doors, also miraculously unlocked, and disappeared through into the corridor beyond. Aaron decided he had no time to try to understand the situation, he had just better keep going and think about it later so he jogged after José and caught up with him at the next set of doors.

Five more doors and corridors later they were outside in the grounds. "Now it gets more complicated." José said, still whispering as he looked at his watch. "Come on."

Staying close to the side of the buildings the two men hurried around two sides of the prison block until they were parallel to the woods outside the perimeter fence.

"That's where we're going through the fence." José whispered as soon as Aaron caught up to him. He glanced at his watch again. "In three minutes we need to be on the grass over there by the fence." He added pointing to the fence directly in front of them but some hundred yards away across open, flat and featureless ground.

"We just going to stroll over there under the glare of all these lovely floodlights?" Aaron could see no way of reaching the fence unseen, the only reason they could not be seen where they were standing was that they were in the shadow of the building.

"Not quite Mano. In 90 seconds the external CCTV and the lights will go off line, we have to get to the fence then. After that, the motion sensors between the fences and all the fence security measures will go off for five minutes, during that time we have to cut through two fences, cover the ground in between and the open ground between the fence and the woods." José was staring at his watch the whole time he was speaking.

"Your cousin can do all that?" Aaron was impressed despite his anxiety levels still being intolerably high.

"No, course not." José shot Aaron a *'don't be so stupid'* look in the brief second he allowed himself to stop looking at his watch. "They are having a system wide software update in the whole prison tonight. They do it at night because it means the whole system cycles off as it updates. They station guards on every landing so if any inmate happens to be awake and hears his door unlock, he'd only get as far as sticking his nose out the door before he had a gun in his face. That's why we had to get out here as quick as we did, any longer inside and we'd have run into the guards who were just getting their positions allocated when we came out." José glanced at his watch again. "The whole process takes around ten minutes, and the perimeter CCTV will go off in exactly fifteen seconds, get ready to run."

Aaron had little time to ready himself as José suddenly jerked his sleeve, pulling him away from the wall in the direction of the fence opposite. They covered the hundred yards at a flat run and as they hit the ground beside the fence on their bellies they discovered two pairs of wire cutters sitting neatly in the grass just to the right of the upright post, exactly where José had expected them to be. Aaron grabbed the nearest pair and was about to start cutting when José's hand grabbed the cutters by the sharp end.

"Not yet." He hissed, again studying his watch, this time Aaron could see José counting off the seconds silently as he watched the hands crawl round. "Now!"

Both men started to cut the wire, unspoken they started at either side of what would be a man sized hole and quickly and silently they met in the middle. José scrambled through into the long grass between the fences and still on his belly he headed directly for the outer fence. Aaron was right behind him and within a few seconds they were again working from either side to create a hole in the outer fence. José kept glancing nervously at his watch.

"How long?" Aaron panted, the sweat on his forehead belying his slight state of panic rather than any effects of the exertion.

"90 seconds left." José answered, "Cut faster!"

After what seemed like an eternity the wire cutters snipped the final wire and both men again scrambled through the hole they had made, without pause they both rushed headlong into the woods some fifty yards away, neither stopping until they were well concealed by the trees. José took a last look at his watch.

"And the whole security system is back up and running....Now!" He turned to grin at Aaron. "So far so good, let's get the hell out of here."

"How long before they notice we're gone?" Aaron asked as they jogged away from the prison and further into the woods.

"Hopefully at least four hours, just before breakfast." José replied, "Assuming they don't discover our empty beds before that for some reason. We'll be well away by then."

"Will they set the dogs on our trail?" Aaron had seen a great many movies but had never thought about the reality of a prison break.

"Yup. But don't worry, we're heading for the river, it should be about half a mile south of us, Padre will have left us a parcel, some money and stuff, and we can follow the river north for several miles, way long enough to throw the dogs off the scent."

Satisfied that José seemed to have everything covered for now Aaron decided to quit talking and put all his energy into putting as much distance between themselves and the potentially chasing dogs as they could in the time they had.

It took them ten minutes of good paced jogging to reach the banks of the river. To the left, a few hundred yards further along the bank they could just make out the shape of a bridge in the dark half moonlight.

"Parcel should be under that bridge." José panted and Aaron was glad to hear he was as short of breath as he was rapidly becoming.

"I hope it's in the shape of a boat!" Aaron tried taking deep breaths to regulate his heaving chest.

"If it is, I hope it's got an engine coz we're going up river, I'd rather jog than paddle against the current." José threw over his shoulder as he headed for the bridge.

Underneath the bridge the good Padre had kept his word. They found a backpack containing sweaters, waterproof coats, a compass and map together with a substantial quantity of cash.

"Good old Padre." Aaron exclaimed after pulling on a welcomingly warm sweater and the waterproof. "At least we might not freeze to death now."

"Don't get too excited. We have to get in the water now if we want to throw the dogs off the trail. I don't think the water will be very warm!" Said José, stuffing his sweater and waterproof back into the backpack and slinging it over his shoulder.

"Shit!" Aaron exclaimed, pulling off the nice warm garments and handing them back to José to put in the bag. "How far d'ya think we need to go?"

"Dunno, far as we can I guess, the dogs will bring them to the river for certain but I've no idea how many miles either way they'll go before they give up." With that he waded into the knee deep water a couple of yards from the bank, hoping he didn't have to go any further or deeper in and risk all this clothes getting wet with freezing water, and set off up river.

Aaron reluctantly followed, gritting his teeth against the cold of the water and thanking whatever God there was that the river's current did not seem to be too strong, even so, walking against it in this cold was going to be arduous work and the thought that kept Aaron going was that this would lead to him watching Abigail Storm die. He trudged on.

They had probably covered only about a mile but the cold was sapping their strength and they were both struggling to walk against the current when José spied something jutting out from the bank up ahead.

"Come on Aaron, there's a boat house up ahead, you up to stealing a boat?" He grinned, trying to inject some enthusiasm into Aaron's flagging frozen spirit.

"If there's a boat with a motor in that shed I'll kiss you José!" Aaron replied through chattering teeth as he ploughed on towards the outline of the boathouse up ahead in the dark.

"No need for that!" José joked as he pushed his frozen legs forward the last few yards to the boathouse.

As the pair rounded the side edge of the wooden structure they almost shouted with joy at the sight before them. There, bobbing in the lapping current was a small wooden dingy, complete with outboard motor. Hurriedly they dragged themselves over the side into the small boat and began to untie its mooring rope, taking care not to touch anything inside the shed which could hold their scent they allowed the boat to drift slowly out into the current.

"Maybe we should go south." José muttered almost to himself.

"I thought Boston was north?" Aaron said, puzzled.

"It is but, the dogs will lead them to the river. When they find our scent under that bridge they will assume we went north, then, someone will report this boat missing, further north, and they will hopefully be convinced then that we went that way. So, if we now go downriver, first, we'll be travelling with the current and so we'll go faster, and second, we'll put more distance between us and them hopefully, we can turn north later. What do you think Mano?" José looked at Aaron, hoping he could see the sense in the argument.

"Sounds like a good idea, how long until they discover we've gone?"

"Good couple of hours yet, it's only just after 4 am." José replied looking at his watch.

"OK, let's do it." Aaron decided and reached over to pull the sweater and waterproof from the backpack, at least the top half of him could get warm for a while.

José started the outboard and set the little boat out into the centre of the river where the current was strongest. He motioned to Aaron the take the tiller while he too donned a sweater and coat and soon they we're travelling at a good pace back the way they had come.

In what seemed like no time at all they passed under the bridge where they'd started their icy trek.

"Christ, is that all the ground we'd covered?" Aaron was genuinely surprised, it had felt like they had gone miles in the freezing water. "We can't have done more than a mile!"

"Thank God we found this."   Agreed José, knowing that if they didn't get out of their wet pants and shoes soon, no amount of warm top half was going to stop them from getting hyperthermia, he gunned the little engine to its maximum, determined to put as much distance between them and their would-be captors as possible before they simply had to stop and find dry clothes.   They wouldn't get anywhere near Boston if either of them ended up in hospital.

~CHAPTER THIRTEEN~

"Boss?" Sean heard Frank's voice calling from the outer office. For Frank to risk interrupting him he knew it had to be urgent.

"What's up Frank?" He answered as soon as he saw the toecap of Frank's boot preceding him through the office door.

"We got a problem Boss." Frank was his usual taciturn self and Sean merely waited for him to continue. "Steele's out!"

"In English Frank." Sean raised his eyebrows indicating he needed more information.

"Aaron Steele escaped from prison last night. State police, dog handlers and US Marshals are all out looking but no sign of him yet, looks like he got clean away."

"Alone?" Sean was sure Steele did not have the wit to pull off an escape alone.

"No Boss, Mexican called José Menendez was with him."

"Connection?"

"None the yanks have found so far Boss. I've put the word out we want information, but it's only been a few hours, be later on before we find out more." Frank shuffled his weight from one foot to the other, always a sure sign he had something more to say.

"What is it Frank?"

"Er...not really my place Boss." Frank looked uncomfortable.

"Spit it out Frank, you know I value your opinion more than anyone's, so it's *always* your place."

"Well Boss, it's just Miss Storm Boss."

"What about her Frank?" There was no way to rush Frank, Sean knew from years of experience, you simply had to encourage him to continue.

"You think that scumbag will come after her again? You think maybe we should be watching her again?" He blushed slightly as he spoke and Sean couldn't help but smirk.

"You've taken quite a shine to Abigail haven't you Frank?" Sean smiled up at his longest serving employee and, although Frank would be the last to acknowledge it, his friend.

"Not...not like that Boss..." Frank was suddenly agitated, "Just feel a bit protective is all." He added hurriedly.

"Frank, sorry, I didn't think for a moment you had, or ever would have, any inappropriate thoughts about Abigail, so calm down. I'm very glad you like her, I hope to keep her around, if she'll have me, but that's another story. Today we do have a problem. You're right, no doubt that waste of skin will have his sights set on finishing what he started, so, in answer to your question Frank, yes, organise someone to watch Abigail 24/7, but quietly Frank, I don't want her to know, it'll frighten the life out of her. I'll tell her when we know what's going on."

"Yes Boss." Frank turned to go.

"And Frank…"

"Yes Boss?" He turned back.

"What's the fastest he could get here?"

"Well Boss, his best bet would be if he can get to New York, shipping time to Liverpool would be about 8 days. If he heads for Boston it'll take a lot longer, ships tend to bounce around the east coast a bit so could take as long as 28 days from there."

"You don't think he'll try to fly?" Sean knew Frank had a reason for assuming Steele would come by cargo ship.

"Not these days Boss, no way anyone would recommend travelling by air on false papers, not with today's security levels. No Boss, my guess is he'll come by ship, s'what I would do." Frank added with a shrug.

"OK, so we should have at least a week before we need to worry, we got people who can watch the ports?"

"Yes Boss, they're on it already." Frank nodded.

"For now we'll have to assume Steele is being helped…"

"Seems most likely Boss."

"Which means he's not going to find it as difficult as it should be to travel but, as you suggested, he is going to need false paperwork." Sean looked up at Frank as he spoke, their relationship was such that he knew he wouldn't need to clarify the thought.

"Already on it Boss, not many decent forgers on the eastern seaboard, all getting a visit this afternoon."

"Good job Frank, keep me informed."

"Yes Boss." Frank turned and marched from the room.

After Frank had gone Sean stared unseeingly out of his office window. He had a fabulous view of the whole development which was now Salford Quays. He could see media city just across the Manchester Ship Canal part of which ran past the front of his office building and in the distance he could see the red lights atop the Hilton Tower. But today he wasn't seeing the view, all he could see was the battered and bleeding form of Abigail Storm, the last time Aaron Steele had come after her in the hospital back in Boston. He was not going to let that happen again so, if Frank thought Steele could be here in just over a week he would make sure Abigail was not here when Steele arrived.

Making the kind of instant decision he was famous for he reached for the phone. She answered on the third ring.

"Sean, hi." She said brightly, her voice making his heart constrict as always. "I thought you were going to give me a few days to think about how to implement your proposal?" She added trying to be stern but he could hear she was smiling.

"Ah, yes, well, I was going to but erm...something's come up and I need to fly to Gabon day after tomorrow, I could be there for a few weeks and I would really love it if you'd come with me. I know it's short notice but I think you'll be glad you came." He knew he was speaking too fast but he wanted to get her to agree before she really thought about it, knowing she wouldn't back out if she agreed to come. "So what do you think? Can you be ready in thirty six hours?" He crossed his fingers, held his breath and waited.

"How many weeks?" Abi asked hesitantly, she hadn't really convinced herself to fully take up Sean's proposal yet, he was far too sexy and being around him confused her, she had been wondering whether to shadow him on a limited basis would work. But she hadn't been able to convince herself to decline either, something about him drew her in, despite her sensible side telling her that whatever he said, gangster ran in his blood.

"At least two or three, maybe even four." Sean answered, still not daring to breathe but hoping the prospect of not seeing him for that long might sway her to his side rather than dissuade her from coming at all.

Sean could read her well enough to know she was attracted to him, he was also well aware she would fight it for as long as it took for him to make her trust him. He didn't care how long it took, he was willing to put in however many hours of patient and genuine understanding she needed to become the confident, beautiful, whole human being he knew lurked somewhere inside her. If it meant he was only ever her friend then so be it, he would settle for that although his dream would be for their relationship to be much, much more.

"Do I need jabs?" She asked tentatively, Sean smiled, he had her.

"Yes a few, and malaria pills, but I can arrange all that for you this afternoon when we go into Manchester to get you the clothes you'll need." Sean smiled into the phone, he knew she was going to protest but had already decided to come with him.

"Why do I need clothes?" Her suspicions rising yet again, just as Sean had predicted.

"You'll see." Was all he would say. "I'll pick you up in half an hour and we'll go shopping, then get some lunch, then sort your vaccinations out. Your passport is still valid I hope?" He added, more than pleased she had agreed, and not just as a means to put distance between her and the possible visit of Aaron Steele.

"Yes, my passport has another five or six years on it." Abi realised she had inadvertently agreed to the trip but she wasn't displeased with the thought, seeing Africa, or at least part of it, was definitely on her list of things to do before she died and going with Sean would mean she had a guide who knew his way around.

"Great, I'm on my way then." Sean was very pleased with himself and it showed in his voice, although Abi thought she detected a slight undercurrent she couldn't quite put her finger on. "Is everything OK Sean?" She added, curiosity getting the better of her usual timidity.

"Everything is fine Abi, I'll see you in half an hour." Sean answered swiftly disconnecting the call, slightly disconcerted that she had seen through his jolly façade. He was also delighted of course, for her to detect that his mood was anything other than he projected, particularly over a telephone line, meant that whether she liked it or not she was starting to tune in to him.

Sean was also aware that lying to her, or more accurately, her finding out he was lying to her, would do serious damage to their relationship both now and at any time in the future, however, telling her about Aaron's escape now would only frighten her so he decided to tell her when they were safety in the air, when hopefully he would also be able to convince her she would be safe in Africa, Aaron would never find her there.

~CHAPTER FOURTEEN~

Bruce Harrison stepped from the elevator into the air conditioned lobby of the *Hotel le Cristal* in Libreville, capital city of Gabon. This hotel was one of the few five star hotels within the city limits, being just less than a mile from the city centre. It was also one of the few hotels in the area which boasted presidential suites, even if there were only two in the entire building.

Today he had a meeting with the government official in charge of drilling and mining rights in the areas he was interested in. He knew the meeting was merely a courtesy as the government had already indicated they were more than happy with how Sullivan Industries were running their operations. However, if Harrison's plan was to succeed he needed to be viewed as the second favourite independent contractor, so when Sullivan fell out of favour, he was ideally placed to pick up the ball and run with it.

As he climbed into a taxi outside the hotel's front entrance he saw, in his peripheral vision, a black windowed limousine pull up behind his ride. He glanced behind as his taxi pulled away and was both surprised and mildly alarmed to see John Sullivan climbing out of the back of the executive vehicle. As he watched,

Sullivan turned and offered his hand to help another person alight from the car. Harrison's blood ran cold as he recognised her instantly, it was Abigail Storm.

"Shit, shit, shit!" He exclaimed, hurriedly digging his mobile phone from his pocket.

"Pardon Monsieur?" The shocked but polite driver enquired.

"Nothing just drive." Harrison snapped, then seeing the driver's uncomprehending look he waved his arm frantically and shouted "Allez!" The driver got the message and pulled away into the traffic.

Calculating quickly that direct contact from his phone here in Gabon to Burt Tomasino, however urgent his message, might one day come back to haunt him, Harrison quickly dialled a different number.

"Ray?"

"Bruce? I thought you were in Africa?" Raymond Cabot answered groggily. Harrison had failed to consider the time difference and it was only 4 am in Boston.

"I am, sorry to wake you Ray but this is urgent. I need you to call Burt Tomasino. Do you have his number?"

"Yes, you gave it to me a while back when I needed some security matters dealt with. Why do I need to call him?" Ray still wasn't fully awake but he had detected the urgency in Harrison's voice so held off on chastising him for calling at such an ungodly hour.

"I need you to give him an urgent message. Tell him, there is a storm in Africa!" Harrison paused for Ray to catch up.

"What'll he care what the weather in Africa is doing? Is he coming over there to meet you?" At this time of the morning Raymond Cabot didn't really care if it was raining in Africa, he just wanted to go back to sleep.

"No, Raymond, he isn't coming out here but the message is very, very urgent, repeat it back to me." Harrison demanded.

"It's raining in Africa!" Ray Cabot was getting a little cross now, who the hell did Harrison think he was, ringing at this hour with a weather forecast then challenging him to remember it.

"NO! Raymond, listen, *there is a storm in Africa.* Those are the exact words I need you to use. Burt will know what to do. Now, repeat it to me."

"OK, *there is a storm in Africa*, I'll call him first thing and tell him. Now can I go back to sleep please?"

"Now Raymond, I need you to call him now then ring me back. OK?" Harrison rang off before Cabot had any chance to argue further.

Five minutes later the phone in his hand rang, it was Cabot.

"OK, I called, I gave him the message, he said 'Oh Shit' and hung up. So, would you like to tell me what that was all about please Bruce?" Cabot's tone suggested he was now fully awake but Harrison was in no mood to explain, besides, the less Cabot knew the better.

"Not really Ray, you don't need to know. You can go back to sleep now. Thanks." With that Harrison hung up and leaned back against the seat. Sullivan being here in Gabon was not part of the plan. The whole point of getting Aaron Steele out of prison was to keep Sullivan's eyes firmly fixed on Abigail in the UK while Harrison's hired thugs did their jobs here. Sullivan was supposed to be too preoccupied and too far away to rectify the situation in time to rescue his contracts when the government decided he didn't have control of the situation.

Now the entire plan hung on Burt Tomasino, a scenario Harrison was not happy with at all. But there was no more he could do right now, he would just have to go to his meeting and hope Burt could salvage the situation.

In Boston, Burt sat on his bed staring at his phone, trying to reorganise his carefully laid plan to accommodate this new and unfortunate information.

"What the hell is Abigail Storm doing in Africa? She's supposed to be in bloody Manchester!" He said aloud to the reflection of himself in the mirror on the front of his wardrobe. "Bollocks!" Glancing at the clock he winced at the hour but climbed out of bed anyway. He was going to have to go personally to sort this out. Not what he had planned for. He pulled on his clothes, tucked his handgun into the back of his pants and shrugged into his old faithful leather jacket. Grabbing his car keys on the way out he headed for the Seaport District and the docks.

Burt knew José and Aaron were due at the document forgers sometime today, he hoped they would be there early, preferably before dawn, he didn't fancy sitting there all day waiting for them.

When the Padre had spoken to José yesterday he had learned that the fugitives had apparently decided to spend their second full night of freedom at a motel just outside the city limits. As they had been on the move for the majority of the previous two nights and had laid low during the days for fear of being spotted, Burt could hardly begrudge them a comfortable bed and a shower before the final leg of their journey into Boston. Given they had plenty of cash it wasn't as if they were going to have to walk to the docks.

According to the Padre they had followed the river down as far as Taunton, Massachusetts, then hitched a ride on a road train heading for Portland in Maine. They were dropped off just west of the city some time yesterday and decided to get some sleep before heading in this morning.

The Padre was supposed to meet them at the forgers but Burt decided he was going to have to do it himself. The Padre already knew more than Burt would ordinarily be comfortable with, and he was only supposed to ensure their introduction to the forger and then put Aaron on a container vessel heading to the UK. He didn't need to know this latest development, that way, if the FBI ever did catch up with him the trail would go cold with the little information he could give.

As Burt pulled up outside the lockup which served as the document forger's home and place of business it was still only just after 5 am. Sitting in his car across the street Burt used the time to work out how the hell he was going to get Aaron to Africa, at least he would be able to tell Steele which hotel to try, it was the best in Libreville and he knew both Harrison and Sullivan used it regularly. The plan to get Steele to England had been easy, he was just going to board a train to New York where he would catch a freighter and sail straight into Liverpool docks. He was sure even Aaron Steele could manage to catch a train or hire a car or some such to get himself to Manchester from there. But Africa? That was a whole different ball game. He'd have to check but Burt was fairly sure there wouldn't be any freighters going to Africa from Boston or even New York docks.

Using the google app on his phone Burt started to research his options and it soon became obvious that trying to get Aaron to Africa by ship was going to take weeks and even then the best he could do was get him to South Africa, which was a hell of a long way from Gabon.

Finally Burt had to give up on the idea of a freighter altogether, it was nigh on impossible anyway and as his mind churned over the possibilities he suddenly remembered the Mexican. José had been due to meet his maker after Aaron was safely shipped out to the UK but Burt now saw he may well be the answer to his immediate problem. No doubt José had planned to get back to Mexico by whatever means Burt didn't need to worry about.

An idea was fast forming in Burt's mind. An associate of his had a Cessna TTx, allegedly the fastest fixed gear single engine plane in the world. For a fee Burt was sure he could be persuaded to fly two anonymous passengers down to southern Texas, somewhere near the border with Mexico. He pulled out his mobile phone and flicked the power on, the display told him it was almost 6 am, very nearly a civilised hour to make a phone call.

The call was answered on the second ring, a voice definitely not just woken from sleep greeted Burt as the old friend he was.

"What can I do for you this fine morning Burt?"

"Morning, Alfie, busy today?" Burt had yet to meet another man who was as cheerful as Alfie no matter what time of day or night it was.

"Nothing I can't put off until tomorrow." Alfie chuckled, "No doubt whatever you have in mind is urgent?"

"You know me well Alfie. Yes, I have urgent cargo for South Texas."

"How much urgent cargo?"

"Two packages."

"Hot?"

"Very!"

"It's gonna cost." Alfie warned seriously. "And not just the fuel."

"Name your price." Burt knew it would be expensive, but it would be so worth whatever it cost to have Steele out of the country and on his way, no longer Burt's concern.

"Well, it's about 1900 miles, that's a good tank and a half each way, that's somewhere around 500 dollars just in fuel. Then there's my time, there and back'll take me two days, can't fly both ways without a stopover, so there's a hotel too…"

"Alfie how does $10,000 sound?" Burt couldn't wait any longer for Alfie to do his maths.

"Oh now Burt, it ain't gonna cost that much!" Alfie was astonished at the figure Burt suggested.

"Alfie, I'm offering you $10,000 to do the job today, you interested or not?"

"Would that be cash dollars?"

"Cash dollars, all upfront."

"You got yourself a plane Burt, it's at the airfield as usual, that good for you or you want it somewheres else?" Alfie was delighted, $10,000 in cash to fly his favourite little plane was a great deal, legal or not he didn't care who his passengers were, he'd just drop them off and head for home, or maybe Vegas.

"Airfield is fine Alfie, I'll give you the heads up when we're on our way." Burt hung up, just as he noticed two scruffy looking characters heading for the door to the lockup across the street from where he was parked. He climbed out of the car and scanned the area for the Padre, he was supposed to be here somewhere too.

Moments later the Padre arrived and escorted the two ex-prisoners into the forger's domain. Burt hung back, he wanted to catch the priest as he left, no need to let the guys inside know he was acquainted with Father Delgado.

Sure enough, as soon as the Padre had introduced Aaron and José to Luis the forger he made his excuses and left. Burt was waiting for him outside the door and informed him that his services were no longer needed. The look of relief on the priest's face was palpable as was his delight when Burt handed him a thick brown envelope containing the agreed fee for his services.

Father Delgado hurried off into the predawn light as Burt let himself into the lockup. Luis had been under his protection for a long time and there was no need for him to knock.

In all the time he had been parked outside he had not noticed the shadowy figure leaning against a fence to the rear of the lockup next to Luis'. As soon as Burt disappeared inside the figure brought out his own mobile and put it to his ear. He spoke quickly and quietly into the instrument, nodded twice as he received a reply, hung up and stuffed the phone back into his pocket. But still he didn't move, just watched Luis' lockup from the shadows where he had been for the past two days.

Almost six thousand miles away on the other side of the Atlantic, Frank too hung up his phone and decided that the news could wait until he had more concrete information, perhaps he would know more by the time Sean and Abi returned to the hotel later tomorrow afternoon, unless he could get a moment alone with Sean before that, then he could tell him what little extra he now knew. He was aware Sean had told Abigail, during their flight down from Manchester, that Aaron had escaped custody but he was unaware how much more Abi knew and didn't want to compromise the situation by telling Sean what he now knew in front of her. What Sean told her was up to him.

~CHAPTER FIFTEEN~

As Sean glanced back towards the helicopter they had arrived in he noticed Frank just coming off the phone, even at this distance Sean could see Frank's expression was less than pleased. Catching Frank's eye he raised an eyebrow. In reply Frank looked at Abi then shook his head conveying clearly the news was not good and Sean may want to hear it without Abi in earshot.

Frank had arrived in Sean's life when Sean was a mere boy of ten. Sean's father, although promising to keep Sean away from the organised crime side of the business, knew his son would still be a target for would-be rivals.

Frank had been twenty seven at the time, he had been a US marine, this despite the fact he was born and brought up in Manchester in the UK, before going into the private close protection business. Rumour had it that he was once bodyguard to the wife of an extremely wealthy then senator who had since become an ex-President of the United States, a rumour he would neither confirm nor deny, although Sean knew the truth.

So the ten year old boy had acquired a friend and mentor, although Frank had been careful never to step above his perceived position of employee, Sean knew he was aware of how fond Sean had always been of him. For his part Frank had taught the young Sean how to defend himself in any situation, he taught him to fight, to handle weapons of all varieties and, most importantly he taught him to read faces and body language. It was a skill which not only gave Sean a fighting advantage by knowing his opponents next move before he made it, it was also a serious advantage in business, as Sean had proved many times over the years.   Sean had been willing student and by the time he was 21 there was no way Frank could beat him in a fight, either armed or otherwise.

The twenty seven years they had spent together meant they could often communicate without speaking and this was one such time. Sean knew if Frank's bad news had been urgent he would have found a ruse to separate him from Abi and told him. The fact that he hadn't meant it could apparently wait.

Sean returned his attention to Abigail, and the man he had been about to introduce her to a moment ago.

"Miss Abagail Storm, this is Koudjo, General Manager of Sullivan Industries N'Goutou Mining operations." Sean formally introduced Abi to the tallest, widest, blackest man she had ever seen. He would have been intimidating but for the enormous smile he sported, showing perfect rows of gleaming white teeth, and the sparkle of mischief dancing in his eyes. Abi couldn't help but smile back at him.

"Lovely to meet you Koudjo." She said extending her hand to shake his.

"The pleasure is mine, Mademoiselle."   His unmistakable French accent mixed exotically with his African Bantu heritage.

"Koudjo." Sean leaned in to extract Abigail's hand from the massive grip of the still grinning Bantu, shooting him a slightly disapproving but jovial glance.

"Ah, Massa, you bring me such a beautiful lady, Koudjo can't help it."

Abi blushed scarlet right up to her hairline and tried to turn away to hide it from both men. Koudjo roared with laughter and slapped Sean heartily on the back.

"I approve Massa." He said and turned abruptly around, heading towards the long low building to the right which Abigail assumed housed offices of some sort.

"I apologise for Koudjo." Sean said, although Abi could see he was supressing a smile. "He is quite irreverent, but he has worked for me for fifteen years and he's the best General Manager I ever employed."

"No need to apologise, actually I quite like him, just caught me a bit by surprise that's all." Now that her embarrassment had subsided Abi could see the humour in the situation, there had been not a trace of malice in Koudjo's eyes and although he had appraised her she had not seen any hint of sleazy leering, merely open interest and approval. "Although, calling you Master? What's that about?"

"Don't worry, I'm not into slavery or anything here. He is a properly paid and contracted employee. They all call me Massa, at first I thought maybe they were taking the piss." He smiled as he remembered the first time he had come here. "But when I asked Koudjo he said it was just a term for Boss which they all felt comfortable with, so that's what they all call me."

Sean and Abigail had taken the long helicopter flight, across most of the expanse of the country of Gabon, to N'Goutou after checking into the hotel in

Libreville earlier in the day, after flying overnight from Manchester. It seemed having private jets and helicopters at your disposal meant you could go anywhere, anytime, with the minimum of the usual travelling inconveniences. It was a state of affairs Abi knew she could very easily get used to. Although, their speed of departure had meant she'd had vaccinations for cholera, typhoid, hepatitis and yellow fever injected into both her arms and a polio vaccine into her mouth without the sugar lump, which was completely revolting. The combined effects of which, together with the malaria tablets she was now taking, had given her two severely aching arms and a feeling of sick, flu like symptoms in the rest of her body. Sean assured her it would all wear off soon but in the meantime regular paracetamol was helping.

Not that she was complaining, so far Africa had proven to be all she had ever dreamed it would be. When they landed in Libreville it was early morning and the heat of the day had not yet settled in. Abi had stepped from the dim coolness of the Gulfstream and fallen immediately and permanently in love with Africa. It had been a feeling she would struggle to explain when she tried to tell Ginny about it but the whole place felt and smelled exotic, foreign and comfortingly welcoming, like the continent itself welcomed her, not just its people.

During both the drive to the hotel in the car and the helicopter ride from Libreville to the mine, Sean had pointed out incredible things for her to look at, from huge elephants forging paths through the rainforest to herds of buffalo grazing on the grasslands. Even passing overhead as swiftly as they were travelling Abi had seen colourful birds flying around the rainforest canopy and she was sure she had glimpsed monkeys in the trees.

She was captivated and despite feeling slightly ill and exhausted from travelling was excited to be here and was already hoping their trip turned out to be the *'maybe four weeks'* Sean had suggested it might.

As she wandered with Sean towards the building into which Koudjo had now disappeared a loud, piercing siren suddenly blared from speakers she could see set atop poles around the works.

"What's that mean?" She asked Sean, alarmed it might denote an accident of some sort, she was well aware mines were very dangerous places.

"Shift change." Sean replied nonchalantly. "Koudjo will oversea the handover while I tell you a bit about this place and how it all works, then we'll go home with him." He added with a smile.

"We're going home with Koudjo?" Abi echoed, a touch of disbelief in her voice. Sean hadn't sounded like he was joking but she was sure he must have been.

"Yes." Sean confirmed, his smile widening at her obvious incredulity. "It'll be dark in less than an hour, we can't look around this place in the dark, nor can we fly back to Libreville in the dark. So, we are staying with Koudjo and his family in their village which is a few miles from here."

"Oh...er...OK." Abi replied with not just a little trepidation.

"Don't worry, you'll love it." Sean assured her with a grin. "They are some of the nicest people you could ever hope to meet. You'll have an interesting night I promise."

As she did not appear to have much choice in the matter Abi resolved to put her fear of strangers aside and trust that Sean would not deliberately put her in a situation which would endanger her. As for her reluctance to meet people, she would just have to swallow that down and hope for the best, it was something she was well used too, having had to do it many times before.

Sean watched her swallow her fears, wondering if she was aware her every emotion showed in her eyes. He knew he was pushing her out of her comfort zone yet again but hoped he was not pushing her too far or too fast. In order to build her self-confidence Sean knew she had to face situations which frightened her, so that when she came through them unscathed she could be rightly proud of herself. She could not build confidence by avoiding the things she feared. His hope was that by leading her into these situations and supporting her through them, he could help her relax and see how wonderful she really was.

His feelings for her seemed to grow stronger and deeper every day, but he had vowed to himself he would never be the cause of any more distress to her and so he would wait until he knew she was absolutely ready for him to make advances of that nature. Right now she needed a friend, someone she could rebuild her sense of trust with, someone she could rely on if Ginny decided to move to Boston with Sam. He knew trust was something he was going to have to work hard to earn from her but he did not care how long it took. She was the most remarkable woman he had ever met and if it took him until his last day on earth he was going to make her see that.

Placing his hand gently in the small of her back he gestured towards the black, remarkably clean Range Rover parked alongside the buildings, "We can wait and talk in the car, he won't be long."

Abi allowed herself to be led over to the car as she tried to still the tumbling thoughts in her mind. His touch was almost electric, and every time she felt his hand on her she jumped, whether it was like a moment ago when he was merely guiding her in a different direction, or earlier that day when he had offered her his hand as she climbed from the car. Every time he touched her sensors went off all over her body, the sensation both excited and scared her at the same time. Half of her wanted to throw herself into his arms and find out if they really were, as they looked to be, arms which could hold her so tightly they would stick all her broken pieces back together. The other half of her was terrified of letting her guard down, of letting him into her inner self where he could do the most enormous damage just like the other men she had allowed to influence her life.

Coupled with the fact that the whole crime boss or not thing still bothered her immensely, her feelings and thoughts about Sean were a mess. If anything, the more she saw of him the more confused she became.

Having seen the beautiful and luxurious but very separate bedrooms he had procured for them in the presidential suite at the hotel this morning her fears had subsided somewhat. But now, they were to sleep who knew where, in a village, in the African bush and their host seemed to be under the impression they were 'together', at least that was the understanding Abi had drawn from Koudjo's '*I approve*' comment.

She was still stewing over the possibilities when Koudjo arrived at the car closely followed by Frank. The four of them climbed in and set off out into the rapidly darkening bush leaving the lights and noise of the mine behind them.

At this latitude the sun went down alarmingly fast, it seemed that one minute it was daylight, the next it was pitch black. In truth they were almost sitting on the equator where the sun appears to drop out of the sky and disappear below the horizon in just two minutes.

After a very bumpy twenty minute drive Abi began to see lights in the distance.

"My village." Koudjo smiled proudly at her.

"That's amazing, there are lights on." Abi was stunned, she had imagined a series of mud huts in the middle of nowhere with nothing but a cooking fire and half-naked children running around chasing skinny goats. What she was actually seeing was a cluster of buildings, some with lights on she could tell were made up of wooden walls and corrugated tin roofs. Dotted between these were others obviously built in a more traditional African style, but they too had lights on, both inside and out.

"Yes, lights now, we have electricity now, in all our homes and in our school and in our medical centre." Koudjo was beaming, obviously delighted to have stunned his guest so considerably.

"How?" Abi was genuinely astonished, knowing there was no way any power companies would run cabling out this far into the bush.

"Massa did it!" Koudjo stated, beaming his brilliant smile over his should at Abi.

"Koudjo!" Sean laughed, "Stop it!"

Koudjo roared with laughter again, his laugh was infectious and soon the three of them were laughing with him.

"But Massa, it's true." Koudjo was suddenly serious. "Mam'zel Storm it was Massa who got us the water wheel, and the solar panels. The water wheel is in the river behind the village and the solar panels collect sunshine all day long. I show you tomorrow when it's not so dark."

"Actually, it was about getting a stable supply of electricity for the medical centre, so the equipment worked and the fridges kept things like vaccines and antibiotics from spoiling. We discovered it was as simple to electrify the whole village as it was to just provide for the medical centre. So that's what we did." Sean explained quietly, trying to play down his role and neutralise Koudjo's apparent hero worship at the same time, he knew he was only doing it for Abi's benefit anyway.

"I'm very impressed Koudjo." Abi said to the back of his head as he carefully parked the big vehicle in front of a large round wooden building.

"This is where you sleep Mam'zel Storm. You have travelled a long way today, you want shower? Or lie down? You meet my wife and children at dinner in one hour. Massa will show you the way." With that Koudjo hauled his bulk out of the car and ambled off in the opposite direction.

"Come on." Sean said, climbing out of the car too and wandering round to the boot where he retrieved two bags. "Come and see your bedroom, *Mam'zel!*" He added mischievously.

Abi giggled and followed him inside the wooden hut. What she found amazed her further. It was indeed a bedroom, although a partition to one side screened off a small but beautifully appointed shower room and a toilet. Abi noted the modern fittings set against the old and traditional wood and mud walls and couldn't help but marvel at the ingenuity of the builders. The rest of the hut was arranged around a large bed, covered in crisp white sheets already shrouded by the draped mosquito net. In the ceiling was a large, colonial style fan, rotating lazily to create a gentle breeze which ruffled the mosquito net and the thin voile curtains adorning the only window. Other than the bed, furniture was sparse. A bedside table, with a lamp and what turned out to be a small fridge underneath containing bottles of water and a chair, on which Sean gently placed one of the bags.

"What's in the bag?" Abi's curiosity got the better of her.

"Your clothes." Sean replied with a chuckle, as if it were the most obvious thing in the world.

"I didn't pack any clothes." Abi said, her suspicions rising again.

"Don't panic." Sean held up a hand to deflect her inevitable protest. "I knew we'd be staying, I wanted to see your face when I told you we were staying with Koudjo, I apologise if that worries you but it really doesn't need to. As for your clothes, I packed your pyjamas, your toothbrush, make up bag, toiletries, clean underwear and a change of outfit. I hope you approve of my choices."

"Why did you want to see my face? What were you expecting?"

"I was expecting exactly what I saw, you panicked, you controlled that panic and you forced your fears aside. It is a miraculously beautiful thing to witness, I have seen it before, the strength of character it takes for you to just stand up in front of everyday things which scare you so much amazes me, I hope one day it will amaze you too." He added quietly.

Abi could not decide whether she wanted to cry or hug him. What he said was absolutely true, but to know he could read all that from her face was unnerving in the extreme. Suddenly another terrifying thought struck her, and she couldn't help but look from his face to the bed and back again.

"Er...are we...?" She started but before she could finish he had crossed the room and now held her face between his hands. His lips so close to hers she could feel the warmth of his breath on her skin.

"Abigail..." He breathed. "Yes, I would very much like to make love to you in that bed tonight, in fact, I can hardly think of doing anything else right at this moment." He paused for long enough to force her to look up and into his eyes. "But you are so far from ready for that I would be no kind of man if I pushed you. Abigail, I swear to you, never while I see fear in your eyes!"

"Sean...I..." Abi stammered, feeling she ought to say something but having no idea what.

"SShh..." He brushed his thumb across her lips as he spoke. "I know. And one day I will teach you how to trust me, I promise." He smiled into her eyes, seeing her fear retreat ever so slightly, and planted a soft, quick kiss on her lips before he let her go, hoisted up the second bag and strode over to the door. "I'm next door, shower, change, whatever you want to do and I'll be back in half an hour to take you to dinner."

"Thank you." She whispered as he disappeared through the door, willing herself to stop trembling and wondering, not for the first time, how she was ever going to work out how she felt about this man.

Once outside Sean found Frank leaning up against the side of the Range Rover.

"What's up Frank?" He said as he strolled over to join him. "That phone call earlier bad news?"

"Yes Boss. Think so anyway." Replied Frank as the pair headed into the hut next door to Abi's.

"Spit it out then Frank." Sean commanded gently, throwing his overnight bag on the chair next to his bed while Frank did the same on the other side of the room. Abi definitely had the presidential suite tonight, no doubt Koudjo had expected Sean to stay in it with her but bunking in with Frank suited him just fine.

"Well, Boss, you know I had a call earlier saying Steele and his Mexican friend had turned up at Luis the Forger's near Boston Docks and Burt Tomasino turned up right after them."

"Yes Frank, you told me that."

"Well, my man followed them when they all left and they went to a private airfield somewhere south of the city. He couldn't get a hold of a flight plan or anything without breaking cover but he reckoned they was headed south."

"Mexico?"

"Would be my guess too Boss. Anyway, he went back to visit Luis then and Luis said they was all in another room while he made up passports and the like but he heard odd words of their conversation."

"Odd words like what Frank?" Patience was the only way to get Frank to tell a story coherently.

"Well apart from the swearing and stuff, the only real words he got were Africa and storm." Frank looked up at Sean's face as he relayed this last comment, knowing Sean would make the same connections he had made.

"Shit!"

"Yes Boss." Frank agreed.

"You don't think that's a coincidence either do you?"

"No Boss.   Never was much for coincidences Boss."

"Me neither Frank, me neither." Sean sat down heavily on the bed, his face a mask of concern mixed with bubbling rage. "How the fuck does Burt Tomasino know she's here?"

"Shouldn't that be *why* does Tomasino know she's here?"

Sean looked up a Frank, he seemed to try hard to pretend he was just a chunk of muscle, but underneath the façade he was really as sharp as they came.

"Why exactly, Frank.   Would tend to suggest Steele's breakout was orchestrated for a purpose, don't you think Frank?"

"Yes Boss, never thought he'd have the stones or the brains to come up with it on his own Boss."

"Well it sure as hell wasn't Burt's idea either. That leaves one other obvious possibility."

"Harrison." Frank agreed nodding.

"Yes, Harrison. But, no way he did this just for revenge against Abi, not Harrison's style at all, and anyway, apart from costing him a few quid, of which he has ample reserves, and forcing him to change his plans, she hasn't really done him any damage.   That story inconvenienced him is all, it was Cabot and Steele who paid the price."

"You think he did this for Cabot?   Kind of consolation prize?"   Frank didn't look like he had convinced himself of that possibility and Sean shook his head.

"No, Cabot doesn't mean enough to him to risk it."

"So, it's about you then." Frank stated bluntly.

"It would certainly make more sense Frank." Sean agreed sighing heavily. "Bollocks! How am I supposed to get her to believe I'm not some thug gangster if I now have to tell her that Harrison sprung Steele so he'd go after her to get to me. It's just going to confirm to her I'm someone to fear."

"Maybe you shouldn't tell her Boss?" Frank suggested, trying to be helpful.

"I have to tell her Frank. Keeping this from her would be the same as lying to her in her eyes. She'll never trust me if she thinks I'll lie to her. We need a plan Frank."

"Yes Boss, I say we take her home."

"You think we can protect her better in Manchester than here?"

"Definitely Boss, we brought her here to hide her. Well, somebody's telling the other side where she is anyway so we're better off back in Manchester. We got more manpower for a start."

"Yes, you're right there Frank, OK, we head back to Libreville tomorrow but it'll be too late when we get there to leave tomorrow night so we'll fly home first thing the following day. By the way, did our man in Boston inform the relevant authorities about having seen Steele on Boston Docks?"

"Yes Boss, he even said he heard them say they were heading for Mexico but you know that's no guarantee the Feds will catch up with him in time to stop him getting over the border."

"We got anybody in Mexico we can use?"

"We have but it's a big place and we got no idea where he'll try to cross the border so the chances of us finding him there are a bit slim I think. I also got a man at the airport here in Libreville in case he manages to get here before we get out."

"Good job Frank, well there's nothing else we can do at the moment, I'll tell Abi after dinner. We'd best get showered and changed or we'll be late for Koudjo's spectacular feast."

"I hope it's hog roast again, the last one was fantastic." Frank muttered as he grabbed his towel and wash-bag and headed out the back of the hut leaving the bathroom for Sean to use.

~CHAPTER SIXTEEN~

When Aaron's plane touched down in Libreville it was almost 11pm local time. He had been flying for what felt like days and having lost 7 hours in time zones his body had no idea what time of day it thought it should be.

After an otherworldly visit to Luis the Forger somewhere in the Boston docks area all Aaron's plans had changed. Instead of heading for the coast of England on a freighter, he was suddenly heading for Africa. Not that he was bothered in the slightest, this way meant far less rigorous security checks for his forged passport to get through and the added bonus was he would get to Abigail Storm way faster than he would have done had he followed the original plan.

Aaron had no idea who the guy was who had turned up on the docks and told him Abi was in Africa. As usual, Aaron's total lack of journalistic curiosity had prevailed and he had not even thought to ask. Nor had he given much thought to who might be providing all the money he and José had used and were, for his part, still using since escaping from prison. José had said his cousin had left the parcel under the bridge and that same cousin, the padre, had given them another parcel when they had first arrived at Luis the Forgers.

As far as Aaron was concerned his mission to seek revenge for Abi's offences was his right. It was something he was entitled to do because he had been severely wronged by her. If José or his cousin wanted to fund that why would he argue, surely that was just more proof positive that he was right, and Abigail Storm should pay for her crimes.

It had not occurred to him to ask why she was in Gabon, a country he had never before heard of save its mention in the story Abi had stolen from him. He certainly had no idea where in the world it was. Had he thought to ask a few questions he might have discovered she was with the man who, it was widely surmised, had thwarted his last attempt to seek his revenge. Whether this would have given him pause was however so debatable as to negate the value of the question in the first place.

From Boston docks he had been driven to an airfield, bundled aboard a Cessna TTx and flown for seven hours almost due south to the US side of the border between Texas and Mexico, apparently to fly the little plane over the border would have attracted way too much attention from the authorities, so they were dropped off just a couple of miles inside the US. He and José had crossed the border without incident, picked up a car left for them on instruction of José's cousin the Padre, and driven further south into Monterrey. They had parted company at Monterrey's International Airport where Aaron had boarded a flight to Luanda in Angola. Where José had gone then Aaron did not know, nor, despite the little Mexican's ample assistance in getting Aaron to this point, did he care.

Touching down in Luanda after an almost seventeen hour flight Aaron had immediately boarded yet another plane for the two hour hop to Libreville.

He had spent most of the long flight from Mexico sleeping, having had little for the previous couple of days since the breakout, so when he finally found his way out of Libreville airport in his newly acquired hire car at a little before 1am he was wide awake and wired. He knew Abi was almost close enough to touch now and nothing was going to delay him further.

It wasn't a long drive to the *Hotel le Cristal* where he was assured Abigail would be staying. He pulled up in front of the hotel in the little blue Fiat POS which had been the only car available to rent at such a late hour, all the regular car rental firms had closed their shutters at 9pm apparently. Climbing from the car he strode purposefully into the lobby. A lone clerk was at the front desk but smiled accommodatingly as soon as he saw Aaron approaching.

"Do you have a reservation Sir?" He enquired politely, again Aaron's lack of interest in his surroundings failed to alert him to the fact that the clerk spoke to him in English not the French he ought to have expected.

"I don't actually." Aaron replied, his fake smile failing to reach his eyes. The desk clerk was so used to fake he hardly noticed.

"Then would you like me to check if any rooms are available Sir?" The clerk continued.

"No. Actually, my fiancée is staying here at the moment on business and I have flown all the way from the States to surprise her. It's her birthday tomorrow you see." He flashed the clerk his best TV smile and continued. "So, I would be really grateful if you could just tell me what room she's in so I can go up there and give her a fantastic birthday surprise."

"I'm really not supposed to do that Sir..." The clerk began but Aaron had anticipated his reluctance to help and was already sliding a crisp $100 bill across the counter top. "However, as it's such a special request, what is your fiancée's name Sir?"

"Storm, Abigail Storm." Aaron said clearly, almost breathlessly, he was so close now he could almost taste her.

After tapping his keyboard a couple of times the clerk looked up at Aaron, an apologetic look on his face as he pocketed the $100 with his left hand. "I'm sorry sir, nobody by that name is booked in here."

"Oh, of course not, it'll be under the company name." Aaron was floundering, he of course had no idea what name she could be staying under as he hadn't bothered to ask. "Except..." He continued, feigning deep thought, "She's probably booked in under the client's company name. Damn, I have no idea what that could be. She's freelance you see..." He started to explain to the bemused clerk. "She advises other companies, these trips are almost always booked and paid for by them not her. How stupid of me." He pretended to think for a moment then smiled at the clerk as if a thought had just occurred to him. "Perhaps you've seen her, 5ft 7, blonde, blue eyes, fantastic figure..."

"English not American?" The clerk added with a smile.

"Yes!" Aaron looked delighted. "So you know where she is then?" He asked quickly.

"Room 14 Sir, take the elevator round the corner to your left and follow the signs. I hope she enjoys the surprise Sir." With that the clerk went back to tapping on his computer and Aaron headed for the lifts as he had been instructed.

Riding up in the lift Aaron wondered how he was actually going to get into her room. He half thought of going back down to the desk and asking for a key but decided he might be pushing his luck there. By the time he found himself standing outside the door with a *14* sign on it he had narrowed it down to two choices. He either had to try to break down the door, hoping the noise did not arouse any suspicious neighbours who might come out of their rooms to investigate and therefore get in his way. Or, he could knock.

Raising a clenched fist to knock on her door another thought occurred to Aaron. The door had an old fashioned key operated lock, not the usual swipe card system found in most hotels these days. That meant Abi actually had to lock it from the inside, it wouldn't lock automatically. Reaching for the handle, Aaron wondered if she had been as stupid as he knew her to be and left it open for him.

Slowly and silently Aaron pushed down on the handle, not daring to breathe, hearing a faint click he pushed gently at the door and was elated to find it swung silently inwards. He stepped quickly into the room and closed the door behind him, feeling for the key in the dark and turning it in the lock. His breathing was coming in short pants now, the prospect of taking out his frustrations and anger on the one person in the world who so deserved it made him excited beyond belief. His erection was so hard it was pressing against his trouser leg, vying for its freedom.

He waited by the door as his eyes adjusted to the darkened room and soon outlines of objects became clearer and more defined. He could see the shape of the bed in front of him, with the obvious form of a body on top of it. Silently he started across the room towards the bed, knowing his best chance of subduing her was to immobilise her on the bed then hit her hard, just like last time. Even if he didn't knock her out completely it would subdue her long enough for him to get the sedative into her. Only after he rendered her unconscious would he turn on the lights and work out how to get her down to the waiting car. He had no intention of finishing her off here, what he had planned for her would take far too long and make far too much noise. No, he just wanted to grab her and go.

Suddenly, a foot from the bed, the body turned, the lights went on and Aaron found himself staring straight into the eyes of a very angry looking man.

~CHAPTER SEVENTEEN~

Abi lay on the bed under the mosquito net in the semi darkness, the light outside the hut filtering faintly under the door. He was standing watching her, she could see his outline and hear the steady rhythm of his breathing.

She was flushed with excitement, all her fears seemed to have melted away replaced by a hot longing radiating through her body. She was ready for him, she wanted him, in truth she knew she had wanted him from the start, and yet still she couldn't move.

She wanted to throw off the covers and lift the net to allow him to get to her, so he could touch her and slide into the bed beside her.

She wanted to hear him breathe her name, to feel his body against hers, hard and powerful. She tried to speak but no words would leave her mouth. Panic began to rise as she realised all she could move was her eyes.

As soon as she realised this he moved the net aside, his eyes finding hers in the semi-darkness, smiling, reassuring grey-blue eyes. Relief began to flow through her, Sean would see her panic, he would know what to say to allay her fears. His hand on her neck began to caress her skin, she tried to swallow her fear, like she knew he wanted her to but suddenly, every hair on her body stood on end, the hand on her neck began tightening its grip and the only things she could see in the darkness were his eyes, his livid green eyes.

"Abi...Abi...Wake-up.   You're   having   a nightmare."   The voice which came crashing into her consciousness was definitely Sean's.

Abi opened her eyes, the terror of a moment ago still flooding her nervous system, she looked wildly around her, quickly focusing on the grey—blue eyes only inches from her face. She became aware of his hand caressing her neck, a calming, gentle sensation for which she was so grateful she could have wept.

"It's OK Abi, it was just a dream." He reassured her again, as he felt her heartbeat hammering in her neck. "If I lay down beside you and hold you will you panic more or less?" He asked quietly.

"Less." Abi managed in a croaked whisper, the adrenalin dump of her nightmare still affecting her physically.

As Sean climbed onto the bed and lay down beside her he wrapped his arms around her and held her, she could feel his steady breaths on her neck and she snuggled into his chest as far as she could bury herself.

"Close your eyes, try to get some more sleep." He whispered, "It's been a long day, you're exhausted."

It had indeed been a very long day, well over twenty four hours ago it had started when Sean had told her Aaron Steele knew she was in Africa.

"We need to assume the worst Boss." Frank had insisted for the fourth or even fifth time. "It's a long way from Mexico to here you're right there Boss, but we know he's probably flying and we know he has help. I worked it out, the timing is possible, he could get here before we leave."

Sean, Abi and Frank were all in Abigail's bedroom at Koudjo's village having just eaten the most succulent spit roast pig Abi had ever tasted. They'd had a great night, Koudjo and his family could not have been more hospitable and his children were adorable, all of them fascinated with Abi's long blonde hair.

But now Sean had told Abi what Frank had reported to him earlier and they were planning what they should do next.

While Frank and Sean discussed the possibilities Abi was trying to process the reasoning behind Sean's assertion that Harrison was bankrolling Aaron's escape as a means to get to Sean. But as Sean had also assured her again, he was not into organised crime and neither was Harrison as far as he knew, it just didn't make any sense. If it wasn't revenge it was business, Harrison had nothing personal to gain by Sean being upset if Aaron actually managed to kill her, so, she reasoned, it had to provide him with some sort of business gain.

"You said Harrison had business interests here?" She interrupted whatever conversation had been going on between Frank and Sean.

"He doesn't really have any as yet. He's been trying to get drilling and mining rights but the government aren't playing ball and anyway I already have the ones he really wants." Sean said looking over at her from his position in the room's only chair. Yet again she had amazed him, she had taken the news of Aaron's impending arrival with first shock, then terror, then she had sucked up her strength and got down to discussing the options with him and Frank. Whatever she felt inside, she was determined to not allow it to paralyse her.

She pondered Sean's answer some more before the pieces suddenly clicked into place in her head.

"I'm just a distraction!" She exclaimed, loudly enough to stop both men from continuing the heated discussion they had been engaged in.

"Come again?" Sean asked.

"I'm just a distraction. I've been trying to work out why Bruce Harrison would go to all the trouble and risk and expense presumably of getting Aaron out of prison and over here to do whatever nasty deeds he has planned for me. I mean, it just didn't make sense. As you said, he wouldn't do it for Aaron's sake, he couldn't stand the man, and he doesn't care for Cabot much either so he wouldn't do it for him. I didn't really do him any great damage, just made him change his plans so, yes he could be a bit pissed off but he'd have to be unhinged to be doing all this for revenge. So that just leaves business, but that didn't make sense really either unless I am just a distraction. If you are busy protecting me from Aaron Steele, you're not busy protecting your business." She looked directly at Sean as she spoke, challenging him to disagree with her. "Don't forget, without Frank's information. Steele could have just turned up anywhere and caused havoc, if we hadn't known he was coming."

"And they were expecting you to be in England. If Steele had come after you there you're right, it would have kept my focus over there and anything could've happened here before I had any chance to do anything. That bastard is planning a coup." Sean leapt up from the chair and began to pace the room.

"Sorry." Abi whispered into her hands which she was now twisting nervously in her lap.

"What on earth for?" Sean was instantly on his knees at her feet, trying to look into her downturned face, before he had finished speaking.

"If I hadn't written that story none of this would ever have happened." She stated bluntly, tears of self-loathing stinging the backs of her eyes.

"Abigail, look at me." Sean lifted her chin gently to try to get her to look into his eyes, she resisted. "Abigail Storm, look at me!" He said, more forcefully this time. Reluctantly she raised her eyes just enough for him to see them. "This is not your fault. This is not even anything to do with that story. Bruce Harrison has wanted drilling and mining rights here for years but the Gabonese government don't seem to like him very much. Senator Cabot was supposed to oil the wheels when he became president but now that's not happening he's had to think of another way to get those contracts from me. Harrison would use anybody I care about if he thought it would get him what he wants, so if it's anybody's fault it's mine, for caring about you." He smiled into her eyes, willing her to see the logic in his words.

"But Steele doesn't even know you. He is coming after me!"

"Abigail, sweetheart, Steele was hitting you long before you wrote that story. As far as I can tell people like him only get worse, so chances are he would have put you in another life threatening situation sooner or later, story or no story. Just because his psycho agenda helps Harrison with his, still doesn't make it your fault!" He said with a finality he hoped would shake Abi out of her doubt ridden bubble.

As she finally looked up properly and he could see into her eyes he saw the enormous effort she put in to composing herself, he wished, not for the first time, she could see her own strength like he did.

"We will never let that bastard harm you again, Abi." He added, still holding her chin although it was unnecessary now she was looking up at him of her own volition.

"We?"

"You and me."

"And me!" Frank chimed in from over near the window.

"And Frank." Sean added with a reassuring smile. "OK?"

"OK." Abi took a deep breath and swallowed hard, Sean resisted kissing her by the skin of his teeth and stood quickly and walked back over to his chair before the temptation got the better of him.

"OK." Sean blew out a long breath, trying to slow his hammering heart, being close enough to touch Abi but having to restrain himself was an exquisite torture he would gladly endure for as long as it took, but he couldn't help his body's reaction to her. "We leave first thing after breakfast, I'll warn Koudjo to keep an eye out for anything out of the ordinary, hopefully, if he knows to expect trouble, he'll be able to nip it in the bud."

"You think they'll try stirring up the workforce or something?" Frank asked following Sean's lead to keep Abi from dwelling on Steele's intentions.

"I can't see how else he could legitimately get the ministry to reassign those contracts. If he can get a workforce rebellion of some sort going then he can step in and tell the ministry I've lost control or something?"

"Your workforce?" Frank raised an eyebrow.

"You don't think it's likely?" Sean stopped pacing and looked directly at Frank.

"You look after them so well Boss I've sometimes thought of coming to work here myself." Frank replied in a rare moment of candour, Abi was obviously affecting him too.

"What then?" Sean asked.

"If it was me, I'd be thinking sabotage, some kind of industrial disaster...something along them lines anyway." Frank concluded quietly, knowing how alarming this possibility would be to Sean.

"Shit!" Sean slammed a fist into the nearest solid object, which happened to be the partition to the bathroom. "Fatalities, of course, what better way to have the government looking for a scapegoat!"

"You should stay here." Abi had announced. "I can fly home on my own, that way you can concentrate on preventing a catastrophe here instead of protecting me."

"No way." Frank spat, before Sean even had time to form the words.

"Ditto!" Sean agreed. "The three of us are staying together, and we're all going home tomorrow."

"But if Steele thinks I'm in Africa he could spend weeks looking for me here while I'm safely at home." Abi tried to reason, even though she was utterly terrified of the prospect of going home alone.

"For Steele to know you are here now he has to be getting help. We're going to have to assume he will know about your every move, at least until we figure out where his information is coming from." Sean flashed a reassuring smile at Abi before continuing. "Anyway, Koudjo can handle things here, he'd spot something out of place or unusual long before I would as he's here all the time. He just needs to be alerted which we'll do before we leave."

"On the subject of Steele getting information Boss."

"Yes Frank, idea?"

"Well, you think he'll know which hotel we're in?"

"We should probably assume he does. Good thinking Frank." Sean pondered the problem for a few more moments. "OK, we warn Koudjo in the morning, then take the chopper back to Libreville, clear out of the hotel and spend tomorrow night on the Gulfstream, no way we'll make it there in time to take off tomorrow, at least not before it's too late to fly all that way and land before they close Manchester airport for the night."

"Yes Boss, I agree, I'll slip the desk clerk a little misdirection encouragement before we leave, get him to send him up to any old room and call the police as soon as he's out of sight, should keep Steele busy until we're out of the country at least."

All had gone to plan so far except the Airport authorities had refused to allow them to sleep on the Gulfstream. Abi now found herself lying in Sean's arms, in the almost luxury surroundings of Libreville Leon M'ba International Airport's VIP lounge, trying to get some more sleep before they departed for Manchester as soon as air traffic control opened the airport in the morning.

Abi closed her eyes, trying to ignore the sensation of having Sean's body pressed up against hers, he was right, she was so far from ready to be sleeping with him it wasn't funny but the dream she had been having before Aaron had invaded her subconscious, had suggested it might only be a matter of time.

~CHAPTER EIGHTEEN~

Abi slept fitfully for the next few hours but by 4.30am she decided to get up. Being wrapped in Sean's arms had been comforting and safe and had staved off further nightmares but it had its disadvantages too. She hadn't dared to move for several hours and the hip she had been lying on was now quite painful, definitely preventing any further sleep. As carefully as she could she slid out of Sean's embrace and off the wide sofa which they had been using as a bed.

Sean stirred and opened his eyes, seeing Abi heading for the bathroom he assumed she was just going for a toilet break and he rolled over and went back to sleep.

Frank stirred at the sound of Abi padding across the room too. He saw Sean stir then go back to sleep and was about to do the same when Abi returned from the bathroom but instead of climbing back into bed she had her shoes in her hand and was heading for the door.

"Not wise Miss." He said quietly as she tiptoed past him.

"Just going to stretch my legs Frank." Abi whispered, surprised to find Frank awake.

"Wait up I'll come with you." Frank said, stifling a yawn.

"You'll do no such thing Frank, go back to sleep, it's 4.30 in the morning, I just need to walk around a bit, clear my head, I won't be long." She said, pushing Frank back down onto the bed he was heaving himself up from.

"But..." Frank started to protest.

"But nothing Frank. You said yourself, if Aaron managed to get here this fast, and if he turned up in my hotel room at any point tonight, the resulting uproar would have him in police custody faster than he could blink, where, even with whatever anonymous help he seems to have, he'll stay until we are well on our way in the morning. Therefore, I'll be quite safe going for a little wander to stretch my legs." She said with finality and hurried from the room before Frank could argue further. She knew he was only trying to protect her and she was grateful for that but she hadn't had a moment to herself since finding out Aaron had escaped and she just needed some space to breathe and to try to be able to think straight for a while.

Abi wandered down the stairs from the VIP lounge onto the airport's main concourse, there were a few dozen people strewn around, most trying to sleep on the hard bench seats, presumably waiting for early fights just as Abi was. The odd worker pushing a mop around added to the subdued sounds of an airport barely awake. It was a far cry from the constant motion which seemed to engulf Manchester airport whatever time of day or night you found yourself there.

When they had arrived earlier Abi had, in true girl style, noticed a row of shops spanning the far end of the concourse and this is where she headed. She knew they would be closed at this hour but there was nothing quite like a bit of window shopping to take your mind off your troubles for a while.

She had examined the contents of the clothes shop and discovered it contained some fabulous tie-dyed sarong style garments which she hoped she'd have time to come back to buy before they left, noting the opening time of the shop was 8am she decided to ask Sean if they would have time. Moving on she arrived at a leather shop selling traditional African leather goods. From the window she could see at least three or four items she very much wanted a closer look at and was just wondering whether she could insist they didn't leave until she had chance to view these shops open when an arm suddenly appeared and held her tightly around the waist.

"Don't move or scream or you will die right now!" A very familiar voice hissed in her ear whilst something very hard was pressed painfully into her left kidney. "You didn't really think that little stunt at the hotel would stop me did you? Stupid Abigail, that pathetic little desk clerk was no match for me, obviously his injuries are now your fault too."

Abi's blood froze in her veins, causing every hair on her body to stand on end and her bowels seemed to liquefy all in the split second it took her to recognise Aaron's voice.

"Now Walk!" He commanded, digging whatever he was holding harder into her side and pushing her round to her left away from the shop window she had been admiring.

Abi did as she was told, walking past the sleeping passengers she was willing at least one of them to wake and look at her, she was out of luck and had not managed to catch anyone's eye before Aaron propelled her through the outer doors, across the access road and into the carpark beyond.   She had no idea if he possessed a gun but whatever he had sticking in her side certainly felt like she imagined a gun would feel. With her heart beating wildly she had no choice but to obey his commands, wishing she had listened to Frank and praying that one of them would come looking for her right now.

"Stop!"   He barked as they arrived beside a battered blue Fiat and before she could register anything further he removed his right arm from around her waist and shoved her hard against the side of the car. Seconds later she felt a sharp stab in the right side of her neck before her entire world faded to black.

~CHAPTER NINETEEN~

From the moment Aaron had come face to face with a complete stranger in what was supposed to be Abigail's bed, he had known his purpose and whereabouts had been compromised.

The unfortunate man in the bed had rolled quickly over the side of the bed onto the floor and reached for a gun resting in a holster draped over the bed post.

Aaron had reacted instinctively, kicking the man hard under his chin. The half-naked man had slumped to the floor, Aaron neither knew nor cared whether he was alive or not.

Grabbing the gun out of the holster Aaron had swiftly tucked it into his pocket and left the room, retraced his steps to the elevator and as he was about to press the button to call the car he realised something else. The desk clerk had to be in on the deception as well as Abi, he must surely have known she was not in that room. With his adrenalin pumping Aaron felt invincible, it was a feeling he had not had for a long time and he was enjoying it immensely. Whether this heightened his usually sedentary thought processes too he was unsure but something told him to use the stairs not the lift.

He charged through the door denoting access to the stairwell and took the stairs down two at a time. When he reached the doorway marked *reception* he pulled up fast behind it. Opening it just a crack he saw, to his relief, four heavily armed uniformed policemen stepping into the adjacent lift.

As he had thought, the desk clerk must have called the police, expecting mayhem to have occurred in room 14. He waited for the lift door to close with a hushed ping and counted five beats before he pulled open the door fully and rushed headlong towards the reception desk.

The desk clerk's eyes widened in horror as he saw Aaron coming at him, a murderous look on his face, but he had nowhere to run. Aaron vaulted the counter and, grabbing the little man by the lapel he dragged him into the room he had seen behind the counter. Slapping him so hard he left a handprint on his cheek, Aaron pushed him down into a chair and retrieved the gun from his pocket.

Pushing the tip of the barrel hard against the terrified clerk's left eye he placed his other hand in a vice like grip around his neck.

"You were paid to send me up there weren't you?" Aaron hissed malevolently.

"Yes." Came the strangled and obviously petrified reply, it was clear this clerk would put up no resistance at all.

"Where is she?" Aaron watched as the panic flooded through the clerk's body. He thought vaguely it was a shame he didn't have time to enjoy this as images of what he could do to this pathetic worm filled his mind.

"I...don't...know." The clerk's eyes were starting to bulge, Aaron released the pressure just a little, enough to keep the oxygen flowing for now.

"Wrong answer!" He stamped hard on the clerk's foot, hearing a satisfying crunch as a howl escaped from his prisoner's mouth. "Try again."

The clerk tried to swallow but found he could not, as he struggled to breathe, spittle started to dribble from the edges of his gasping mouth and he began to claw at Aaron's hand still firmly gripping his neck.

"I was just told to send you up there and call the police." He managed through gritted teeth, the pain in his obviously broken foot was excruciating.

Aaron stamped on the other foot.

"You're lying. You know where she is. You must've given her another room." Aaron was incensed, how could this stupid, little, excuse for a man still be lying to him, he wouldn't have thought he'd have the courage.

"No, no I didn't." A ray of hope seemed to flicker in the desk clerk's eyes. "They checked out."

"They?"

"The lady, and the two Englishmen with her." The clerk truly believed his ordeal would now be over, there was nothing more he could tell the crazy American about people no longer in his hotel.

Before Aaron even processed this new nugget of information he had determined the clerk was no longer of any use. He pistol-whipped him hard across the side of the head and was gratified to watch as he slumped into unconsciousness, sliding down and off the chair, banging his head hard against a filing cabinet as Aaron released his grip of his throat. Again, it had never occurred to Aaron to check if his victim was alive or dead, he just spun on his heel and left the room and then the hotel, aware that the armed police would not take long to discover he wasn't upstairs where they thought he was.

He climbed back into the little blue fiat and drove away as sedately as his fully pumped, adrenalin soaked body would allow, not wanting to draw attention to his departure.

When he was sure he had put enough distance between himself and the hotel and therefore police he pulled over.

Taking stock, it was still only just after two in the morning and apart from not knowing the names or whereabouts of any of the other hotels in town, it could take days for him to find and visit them all looking for Abigail. He really did not like the idea that she was holidaying with two men but she was a lying, thieving whore so what more could he really expect from her. It was just another thing he was going to have to punish her for when he got hold of her.

Sitting in the car weighing up his options he decided he was going to have to be a little more patient. Even though he had rushed over here to get to her as soon as possible, without an exact location the reality of finding her was slim.

He decided to make his way back to the UK. He had plenty of money and a fake passport which had so far proved to be worth the money he had paid for it. He decided to head for the airport and try to get a flight to somewhere on Africa's northern coast, somewhere he could get a ferry to southern Spain. Once in Europe getting back to England shouldn't be too hard as long as he avoided airports where security was way too high to risk waving his false papers around.

After arriving back at the airport he had parked in the car park mere yards from the building entrance with the huge *'departures'* sign hung outside. He had half thought about taking the hire car back but that was way over the other side of the airport and he decided to just leave it for them to find. It wasn't as if they could trace him after all, the copy they had taken of his passport was hardly going to get them any useful results.

He strode through the revolving door into the air-conditioned cool of the airport and cast around looking for an information desk. Spotting it off to his left he ambled across and made enquiries of the petite, very tired-looking but still inordinately pretty clerk whose name was Petula according to her name badge.

"I'm touring around Africa and have just heard that a family member has been taken seriously ill in Gibraltar. Can I get there from here?" He turned on the charm as well as his devastating smile.

"I'm sorry Sir, we don't have any carriers who fly to Spain from here. You could get to Paris, on Air France but that's quite a way north of Gibraltar. The best I could suggest is Casablanca in Morocco. You can probably get a connecting flight there but if not I'm sure there will be a ferry from northern Morocco to Spain or Gibraltar."

"Thank you that's very helpful, where can I book a seat to Casablanca." As far as Aaron was concerned Morocco was perfect, he'd work out the rest when he got there.

"You'll need to wait until the Air Maroc desk opens at 8 am Sir, it's just over there to the right of the shops." She replied with a smile and Aaron followed the direction of her pointing finger with his eyes.

There, standing not three feet from the desk in question was the unmistakable form of Abigail Storm.

"Thank you." Aaron replied, trying to supress his sudden surge of excitement. "I guess I'll just try to sleep for a few hours until it opens then." He added as he wandered away from the beautiful Petula.

He circled round the back of the concourse, keeping an eye on Abigail as he tried to determine which two of the sleeping figures she could be with but none of them seemed to fit the bill. Most of them were African and he immediately discounted all of them as the hotel clerk had called them Englishmen.

As far as he could tell there were only two sets of two white men, all were sleeping. Aaron silently crept up to the nearest two and allowed his bag to bump one of them as he passed.

"I am so sorry." He whispered to the half-asleep face which had turned suddenly to see what had bumped him.

"Pas de problem." It replied groggily and settled down to sleep again.

The last two possibilities were a long way over the other side of the concourse and were obviously asleep. Aaron took a second to weigh up his options. If he risked crossing the entire expanse to check whether they were her friends or bodyguards or whatever he ran the risk of her seeing him. As it was he was behind her and he could approach her unseen from here. He knew his best chance of getting her out of here alone was if the 'friends' stayed asleep so his decision was made.

Closing the distance between Abigail and himself with half a dozen purposeful strides, he drew the gun from his pocket as he grabbed her from behind around the waist. Making sure the barrel of the gun was pushed hard up against her left kidney, he leaned in beside her, the familiar scent of her immediately intoxicating him, driving his desire to harm her ever higher.

~CHAPTER TWENTY~

The annoying incessant beep of Sean's iPhone alarm going off roused both him and Frank simultaneously. It was 5.30am and both men instantly realised Abi was not in the room.

"I'll check the bathroom." Said Sean rising hurriedly, any grogginess he had felt dispelled without a moment of thought.

He was back seconds later, he looked at Frank and shook his head.

"She went for a walk Boss." Frank said as soon as Sean had determined she was not in the bathroom. "I tried to stop her Boss but she wasn't having it."

"I know Frank, I heard you." Sean smiled reassuringly at Frank. "My fault, I should've backed you up but to be honest I thought she'd be safe. Steele has got to be still with the police, if he even managed to get to the hotel last night. So she's probably just looking at the shops or having a coffee or something. C'mon, let's get out there and look."

He strode over to the door with Frank right behind him. Through the door and along a short corridor and they were standing on a mezzanine with a view of almost the entire concourse save the area directly beneath them.

Both men scanned the area, finding it much the same as Abi had an hour earlier. Passengers asleep on chairs, janitors still mopping, shops still closed and no sign of Abi anywhere.

"I'll check underneath." Said Frank, making for the stairs at a run. Seconds later he appeared below Sean shaking his head, "Not under here Boss, I'll go check if she's gone outside for fresh air or something."

Sean watched him head out of the revolving doors but as the entire front of the building was glass he could see for himself she was not out there.

He scanned the expanse of the concourse again, this time he was not looking for Abi, he was looking for a security office. A feeling in the pit of his stomach told him what had happened and he knew time was not on their side now. He located the security office in the far corner and was half way across the concourse when Frank joined him from outside.

"Nothing Boss." Frank confirmed what Sean already knew.

"Security, in the corner to the right, they must have CCTV all over this place." Sean replied breaking into a jog.

Arriving at the door marked *Sécurité* neither Sean nor Frank elected to knock, they just walked in startling the sleeping security guard seated in front of a bank of about a dozen TV screens showing various views of the concourse and beyond.

"Allez!" The startled guard cried. "Vous n'êtes pas autorisé en ici!"

"English?"

"Yes."

"That camera, one hour ago." Said Sean pointing at the screen with the view of the stairs from the mezzanine.

"I can't do that Sir." Replied the guard apparently unused to having civilians barge into his office and bark orders at him.

"I can." Said Frank, reaching for the machine under the monitor in question and pressing rewind.

"There!" Sean shouted as an image of Abi on the stairs flashed into view. "Go forwards, can we see where she went from there." But the camera angle was unhelpful and she went out of view as soon as she descended the final step. "Do them all." Sean instructed Frank.

As Frank rewound each camera to around an hour earlier, images of Abi appeared on several screens.

"Run the one outside the shops on double speed Frank." Said Sean staring at Abi as she gazed through the shop windows, two minutes later both Sean and Frank gasped as a man came into shot from behind Abi and grabbed her around the waist. "Shit! Shit! Shit!" Sean shouted as they watched the back view of Abi and what had to be Steele turn and walk away to the left, affording them a clear view of the gun aimed precisely at her kidney.

"How far do the cameras reach outside?" Frank aimed his question and the now placated guard.

In reply the guard started pressing buttons on his console and a few seconds later an image of the access road outside the building appeared on the screen in front of them, running the tape fast they soon saw Abi and Steele emerge from the revolving doors, cross the road and stop at a blue Fiat just inside the carpark. They then witnessed something which made Sean's heart stop. Abi crumpled into Steele's arms and was bundled unceremoniously into the back of the car.

"Did you see blood?" Sean demanded of Frank.

"No Boss. Anyway, his hand was high, like he was touching her neck." Frank replied, knowing the only way to keep Sean focused was to be as professional as possible.

"Sedatives again?"

"Would be my guess yes Boss." Frank agreed. "How far do these cameras go?" He asked the guard who now looked shocked beyond comprehension.

"That's it." He replied.

"We can't see where they went after the carpark?" Sean demanded.

"Not with cameras no. I'll call the gate guard, he might remember." The guard picked up the telephone on the desk in front of him and dialled while Sean hoped the guard on the gate had been a little more awake than this one. "Gate says small blue Fiat left almost an hour ago and headed north."

"Get us a car Frank." Sean barked and Frank was out of the door and heading across the concourse before Sean had turned back to the guard. "What's north of here?"

"Nothing much after the airport complex." Replied the guard scratching his head. "There's Akanda National Park and the Sea."

"Towns? Villages?" Sean prompted.

"No. Maybe one or two residences dotted around but no towns or villages. You want me to call the police?" Asked the guard helpfully. "Your friend, she's in trouble, No?"

"How big is the national park?" Sean asked.

"About five or six hundred square kilometres I think. It is a big place, all trees and rivers and animals." The guard beamed, glad to be able to provide information.

"OK. No, no police." Sean headed for the door, seeing the confused look on the guards face he added. "Corporate team building game – gun's fake." And with that he left the bemused guard to his thoughts and ran for the main door to the terminal, stopping briefly to buy a map from the display on the desk at the information kiosk.

Outside he was gratified to find Frank just driving up in a 4x4.

"Figured this might be useful." Frank said as Sean climbed into the passenger seat. "All our bags are here too, had a very helpful janitor collect them for us while I sorted this out."

"That must've cost you?"

"Hundred bucks!" Frank grinned. "So, what's north then?" He asked eyeing the map in Sean's hand.

Sean spread the map as best he could in the confines of the car, there was no way he and Frank were going to waste any more time by stopping to spread it properly on the bonnet or some such useful place. Steele already had almost an hours head start so Sean would make do while Frank drove north.

"Guard says nothing but a national park and the sea." He said absently as he tried to locate their position and fold the map to a manageable size all at the same time. Finally he got organised and scrutinised the area north of Libreville airport. The guard had been correct, it was a peninsular, most of which was made up of Akanda National Park and the road they were on went straight up the west side of the peninsula to the sea. "He was right, nothing up here." He added for Frank's benefit.

"I think he's winging it Boss." Frank offered.

"What makes you say that?"

"No way he could know we hadn't just changed hotels. His choices would be try to find her in any one of God knows how many hotels in Libreville, or head for home and wait for her to return." Sean couldn't fault Frank's reasoning.

"Except, whoever's helping him has a spy somewhere, how else would he know we were in Gabon?" This fact worried Sean most of all, he had no doubt that alone he and Frank could outsmart and overpower Steele, but without knowing who was helping him and how much, they could just be walking into an ambush.

"Nobody has been following us Boss. I checked since the moment I heard Steele had escaped, all the time, we've not had a tail anywhere."

"So how the hell did he know to come here?"

"Can I make a suggestion Boss?"

"Course you can Frank, you know you don't have to ask."

"Find out where Harrison is?"

"Why?"

"If this is being orchestrated by Harrison to distract you as Miss Storm suggested yesterday, it makes sense he would be around somewhere, he can't charge in and save the situation from Texas!" Frank glanced over at Sean before fixing his eyes firmly back on the road.

"He'll be staying at the *Hotel Le Cristal* if he's here." Said Sean pulling out his mobile phone and scrolling through his contacts.

"Always does Boss." Agreed Frank.

Five minutes later Sean came off the phone, a grim expression on his face.

"Trouble Boss?" Frank had heard one side of the conversation and knew all was not well.

"Steele killed the desk clerk." Sean said without preamble.

"Shit!" Frank exclaimed. "And Harrison?" He added, nothing else he could say about the fate of the desk clerk.

"He's there OK, arrived the night before we did. So, chances are he saw us and that's how Steele was warned where we were."

"Sounds most likely Boss." Frank knew Sean would be relieved they didn't have a spy in their camp. Trust was an important trait in Sean's business and personal life.

"Apparently the poor guest who got a visit from Steele tonight was an off-duty security guy, it's his gun the bastard had sticking into Abi's kidney. Which brings us back to Steele winging it." Sean concluded, picking up the thread Frank had started.

"Which should mean he's driving up this road somewhere looking for a suitable place to do whatever he's got in mind."

"This national park is over five hundred square kilometres Frank, he gets in there it could take weeks to find her." Sean studied the map, looking for any possible locations which he thought might appeal to Steele.

"He's in a Fiat POS Boss, he ain't going to get far off road in that thing." Frank chimed in, optimistic as ever.

"Unlike us, in this very handy 4x4." Sean remarked, looking over at Frank. "Where did we get this by the way? Can't have been many hire places open at this hour?"

"Borrowed it from the car park Boss, figured we needed it more than the owner." Frank grinned as he drove.

"We'd best try not to bend it too much then." Sean added, also with a smirk as he went back to studying the map. "Well, according to this map the road just stops about five hundred yards from the sea, looks like it's a forest area, if I were a nutter hell bent on causing a beautiful woman harm I'd be looking for somewhere easy to get to with the possibility of somewhere to dump her body without much danger of her being found too soon. The end of a road to nowhere seems like a good choice to me." Sean looked over at Frank in time to see he was nodding his approval of Sean's deductions.

"Straight on it is Boss."

"We do have one other problem Frank."

"Yes Boss, I know, but, a gun is only any use if you know how to use it, and there's two of us and one of him. We can take him." Frank asserted confidently. "How far to the end of this road then?"

"Map says it's about 20 miles from the airport to the road end, can't be far now, another ten minutes maybe?" Sean settled back in his seat, it was rapidly approaching 6.30 am and the sun was about to rise, then they'd be able to see where they were and hopefully be able to work out where Steele had taken Abi.

Sean kept his eyes firmly fixed on the lightening sky, forcing his mind not to imagine what Steele could be doing to his beautiful Abi, or the fear he knew she would be feeling.

~CHAPTER TWENTY-ONE~

Aaron drove as fast as the little Fiat would allow over the less than perfect Gabonese road surface. He had elected to go north from the airport as according to his map there was very little up there. Going south would have meant going back through town and he had no idea how long he had before her 'friends' discovered she had gone and came after him or sent the police out looking for him.

He reasoned there would have to be somewhere at the end of this road where he could keep her while he satisfied all the fantasies he had been entertaining since she had so callously and selfishly damaged his life. A hut in the forest would do or even by the beach if there was one.

"*That could be quite nice,*" he mused, "*Abi trussed up in a beach hut would mean I could nip out for a swim whenever my exertions make me too hot.*"

It was still dark when he reached the end of the road but he pulled off into the forest anyway, glancing at his watch he realised it wouldn't be light for at least another hour so he attempted to drive as far as he could with just his dim Fiat headlamps showing the way.

As he had surmised, the car was no off-roader and the going was very slow but he plodded onwards, reasoning every yard further he got was a yard less he would have to carry the bitch and a yard further from the road and therefore further from discovery should anybody happen to drive up that way.

Eventually the undergrowth became too thick for him to force the little car through any further so he climbed out, leaving the lights on so he could get back to the car in the dark, he made a wide circle around the car to see if there was anything to see. He was about to go back to the car when he saw the outline of something dark up ahead through the trees. Checking he could still see the car behind him he struck out in the direction of the shape.

Ten minutes, many scratches and an almost turned ankle later he stood outside of what he could just make out was a house of some sort. In the darkness he could determine no more than that but on checking his watch he realised it would be getting light in less than half an hour. He decided to go back to the car and wait for dawn, then he could check out his discovery properly and if it proved as useful as first impressions suggested, he would drag Abi in there, leaving the car where it was.

Sitting in the car waiting for dawn to break Aaron wondered at the latest turn of events. After the hotel he had been sure he was going to have to wait, possibly weeks, before he would get another crack at Abi, and yet, here she was.

He had not been able to believe his luck when he'd seen her, large as life in the airport. Standing there with her back to him she could almost have been waiting for him to grab her. It had been pure luck he still had the syringe of sedative in his pocket. He had acquired it just outside the airport in Luanda before he had boarded his plane for the short hop to Libreville. It was truly amazing what a person could buy with enough US dollars and the right questions. He had been going to use it at the hotel and, having failed to find her there, had meant to throw it in the bin on the way into the airport in case security wanted to know what it was.

He glanced over into the back seat, Abi was still sleeping but she should be stirring soon. He had only used enough sedative this time to knock her out for a couple of hours or so, he wanted her wide awake while he administered the punishment she so deserved.

Risking opening the window again and letting in the deafening noise of the cicadas, Aaron glanced up at the sky. His watch told him it was almost 6.30am so the sun should be up very soon. Sure enough, the sky was beginning to lighten, as he looked up he could see the vegetation was not nearly as dense as he had thought it to be. In fact he could see great swathes of rapidly lightening sky through the quite sizeable holes in the canopy, soon it would be light enough for Aaron to retrace his steps to see what in fact he had found and whether it was a suitable structure to hold Abi in, ideally for several days although if that plan was to be realised in full he was going to have to find a source of food and water, if only for himself. He wondered idly whether he could reverse the Fiat back the way he had come and if he did, would he be able to find the hut again on his return.

Seeing the sky was now light enough to be able to make out his surroundings, Aaron decided to shelve the problem of food and water until he needed it. It was time to go and see if he had found a suitable hiding place. He climbed out of the car and made his way through the forest again, this time he headed straight for the building he'd found, arriving in under five minutes now he could see where he was going.

As he approached what he could now see was a mud and straw hut he was careful to be as silent as he could, just in case the hut had inhabitants. As he got closer he could see a door round to one side, it was closed but had quite a growth of creepers up it, suggesting to Aaron that the hut was long abandoned.

He tentatively pushed at the door, finding it stiff and difficult to move he just managed to get it fully open. This further added to his conviction that the hut was in fact uninhabited.

Inspecting the inside he found very little, an earth floor with signs it had once housed a fire in the middle. There was a small window on the opposite side to the door but it was covered with wooden slats preventing much light and, more importantly Aaron thought, small animals from coming in. There were a couple of iron rings embedded in the mud walls, presumably for restraining animals or some such, Aaron had no real idea but they were ideal for what he had in mind.

Retracing his steps back to the Fiat he hauled Abi unceremoniously from the back seat. Dumping her on the ground he grabbed his bag from the boot and locked the car. He chuckled to himself as he looked down at the keys in his hand.

"Like it's going to get stolen out here!" He chastised himself good humouredly, he hadn't felt this good in months.

After throwing his rucksack over his shoulder he grabbed Abi by the ankles and proceeded to drag her over the rough foliage and tree roots to the hut. By the time they arrived her back and arms were bleeding nicely from a series of superficial but probably quite painful cuts.

Between the border crossing in Mexico and arriving at Abi's hotel in Libreville Aaron had made a number of purchases, all of which were now residing in the rucksack he had just retrieved from the car.

The first item he pulled out was a packet of cable ties with which he proceeded to tie her, one wrist at a time, to the farthest apart of the iron rings inside the hut. With her arms immobilised, her wrists two feet apart, he discovered to his delight that the rings were just far enough from the ground for her to sit on the floor, arms above her head and slightly to each side, a position he was certain would make her shoulders ache after a time. He spread her legs as wide as they would go, he would have liked to tie them too but there was nothing to attach them to. For now this would have to do, he would have to move her around anyway in the course of his ministrations but when she woke he wanted her to realise instantly she was powerless against him. He began to cut off her clothes, first her shirt, then her trousers. He discarded the garments across the other side of the hut, not that they would have been any use to her even if she could reach them, both garments were cut in half.

After removing her bra he allowed himself a brief fondle of her breasts, heat rising in his loins as he remembered how much he had longed for this moment.

Sliding his knife into the elastic of her knickers he paused, licking his lips he decided that could wait until she was awake, he very much wanted to see her face as he removed the last vestiges of her dignity.

Leaving her slumped and almost naked he wandered outside and sat down on a large log he found handily propped against the outside wall. He had taken up smoking again since being incarcerated and decided to savour a cigarette whilst waiting for her to wake.

Blowing smoke into the early morning ever-brightening sky Aaron reflected on the last time he been forced to teach Abigail Storm a well-deserved lesson.

He had returned from four weeks in Washington to find she had been a busy little bee in his absence. Not only had she attempted a journalistic story which he had repeatedly told her she was wholly ill prepared for, but she had lied to him about her whereabouts and been questioning ex-girlfriends of his about things which were none of her business.

Obviously he had every right to be enraged, and when she had wandered in to the living room he had no choice but to hit her hard across the side of her head. It had been a punch he had been inordinately proud of and had rendered her unconscious immediately.

He had tied her to her bed, attached her to a drip and catheterised her, this time without the fiasco of bleeding and subsequent emergency room visit he had endured the previous time with Anna Foster.

Unfortunately whilst planning how Abigail's punishment should be administered someone, he still had no idea who but suspected Bruce Harrison, had managed to get into her apartment and spirit her and all her belongings away during the six hour interval between drip bag changes.

He still remembered with a shudder the feeling of utter shock he had experienced when he had entered the apartment at 6 am one Monday morning to find no trace of her or any of her furniture.

It had been several months later when she had returned to ruin his life. Going public with a ridiculous tale about him stealing her story and then, as if that had not been bad enough, she had gone to the police claiming he had raped, battered and imprisoned her. None of which she could prove obviously, although the police had still listened to her for some reason Aaron could not fathom.

He had been presented with another chance to punish her then, when she had been in hospital after he had been released on bail. He had managed to get to her hospital room unseen, he had subdued her friend and tied Abi's arms and legs to the bed. It was the next bit he could not explain in his own mind.

He had been in the process of telling her how wicked she was, he remembered climbing onto the bed where he had her spread-eagled. He remembered the arousal of seeing her staring at him, terrified of what he would do next. He remembered pulling up her hospital gown and unbuttoning his pants, but then someone pulled him off.

The trial documents presented by the police stated that Abi must have pushed him off with her legs, he had fallen to the floor and banged his head, knocking him out and giving him a concussion.

But Aaron knew that was not how it happened. He was absolutely certain he had tied her legs so she would have been unable to push him off with her feet, and anyway he was sure the force he had encountered had come from behind him, not from the front where it would have been had the police's scenario been true.

The upshot however had been that Abigail's punishment had been interrupted yet again and Aaron now had two mysteries for which he required answers before he dealt with her once and for all.

He wondered, not for the first time, how such a waste of space whore could have continually caused him such trouble.

"Not for much longer." He announced to the screeching cicadas. "Not ever again." He threw his now extinguished cigarette butt into the dirt at his feet and walked back into the cabin to find out if his prisoner had woken.

~CHAPTER TWENTY-TWO~

Abi woke slowly, her groggy senses seemed reluctant to engage. Her hearing seemed to kick in first but her brain could make no sense of the loud clicking chirps she could hear. She strained her hearing to try to pick up any other sound but there were none.

Finally managing to get her eyes to open Abi took in her surroundings. In the dim light she could not make out much beyond she appeared to be in a small, unlit room. Glancing downwards she saw the floor was earth, with apparently nothing but her naked legs anywhere else in sight.

Panic started to rise as Abi's memory began to wake. Suddenly she recalled Aaron's arms around her waist, the sheer terror of hearing his voice flashed instantly into her now fully alert mind. It was at this moment she began to feel the tension in her arms and swivelling her head sideways to look up she realised she was shackled to the wall.

Completely aware now she remembered the gun thrust against her kidney, she remembered gazing up towards the mezzanine hoping either Sean or Frank had decided to take a look outside the VIP lounge, she remembered being crushed with disappointment when they hadn't, she remembered the forced walk across the concourse into the carpark and the little blue car. She remembered the sharp sting on her neck, then nothing until now.

To attempt to stem the increasing flow of fear threatening to engulf her Abi tried to concentrate on her surroundings, looking for any possible way out, knowing there was no way Sean could find her this time. He had been asleep when Aaron took her from the airport and although she had no idea how far or which direction she had come she doubted Aaron was stupid enough to have her holed up in a hut within sight of the terminal buildings. Sean and Frank therefore would have no idea where to start looking for her so she had no choice but to try to get out of this by herself.

Looking around she saw faint natural light filtering in through the wooden slats over the window, so it was daylight outside. Having no idea how long she had been unconscious the fact that it was daytime meant little save she knew she must have been asleep for at least two hours. She realised they could have come quite a long way from the airport in that time. Staving off the desperation and despondence she was starting to feel she tried to get a better look at the way in which she was shackled to the wall. She noted the cable ties and knew she would be unable to remove them without a knife of some sort. However, they were attached to some very old looking rings embedded in the mud wall.

She pulled against the cable ties but all she managed to do was make them dig painfully into her skin, the rings had barely moved at all with her efforts. She knew if she could just turn her hand within the plastic restraints she might be able to get a grip on the iron ring itself, with a good grip she may be able to start to wriggle it around.

Putting all of her effort into twisting one wrist within its restraints Abi tried hard to ignore the pain it caused her, even as blood began to trickle down her arm, she continued to twist, moving barely millimetres with each effort.

She had almost managed the turn when a noise from her left caused her to snap her head round in alarm.

"And what do you think you're trying to do there whore?" Aaron's voice dripped acid and Abi's blood turned cold, her sense of purpose immediately lost in the face of her tormentor. She did not dare speak, although his utterance appeared to be a question, she knew well enough what her punishment would be for speaking without being expressly instructed to.

Instead she pulled her knees up to her chest as best she could with her arms in such an extended pose, trying to cover her near nakedness and make herself as small as possible in his eyes.

With two rapid strides he crossed the small hut and slapped her hard across the face. She tried to bite back the cry of pain but it escaped despite her efforts.

"Did I say you could move bitch?" He shouted, his face mere inches from hers, the smell of his breath and of stale cigarette smoke making her want to gag. "Put your legs back where they were." He added with such venom in his voice Abi knew the next blow would be far worse than the last, she could already taste blood in her mouth, coming from the inside of her cheek where he had forced it into her teeth. Obediently she moved her legs back into the splayed position they had previously been in, having no idea how to deal with the emotions this man made her feel.

Somewhere in her mind she was aware she was going to have to detach herself from the paralysing fear he instilled in her otherwise she would have no alternative than to do whatever his bidding entailed until such time as he was satisfied when, she had no doubt, this time he would kill her. If she continued to live would depend on her ability to resist the manipulative psychological torture he was capable of meeting out to her. Unfortunately in her present state she was unaware she possessed such an ability, such was the psychological damage he and her upbringing had already done to her. She was under his spell from the moment he opened his mouth and without any external stimuli to convince her otherwise, she would spiral downwards until she hit the bottom, without self-belief she was as good as dead already.

She tried to force her mind not to hear him by attempting to recall all the positive and encouraging things Ginny had said to her when she had first been rescued from Aaron's clutches. Ginny had told her repeatedly she was not useless, or selfish, or stupid, nor did she deserve anything Aaron had put her through. Abi recalled these words had helped at the time however, saying them to herself apparently had no meaning as she felt none of the fortifying resolve she had experienced last time.

Aaron Steele had demolished what little self-belief she had ever had, he had systematically tortured her mentally until she was so painfully aware of her shortcomings she agreed with him when he told her she deserved no more than the degrading sex and physical abuse he had administered.

That branding was a difficult mental hurdle for anyone to overcome without professional help. Unfortunately Abigail believed she ought to be able to deal with her life by herself. She was convinced that outside assistance in such matters was proof positive that she was in fact the waste of space she had so often been informed she was, both by Steele and her parents before him.

Abigail tried not to think about the time she had previously spent with Aaron, but just the sound of his breathing sent her mind right back there and made her feel as small and worthless as he had made her feel back then. For every minute of every day they had been together when she had lived in Boston he had instilled fear and self-loathing in her and these emotions now returned with a vengeance.

"This time you are not getting rescued Dog, so you'd best get used to the idea you're going to die here." He hissed, pacing the small hut in front of her, his dilated pupils indicative of his heightened state of both anger and sexual arousal more than the dimness of the hut. To Abi those eyes were paralysing, she had seen them twice before and both times it had ended badly for her. "By the time they find you I will have taken everything I deserve from you, everything you, ungrateful bitch that you are, refused to give me before." She could see him getting hard at the thought of what he intended to do. She did not need to try very hard to imagine what he had in mind, he had tried to demand it of her often enough before.

"Why can't you just leave me alone?" She whispered, knowing that to speak now could cost her dearly.

She was not wrong as she felt the backhand hit her across the other side of her face.

"Leave you alone?" He spat in her face, "I'll leave you alone alright, alone out here to die, when I'm done I doubt it'll take long for you to bleed to death." He smiled with such nastiness Abi's already frozen blood seemed to stop moving altogether.

She allowed her head to drop, resting her chin on her chest her tears flowed freely now. If anything was proof she was exactly the useless bitch Aaron had always told her she was then this was it. She was powerless against him, about to be brutally sodomised together with whatever other delights he had dreamed up to damage and humiliate her, but all she could manage to mumble was 'why can't you leave me alone' it was pathetic and she knew it.

Grabbing her hair he yanked her head back up.

"Did I tell you to look away?" He spat, "Do I have to teach you how to behave AGAIN?" This time he banged the back of her head hard against the wall behind her to emphasise his point.

Wincing at the sudden explosion of pain behind her eyes Abi obediently looked into his. Hard, livid green eyes stared back but Abi could not help comparing them to Sean's. The startlingly clear grey blue of Sean's eyes were full of compassion, care and fun, she remembered once thinking Aaron's eyes were sexy but that had been a long time ago and she knew without doubt she would never find green eyes sexy again.

Thoughts of Sean stuck in her head, she realised suddenly how much she had become fond of him in the last few weeks, the realisation she would never see him again made her want to cry more than ever, but something else happened instead. The selflessness of

Sean's heroic past rescues, now to be rendered futile by the very man he had rescued her from made her suddenly and ferociously angry.

"Fuck off you twisted piece of shit." She spat back, surprising herself by her own venom but she was past caring what he did, something had snapped inside her and whilst her rational brain knew he would overpower her and do whatever he wanted she would at least go down fighting.

"What the fuck did you say?" He whirled round, clipping the side of her head with a backhand once again.

"You heard me you filth." She spat blood as she spoke, her eyes ablaze with all the fury and hatred she had absorbed from this man over the previous three years.

"Don't you fucking dare answer me back you little whore, remember who you are, you're nothing, a waste of skin. You speak when I tell you to or you will be severely punished." He reminded her viciously, grabbing a handful of hair and yanking her head back again.

"Really?" She could barely croak out the words with her head and neck in such a position but she was too angry to stop now. "What? More than rape, sodomy and murder? You going to punish me more than that? Arsehole." Abi had really done it this time, he leapt to his feet and started raining blows down on her wholly unprotected body. He punched and kicked her repeatedly on every surface he could connect with until he was forced to stop to catch his breath.

During the pause Abi managed to lift her head just enough to look at him with the one eye which was still open, the pains shooting messages to her brain from all over her body were unbearable and she knew she couldn't endure much more of this beating. Her vision was swimming but she managed to focus briefly on his face.

"Is that the best you can manage?" She just managed to croak before her world swam into blackness and her chin slid down again to rest on her chest.

Aaron kicked her hard again, frustrated that she was obviously unconscious now and he was going to have to wait until she came round. She was no use to him unless she was awake, he wanted to see the terror in her eyes when he killed her, after everything she had put him through he deserved that much at least.

"Fuck!" He bellowed to his now unresponsive audience and kicked her hard again before stalking out of the hut and pacing around outside for several minutes while his immediate anger subsided to a more manageable level.

When he was sufficiently calm he realised the exertion of disciplining the ungrateful bitch had made him hot and thirsty. He had not brought provisions with him as he had gone to the airport to catch a plane out, not to collect his prize. He decided to use the time he now found himself with to head towards the beach the map told him was on the other side of the trees, hoping he would find some refreshment there, even if it was only a stream.

He set off through the forest, away from the hut and even further from the car. According to the map the distance between the end of the asphalt and the beach was only about 1 kilometre and he must have travelled at least half that distance into the forest in the car, so the beach couldn't be far away.

~CHAPTER TWENTY-THREE~

"Pull over." Sean instructed Frank suddenly.

"What for boss?" Frank asked as he dutifully signalled to pull into the side of the road, not that there was any other traffic to signal to, but it was a habitual move.

"We need intel, the map just shows the road ends in a couple of miles and all it's got is green between there and the sea. We need to know if there's anything useful in that green patch, otherwise we're just searching for a needle in a haystack. So, I'll drive and you call whoever it is you call for this stuff and see what you can get us."

Frank accelerated away again, pulling his phone out of his pocket as he did so.

"Call 'Brad'." He said handing his phone over to a slightly perplexed Sean. "Put it on speaker please Boss." Frank added a little sheepishly.

Sean did as he was told and within a couple of seconds the call was answered.

"Frank? Hi, long time no hear from, how are you?" The inordinately cheerful tones of an obviously native Texan rang out.

"Brad, hi, yeah I'm good thanks but sorry I don't have time to chat. I need info and I need it fast." Frank answered, not taking his eyes off the road which they were rapidly approaching the end of. "I need hi-def imagery of the area surrounding the end of Highway L101, north of Libreville airport in Gabon, West Africa. Can you help?" He asked, noticing Sean's raised eyebrows out of the corner of his peripheral vision.

"West Africa? What the hell you mixed up in now Frank?" Came the less than appropriately surprised reply.

"Mercy mission Brad, nothing to get you any heat, my word on that." Frank replied, pulling the car to a halt as they had now reached the end of the asphalt. "You need co-ordinates?"

"Nope, got your phone signal loud and clear!" Brad replied, his grin translating clearly through the ether. "OK, images en route, on your phone in the next few seconds. Be good Frank or at least be careful, we must catch up soon." He concluded and hung up before Frank had time to speak again.

As the call disconnected the phone in Sean's hands beeped twice, Sean swiped the screen from left to right and an image appeared. It clearly showed the end of a road, surrounded by dense trees and bushes.

"Is this real time?" Sean asked dubiously.

"No Boss, it's a stock image, they only have real time for places where there's something going on. Satellite takes them every pass, computer analyses them and if anything has changed it stores the new image and disregards the old one, unless it's told not to." Frank replied with a small smile.

"I'm not even going to ask how you know Brad." Sean added without looking up.

"Best not Boss." Frank agreed. "Those images are the best hi-def you can get so you can zoom in as close as you like, you'll still be able to see all the detail." Frank added as Sean began to search the surrounding forest on the tiny screen in his hand.

"It's still a hell of an area, this could take a while." Sean said a little down heartedly, whilst Frank was correct, the detail on the images was fantastic, there were still several square miles of forest to look at and time was definitely against them.

"I can probably help you with a starting point Boss." Frank had been studying the immediate vicinity while Sean scoured the images.

"What's that?" Sean looked up expectantly.

"Over there Boss." Frank said, pointing to an obviously flattened section of grass and small shrubs to the left of the tarmac road. "Could just be a coincidence but that looks like somebody drove over it."

"I don't believe in coincidences Frank." Sean replied and immediately found the spot on the image in his hand and began to search in the direction the flattened bush seemed to travel.

"Holy Shit!" He exclaimed after a few more seconds of searching. "Score 1 for Brad." He looked up excitedly and thrust the phone under Frank's nose. "I guess that satellite passed here not too long ago then." He added as Frank digested the image he was looking at.

"Holy hell, that looks a lot like the back end of a little blue Fiat, jammed up against a tree." He chuckled. "Way to go Brad."

Both men jumped from the car and headed into the trees, the need to discuss tactics unnecessary at this stage. They had no idea if Aaron had Abi in or near the car or whether he had gone further after stopping and leaving the car where it was. They both knew an approach in their car would cause enough noise to eliminate any element of surprise and more than likely cause Steele to panic and potentially shoot Abi as a last ditch attempt to put her out of their reach.

The low level foliage was thick and they were almost within touching distance of the back of the car before they spotted it through the greenery. Sean suddenly held up a hand and crouched low, Frank recognised the signal and dropped to the ground too. Crawling up beside Sean, he too peered through the trees to where the little Fiat sat just up ahead of them.

Both men listened intently but could hear nothing more than the incessant chirping of the cicadas. With more hand signals Sean indicated he was going in for a closer look. Frank nodded and gestured to the right side of their position, telling Sean he would circle around and come at the car from the side while Sean approached from the rear.

Crawling slowly and quietly on their bellies the men approached the car, arriving almost simultaneously, Frank on the right and Sean almost touching the rear bumper, inches from the latch for the tailgate. On Sean's signal both men jumped up and yanked at the doors in front of them, both found them locked.

"Bollocks!" Sean exclaimed in a loud stage whisper as he stared through the rear window into the empty interior of the little car, hoping instantly the noise of the cicadas had prevented his voice from carrying far into the forest. "Now where?" He whispered to Frank who was busy examining the forest floor on the other side of the car.

"This way Boss." Frank whispered in reply, he had found more flattened vegetation and as he followed the trail he noticed tiny scraps of white cloth stuck to various protruding roots and twigs. "Miss Storm had a white shirt on didn't she Boss?" He asked as Sean joined him.

"Yes why?"

Frank pointed to the small scrap of cloth on the nearest sharp looking twig. When Sean bent to retrieve the scrap he brushed his fingers over the end of the twig and sure enough it came away with a trace of blood smeared on it.

"Bastard dragged her." He stated unnecessarily to Frank.

"Looks like it Boss, recently too." Frank agreed and both men set off following the trail Aaron had unwittingly left behind. It didn't take them long to reach the small clearing with the hut slightly to the left of centre. They crouched just inside the tree line and listened again but still all they could discern was the chirping cicadas.

Frank took one look at Sean's face and knew exactly what he was thinking, they were too late, if Aaron had still been working whatever evil he had planned for Abi they would definitely have heard her screams from here.

"Only one way to find out Boss." Frank declared and leapt up from his hiding place and ran headlong towards the little hut. Sean was right on his heels, if Aaron Steele turned out to be just inside that hut with a gun in his hand he had better know how to use it because as far as Sean was concerned it would be the last thing the bastard ever did in this life.

They entered the hut one behind the other, Frank quickly surveyed the tiny interior, saw Steele was not there and turned on his heel, almost colliding with Sean who had stopped dead in his tracks, and headed back outside.

"I'll find him if he's still out here Boss." He threw over his shoulder as he went.

Sean was instantly transported back to the apartment in Boston, icy fingers seemed to squeeze at his heart as he took in the obviously battered state of Abi. Seeing her like this again reminded him of Abi's previous ordeal at Steele's hands, he quickly crossed the little room and placed his fingers gently, almost reluctantly, against Abi's carotid artery. There, to his overwhelming relief, he felt a faint but steady pulse. He blew out the breath he had been holding, they were not too late after all, she was still alive, very beaten but alive nonetheless.

Pulling his keys from his pocket, he unhinged the tiny penknife from the key-ring and hoped the blade was up to cutting through cable ties. He had always thought this little knife was useless but his mother had given it to him years ago so he had kept it more for sentimental than practical reasons.

There was little room between Abi's already damaged flesh and the plastic ties holding her wrists and Sean was glad she was unconscious as he wedged the little knife between her bleeding skin and the restraint, knowing that a swift upward stroke would put more stress on the plastic than if he tried to cut it from above. He also knew it would be significantly more painful for Abi, hence being glad she was unconscious.

To his immense relief the little blade found its way through the plastic after only three passes and he immediately went to work on the other arm. Moments later she was free and Sean caught her deftly as she slumped to the side, having nothing now to hold her in place. Briefly Sean allowed himself to hold her, closing his eyes and wrapping both arms round her gently but firmly, careful not to squeeze in case anything was broken. As he held her he heard footsteps approaching outside, he was about to lay her on the ground and ready himself to face Steele's return when Frank appeared in the doorway.

"No sign of him Boss." He panted. "How's Miss doing?"

"Unconscious but breathing." Sean replied. "Let's get her out of here." He added, taking his shirt off to wrap around Abi's naked torso. "She's going to need a doctor at the airport Frank, I want to take her straight home but we need to know if anything is seriously damaged inside before we take her on an eight hour flight. Get on to Dominic and ask him to sort something before we get back to the airport."

"OK Boss." Frank had recovered his breath now and immediately pulled out his mobile phone to call Dominic, the pilot of Sean's Gulfstream which was waiting in a hangar at Libreville airport. When he was finished he collected Abi's tattered clothing and Aaron's belongings from inside and outside the hut.

"No point leaving him anything useful if he ever comes back." He said with a grin at the slightly confused look on Sean's face. "OK, you bring Miss Storm Boss and I'll high tail it back to the car and bring it in to get you." He said and set off at a run back the way they had come.

Sean carefully rolled Abi on to her back and with one arm under her shoulders and the other under her knees he lifted her gently and set of at a steady pace in the same direction as Frank.

~CHAPTER TWENTY-FOUR~

"Well Mr Sullivan, as far as I can tell without x-rays I would say the lady has at least one possibly two broken ribs, neither appear to have punctured anything so far however, I would strongly recommend a trip to hospital for x-rays as soon as you get her home." The doctor had finished his examination of Abigail on board the Gulfstream as they waited for clearance to take off.

"So she's OK to fly?" Sean enquired seriously.

"As I said previously Mr Sullivan, I would prefer to take her to hospital here first but as you have expressed a wish to go straight home I have examined her as best I can and determined she does not so far appear to be bleeding internally, her belly is soft, her heart beat is strong, her blood pressure is good, her pupils are reactive and her lungs sound clear. For these reasons I would say she is OK until she reaches the UK but would strongly advise a trip to hospital as soon as you get there. A beating such as she has taken can cause all sorts of internal injures which will only be determined with the proper x-rays and scans." The doctor looked seriously at Sean, waiting to hear his agreement.

"Doctor, I promise, the first thing we will do when we land is take her to hospital for a thorough check-up. I'd be happy to call you and let you know how that goes if it would put your mind at rest." Sean added with a relieved smile. To know Abi seemed to have sustained relatively minor injuries when compared with what Aaron had presumably ultimately planned for her was a miracle in itself and he was quite prepared to jump through whatever hoops this doctor wanted him to jump through in order to get her onto home turf where he could protect her properly.

"I would be grateful for an update yes please Mr Sullivan." Replied the doctor with a smile as he exited the plane and started down the steps. "Can I suggest you move her as little and as carefully as possible until you get those ribs looked at? And when she wakes try to get some fluids into her." He added and then was gone without waiting for Sean's reply.

"Let's go Dom." Sean said to the waiting pilot as soon as the doctor had cleared the steps and Frank had hauled them up and secured the door. "Put your foot down, let's get home as soon as." He added. "And have we got any food on board?"

"Fridge is full Sir." Replied the unflappable Dominic, "We're cleared for take-off in five minutes so strap in please, and can you put a lap belt on Miss Storm too please Sir, she shouldn't roll too much then and risk damaging those ribs." With that he headed for the cockpit to finish his pre-flight checks and get the bird in the air.

About an hour into the long flight Abigail began to stir. At first she just rolled her head from side to side a couple of times, moaning gently but making no attempt to open her eyes. Sean was at her side instantly, taking her hand gently and waiting for her to come to full consciousness, he knew she would be in pain when she came round.

After what felt to Sean like an age she managed to open one eye, the other being swollen shut and turning angry shades of purple and black. He watched as she struggled to focus her one eye on his face and a smile crept across his features as he saw the recognition blossom as her brain finally made sense of the image it was seeing.

"Again?" The tiny croak would barely have registered on a decibel meter but Sean heard it loud and clear.

"Always." He confirmed gently, risking planting a soft kiss on her forehead. "Don't try to talk sweetheart, you must be in a lot of pain?" He watched as she nodded agreement. "I have morphine which will help a lot but it will probably send you back to sleep. Would you like a drink before I give it to you?" Again he saw a nod, this time accompanied by a silent tear which slid from the corner of her good eye. "You're safe now Abi, we're going home and either Frank or I will not take our eyes off you for a second, I promise." He brushed the tear away softly and then slid a hand gently under her head to raise it slightly so she could take a few sips of the water he had ready for her.

He gave her a shot of morphine from the on board medical kit and watched as she gently drifted off to sleep again.

"Frank?" He said, as he sat back down in his seat across the aisle from Abi.

"Yes Boss?" Frank knew what was coming next.

"How long do you suppose it'll take that scumbag to get back to the UK?" Neither man even entertained the notion that Steele wouldn't try to come after Abi again.

"Well Boss, it would've taken a damn sight longer if his passport had been in this bag of his." Frank replied indicating the belongings he had brought with him from the hut. "He must've had it in his pocket or something, that and whatever money he's got. Only things in here are a few clothes, map, knife and more of them cable tie things."

"So how long?" Sean asked again.

"Well, even Steele's not stupid enough to try to fly into Britain on a dodgy passport. My guess is he'll enter the EU at some easier border and then he can travel freely anywhere he wants."

"What a fantastic system we have!" Replied Sean with copious sarcasm. "Sorry Frank, go on."

"My best guess would be to get a ferry across from northern Africa to southern Spain, not Gibraltar but somewhere on that coast. Then, if it was me, I'd get up to Paris by road or rail, get the Eurostar from Paris to London and then probably hire a car when he hits the UK, he doesn't appear to be short of money so far so we have to assume lack of funds won't hold him up anywhere. I'd say three days at the most if he's on a mission and doesn't waste any time sightseeing." Frank concluded looking directly at Sean.

"OK. So we have three days to get my house as secure as is humanly possible or to hide Abi somewhere we're sure he can't find her." Sean was almost talking to himself although he knew Frank would be listening intently to every word. "My house is preferable I think."

"Agree Boss." Frank nodded. "He's getting help, and that help is going to send him right to your door." Frank knew Sean would prefer to know that Aaron would definitely turn up rather than be hiding out somewhere never knowing whether Steele would find them or not.

"Absolutely Frank, we need to take him on head on, none of us want to be looking over our shoulders forever, least of all Abi. So we beef up security and wait. Maybe put a man at St Pancras to watch the Eurostar arrivals, might spot him getting off a train and give us a heads up?"

"Worth a shot Boss although it's a long shot. Busy place St Pancras, and the only photograph we can give them for recognition is a grainy CCTV shot we can pull off this security tape I lifted from the airport." He said waving a small analogue video tape he had apparently stolen from the security office in Libreville airport.

"Well done Frank, I'd not thought of that." Sean said with an approving chuckle. "Still, you're right, it is a long shot, especially if he has the wherewithal to shave that ridiculous beard off somewhere along the way. Oh, and speaking of lifting things, did we leave money in the car to pay for the scratches we made?" Satisfied with Frank's nod in reply, he continued. "Good, anyway, get some sleep Frank, we've a lot to do when we get home."

~CHAPTER TWENTY-FIVE~

Aaron was sweating profusely when finally he managed to push his way through the last bush barrier and emerge onto a deserted pristine beach. The Atlantic Ocean was relatively calm today with knee high waves breaking gently onto the crisp white sand. He removed his shoes and socks and paddled along in the shallows until he found a small trickle of a stream running across the sand to meet the sea.

He followed the stream back from the opening where it emerged from bush until he found a spot where it had made a small pool, with a miniature waterfall at one end. The water was clear as it ran over the rounded pebbles resting on the bottom of the pool.

Having bent down to drink Aaron suddenly realised he would have been better bringing some sort of receptacle to carry some water back with him in. After all, Abi was not going anywhere and he intended to make the most of his time with her. The anticipation he felt was exquisite, he realised he had finally found his ultimate fantasy, and the best of it was nobody would ever be able to connect it to him and therefore stop him from pursuing this newly revealed passion, a passion he was quite sure would not end with the death of Abigail Storm.

Conscious though he was that the law would frown on his activities, he found it an unreasonable truth to live with. As far as he was concerned he would be fulfilling his rights as a man in taking his pleasure from Abi in whatever way he saw fit, then by ridding the world of her he would be doing all other men a favour as she would no longer be around to pollute others' lives with her feeble, selfish, nothingness. His heroics therefore should be something he could lay claim to, not have to hide from the law or anyone else. It was a conundrum he had yet to establish the best answer to but it would occupy his mind until he did.

Knowing how compliant Abigail became after a period of incarceration, as it had worked many times before, Aaron decided not to hurry back to the hut. He lowered himself, clothes and all, into the pool, the refreshingly cool water instantly chilling the sweat he had worked up already. He lay back with his head on a rock and allowed his mind to drift, a scene he had not thought about for a long time suddenly sprang to mind.

He was back in Texas, over ten years ago, and he had Anna Foster tied, face down on the bed. He recalled his excitement as she struggled to be free, and the thrill which rippled through his body as he entered her anally feeling her flesh tear as he went in, accompanied by the gratifying scream she emitted. Then there was the blood, a situation he had not planned for. He remembered packing wads of toilet paper into her to stem the flow, annoyed that she would not stop screaming so he had to gag her. Recalling the dilemma he had then faced about how to keep her immobilised and away from any means of contacting anyone, not that she had any friends, he had patiently explained to her how insidious they all were and she had obediently dropped them all.

In the end he had decided just to leave her tied to the bed until she stopped bleeding which would then allow the tear to heal, which was when the idea of the catheter had arisen. Another mistake he had learned much from. Unfortunately for Anna the placing of the catheter had gone badly wrong, with only a bad diagram in a cheap text book to work from Aaron had misplaced the tube, and more blood had begun to pour from Anna's body.

To his shame Aaron had panicked at this point and, instead of leaving her to bleed out and therefore be unable to cause him the grief she subsequently caused, he had taken the stricken woman to the emergency department.

He had known at the time that the doctors did not believe the story he told about the damage happening merely as a result of completely normal, if a little robust, sex, but he had threatened Anna with far worse treatment if she ever said a word and she had stuck to the story he had given her.

Thinking on it now as he lay in the cooling water Aaron realised he had just selected his next victim, after all, she had brought it on herself by going to the police, he had no recollection of setting a time limit to his threat.

Realising he had been daydreaming for some time he hauled himself out of the water, making a mental note to bring a bottle of some sort next time he came for a drink, then he wouldn't have to struggle through the undergrowth every time he became hot or thirsty while he administered Abi's long overdue punishments.

He followed the stream back down to the beach then wandered along the shoreline until he reached his original footprints where he had first emerged from the forest. The slight onshore breeze was welcomingly cool as it filtered through his wet clothing and after retracing his footsteps back towards the hut he managed to reach it without getting overheated again. Maybe he would not take a bottle next time, wet was, it seemed, a far more comfortable way to be and he resolved to go back and get wet again as soon as he had become too hot again in the stifling heat of the aging day. After all, it was still not too long since sunrise but already the heat was building, by midday it would be unbearable and his little swimming pool would be a most welcoming distraction.

Ducking back inside the hut to see whether Abi had come round and, if she had, how compliant her lonely incarceration had rendered her in his absence he was wholly unprepared for what he found.

"For Fuck's Sake!" He exploded, running back out of the hut to search the surrounding bush. "She's like fucking Houdini!" He shouted, although only the cicadas could hear him.

After a fruitless ten minute search he returned to the hut and examined the scene. Not that there was much to examine, he soon discovered his bag was missing along with his prisoner but not a single clue as to how she had escaped was present, there was nothing in the hut to proclaim she had even been here.

As Aaron processed this thought he wondered if there were more huts in the vicinity, if in fact he was at the right one. He again went outside, this time looking for the log he had sat on to smoke his cigarette. Quickly discovering the log was exactly where he expected it to be, together with the discarded cigarette butt, he was forced to conclude Abigail Storm had escaped from him again.

"Just like fucking Boston!" He breathed, furious at his own stupidity in leaving her alone, it was not as if being unconscious and shackled had stopped her escaping last time either. "When I find that bitch..." He was so angry words failed him and he stalked off back through the bush to where he had left the car, thinking that if she had stolen his car his head was likely to turn full circle on his shoulders. "God help her when I catch up with her." He hissed to the unlikely audience of chirping cicadas. "And shut the fuck up!" He yelled at the trees, unable to see even one of the noisy little creatures.

Reaching the car and finding it still locked where he had left it just managed to calm Aaron enough to make him capable of driving, although reversing the little Fiat through the unforgiving undergrowth back to the road was much harder than he had anticipated. By the time the wheels again touched tarmac the little blue car had dents in almost every panel. One back light cluster was hanging by a thread and the front bumper was nowhere to be seen. But, the plucky little thing was still moving so Aaron spun it around onto the road and hurled it back in the direction of the airport.

His aim now was obvious to him. He had to get to England. However Abi had escaped it was more than likely she would now go home and Aaron knew his best chance of capturing her again would be there. So, it was back to the plan he had started the day with. He would go to the airport in Libreville and catch the flight he had already been informed went to Casablanca. He intended to work out the rest of his route as he went, knowing it would be unwise to try to fly into the UK on a false passport.

Just over an hour later, he was sitting in the departure lounge sipping a cappuccino. He had purchased new clothes at the airport shops and had discarded his old ones. His boarding card lay on the table in front of him, next to an ashtray with a lit cigarette.

He had managed over the previous hour to cool his temper, but the burning resentment he felt towards Abi had grown tenfold with the effort. He was dreaming about all the things he could and would do to her when he caught her as he stared out of the window at the runway, watching a very shiny and expensive looking Gulfstream streak its way into the sky and head north west, away from Gabon and off in the general direction he would be headed in just under two hours.

~CHAPTER TWENTY-SIX~

When Abi awoke she found she could only open one eye, her head throbbed, her body ached all over and when she took a breath in it seemed as though someone was stabbing her in the back. As her mind slowly crawled into focus she realised she was yet again, in a hospital bed but this time, someone other than Ginny was holding her hand.

Being unable to see who it was in no way diminished her belief it was not Ginny. The hand folded around hers was far bigger than Ginny's and curiosity forced her to roll her aching head to the side to allow her good eye to see who was there.

Managing just enough of a turn to glimpse the top of a head resting on the bed beside her hand she knew even at this angle it was Sean. As her mind registered surprise that he was apparently asleep holding her hand, the events which had landed her here started to present themselves in her now clearing consciousness.

With horror she recalled being grabbed at the airport by Aaron Steele, where he had materialised from she had no idea but she was sure she remembered something about expecting him to be in police custody not arriving larger than life at the airport. As she recalled waking in that stifling hut, and the state of undress he had left her in her heart rate started to rise, she knew it was stupid but even the thought of Steele and his plans caused a wave of panic to overcome her.

Fighting for control of her emotions she had no idea she was squeezing Sean's hand with a vice-like terror grip and it was not until he leapt up and rolled her fully into his arms that she finally halted the freefalling decline and managed to partially stabilise her feelings.

"Sshh...you're safe now." She could hear Sean muttering softly into her hair as he rocked her gently backwards as forwards. "I promised you one of us would be here every second and I have no intention of breaking that promise." He reassured her, feeling her begin to relax a little in his embrace.

"Which hospital are we in?" Abi felt the need to put some pieces of the fragmented jigsaw together.

"Wythenshawe, it's the closest to Manchester Airport." He answered, glad she had got a handle on her terror, not that he had expected anything less, she was the strongest woman he had ever met. "You've had CT scans, MRI scans and x-rays. You are covered in bruises, including a magnificent black eye, you have a concussion and you have broken your lower left rib at the back. Other than that, you are in good shape." He added, knowing she would need to know what state she was in.

"That would explain the pains then." She murmured, trying to work out if moving would worsen or alleviate the sharp pain in her lower back. She squirmed slightly within Sean's arms, he moved instantly, suddenly aware he was still holding her despite her panic attack having subsided.

"Sorry, are you comfortable?" He asked with genuine concern.

Abi tried to roll over but the pain this caused in what she assumed could only be the area of the broken rib was intense. She winced and tried to move back to where she had come from, the pain only intensified.

"Not really." She managed through gritted teeth. "I need to sit up I think." She added eventually, hoping that if she took the weight off her back it might ease the discomfort.

"OK." Sean replied standing over her. "Cross your arms over your chest and I'll lift you, there's no way you can rise to sitting on your own, you may find you have to roll out of bed for the next few days."

Abi complied and Sean slipped one hand under her back between her shoulder blades and the other under her clasped hands on her chest and lifted. With almost no effort on her part she found herself in a sitting position, apart from the sharp stab when moving, the pain became almost manageable the instant she was sitting. Sean busied himself finding extra pillows and within a minute she was leaning slightly against a soft supporting wall and apart from a slight dizziness she felt much better.

"Did I wake up on the Gulfstream?" She still needed to piece together her fragmented memories.

"Briefly." Sean nodded.

"I had to be rescued again!" She hung her head, the tears now beginning to fall, she remembered the shame she had felt when she had seen Sean on the plane.

Sean suddenly realised this was what she had meant on the plane when she had said 'again?', his heart went out to her and he searched for something to say to make her stop feeling like a failure.

"He had you at gunpoint, then he drugged you Abi, there was not a thing you could have done about it." He hoped his words were reassuring enough to make her hear him.

"I argued with him, I made him angry, that's why he did all this." She gestured to her battered body, her tone indicating she had received no more than she deserved.

"That's fantastic Abi!" Sean exclaimed, knowing how much courage it would have taken for her to even consider fighting back.

"Fantastic?" She looked at him as if he were mad. "Making him do this to me is fantastic how exactly?"

"Abi, firstly you did not make him do anything. He did all this of his own volition, and believe me, he would have done this and a lot more besides before he was finished with you. And secondly, if you argued with him, that means you were prepared to fight back, you, the amazing Abigail, were not prepared to lie down and take his bullshit this time, and that means you have developed some self-belief, which is fantastic! As I said." He finished with a big smile but Abi was unconvinced.

"No, it just means I'm too stupid for my own good, just like he said."

"Oh Abi, I wish I knew how to convince you he's so wrong about you. I wish you could see the Abigail I can see." It was not the first time Sean had expressed these sentiments and he doubted it would be the last.

"How did you find me?" Abi was determined to find out what had happened, even if it meant staring her own failures in the eye.

"Well, as soon as we realised you were missing we examined the airport CCTV footage. That's how I knew you were taken at gunpoint and drugged. The carpark guard saw which way you went out of the airport and we followed. The road Steele took ended just twenty miles from the airport, then he drove that poor little Fiat into the forest, leaving a trail of crushed bushes in his wake, we just followed the signs." Sean decided not to mention Frank's friend Brad, he was not sure why but he sensed Frank would want it kept quiet.

"Simple as that?" Abi stated forlornly, the apparent ease with which Sean and Frank had found her only adding to her feelings of uselessness.

"Not simple at all, we had Steele's lack of stealth and planning and plenty of luck on our side." Sean just wanted to wrap her in his arms and kiss all her pain away but he knew pushing that on her at this time would do more harm than good. He settled for taking her hand in his again and giving it a reassuring squeeze.

"What did you do to Aaron?" Abi whispered the question which had been circling her mind, a part of her hoping Sean said he had killed the bastard, the other wondering if that would just prove he was a gangster after all.

"Nothing." Sean said with regret in his voice. "He wasn't there."

"Not there?" Abi repeated, trying to make sense of the statement.

"No, just you, unconscious and tied to the wall in the hut. Frank went looking but Steele wasn't in the vicinity anywhere. We decided not to wait to see if he returned, just scooped you up and left." Sean replied, dreading the next question.

"He's still alive then? That means…" Abi's whole body began to shake and Sean threw caution to the wind, climbed on the bed beside her and held her as tightly as he dared, trying not to exacerbate her injuries. "He's coming back!" Abi stated in an anguished whisper. "He'll come after me again." She began to sob, each convulsion sending searing pains along her damaged rib.

"I won't let him Abigail. I promise. He will not hurt you again." Sean hoped he could keep this promise, he certainly had no intention of ever leaving Abi unguarded for Steele to find.

~CHAPTER TWENTY-SEVEN~

Later that evening when Ginny arrived at the hospital having driven up from South Cheshire after work, Sean could not have been more pleased to see her. Abi had barely stopped crying since finding out Aaron was likely to come after her again. Sean did not blame her for being frightened but he was at a loss as to what else to say to help her.

Allowing Ginny to take charge he sat down in the chair and watched as she expertly coaxed Abi to dry her tears and then eventually managed to get a small smile out of her. He was just marvelling at how well Abi responded to her friend when Sam arrived, fresh off the plane from Boston.

"I grabbed the next plane as soon as I heard." He explained, dumping an overnight bag on the floor and walking round the bed to kiss Ginny and give Abi's hand a reassuring squeeze. He picked up Abi's medical notes, "Mind if I take a look?" He asked Abi before opening the file. "Well, nothing here which won't mend." He announced with a smile at Abi after a few minutes reading. "No mention of fluoxetine though, you still taking them?" He asked receiving a small nod from Abi he went on. "When was the last one?"

"Er...I remember having one before bed at Koudjo's house." She said in a small voice looking at Sean. "How long ago was that?" She still had no real idea of the timeline of the past few days.

"That was nearly 48 hours ago." Sean informed both her and an expectant Sam.

"Best get you some then." Sam concluded heading for the door, "Missing one day shouldn't do too much damage." He assured Abi as he went to find a doctor to get the medication prescribed for her.

By the time he returned he found Sean waiting outside Abi's door, it was obvious he was looking to have a talk.

"Something I can do for you Sean?" Sam enquired in is usual jovial manner.

"Actually I was wondering if there was something I could do for you." Sean replied enigmatically.

"Oh?"

"Well, watching Abi with Ginny in there it occurred to me there is no way Abi could deal with Ginny moving to Boston. Not any time soon anyway, and I think Ginny is well aware of that." He paused to gauge Sam's reaction. Finding nothing resembling 'mind your own business' in Sam's eyes he ploughed on. "So I was wondering what you thought about moving here? In a nutshell, Abi needs a doctor she can trust and she seems to trust you."

"I'm not sure Abi trusts anyone with the possible exception of Ginny." Sam corrected Sean quietly, not trying to antagonise him in the slightest, but wanting to make Sean understand why Abi was so reluctant to let him in.

"Well, yes, you're probably right there, but she trusts you enough to let you look after her medically, is what I really meant."

"Oh I see, yes I would have to agree with you there then." Sam nodded for Sean to continue, there was obviously a point coming soon.

"So, how would you feel about moving over here and becoming Abi's GP? I could probably buy you into a private practice in Manchester, there are several on John Dalton Street, in fact my own doctor is there." Sean stopped, not wanting to bully Sam but at the same time he was desperate to do something positive for Abi.

"Wow, that's a hell'uv an offer." Sam was stunned, this had not been the point he was expecting.

"What do you think? You must've already given some thought to moving over here, which way were you leaning?" Sean pushed on.

"To be honest I was beginning to like the idea, it was obvious as you say, that Ginny wasn't going to be comfortable leaving Abi any time soon so I have given it some serious thought, I'd actually been looking at being an NHS GP?" He said this as a question to illicit a response from Sean.

"NHS? Well, you could do that too if you like, plenty of doctors have a practice which incorporates NHS patients as well as private patients. Unless of course you were talking about being fully NHS, the pay's not bad these days I hear but you won't make anything like what you're making in the States." Sean concluded, he had his business head on now and Sam could see why he was so successful. He was concise and to the point, covering all bases with the minimum of effort.

"Given the buy-in cost of private practice I didn't think I'd have much choice." Sam began, holding up a hand to stop Sean from interrupting. "But if you're willing to loan me the capital I'll need then I'd definitely be interested." He concluded with a smile, "Although, we should probably run it past Abigail first. If she's ever going to trust any of us we have to be honest and upfront with her at all times."

"Great, yes we'll go and ask Abi now." Said Sean with a smile, extending his hand for Sam to shake on the deal. "And it doesn't need to be a loan, for me it would be money well spent."

"It will be a loan though." Said Sam pointedly, pausing before shaking Sean's hand until he received a curt nod in agreement.

Abi's mood lifted almost immediately when the two men told her and Ginny of their discussions and Sean felt as though a huge weight had been lifted from his shoulders, despite the fact that he still had to protect her from a maniac. He knew she had been worried about which way Ginny would decide to go, he also knew she had not and would not discuss her fears with Ginny so she had been trying to cope alone with them. At least now that particular dark shadow was no longer a threat to her.

For a long time he sat and watched her talk with Ginny, amazed again at how resilient she was and how little she knew of her own strength. She had endured so much in her life that most people only ever hear about and it was remarkable she was not a complete basket case.

He knew she viewed her inability to deal with confrontation, or to defend herself, as a weakness and he hoped in time he would teach her it was simply a defence mechanism she had employed to protect herself from bullying and abuse first from her parents and then Aaron Steele.

Occasionally as he watched her she glanced in his direction, catching his eye and blushing slightly, Sean thought it the sexiest reaction he had ever triggered in a woman and he had to look away for fear she might notice the effect she had on him.

Eventually he could keep his eyes open no longer and drifted off to sleep, safe in the knowledge that both Sam and Ginny would be staying for some time and Frank was due back to watch the door in a few hours. Abi would not be left unguarded, never again.

"Thank God for that." Ginny whispered conspiratorially to Abi, "He's asleep."

"Why thank God for that?" Abi whispered back.

"Coz, now you can tell me how the trip went, I mean before the mad bloke turned up obviously." Ginny replied with a grin, looking over to where Sam was also sleeping to check he was still away in dreamland. She had woken him at 3am after Sean had called to say Abi was in hospital again and the wonderful man that he was had got up and come straight over, he was obviously knackered.

"I've no idea what you mean." Abi tried to reply with innocent aloofness.

"Give over, you didn't fly out there on his private jet and get up to God knows what and think you could get away with not telling me about it did you?" Ginny chastised her friend gently. "Come on, spill!"

"What do you want to know?" Abi asked with resignation, knowing she would now be questioned until Ginny was satisfied she had all the information she wanted.

"Well, most importantly, did you sleep with him?" Ginny whispered, trying to keep her voice down so as not to wake either of the sleeping men.

"No, of course I didn't!" Abi giggled despite herself, Ginny was nothing if not straight to the point.

"What d'you mean, 'Of course'? There's no 'of course' about it!" Ginny was genuinely surprised.

"We just don't have that kind of relationship." Abi began, noticing the unstoppable giggle threatening to spill from Ginny's eyes. "What?" She asked.

"My darling girl, *you* may not have that kind of relationship but I guarantee, *he* does." She said cocking her head towards the now slumped form in the corner.

"No, he doesn't." Abi assured her. "We're just friends."

"Abigail Storm," Ginny put on her best 'mother knows best' face, "He is nuts about you." She stated, "And, for the record, you're pretty fond of him yourself." She added while watching Abi shake her head in denial. "Deny all you want my girl, he has wedged himself firmly under your skin."

"No he hasn't." Abi insisted, less sure of herself than she had been a moment ago. "And anyway, I haven't decided if he's really a gangster or not yet." She added seriously.

"I'd say the gangster/not gangster question is irrelevant now, it's only a matter of time before he tells you he wants to sleep with you." Ginny asserted, stopping short as she saw the guilty look sweep across Abi's face. "Oh, I see he already has!" She added triumphantly. "When did this happen?"

"In Africa, we were staying out in the bush at his General Manager's home." Abi replied, there was no point denying it Ginny could read her like a book.

"And how come you didn't sleep with him then?" Ginny was puzzled, that kind of declaration would usually result in intimacy, especially if the situation was favourable, which it sounded very much as if it was.

"He said, 'never while there is fear in your eyes'..." Abi whispered, realising Ginny was correct, in that moment he had declared his love, his intentions and his compassion. In one sentence he had told her exactly who he was.

Ginny smiled and hugged Abi, there was no need for her to say any more, she had seen the realisation dawn in Abi's eyes, what she chose to do with the knowledge was now up to her.

~CHAPTER TWENTY-EIGHT~

"We need to be ready to move in the next twenty four hours." Bruce informed the bald headed, dark skinned man standing before him in his hotel suite, doubling up as an office during his stay in Gabon. Until he managed to get government agreement for drilling and mining rights there was little point outlaying the expense of a permanent office arrangement.

"We ready Sir, just say the word and we can go." The intimidating black man known to his friends as Tore, meaning *supreme god* in his native Congolese, confirmed with a slight bow, his deep baritone resonating as he spoke.

"And you're sure the General Manager and the shift foreman know nothing?" Harrison asked, possibly for the fourth time during their brief conversation.

"No Sir, nothing. I am sure." Tore confirmed, again with a slight bow of his head.

"Very well, I will give the go signal soon, keep your phone with you at all times, you will receive a text containing your name only."

"Yes Sir." Tore turned, having received his instructions, he knew better than to ask about payment, this would follow when the job was done. He left as quietly as he had arrived, Harrison was again surprised that such a bulk of a man could move so silently.

Turning to the window Harrison considered his plan again, going over every detail to make sure there was nothing he had missed.

His spy at the airport had informed him yesterday of Steele's fortuitous find after having totally missed Miss Storm at the hotel. Quite how Sullivan had known Steele was coming was still a mystery to Harrison but it was obvious he had found out somehow, there was no other reason for the trio to spend the night at the airport instead of the comfort of their five star hotel.

Unfortunately his spy had also informed him that Steele had failed to get very far with Miss Storm, as several hours later she was back at the airport with her guardians, albeit a little the worst for wear after her encounter. They had left for Manchester on Sullivan's Gulfstream and would have been back there by late evening the previous day.

Having no way of knowing how badly injured Abigail was, Harrison had placed a call to the nearest hospital he could find in the vicinity of Manchester Airport. When he had finally convinced the switchboard he was Abigail's brother, they had reluctantly put him through to a ward Sister who had informed him of his *sister's* condition.

Although not as serious as he would have liked, the broken rib would put her out of action for a while, and hopefully that would mean Sullivan was preoccupied with her for the time being. The knowledge that Steele was also apparently heading for England would, he knew, also prey on Sullivan's mind. So, whilst not ideal, Steele would seem to be doing the job he had been sprung for.

Harrison turned his attention to Tore. The man had been employed by Sullivan for the past three years, his employment record was unblemished. He had always been Harrison's back up plan. Had the Senator succeeded in becoming President, Tore's job would have been to assist the US ground troops with whatever their President told them to do. As it had turned out, Tore was now to be the catalyst to start the fire sale to give Harrison the opportunity to step in and rescue the situation before the Gabonese government lost control completely. Thus, putting Sullivan out of favour and himself into favour.

Such was the contentment of Sullivan's workforce, apparently the company treated them well, it had been very costly to keep Tore and his little gang of helpers from throwing in their hand and defecting to Sullivan's side entirely. The big Congolese had assured Harrison all was well with his attack force, none would jeopardise the pay-out he was promised.

Harrison turned away from the window, all seemed to be in place, now all he needed to do was light the fuse at the appropriate time. That moment, he judged, would be about an hour before his scheduled meeting with the Minister for Mines and Energy, which he had arranged for three pm that afternoon. He judged it would take this long for the information to filter through to the minister, any earlier and the meeting could be cancelled, any later and the meeting could be over before Harrison had chance to offer his services. He set an alarm on his phone to go off at 1.50pm.

~CHAPTER TWENTY-NINE~

"Sorry Massa, I know you just left but I think you need to come back." The unmistakable lilt of Koudjo's deep voice echoed through the phone in Sean's hand.

"What's up Koudjo?" Sean was instantly alert, knowing Koudjo would not be bothering him for nothing, especially after the orders Sean had left him with two days earlier.

"We've found a bomb down one of the pits. I've evacuated all the workers and called the army who say they'll send the bomb squad but they're not going to want to deal with me Massa, the government officials who are bound to turn up will want to see you."

"Holy shit, how did you find it Koudjo?" Sean was aghast. Detonating a bomb in a mine shaft could have killed countless men, not to mention trapping many others. He had always known Harrison to be a ruthless businessman but this was a step too far even for him.

"You told me to be vigilant Massa, look for anything out of the ordinary..." Koudjo began. "So when I saw one of the night gang come up the wrong shaft this morning I decided to go down and see if anything was amiss." Sean could almost hear Koudjo shrug from eight thousand miles away.

"And it was just sitting there?"

"No Massa, it was hidden in amongst a pile of tools and old cap blocks, it was the cable as gave it away Massa." It had been a cable running along the bottom edge of the pit shaft and into the pile of debris which had caught Koudjo's attention, knowing it wasn't a power cable as they were all strung along the shaft roof out of the way of feet, tools, pit carts and the like, and therefore out of harm's way.

"A cable? Like a detonator cable?" Sean was too stunned to process the information properly.

"I suppose so Massa, it ran all the way to the cage shaft and was attached to the telephone apparatus at the bottom." Koudjo confirmed. "I suppose they couldn't use a mobile signal down there so this must be the next best thing?"

"Sounds about right Koudjo. Is the cable still in place?"

"Yes Massa, I don't know about bombs, didn't know if taking it out would set the bomb off."

"Wise move Koudjo, best leave that to the experts. Where is the man you suspected in the first place?"

"We picked him up at his home a little while ago Massa, he's locked in the infirmary now, apart from my office it was the only place we could put him and lock him in." Koudjo explained adding, "You want me to turn him over to the police when they arrive?"

"Not yet Koudjo, I'm on my way, tell the police you were just doing a routine inspection when you found the device, I want to speak to him long before police do."

"Right Massa, I've had a gang working on the runway here for the past two days Massa, it'll be long enough by the time you arrive."

"Good job Koudjo, I'll call you as soon as I know when I'll get there." With that Sean hung up, the look on his face still told of total disbelief at what he had just heard.

"Trouble Boss?" Frank had been watching from the other side of the room having recently arrived to do his shift protecting Abigail while Sean went home for some rest and a shower.

"Koudjo's found a bomb down one of the shafts, I have to go back as soon as I can get hold of Dom and get the plane ready." Sean looked over at Abi who was sleeping soundly in her hospital bed, it was almost 8am and she had finally dropped off to sleep at about midnight after Ginny and Sam had left. "Get her out of here as soon as the doctors will let you." He instructed Frank, standing and throwing his coat around his shoulders. "Take her to my house, if she wants to go home and collect some of her stuff that's fine but go with her. And I mean go with her, DO NOT wait outside."

"Got you Boss." Frank nodded. "I'll watch her. Don't worry, I won't give him a chance to get to her."

"Pull in more manpower if you need to Frank, there's plenty of blankets and pillows and sofas they can sleep on. And make a start on the security, cost is irrelevant." He looked pointedly at Frank who was nodding his understanding. "HE doesn't touch her again Frank." He warned, knowing it was unnecessary but it made himself feel better about leaving her. "Tell her I'll call as soon as I can." He added as he headed for the door, pulling his mobile phone out as he went.

"Dom?" He said as the phone was answered at the other end. "Have you slept?"

"Er...yes Boss, actually I'm still in bed, apologies but I didn't think you'd need me today." Dominic Green answered sheepishly, it was rare he was caught off guard.

"No apology necessary Dom, I didn't think I'd need you either but shit's happening and I need to go back to Gabon ASAP. How soon can we leave?" He asked, climbing into a waiting taxi outside the hospital and directing it to his home.

"I can be there, refuelled and checks done it just over an hour Sir, it'll just be down to air traffic control after that, I'll put in a flight plan as soon as I've finished talking to you but there are no guarantees, they'll have to shoehorn us into an already busy schedule."

"Yes Dom, I know, do what you can, I'll be there in an hour. Thanks." Sean hung up and as he sat back in the taxi he contemplated how he was going to manage the situation Harrison seemed determined to put him in. Momentarily he felt guilty about leaving Abi after having promised to look after her but, he consoled himself quickly, there was no way Frank would leave her side, his loyalty was unwavering, she therefore could not be in better hands and this trouble in Gabon definitely needed his attention right now.

Almost exactly an hour later he was seated in the Gulfstream, she was ready to go and he and Dom were just awaiting permission for take-off from the tower.

He had spent the time since receiving Koudjo's call wondering what on earth could be so important to Harrison he was willing to take lives for it. It was true, Sean made a considerable amount of money from the mining operations in Gabon but Harrison was no minor league player when it came to fortune counting. At a guess Sean would have put Harrison's own personal worth somewhere on a par with his own, and that put it somewhere in the two and a half billion range.

Whilst Sean was well aware there were people in the world for whom no amount of money would be considered enough he felt Harrison was unlikely to be such a man. If it was just money he was after he would surely have looked to mine elsewhere, somewhere he could get mining rights without having to resort to such inhumane tactics, not to mention the unproductive cost of his current activities. Sean felt that money could have been far better spent on developing mining interests elsewhere.

Sean possessed drilling rights for oil and mining rights for Manganese, Diamonds and Gold, all of which could be found in various parts of Gabon, not just Sean's mines, together with many other locations around the world. It was a puzzle Sean could not work out but he knew, if he could figure out why Harrison was so hell bent on relieving him of his drilling and mining rights he might just get a handle on how to prevent it.

Leaning back in his seat he felt the engines shudder into life, they had obviously received permission from Air Traffic so Sean settled in for the long flight back to Africa.

~CHAPTER THIRTY~

"Morning Frank." Abi mumbled opening her good eye and seeing him sitting on a chair by the door.

"Morning Miss." He replied immediately rising and coming towards her. "Can I get you anything?"

"They been round with the coffee yet Frank?" She asked hopefully, nothing could wake her like a nice cup of coffee.

"Not sure they do that anymore Miss, but there's a machine just outside your room, I'll go and fetch you one. How do you like it?"

"Milk one sugar please Frank."

"Yes Miss."

By the time Frank returned Abi had managed to roll off the bed, just as Sean had predicted, and climb back on into a sitting position, there was no way she could sit straight up from lying without assistance.

"Did Sean go home for some rest Frank?" Abi enquired as he came back with her coffee. "Sleeping in that chair can't have been very refreshing for him."

"Er...Boss had to go back to Africa Miss." Frank replied, trying to soften what he assumed would be bad news for her. "Trouble at the mines."

"What kind of trouble?"

"Er..." Frank hesitated.

"Spit it out Frank." Abi encouraged with a smile, taking a sip of the hot coffee as she did. It almost scalded her tongue and tasted vile but it was hot, wet and caffeinated so it would just have to do.

"Er...Well Miss, seems they found a bomb down one of the pits." Frank said hurriedly as if saying it fast would make it better somehow.

"Holy shit, a bomb?" Abi was astonished. "No way, Harrison cannot be that desperate."

"Miss?" Frank was confused.

"Sean produces manganese and oil from Gabon right?"

"Yes Miss."

"And there's potentially gold and diamonds there too?"

"Yes Miss."

"But it's hardly the Transvaal is it? Sean doesn't think the diamond or gold deposits are commercially viable. He told me if they happen to unearth something while mining the manganese then great but he wasn't going looking for anything else. Is that right Frank?" She looked hard at him, daring him not to lie to her.

"Yes Miss, that's what he told me too." Frank agreed, surprised she had remembered so much of Sean's narrative when she had been touring the mines with him. Especially after the bump on the head she had suffered since.

"So, why is Harrison so desperate to get control of Sean's mines that he would sanction mass murder when there's nothing there he couldn't find elsewhere? Sean says manganese deposits, although lucrative, are not especially rare, and Harrison has oil coming out of every orifice from Texas, he couldn't possibly have his eye on

the oil fields. It just doesn't make any sense Frank."
She concluded, looking to him to see if he could shed
any insight.

"See what you mean Miss, put that way it does
seem a bit extreme." He could not fault Abi's deductions
at all.

"Could it be personal?" Abi asked. "You've been
with Sean a long time, does he have any history with
Harrison?"

"Not sure he's ever met him."   Frank was
obviously trying to recall any incident involving both
men. "Sure he's never done business with him though,
even at a distance. No..." he concluded. "It can't be
personal, I don't reckon."

"There surely has to be a compelling reason for a
man like Harrison to want to murder many innocent
men."   Abi mused, draining the last of her coffee.
"Maybe we could try to find out while Sean's off fighting
fires in Gabon?"

"Miss, my orders are to take you to Boss's house
as soon as the hospital will let you leave, and watch you
round the clock until Boss gets back. No mention of
solving puzzles or anything of that nature."   Frank
jumped in quickly, he had no idea what she had planned
for how to find out what Harrison was up to, but that
was not part of the instructions he had been given.

"You going to imprison me Frank?" Abi asked,
with raised eyebrows, knowing she would make Frank
squirm and feeling a little guilty for it but not enough to
put her off.

"No Miss!" He exclaimed, blushing slightly at the
thought.

"So how are you going to prevent me from investigating Harrison's motives?" She added with a sweet smile, adding to poor Frank's discomfort.

"Er...I don't know Miss, I suppose that depends what you need to do for this investigating?" He hoped and prayed she said she'd need a computer and an internet connection.

"I'm going to Texas, I'll never find out anything from here." She declared, "Don't worry Frank, we'll be back before Sean even knows we've left."

"We...er...Miss...I'm not sure..." Frank stammered, unsure how much authority he carried with his feisty charge.

"Frank, your orders are to protect me right?"

"Yes Miss."

"Well, I'm going to Texas, so if you're going to protect me you'll have to come too." She stated flatly. "Now, do me a favour and go and find a doctor while I get dressed, I'm going to need discharging." And with that she began the painful process of sliding off the bed, the hospital gown sliding all the way up her legs as she did so. She couldn't help the chuckle which escaped as she saw Frank rush for the door, his indecision overridden by his embarrassment.

It took a lot of cajoling and plenty of promising to take things easy and not lift anything heavier than a coffee cup before Abi finally persuaded the doctor to allow her to be discharged. He was still concerned about her concussion and told her in no uncertain terms that if she experienced any of a list of symptoms she was to come straight back to the hospital.

"Of course doctor." She had agreed whilst glaring at Frank, daring him to say something about how difficult it would be to return to the hospital from Texas.

Wisely, Frank kept his mouth shut, unbeknown to Abi, Frank had spoken to Sean and informed him of her plan.

"Well Frank, can't say I'm happy about it, but I doubt you'll stop her, whatever you do, and in some ways it's better, I mean, there's no way Steele is getting into America on false papers, not by any direct route anyway so she's probably safer there than in Manchester." Sean had said after a moment of thought.

"I thought of that too Boss, but she'll be poking around in Harrison's back yard and if it is him financing all this then he's going to be none too chuffed." Frank had complained. "At least I know what Steele looks like, if Harrison sends someone else after her I won't know who they are."

"True enough Frank so you'd better stay on your toes. Anyway, as far as we know Harrison is in Gabon waiting to pick up the pieces of the mess he's causing so hopefully he won't have too much of an eye on what's happening back home. Look after her Frank, got to go we're on the runway now, call you later."

When eventually Abi was discharged she climbed gingerly into the car Frank had driven round to the hospital entrance, a bottle of prescription painkillers clutched in her hand.

"We need to go to my place first Frank please, I can pack a few things then we'll go to your place and get yours. Then I'll book us some flights, I'm guessing Sean took the lovely Gulfstream so we're going to have to go normal class." She grinned over to Frank, trying to lift his pensive mood. It did not work.

"Come on Frank, work with me a little." She cajoled, "I need to do something Frank, I can't sit here and twiddle my thumbs waiting for Aaron Steele to find me again, I'd go mad." This statement finally made

Frank look at her, he saw the truth of her sentiments in the tears which had formed suddenly.

"Ok Miss." Frank took a deep breath, she was right, she needed to be busy and he had promised to protect her no matter what. "Let's go to Texas." He was relieved to see her grin return as she wiped the rogue tears away with the back of her hand.

~CHAPTER THIRTY-ONE~

"I've just spoken to Harvey Craine, he's the boss at the Boston Globe." Abi told Frank as she wandered into the living room area of their hotel suite. Frank had insisted they either had a suite with two bedrooms or he was sleeping with her. She hadn't put up a fight. "I told him we think Harrison is behind some problems with mining in Gabon, and no I didn't tell him about Steele, I figured I'd save that for another time."

"Not to mention we'd be breaking the law if we knew the whereabouts of a fugitive and didn't tell the proper authorities." Frank replied, Abi smiled, it was the first time Frank had dared to be glib with her, it showed he was starting to relax around her, she was glad about that.

"Yeah, that too." She agreed with a smile. "Anyway, he says he has a guy working undercover at Harrison Oil. Apparently this guy came to him after my story broke and said he thought there was more to it than I'd found and he's been working on it ever since."

"He got a name?" Frank asked.

"Gerald Goldblaum." Abi replied, "GG to his friends apparently."

"And do we know where to find him?"

"Harvey is going to call him and give him my number, he'll contact us here, probably be tomorrow now." Abi said, looking at the clock on the wall, it said the time here in Austin was almost ten pm, although as far as Abi's body was concerned it was some ungodly hour in the morning. "I think I'll turn in." She added with a yawn. "You heard from Sean since we got here?"

"No, we were flying when he landed in Africa, and it's even later there than in Manchester, he's probably asleep now, I'll speak to him tomorrow." Frank said, also with a yawn. "Night Miss, sleep well, you need anything just holla. OK?"

"Ok." Abi confirmed, "Night Frank." She wandered back into her bedroom and closed the door, switching her phone to silent as she went. She loved her iPhone but at night she could not stand to be woken every time it beeped that a message had arrived or an email or other communication she did not need to know about in her sleep.

As she placed it on the nightstand and prepared to change into her pyjamas the screen began to flash, it was receiving an incoming call. She smiled, despite her tiredness, it was Sean.

"Hey." She said quietly, conscious Frank was still just outside her door.

"Hey yourself." Came the reply from half a world away. "You doing OK?"

"Bit sore." She replied, trying to get her clothes off with her one free hand and without bending too much. "Turns out sitting in an airplane seat for thirteen hours with a broken rib hurts a bit." She said, trying not to giggle at her own lame attempt at a joke.

"Only a bit?" She heard Sean chuckle down the phone. "And what about the rest of you?" He asked with concern.

"I'm ok, really, I told Frank I needed to be busy and just sitting around at your place waiting for disaster to strike would drive me insane. I know you're all worried about my mental state, especially after that daft episode last year but I'm ok, really." She was trying to assure herself as much as him and he knew it, but he was relieved to hear she was at least aware of the potential damage her mental state had sustained, it was good to know she wasn't shrinking away from the possibility.

"Good to hear." He said softly, the exhaustion evident in his voice.

"What's happening there?" She asked immediately worried about him. "It must be some horrible hour in the morning there, why are you even awake?"

"It's been a hell'uv a day here Abi, did Frank tell you about the bomb?"

"Yes." She confirmed.

"Well, turns out we were supposed to find it, then when all the law enforcement and army bomb squad and government officials were here, the evacuated men were drawn, by several agitators we think, into a massive fight. One man died, forty-two are injured and the government have closed the mine down while they investigate. It's a mess." Abi could hear the emotion in his voice, it tugged at her heart strings.

"Oh my God, a man died? Are the injured going to be OK?" Abi was horrified at the thought such things could happen in a place only days ago had been a calm, well run place of work.

"Yes, most of the injuries are superficial, cuts, few bangs on the head, stuff like that. We have got a couple of broken bones but they'll all heal. I tell you Abigail, if you can find out anything about why Harrison is doing this that'll be great because I haven't got a clue."

"I know, I told Frank it just didn't make sense. Harrison surely can't be this desperate to take control of your mines." Abi agreed with Sean, having finally managed to get out of her joggers and into her pyjama bottoms, she climbed into the big bed.

"I'm glad you called." She said then nearly bit through her own lip when she realised she had said it out loud. She held her breath waiting for him to answer, hoping he maybe had not noticed her slip. No such luck.

"I'm glad I called too." She could hear his smile as it lifted his tone. "I'm also glad you're glad..." He trailed off, letting the silence hang between them.

"I realised what you said in Koudjo's house meant far more than you actually said." She decided she was far enough away to get away with this conversation and she knew it was something she needed to tell him.

"What did it mean?" He said softly, every inch of him longing to be in Texas instead of the African bush.

"You were trying to tell me I can trust you, forever, that you would never push me around or demand anything I was not willing to give you." Abi replied, gingerly laying back against the pillows as she spoke, trying not to let the pain make her wince at this tender and important moment.

"That's all true Abi but I was trying to tell you something else too." Sean replied, hoping she had understood that too and that she was as comfortable as she sounded with the knowledge.

"I think I worked that out too." She whispered, feeling closer to him than she had ever felt to anyone despite the eight thousand miles separating them.

"I love you." He confirmed, also now whispering, his heart hammering against his ribs, he felt like a teenager waiting for his first girlfriend to agree to let him hold her hand.

"That's what I thought you said." She had no idea why she was crying now but the tears rolled down her cheeks nonetheless. "I'm supposed to say I love you back now aren't I." She started but he interrupted her.

"Only if that's what you feel Abigail. It has no meaning if you don't feel it too."

"I...I don't really know what I feel at the moment." She confessed, hoping he did not think she sounded ridiculous.

"I know that Abi, you've been through so much I think it will probably take a good while before you sort your feelings out and I don't just mean about me. For now I'm happy in the knowledge that I've told you I love you and you haven't run screaming from the room. For me that means you're ready and willing to see where we lead, which also means you are a long way from when you thought I was just a thug gangster. Am I right?" He asked.

"You're right." She confirmed with a smiling whisper. She had definitely decided he was not a thug gangster, or at least she had decided she didn't care either way, she wanted to be close to him and she wanted to see if a relationship with him would lead somewhere. "Although, I still think you'd help out if they were short-handed!" She added cheekily with a giggle.

Sean laughed out loud, despite the rough few days they'd both had she was amazing, even at eight thousand miles distance she had made him feel better than he'd felt for ages. He knew tomorrow was still going to be a stressful and trying day but he could face it now with a calmness of soul which could not fail to help the situation. His body however, craved sleep, it was almost four in the morning and if he did not sleep soon it would be time to get up again and face the day.

"I love you Miss Storm but, part-time gangster or not, I must sleep now." He was unable to stifle a yawn.

"Call me tomorrow?" She whispered.

"Count on it." He replied.

~CHAPTER THIRTY-TWO~

Sean woke to the sound of gunfire. He leapt off the make-shift bed he had cobbled together out of two benches and a packing crate, threw on his pants and shirt and just managed to remember to shake his boots upside down to check for sleeping scorpions before stuffing his feet into them and running outside.

He was met by a worried looking Koudjo.

"I don't know what's got into them Massa." He said shaking his big head in disbelief. "They are behaving like animals, I know it's caused by just a few but the way they are going it's impossible to separate the good from the bad."

"I heard gunfire?" Sean demanded an explanation.

"Army boys have them all corralled on the waste ground at the back Massa, they started fighting again so soldiers fired over their heads to get them to stop. They have them all sitting on the ground now with their hands on their heads." Koudjo sighed, he had never seen the workforce so riled. He knew the vast majority by name but not one of them would look him in the eye today. "I took a couple of boys off on their own but they won't talk

Massa, whatever Harrison's lot have said to them, it's got them worked up like I've never seen."

"We have to get to the bottom of this Koudjo, it's going to tear the place apart otherwise. Have you tried explaining to them how their lives will change if Harrison takes over, assuming it *is* him behind all this, I'm damn sure he won't be paying for their medical centre and their school."   Sean was at a complete loss.   His workforce had always been well looked after, he had never had any kind of industrial protest before, there simply had never been a need. All his workers knew he expected them to work hard when they were on shift, in return he paid them well, made sure all the safety equipment was up to date and working properly and looked after their families. They fared far better than most other mines he had seen in this or any other country.

"I've tried Massa, but until we can sort out who's leading who we're not going to get anywhere. Maybe let them sit where they are for a while, when they start getting hot and thirsty maybe somebody will start to talk."

"I think that's probably called torture Koudjo." Sean said through gritted teeth, the idea of treating men like animals grated on him, even if they had been behaving like animals. "And in the meantime the man from the ministry is taking notes and reporting back to the Minister that we can't control our men. We need to get a plan together Koudjo. And fast!"

"Yes Massa, I'll meet you in the office in five minutes, need to check on the man from the ministry first, we haven't seen him yet this morning."

"Don't wake him if he's still asleep, the less he sees the better."

"Massa."

As Koudjo ran off in the direction of the canteen, where all the non-mine personnel had bedded down last night Sean's mobile began to ring.

"Frank, is everything OK there?" Sean said as soon as the connection was made. "Abi OK?"

"Yes Boss, all fine, she's sleeping now, but it is only 3am here." Frank replied. "You said to call you as soon as possible, I figured you had to be up by now so I called."

"I didn't mean to stay up all night Frank, when you got up would have done. Anyway, I'll have to be brief, it's all kicking off again here this morning. I spoke to Abi last night and she seems in good spirits considering. Keep a sharp eye on her Frank, after what she's been through she could go downhill fast."

"And what do I do if that happens Boss?" Frank was worried now, it had been a very long time since he'd had a real relationship with a woman, almost thirty years to be exact, and he was not entirely sure if he remembered anything about how to handle emotional situations.

"Just call me, we'll work it out." Said Sean realising he had probably just worried Frank half to death. Put Frank in a life or death situation and he was cool as a cucumber, planning, strategy, hand to hand fighting whatever, he was a good man to have around but, when it came to people skills, especially women, Frank seemed to have turned whatever abilities he had once possessed completely off. "Anyway, I'd best go Frank, I've a situation to sort, not that I've managed to figure out what the fuck's going on but I've still got to sort it."

"For what it's worth Boss, you can only have a few agitators in there, the majority are loyal to you, if you separate them out you should be able to get a handle on it." Frank offered helpfully.

"That's the idea Frank, unfortunately we don't seem to be able to work out who's who at this point, it's a fucking mess. When I'm done here I think you and I need to pay Harrison a little visit."

"Count me in Boss."

"Gotta go Frank, I'll call later."

"OK Boss."

Frank had just disconnected the call when Abi sauntered out of her room. She had obviously just showered and was dressed in sweatpants and a t-shirt.

"What you doing up Miss? It's still the middle of the night." Frank asked, surprised to see her dressed as if it were morning.

"My body has no idea what time of day it is Frank, I woke up an hour ago, couldn't get back to sleep so decided to shower and get dressed, was that Sean?" She asked smiling at Frank as she gently rubbed the throbbing ache in her lower back.

"Yes, that rib giving you jip?" He asked. "Taken your painkillers this morning?"

"Hmm, I was trying not to."

"Well don't, no point suffering more than necessary." Said Frank striding past her to retrieve the bottle of pills from her room. "They gave you these horse pills coz it's going to hurt like a bastard for a while, ribs heal slow, so take the pills while you've got them." He said handing her the bottle.

"OK Sir." Abi stuck out her tongue at him as he walked away from her. "So how is Sean doing?"

"Not good, he can't work out how to separate the good guys from the people winding them up." Frank looked worried as he related Sean's dilemma to Abi.

"Sorry Frank, I know you feel you should be protecting him not me." She smiled faintly, feeling burdensome and unworthy.

"Not at all Miss." He declared. "No Miss, I'm not worried about his safety, no Koudjo will take good care of him there and I know there's not another man on the planet he'd trust to look after you. No Miss, I'm worried coz he's worried, he doesn't know what to do for the best and that's not something usually happens to him."

"So it's not as simple as the bad guys being the ones they've recently hired?"

"No Miss, Boss says it's like they're all hell bent on ruining him, but even Koudjo can't get any of them to talk. It sounds to me like they've been threatened or something, they're too good a workforce to be doing this of their own volition." Frank mused, as confused as Sean and Koudjo as to the origins of the apparent anger of the usually compliant workforce.

"Do all the men come from Koudjo's village?" Abi asked, an idea beginning to form in her mind.

"Not all of them, a lot of them do, the others are from neighbouring villages, why?" Frank could tell she was thinking about something.

"I think I may have an idea." She said with a smile as she pulled out her mobile phone and searched for the appropriate number.

~CHAPTER THIRTY-THREE~

"Oui?" The clear, confident voice answered the phone.

"Sephora?" Abi asked.

"Oui, et vous?"

"It's Abigail, Sephora, we met the other day." She hoped Sephora's English was up to this conversation as Abi's schoolgirl French was very bad.

"Ah, yes, Miss Abigail, you are well?" Abi need not have been worried, Sephora as with many other Gabonese spoke French, her native Bantu and extremely capable English. "My Koudjo, he said you had trouble."

"Yes Sephora, some trouble but I am well thank you. But Sephora it is Koudjo I am calling about. He and Sean are in trouble at the mine."

"My husband is he hurt?" Sephora was immediately concerned, the emotion clear in her voice.

"No, no, they are not hurt, but all the men of the mine are fighting each other, the man from the ministry has closed the mine and the army are trying to control the men. Sean and Koudjo think there are just a few bad men in amongst the good ones but they can't tell who they are. If they don't get this sorted quickly the ministry might make Sean give up the mine and give it to someone else." The words tumbled out of Abi in a rush, as if just by saying the words the situation automatically became more urgent.

"Sorry, Miss Abigail, please repeat but slower, please." Sephora said apologetically and Abi realised how difficult she must have been to understand. She went over the details much more slowly with Sephora acknowledging her understanding as she went.

"But there are no bad men from the villages." Sephora assured her when she was sure she understood everything Abi had said.

"I thought so too Sephora that is why I think you may be able to help."

"How so?"

"If you were to go to the mine, all of you, all the wives and children from the villages would your good men stand with you?" Abi crossed her fingers for Sephora to be on the same wavelength as she was.

"And only the bad would remain?" Sephora smiled through the ether. "You are a smart woman Miss Abigail, I see why Massa loves you so."

"Do you think it could work Sephora?" Abi asked excitedly.

"Without doubt."

"How long will it take you to get all the women and children moving? It's quite a way to the mine, how will you get there?"

"Don't worry Miss Abigail, it will not take long. I go now, I have things to sort out." Abi could tell Sephora had a mission plan so there was no more left to say.

"Good luck." She just managed before the line was disconnected. "I hope it doesn't take her too long to get organised, it sounds like Sean and Koudjo are running out of time." Abi said to Frank, aware he had listened to the entire conversation so there was no need for her to explain.

"You ever heard the war cry of a Bantu?" Frank chuckled as he imagined Sephora spreading the word throughout the village, "It would take about twenty five seconds for every single person to hear. Then runners will be sent to the other villages, I reckon they'll be at the mine within the hour."

"Do you think it'll work Frank, or have I just thrown more wood on the fire?"

"I honestly don't know Miss, but it sounded like a great idea from where I was sitting." Frank smiled, "Well, I don't suppose either of us is going back to sleep now so shall I order us some breakfast?"

"Breakfast at 3.30am? Surely there won't be anybody in the kitchen now?" Abi looked at Frank as if he were daft.

"This is America Miss, there's *always* someone in the kitchen."

Abi started to laugh but winced in pain as the sudden movement set off the sharp stab in her lower back. "Bloody rib." She cursed, opening the pill bottle and shaking two out onto her hand.

Frank just handed her a bottle of water from the fridge, to his credit he didn't say a word.

The pair then settled in to wait, ordering breakfast of pancakes and coffee, and hoping to hear some good news from Africa before too long.

In N'Goutou, eight thousand miles away Koudjo had caught up with Sean, the man from the ministry was indeed still sleeping and the order to wake him had not been given.

"We could try talking to the bomber Massa. In all the chaos I clean forgot about him, we moved him from

the infirmary because we needed it for the injured men."
Koudjo suggested, wondering if the man actually knew
anything useful or was just an expendable asset, paid to
do his part and no more.

"Where is he now?" Sean asked, knowing he was
probably thinking the same thing as Koudjo but at least
they would be doing something to try to help the
situation. Right now he felt as though they were just
waiting for further disaster to strike.

"We put him in one of the outhouses, tied to one
of the old counter weights from the redundant shaft."

"How long has he been out there? Has he been
given anything to eat or drink?" Sean looked up at
Koudjo although he already suspected he knew the
answer. "Koudjo!" The big man's face confirmed Sean's
fears. "We'd better go and see if he's still alive then
before we try to question him." He set off out of the
office building and across the compound at a flat run,
Koudjo trotting along behind had grabbed a bottle of
water as he left the office.

On reaching the outhouse Sean was gratified to
see the door was open at least, these sheds were made of
corrugated steel and the interior soon became
unbearable in the heat of the day, at least with the door
open the occupant would have had some air circulation,
although, without water that was by no means a
guarantee of survival.

The prisoner lay prone on the floor, his leg
tethered to the counter weight stretched out behind him,
he had obviously tried to get his head as close to the
open door as he could. Stooping quickly Sean felt for a
pulse.

"He's alive." Sean breathed a sigh of relief.
"Koudjo unshackle his leg and let's get him out of here."

"Where to Massa?" Koudjo asked, unlocking the padlock holding the chain manacling the man's leg to the immovable weight, and lifting him onto his back as though he weighed almost nothing at all. "Infirmary is full Massa."

"Yes, take him to the office, I'll go and see if can find some ice, we need to cool him down and get some water into him."

Five minutes later Sean, the site doctor and Koudjo had laid the unfortunate man out on the desk in the General Manager's office. They had ice packs on his groin and underarms and the doctor was attaching a drip catheter to his arm.

"His pulse is a little stronger than it was when we found him." Sean informed the doctor as he held his fingers to the man's neck.

"Yes, he's not in too bad shape considering, once this drip starts running he should come round fairly swiftly." The doctor seemed wholly unruffled by the man's condition, this calmness allowed Sean to relax a little. Despite his crime Sean had no wish to do any harm to this man, the authorities would deal with him however they saw fit. "It may be a while before he can speak though, Mr Sullivan, his throat will be dry and sore, I suggest you let him drink first."

"What makes you think he'll talk Doc? Sore throat or not, nobody seems to be talking." Sean replied with scepticism.

"This one will talk Massa." Koudjo agreed with the doctor. "You could've left him out there to die but you didn't, his honour will make him talk now."

"His honour didn't stop him planting a bomb in my mine Koudjo, I very much doubt he takes notice of his honour." Sean concluded, his mouth set in a grim line.

"Not so Massa, if his honour had anything to do with the bomb planting then it was the fulfilment of something he promised, therefore his honour was assured." Koudjo said with a small smile, knowing the reply he would receive.

"So his honour is fine with criminality but not with breaking a promise?" Sean would never really understand the African way, he had heard such incongruities many times before but they never ceased to amaze him.

"He is Bantu, Massa." Koudjo just shrugged, as if this in itself was enough explanation.

"Can you stay with him doctor? I know you have a full infirmary." Receiving a nod from the doctor in reply he continued. "Come on Koudjo, there's nothing we can do here until he can speak, we had best get outside and see what other disasters are to happen today."

Outside the sun was high in the sky and the heat was becoming oppressive.

"If we don't get this lot out of the sun soon we're not going to have enough drips to deal with them all." Sean muttered as the two men approached the mass of seated miners surrounded by armed soldiers.

"There is nowhere under cover we can put them Massa, even if they would stay calm enough to be in a confined space together." He was about to say something else when he noticed a dust cloud just appearing above the dip in the approach road. "Someone comes Massa." He pointed for Sean's benefit. "Dust cloud that size means many vehicles."

"Oh God, now what?" Sean groaned, praying the man from the ministry had not summoned reinforcements. "Sounds like trucks?" He added, seeing Koudjo nod his agreement.

As both men waited the trucks abruptly halted, just under their line of sight. The engines were switched off and there was near silence for several minutes. Then, over the crest of the dip both Koudjo and Sean were amazed to see a mass of women and children begin walking towards the mine gates.

The men on the ground noticed too and each turned to watch the unusual sight unfold.

As the women drew nearer it was Koudjo who first recognised one of them. "Sephora, my wife, leads." He informed Sean, his face an unreadable mask. "We should open the gates Massa."

"Koudjo, those gates are the only thing between hundreds of women and children and our murderous workforce. I'm not sure opening them is a good idea." Sean replied with alarm.

"Those women and children are the wives and families of our murderous workforce Massa, I think these women know their husbands, open the gates."

Sean looked hard at Koudjo, trying to work out whether he should do as his General Manager had suggested. He had no desire to have the women and children embroiled in the fighting the men had been engaged in but he trusted Koudjo implicitly. As he looked, Koudjo's face broke into a huge grin.

"Somebody is a genius Massa." He beamed. "Open the gates."

Realising he was to get nothing more helpful from the man beside him, Sean waved a signal to the gateman who nodded once and engaged the pulley's which opened the gates.

By this time the women were massed in the road just outside the compound, they stopped and stood silently and still. Not one of them moved or spoke and nobody crossed the threshold into the mine property. They simply stood and waited.

"Now what Koudjo?" Sean still had no idea what they were trying to achieve.

"Tell the soldiers to shoulder their weapons." Koudjo said quietly.

"Really?"

"Yes Massa, really." He replied, completely calm, without even a hint of hesitation.

Sean shrugged, still not convinced he was not about to witness carnage on an industrial scale, he signalled to the most senior soldier to tell his men to stand down. The Major in question was apparently not on the same page as Koudjo either, as Sean had to give the signal three times before the man complied. It was fortunate that the man from the Ministry had still not made an appearance, as Sean doubted the Major would have taken his order at all if a government official had been present.

As soon as the guns were no longer trained on the seated men they, one by one, began to rise. Very slowly, as though to ensure no sudden movements made anyone panic, they each walked the fifty yards to the gate where the families still congregated, individually they found their wives, picked up the smallest of their children or held the hands of the others and stood, silently beside their wives.

Within five minutes all but five of the mine workers were standing surrounded by women and children just outside the mine gates. A voice from the back of the crowd began to sing, loud, clear baritone voices joined in until all the men were singing, except of course the five still seated on the waste ground within the perimeter fence.

The resonance of over a hundred deep African male voices filled the air around them and every hair on Sean's body stood on end. It was truly a beautiful moment to behold.

"And only the bad remain." Koudjo indicated the five men still seated. The Major had apparently had the same thought as his men now had their weapons back in their hands and trained on these last few.

"Amazing." Sean breathed, huge relief evident in this voice. "I think it's fair to say your wife is definitely a genius Koudjo." He added.

"I would like to agree Massa, but my wife could not have this idea." The big man replied with a shake of his head. "I have not called her since this started and I don't know how else she could know."

"Then we'd better ask her, I'd put money on it being her who brought them here."

"It is a puzzle Massa, I will ask." With that the big Bantu strode away towards where his wife stood at the front of the still singing men.

~CHAPTER THIRTY-FOUR~

"Mr Minister, Mr Harrison is still waiting outside Sir, he is demanding to see you this morning." The petite personal secretary to the Minister for Mining and Energy said with an apologetic look as she entered the Minister's office.

"Still? Can the man not take a hint?" Salomon Avomo complained looking up from reading his newspaper. "Have you told him I'm busy?" He asked.

"Yes Sir, many times." She confirmed. "He says it is vital he speaks with you."

"Vital? Surely not." Avomo sighed, he had detested the Texan on sight and no amount of meetings since had made him warm to the man. He had detected a ruthless streak bordering on callousness which, in Avomo's eyes was a major character flaw. He had no problem with driven businessmen, in fact, he liked to see a man be passionate and resolute in his business dealings, but he had no time for cruelty or maliciousness of any kind. For Avomo neither trait had any place in the world.

"OK, Marlene, what do I have on today?"

"You have a lunch meeting with the PM at 1.30pm and a newspaper interview at 11.30 this morning. Nothing else Sir." Marlene replied smiling.

"Right, give me five minutes then show Mr Harrison in, I'll give him ten minutes and that is all." Avomo replied looking over his glasses at Marlene, trying not to imagine what lay beneath the exquisitely curvy tie-dyed dress she was wearing.

"I will inform him now Minister." Marlene giggled and purposefully wiggled her behind at him as she left his office. As always she had read his mind.

Five minutes later she ushered a somewhat flustered looking Bruce Harrison into the Minister's office. After ensuring neither man required coffee or other beverages she left them to it.

"So, Mr Harrison, what is so urgent you have to camp out in my secretary's office for two days, I had thought I had made the government's position clear at our meeting the other day?" Avomo opened the conversation, as far as he was concerned the sooner Harrison got to the point the sooner he could be rid of the obnoxious Texan.

"My apologies Minister." Harrison began, his attempt at humility coming across as obsequious and insincere. "I realise you are busy but there is a matter I must discuss with you most urgently."

"What it is?" Avomo had no intention of allowing Harrison to get comfortable.

"It is the matter of the mining licences for the N'Goutou region."

"What of them?" Avomo was suddenly all ears.

"Well, I believe they will be up for renewal next week and I want to tender my company's bid for those contracts." Harrison said with a smile which did not reach his eyes.

"So despite the conversation we had three days ago you assume the current contractor will not be renewing then?" Avomo raised his eyebrows at Harrison.

"Er...well Minister, I heard the ministry may not allow the current contractor to continue." Harrison said hurriedly, he had not anticipated the stonewalling he was getting. He had expected the Minister to tell him that Sullivan would not be getting his contracts renewed. Harrison was sure the Minister must have been informed of the mayhem currently going on in N'Goutou.

"Why would that be Mr Harrison?" Avomo was now glaring at Bruce, he seemed to be enjoying watching the oil billionaire squirm.

"A rumour Sir." Harrison hoped the minister would accept this and move on. He was wrong.

"A rumour?" Avomo was furious now, did this revolting Texan fool think he was stupid? Did he really think he would not connect this conversation to the report he had just this morning been reading about massive unrest at the Sullivan Mining Operations, a place which to date had never before suffered any kind of workers' strike or even minor protest. "And where would you have heard such a rumour Mr Harrison?" He asked.

"I believe I saw something in a newspaper Mr Avomo, something about Mr Sullivan having trouble controlling his men." Harrison offered with another insincere smile.

"I very much doubt that Mr Harrison, you see, I have expressly forbidden the newspapers from reporting anything until the matter is resolved. So, again Mr Harrison, how are you aware of any situation arising in N'Goutou, a place which, as far as I am aware, is none of your concern?" Avomo glared at Harrison over his glasses.

Before Harrison could speak there was a tentative knock at the door and Marlene appeared.

"Apologies Minister but I have an urgent message for you." She stated proffering the piece of paper she held in her hand.

"Bring it." Avomo was too angry not to let it show.

"So sorry Minister." Marlene said as she hurried across the room to put the paper in Avomo's hand.

Avomo instantly realised she thought he was angry with her, he caught her eye as she turned to leave and the look he gave her reassured her completely. He read the message she had given him as she hurried out of the office and closed the door behind her.

Turning the paper face down onto the desk so Harrison could not see its contents he continued. "You were saying Mr Harrison?"

This meeting was not progressing in anything like the manner Harrison had planned for it to go. The minister was supposed to just listen and agree with him, he was even prepared to have to grease the wheels a little but it seemed all his information regarding Mr Salomon Avomo was lacking, far from the stereotypical ex-colonial jobsworth he was expecting, indeed, their previous meeting had been too short to change his expectations, Mr Avomo was in fact an astute and busy Minister for a prosperous and growing country. This fact made Harrison's prospects of getting what he came for seem unlikely at best. He decided to try appealing to Mr Avomo's sense of patriotism.

"Surely the Gabonese government can't be seen to endorse a mining company with such scant regard for its workforce that one of them has been killed in fighting on the premises." Harrison watched Avomo's eyes narrow with rage, and could not help feeling relief flood over him, he had apparently hit the little official in a soft spot and was sure this would now swing the conversation in his favour.

"As you seem to be so well informed Mr Harrison, you will also be aware that Sullivan Industries' record for all its activities in this country is exemplary." Avomo's voice was low and loaded with contempt. "There will be an inquiry as to what went wrong in N'Goutou over the past few days and your apparent knowledge of an, as yet, unpublicised situation will be noted. And..." He held up a hand to prevent Harrison from responding. "...before you completely disgrace yourself by offering me some kind of bribe, know this, if you do I will have you bodily thrown from this building."

Harrison opened his mouth to speak but no words came out so he closed it again.

"For your information Mr Harrison, Mr Sullivan now has the situation fully under control. This government has no reason to believe this incident will have any long term repercussions and I personally see no reason, at this stage, to rescind Mr Sullivan's contracts. If the inquiry finds you had anything at all to do with this debacle I will make it my mission to make sure you never receive government sanctioned contracts in this country, not even for toilet cleaning! Are we clear Mr Harrison?" Avomo stood as he finished speaking, pushing a button on his telephone console which brought Marlene back into the office.

"Mr Harrison is leaving." Avomo said without taking his eyes off the oilman.

Harrison left the room and then the building without another word. Emotionally he had no idea what he felt, he was angry, he was humiliated but above all he was terrified. His buyers, who had expected deliveries within the year, were going to be seriously unimpressed when he told them he could not source their awaited product. He very much doubted their reaction would be merely a dressing down, he assumed, with good reason, it would be painful in the extreme, if not fatal.

~CHAPTER THIRTY-FIVE~

The diner turned out to be one of those traditional sixties types, with waitresses wearing beehive hairdos and short pink skirts. The décor was brash and plastic with lots of shiny chrome fittings everywhere. Abi smirked as she entered, wondering whether this was meant to be taken seriously or tongue in cheek.

At the far end of the diner there were several booths with wraparound bench seating in red PVC around chequerboard Formica topped tables. In the end booth Abi could just see a man seated as far back and as out of sight as he could get. She wandered over to get a better look and as he came into view she also spied a copy of *The Globe*, folded neatly beside him on the seat. This was the signal they had agreed so she slid into the other side of the booth, pushing her sunglasses up onto her head as she did, hoping the makeup she had applied earlier was hiding her now purple but no longer swollen black eye.

"Mr Goldblaum?" She asked, extending her hand in greeting.

"Just GG if you don't mind Miss Storm." He replied with a smile, "Mr Goldblaum is my father! Hey, you didn't say anything about bringing company." He exclaimed suspiciously as Frank sat down next to Abi.

"Frank is my bodyguard GG." Abi replied calmly. "I'm sure you've heard what happened to me the last time I was in America?" She let the question hang in the air, raising an eyebrow at GG which suggested he did not argue further. He merely nodded in reply, even if he had not been a journalist he would have heard about what Steele had tried to do to her.

"OK, you want to order before we get started? I'm starving." GG waved the waitress over as he spoke.

"Just coffee for me thanks." Abi nodded her order to the waiting 'Polly' according to her name tag. "Frank?"

"Yeah, just coffee for me too."

"I'll have the full house breakfast with extra pancakes and maple syrup. And coffee." GG said, handing the menu back to the waitress with a smile.

Abi and Frank had eaten breakfast of pancakes and ice cream at 4am, much to Abi's surprise, but it seemed the belief that in American you can have whatever you want whenever you want it was in fact true. At least it was true in their particular hotel.

"So, GG, Harvey tells me you've been down here for a while trying to get some more on the story I started last year?" Abi decided to be as direct as she needed to be, no point meandering around the houses.

"Yeah, Harvey called me. How do I know you're not just going to take what I found out and write a sequel to the last piece you did?" GG eyed her suspiciously.

"What did Harvey tell you?" Abi knew this question would have been asked before.

"Er...well..." GG stammered.

"Don't tell me you didn't ask him GG 'cause I won't believe you, not for a second." Abi stared hard at GG.

"OK, he said you're not the type." GG admitted reluctantly, slightly sulky now he had been caught out.

"I think he probably said more than that GG?" Abi waited.

"He said you'd be a fantastic journalist if you chose to but you haven't got an ounce of ruthlessness in you and you're more likely to give me leads I didn't have already than to steal anything I tell you." GG admitted quietly, conveying to Abi at the same time that Harvey may well have torn a hole in GG merely for asking the question.

"So, have you got anywhere?" She asked sweetly. "I'm fairly sure the motive I used, the 'sleeping with the daughter-in-law' angle wasn't the only reason Cabot was in bed with Harrison."

"You're not wrong there Abi, is it Ok if I call you that?"

"Of course." Abi confirmed although she was sure she felt Frank squirm beside her.

"I think I've managed to trace all the company connections between Ex-senator Cabot and Harrison, some of them are in the names of the kids and wives but I reckon they are actually controlled by the men themselves, the maze of cut-outs and shell companies is too complex to even try to explain, but I've managed to verify most of my findings. A lot goes on in countries like the Virgin Islands, where transparency is only a prerequisite for reading glasses. I'd be surprised if any other members of the families even know about them. Anyway, the most worrying one is a company called Sharif International Shipping Corporation. Although as

far as I can tell it has nothing to do with shipping." GG
began in earnest.

"What does it do then?" Frank asked, earning
himself a startled look from GG who apparently expected
the bodyguard to just guard and not speak. He looked at
Abi who merely nodded for him to go on.

"That's the problem, it doesn't appear to do
anything, at least not that I can find."

"So why is it worrying?" Abi was confused.

"Well, two things, first the name. Sharif was a
famous Islamic leader way back when, believed to be a
descendant of the Prophet Muhammad. It also means
'Illustrious' and 'Leader of the tribe' in case that's
relevant."

"So you're worried because there may be an
Islamic connection?" The tone of Abi's voice suggested
she felt the connection was a bit thin to be worrisome.

"Yeah, what's in a name right?" GG agreed, "Bit
odd for a Texan to call his company though."

"I suppose." Abi agreed but still sounded
dubious.

"Problem is I have, I think, found an Iraqi and a
North Korean connection." He paused to allow Frank
and Abi to digest the insinuation.

"You're saying you think Harrison is doing
business with somebody in Iraq and North Korea?" Abi
asked seriously, when she received a nod in return she
added, "Governmental somebodies?"

"Don't think so, at least not directly if it is
governmental. My instinct says it's not though."

"Why?" Frank asked, staring hard at GG's face,
trying to detect if the odd little journalist was being
truthful.

"Well, no way would the North Korean government, however indirectly, have anything to do with an American, they would suspect a CIA trap and just wouldn't do it."

"What if the Iraqi is an intermediary, the North Koreans then wouldn't necessarily know it was American on the other end?" Abi suggested thoughtfully.

"Possible." GG agreed. "Especially as I think there is some sort of business connection between the Iraqi and the North Korean. I haven't got anything concrete mind you, but there seems to be something tying them together. Information out of both countries is a little hard to come by but from what I can establish, both business men have made a number of trips to Kashgar in western China. I should clarify, both at the same time."

"And what's in Kashgar?" Asked Abi.

"At the moment there is a lot going on in Kashgar. A few years ago Beijing named it as a 'special economic zone' and have been pouring money into developing it. Apparently it was on the ancient silk route but once the bottom fell out of that market it just became a bit of a sleepy backwater."

"But not now?"

"No, now it's coming up in the world, major investment and the like happening all over the city." GG confirmed. "However, before you ask, that doesn't seem to be why our Iraqi and North Korean are frequenting the city so much."

"You say frequenting – how often are we talking?"

"At least once a month I can place both men in the city at the same time. I can also place Harrison there on at least three of these occasions in the last twelve months."

"And how do we know this is not just coincidental?" Frank asked the question which was on the tip of Abi's tongue.

GG smiled and reached into the bag which was lying on the seat beside him. He drew out a large manila folder and after flicking through some of the paperwork in it he withdrew three glossy ten by eight photographs.

"This is Kashizhougkun International Golf Club." GG stated placing the first photograph in front of Abi and Frank. "It's just east of Kashgar and runs along one side of Shangyalang Reservoir."

"Very pretty." Abi said with a frown, wondering where GG was going with this.

"This..." He placed a second photograph on the table. "...is one Zaeem Halabi and his good friend Namgung Kwan on the tee at the tenth hole." He paused as he presented the third photograph.

"And that is Bruce Harrison." Abi finished for him, staring at the photograph of the three men obviously having dinner together. "Where was this taken?"

"That my dear is in the clubhouse after Mr Halabi and Mr Namgung finished their round of golf."

"Well, I'd say that rules out coincidence. Wouldn't you Frank?" Abi smiled as she turned to Frank who nodded his acceptance.

"So, GG, it appears our three men are acquainted, any ideas why?"

"No I'm afraid that's pretty much all I've got on these two, except for the meetings they always go to at night after Harrison has gone. And before you ask, no I don't know what these meetings are about. I do know they are held at a private apartment in Kashgar, they always happen at night, usually starting around midnight, there are twelve regular attendees including our two friends here and I have no idea what else happens, but the meeting usually lasts about two hours. I have photos of all the other ten men but so far have been unable to put names to them."

Abi glanced at Frank who shook his head once so she kept quiet, a moment not lost on GG who decided to file it away should he need it later.

"Any clues as to why Harrison is so hell bent on getting mining rights in Gabon then?" Abi decided it was time to get to the real point of their meeting. "Do you think there's a connection to these two?"

"It's a bit of a mystery I'm afraid." GG shook his head. "I've ruled out the oil as Harrison's fields in Texas and elsewhere are doing great, so whilst I'm sure he'd always like more I wouldn't imagine he'd be desperate enough to be bothered with any sites he couldn't get immediate permission for. Anyway, I was going through the other natural resources available in Gabon when I came across a report which Harrison commissioned by a mining surveyor called Angus McBride."

"Scotsman by any chance?" Abi giggled. "And how did you 'come across' a report commissioned by Harrison, was it made public?"

"Sorry but my source is a secret at this stage." GG looked pointedly at Abi, waiting for her to acknowledge his journalistic privilege, her nod was all he required. "This report mentions manganese, gold, diamonds and a few others but the most unusual mention was uranium."

"Why unusual?" Frank asked.

"Because all 'official' reports suggest uranium is no longer mined in Gabon, from what I can gather it was never a major source and was deemed mined out years ago."

"Well, even mined out it's probably still present in small quantities so a mining surveyor would have to include it in his report." Abi suggested, still unsure why GG thought this would be unusual.

"You said Mr Sullivan's mining operations were around the N'Goutou region?"

"Yes, that's right." Abi confirmed.

"Well, that's exactly where this report says the uranium is." GG finished with a flourish.

"You know, Harrison, an Iraqi, a North Korean and uranium would make for a really bad connection or two." Frank said in his understated low voice. "Really, really bad."

"Might well explain why he's so desperate to get those contracts from Sean too." Abi mused, knowing they had little concrete evidence but feeling the same way Frank obviously did. "You've been a great help GG, what I'm going to tell you now is possibly connected to your story too, although again there is little in the way of proof." She smiled at him and added. "But that's your job."

"That's true. Just tell me what you've got and I'll do the rest." GG confirmed.

Abi took a deep breath and glanced at Frank who nodded once. "Before I tell you GG I need your assurance that nothing will go to print until I tell you it's ok to do so."

"Can I know why?"

"Because my life is in danger." Abi said seriously, looking GG directly in the eyes.

"If this goes to print before we're ready it'll make it far more difficult for me to protect her." Frank added just as seriously.

"Done. What have you got?"

"Are you aware that Aaron Steele escaped from prison in Boston?" Abi asked GG.

"Sure, it's all over the papers and TV, big manhunt going on but the feds don't seem to know where to look even."

Abi took a wet wipe from her bag and wiped it gingerly around her eye, revealing the bruising beneath the makeup.

"Holy shit where did you get that?" GG asked with concern.

"Aaron Steele came looking for me." Abi said, swallowing the terror that recalling the incident suddenly instilled in her.

"Where?   Here?"   GG enquired raising his eyebrows.

"No. In Africa." Abi stated and went on to tell GG about Steele tracking them to the hotel then finding her at the airport and the consequences of that. She also told him of their belief that Harrison was behind the escape. She gave him the name of Burt Tomasino and the forger on the docks in Boston so he could do some follow up and try to verify Harrison's connection to Steele.

"So where is Steele now?" GG asked when she had finished.

"Still in Gabon as far as we know." She lied slightly, she and Frank had discussed this earlier and decided it was best to not tell GG that they suspected Steele would try to recapture her in England. Frank had said it would be hard enough to protect her without the added complication of possible police involvement. Abi was less than convinced but assumed Frank and Sean had their reasons for not wanting police involvement, and, after the number of times these two had saved her life she was not about to argue with them.

"Wow, well if this checks out it's going to add some serious meat to my story. Can I ask another favour?" GG added as he stopped scribbling notes in the pad he had produced as Abi had told her story.

"Sure, what's that?" Abi agreed.

"Tell me the rest of the story when it's over?" He directed the question to Abi but was looking at Frank as he spoke. Frank gave a half smile and nodded. "Thanks." GG slid a business card across the table as he packed his notepad and manila folder back into his bag and rose to leave. "Good luck." He nodded and was gone.

"Uranium Frank? You think what I think?"

"I hope not." Was all Frank replied and he too rose from the table and the unlikely pair headed for the door, both deep in thought.

~CHAPTER THIRTY-SIX~

Stepping from the plane onto the tarmac in Casablanca, Aaron felt suddenly deflated. His anger had subsided for the moment and was replaced by an exhaustion he had never felt the like of before. As he waited in line to clear customs, absently praying his false passport passed scrutiny, he calculated that in the seven days since he and José had escaped from prison he had not slept in a bed once. He had tried to sleep on the various flights, but had not managed more than a few hours at one time.

Having no real idea how to get from here in North Africa to Spain with the least amount of security checks he decided to book into a hotel here in Casablanca and spend a few days resting whilst trying to work out his next move.

The anger which had been pushed down into the pit of his stomach continued to grow, feeding on his interpretations of events but for now he had it under control, ready to be unleashed when next he needed it.

Strangely, far from feeling impotent as he had immediately after discovering Abigail had slipped through his clutches for the second time, he felt empowered by his ability to control his raging emotions.

He allowed the anger Abigail had again caused him to fester and feed off itself, knowing it would be a useful tool when next he caught up with her.

He realised getting out of the UK after he had finished with her would be difficult. Whoever was helping her would alert the authorities, and he had to assume that by now they would know it was him and his false identity would not shield him.

Unless, he smiled at his own ingenuity, he took them all down. He had no idea how many people were protecting her, it could be one or many. Equally he had no idea where she lived or how to find her when he got to Manchester however, he was fairly certain after the attack in Libreville they were unlikely to leave her alone. He could therefore get them all together in one go and if he did it correctly there would be nobody to tell the authorities anything. He could be out of the country long before the police worked out who to look for.

Realising he had a lot of information to collect he instructed the driver of the taxi he found at the curb directly outside the airport doors to take him to the nearest five star hotel. He had a bag full of US dollars, which thankfully he had hidden under the seat of the little Fiat otherwise Abigail would presumably have taken it along with his backpack, and he had no intention of scrimping on accommodation for the duration of his time in Morocco.

The *Kenzi Tower Hotel* on Boulevard Mohamed Zerktouni turned out to be exactly what Aaron needed. From his twenty-third floor suite he had an amazing view out over the city of Casablanca all the way to the Atlantic Ocean and the recently completed *Hassan II Mosque* which seemed to stand in the ocean itself.

Aaron stood for many minutes in the marble and glass shower, letting the piping hot water cascade over his aching body and ridding it of the accumulated grime of the past week. He washed his hair and decided the time had definitely come to shave. The raggedy beard he had been growing had been born from a lack of shaving facilities rather than conscious choice.

After a delicious dinner of lamb tagine with dried fruit washed down with a quite acceptable bottle of red wine, all delivered to his room by a smiling Moroccan waiter, Aaron fell into a deep, much needed sleep. It was to be a full thirteen hours before he awoke.

Now feeling much revived he decided to explore Casablanca, he really needed to get his bearings and work out the best way into Europe. He was certain flying was out of the question, although he had flown into Spain in the past and never even had to show his real passport. But that had been before 9/11 and all the major nations' airports had far more sophisticated security now. His fake passport was no doubt good enough for African airport technology but he doubted it would pass European, and absolutely no way would he be able to get into America with it.

He had bought a new shirt, slacks, shoes and sunglasses from the hotel boutique and now as he wandered towards the sea front looking for a bar to have lunch in he looked every inch the sexy, accomplished man he could have been if he had channelled his efforts into being good at something instead of trying to insist the world danced to his tune.

He found a kiosk where he purchased cigarettes and a map, the only one he could find not written in Arabic and he continued to wander through Casablanca's narrow crowded streets, past vendors selling spices and leather goods and knock-off European football shirts.

Eventually the streets opened out and before him was the Atlantic Ocean, turning right he wandered along the coastline until he reached the marina, replete with myriad yachts of varying shapes and sizes. A bar with outdoor tables, their white umbrellas fluttering in the breeze stood slightly back from the edge of the marina. Aaron decided this one looked as good as any but with the weather only a mild 17°C he was beginning to wish he had bought a jacket too, he opted for a table inside.

Ordering a seafood platter and coffee from the most helpful and apparently genuinely friendly waiter he settled down to do some research. Opening his map he spread it on the table and began to work out how far it was from Casablanca to Spain.

"Going anywhere nice?" A throaty feminine voice asked from somewhere off to his left.

He glanced up and, seeing an obviously well healed lady sitting at the next table, he smiled his killer smile and turned to face her, flashing his green eyes to her apparent delight.

"Undecided as yet." He replied slowly, taking in all he could see of her as he spoke. She was slim with dark brown, very long hair which hung over the back of her chair and would, he assumed, reach her waist if she were standing. She had immaculately manicured nails and a large diamond ring on her right hand. She wore no make-up he could discern and had no other jewellery on. Her dress looked to be silk, it was pale green with lemon coloured edges and she had a matching jacket which was slung over the chair next to her. "I'm touring." He clarified. "Next stop Europe but I haven't quite decided how or where yet."

"How exciting." She breathed. "Join me? Maybe I can help you decide." She indicated the chair opposite and Aaron gladly accepted. Apart from needing information about how to execute his next move, he found her inordinately attractive and had instantly realised it had been many months since he had last had any desirable female company.

As they chatted over lunch Aaron turned up his charm offensive. He flirted with her as she flirted back and he used the dazzling asset of his eyes to best advantage. By the time they reached coffee she was hooked, whatever else happened Aaron was destined to spend the afternoon in bed with this most interesting woman.

"So, you have a yacht in the harbour then?" He said eventually after they had spent an hour discussing the merits of almost every town and city on the coast from Casablanca to Tangiers on the opposite side of the Straits of Gibraltar from Spain.

"Yes, actually it's my father's yacht but he had to fly back to the UK on business so I have it all to myself for the rest of the trip." She answered with a mischievous half smile.

"And where does the rest of the trip take you?" Aaron enquired, touching the tip of her finger as it lay on the table tantalisingly close to his.

"Ultimately back to Marseille where the yacht lives." She did not move her hand. "I may stop in Spain somewhere en route though, I haven't decided yet." She added, unable to tear her eyes from his.

"Sounds like a pleasant trip, how long would that take?" He enquired innocently, an idea forming which would take all the effort out of the next few days.

"Depends on the weather to an extent but somewhere around a week I should think." She said with a smile, sure she knew where this was going.

"I've never been to Marseille." He said with a grin, thinking it may be no bad thing to allow some time to elapse before trying to get to Abigail again. They would be on their guard so soon but probably less so if it took him a while to get there. "Should I have it on my list of places to visit?"

"Definitely." She breathed.

"Anything else you think should be on my list?" He asked, reeling her in was so easy, there was something so simple about a woman with nothing better to do than pick up strange men in bars. It never occurred to him she would be using him as much as he would be using her. He assumed as usual she merely found his charms irresistible. His ego was such that he could not envisage anyone having a mind of their own, he thought he was capable of making anybody dance to whatever tune he wished to play.

"Two things." She replied, leaning forward and resting her chin on her hand.

"They are?"

"First." She sipped what was left of her coffee. "You should ask my name."

Aaron could not prevent the small chuckle which erupted from his throat. "You're probably right there." He acknowledged dipping his head almost imperceptibly. "Would you care to tell me your name? Mine is er...Michael, Michael Gresty." In the nick of time he remembered the name on his false passport.

"Good afternoon Michael Gresty." She replied, extending a slim hand to shake his. "I am Amanda

Southerby, pleased to meet you." She added with a coquettish grin.

"Pleased to meet you Amanda." He said dutifully playing her game. "And the second?"

"You should probably come aboard and view the yacht." She smiled. "Before you attempt to seduce me into taking you to Marseille in it that is."

"Attempt? You think I will only attempt?" He said, his green eyes flashing dangerously as he resisted the urge to chastise her for second guessing him. "I don't attempt my dear, I do!"

"What, no denial?" She asked in mock surprise, her hormones getting the better of her judgement, she had seen the danger flash in his eyes but dismissed it in favour of the sexy look he now wore. After all, if he became too much to handle she had the crew to protect her and they could put him off at any port between here and Marseille if the need arose.

"Why deny the obvious." He had lowered his voice an octave and now reached out to cover her hand with his. "Shall we go?"

Taking her by the hand he helped her up from the table as she collected her jacket and bag from the chair next to her.

"We should go via your hotel and collect your things." She said as she signed the bill proffered by the ever present waiter. "My car?" she asked as she passed back the pen.

"Coming round now Madame." The waiter bowed and retreated.

As Aaron and his new lady reached the pavement outside the restaurant a sleek limousine pulled up, the chauffeur leapt out and opened the door for the couple to get in.

"Nice car." Aaron observed.

"Father doesn't do taxis, in any country." She answered by way of explanation. "Your Hotel?"

"*Kenzi Tower.*" Aaron instructed the chauffeur who merely nodded his understanding and pointed the long car into the traffic.

"Would you like me to instruct the hotel to have your bags packed for you?" Amanda asked, for a moment Aaron thought she was joking but looking into her eyes saw she was deadly serious. "We can just collect them and go then." She added with a smile.

"I wasn't aware that service was offered." Aaron said dubiously, unsure he wanted some chambermaid finding the thousands of dollars he now had stuffed in his newly replaced backpack.

"Of course they do." Amanda took his question to be agreement and lifted the telephone in armrest of her seat.

Moments later the request had been made and the concierge had confirmed all would be ready when they arrived in ten minutes. Sure enough, as they pulled up outside the entrance of the *Kenzi Tower*, the doorman stood waiting with Aaron's backpack in his hand.

"That's all your luggage?" Amanda was amazed.

"All I need." Aaron agreed, jumping out of the car and quickly inspecting the contents of the backpack before he threw it into the boot which had been opened from inside by the chauffeur.

A further twenty minutes in the luxurious limousine and they pulled up alongside an enormous yacht moored in the marina, not three hundred yards from the spot on the front where the restaurant they had just met in stood.

"Nice boat!" Aaron exclaimed, walking along the deck following Amanda. "It's huge." He couldn't help but add.

"Yes, father doesn't like to be confined, so this is the biggest he could find." Amanda threw over her shoulder as she began to climb a set of steps to what turned out to be the bridge.

"Captain, this is Mr Gresty. He will be accompanying us to Marseille. Are we still on schedule to depart in the morning?"

"Yes Ma'am." The Captain replied, looking Aaron over with what could only be described as disapproval. "The weather looks good so unless it changes we will be away at high tide. Mr Gresty." He turned to Aaron. "If you could leave me your passport Sir, there will be no need to bother you with customs formalities before we leave."

Aaron couldn't help but grin, this was just getting easier by the second. He handed his passport over without a murmur, smiled gratefully at the Captain and followed Amanda back down the steps and into the main interior of the yacht.

He could not believe his luck. If he had to pretend to be the courteous, grateful, even slightly subservient, man of her moment, Aaron was quite sure he could entertain Amanda in a way she would be hard pressed ever to forget for the week or so it would take for them to reach Marseille. Once on French soil he could board a train to Paris, catch the Eurostar over to St Pancras in London and be up in Manchester within a few hours.

In the meantime, he intended to take his fill of this woman who was obviously in serious need of male attention.

Claire Smith

~CHAPTER THIRTY-SEVEN~

"Where is all the equipment now Angus?" Harrison asked, holding the phone between his cheek and shoulder as he buckled his seatbelt before the flight from Libreville to Austin began to taxi. Wishing, not for the first time, he had actually got around to buying a private jet like Sullivan's to take him where he needed to go.

"All in a warehouse in Libreville Mr Harrison, as you instructed." Angus McBride replied jovially. "Just awaiting the go ahead and we can be on the move in a day or two."

"OK, sites 4, 5 and 6 are a go. Move the equipment into place but avoid the N'Goutou plateau, I do not want Sullivan to know we are there. Do you understand me Angus?" Harrison waited for a reply before going on.

"Yes Sir, we can approach the sites from the north, no need to go anywhere near the plateau." Angus confirmed. "May I ask why Sir?"

"Because, Angus, I said so!" Harrison was unused to subordinates who did not just obey orders. But, realising quickly he needed Angus onside if he ever hoped to pull this off he added. "Sullivan still has the rights to sites 1, 2 and 3, if he gets wind we're mining in his back yard he will complain to the ministry and they've made it very clear what would happen then. Sullivan has half the government in his pocket so we'd be out on our ears."

"Best not let him know then." Angus agreed instantly, this was the best paying job he had ever been offered and he had no intention of having it cut short because he could not follow orders.

"Let me know when you've got all the equipment in place, I'm going back to Austin now, call me there." Harrison hung up before the big Scot had chance to argue with him further. He had taken an instant dislike to the man but he seemed to know his geology very well and as Harrison could not do the job himself he was prepared to put up with the hairy Celt for as long as it took.

He settled back into his seat and waited for take-off. *"Soon."* He thought to himself, *"Soon I'll get my own Gulfstream, just as soon as those mines start producing and the Corporation suddenly needs the tax right-off."* He smiled as he closed his eyes, it was a long flight back to Texas so he may as well try to sleep for at least some of it.

The past few days had been as stressful as they had been disappointing. Tore's failure at the mine in N'Goutou had been total. Not only had he failed to dislodge Sullivan from control, he had been caught as well. Avomo obviously had no intention of ever granting the Harrison Oil Corporation any mining rights in Gabon so Harrison had decided to go in without the necessary permits.

All his equipment was already in the country as was Angus McBride, he therefore merely had to move it all into situ and he could begin work. His buyers wanted results by the end of the year so he had ten months to find the ore and extract it. As long as he, and he alone, knew of the illegality of the enterprise, and the operations could remain secret from Sullivan, he was on the home stretch.

Apart from Sullivan's mines in N'Goutou, there was nothing in that area for miles around, no-one would ever be any the wiser. Harrison smiled contentedly to himself as he drifted off to sleep. *"$5 billion extra will buy me a magnificent Gulfstream."* Was the last thought he had before slipping into a less than refreshing slumber.

Several miles across town from the airport Angus stared into the now dead phone, his Texan boss was nothing if not rude and demanding. But, he was paying him well over a million dollars for this contract, a contract which should be running well within twelve months, after which a general manager could take over and Angus could get back to doing what he loved most, geological surveys. Setting up mining sites was not really his speciality but Harrison had insisted it was part of the arrangement and for this kind of money Angus would have been prepared to do almost anything.

Having recruited a workforce of displaced Congolese Angus was sure the possibility of them mixing with any local villages would be kept to a minimum, ideally it wouldn't happen at all but, in view of what Harrison had just told him he would make sure they all thought they were employed by Sullivan Industries, that way, any such contact would not arouse suspicion.

It had occurred to Angus he should ask to see the government documentation regarding the sites but somehow he felt the request would not be welcomed by

Mr Harrison so he kept the thought to himself. He was better off not knowing if all was legal and above board, his contract was with Harrison and if push came to shove he would just claim to be doing as his contract required.

The sooner he got this operation under way the better so he lifted the phone again and dialled the number he had written on his pad, this connected him with the warehouse on the outskirts of Libreville where his waiting workforce and equipment were ready to go. It would take three or four days to move the ensemble to the three sites just to the north of the N'Goutou plateau, another week to set up all the machinery and equipment and build the barracks for the men. With luck they would be able to break ground in two weeks.

Angus reflected how much easier it would have been had they got sites 1, 2 and 3, where Sullivan already had mines dug and working but what was not to be was not to be so, Angus gave the order to begin the move and started to pack ready to leave his hotel, he would not be sleeping in such luxury for some time to come he mused.

~CHAPTER THIRTY-EIGHT~

Within a week of the start of the unrest, Sean and Koudjo had ironed out all the problems it had caused. The dead man was buried and his family taken care of. The five trouble causers had been taken away by the police but not before Koudjo and Sean had chance to question them. Unfortunately it seemed the only one of these men who knew the person or persons responsible for instigating the violence was Tore, and he steadfastly refused to say a word.

The question of why the workforce had been so mutinous was answered by all the relieved men Koudjo questioned.   Apparently Tore and his gang had threatened that the next bomb in the mine would not be placed anywhere obvious where it would be found and many men would lose their lives if they refused to co-operate with the riotous unrest. Together with the threat to go after their women and children if anyone was stupid enough to think telling Koudjo or Sean would solve the problem, Tore had succeeded in getting the entire workforce to do his bidding.

The would-be bomber had, as Koudjo had predicted, been most eager to point the finger at Tore as the leader of the trouble but he knew no more than that so Sean and his General Manager were still no closer to finding out whether Harrison was indeed behind it. Without proof of some sort there was little Sean could do but get back to Manchester where Abi and Frank had now returned from Texas.

Arriving home Sean was greeted by the tantalising smell of cooking emanating from his kitchen where he found Abi cooking up a storm with Frank assisting. The sight of Frank up to his elbows in washing up suds made Sean laugh out loud.

"Now there's a sight I've never seen before." He grinned as the two suddenly realised he had arrived.

"Don't tell anybody Boss, you'll ruin my reputation." Frank couldn't help but grin in return. Being around Abi had obviously done him good, he was more relaxed than Sean had ever recalled seeing him before.

"Secret's safe with me." Sean nodded to Frank, at the same time gesturing for him to leave the room.

As soon as Frank did as he was bid, Sean grabbed Abi round the waist, careful not to squeeze her broken rib but still determined to hold her as tightly as he could. He kissed her, long and hard and was gratified to note she was kissing him back. He had thought about this a lot on the long flight back from Gabon, and whilst he would still not push her for more until she trusted him, he would kiss her as often and as much as she would allow until then. In short, he was going to kiss her into submission.

He adored her, she was amazing as far as he was concerned and the fact that the arrival of the women and children at the mine had been her idea according to Sephora, just made him love her all the more.

He knew the idea would never have occurred to either him or to Koudjo and would be eternally grateful to her for it had completely defused a very volatile situation which, had it continued, would not only have cost him a great deal of money, but, more importantly, it would have cost a great many Gabonese their jobs and therefore their livelihoods. Sean was certain, whatever he had promised, Harrison would not have looked after the workforce as Sean did.

"Hello." Abi whispered when he allowed her to come up for air. "It's nice to see you too." She giggled.

"I've missed you." He said, still holding her tightly, one arm around her shoulders, his free hand caressing her face. He kissed her again. "I owe you." He said smiling into her eyes.

"Owe me?" She echoed with a raised eyebrow.

"Sephora tells me sending the women in was your idea. It was inspired. Thank you." Without allowing her to reply he kissed her again, this time so softly she found herself leaning in to him to ensure he didn't stop.

"I missed you too." She finally admitted when eventually he broke away from her. She could feel the effect their intimacy was having on him but before she could say another word he cupped her chin in his hand and turned her face up so he could look into her eyes.

"Still fear." He said softly and released her. "What are you cooking then?" He asked suddenly changing the subject. "Smells fantastic."

"Er...well..." She stammered, trying to regain her balance. "Frank said he hadn't had a home cooked roast dinner for many years so I said I'd cook one. We have roast pork, roast potatoes, carrots and swede, green cabbage, Yorkshire puddings and gravy. Or, we will have when it's all cooked."

"Yorkshire puddings with pork?" He questioned light-heartedly.

"Yorkshire puddings with everything as far as I'm concerned." She confirmed with a grin. They were one of her favourites and she did not care they were generally thought to be an accompaniment for roast beef, she cooked them with any roast and sometimes with sausages and mash.

"Sounds delicious, do I have time for a shower?" He added hopefully, he was going to have to undo the effect she had on him somehow before sitting down to such a feast. Seeing her nod as she turned back to her cooking he headed upstairs to shower and change, wondering as he went how he was going to help her to learn to trust him and how long that might take. He envisioned a great many cold showers in his immediate future.

Abi leaned against the kitchen counter as she watched his back disappear out of the room. She touched her lips where he had kissed her, savouring the taste of him but knowing he had been right, there was still fear in her eyes. She could not fault his deductions but her body was beginning to yearn for him.

She wondered if it was in fact possible for her to trust him, or anyone for that matter. So far her life had not presented her with many trustworthy characters, apart from Ginny and her grandmother whom she barely remembered.

Her prolonged and systematic mistreatment by her parents had left deep scars, scars which Aaron Steele had exploited in his quest to control and subvert her to massage his own ego and sense of self-importance.

Despite knowing this was Aaron's aim she could not shake the feeling she deserved his condemnation. She was all the things he had accused her of, she was weak, stupid and lacking in redeeming qualities, although she tried hard every day to make up for her shortcomings she was aware she did not measure up as she should.

So far, it seemed, she had managed to hide this side of herself from Sean, surely he would not care for her as he seemed to when he found out. She understood it was for this reason she was unable to trust him, if she let her guard down for a second he would surely know who she really was and despise her for it just as her parents, and then Aaron had.

Abi felt a wave of guilt wash over her, to hide her true self from Sean was unforgivable really, especially after he kept saving her life. She ought to be honest with him, tell him what she was really about and let him get on with his life without her, it was the only fair and decent thing to do.

As she put the finishing touches to the gravy she resolved to tell him after dinner, when Frank had gone home. She would tell him the whole truth about how ungrateful and selfish she was and then she would go home herself. He would be better off without her in his life and at least he may come to respect her honesty even when he hated who she really was.

~CHAPTER THIRTY-NINE~

The telephone box smelled of stale urine and yesterday's tobacco. The floor was littered with old cigarette butts, a used condom and several hypodermic needles. Aaron was careful not to stand in any of the detritus as he lifted the received and dialled 155 for the international operator.

Having jumped ship in Algeciras on the southern coast of Spain after deciding he could no longer stand the demands of the overly spoiled and very exacting Amanda Southerby, Aaron had been in Paris just over twenty four hours later. The Eurostar presented no problem and he alighted in St Pancras in central London only five days after his arrival in Casablanca.

Unfortunately, hiring a car in the UK had proved impossible as they wanted a credit card for security which Aaron did not have. He had eventually found a used car dealership who was willing to sell him a car for cash and no questions asked, this had, however, used up the last of his cash and he now found himself in Manchester, or somewhere on the outskirts, with no money and no idea where to go next. When the operator answered he gave her instructions for the collect call he wished to make, giving his name as Michael Gresty.

Moments later an angry voice came on the line. "I have no idea who you are Mr Gresty but there had better be a very good reason why I just accepted a collect call from you." Harrison was incensed, not only was a collect call probably the most expensive way to contact anybody but the caller had come through on his private line, which meant somebody had leaked the number.

"Oh, I think you know exactly who I am." Steele replied confidently, savouring the knowledge he had caused Harrison such anger.

"What the fuck are you calling me for?" Harrison exploded, he did indeed know who Mr Gresty was now.

"Well, you see, the thing is Bruce," Aaron paused to allow Harrison's blood pressure to rise a little more, "Although you think I'm the most stupid man you've ever met, I apparently am not quite as stupid as you think. You see, it occurred to me, quite early on if I'm honest, that our friend José didn't quite stack up."

"Who the fuck is José?"

"José is the little Mexican you employed to help spring me from prison." Aaron waited to judge Harrison's reaction, this would determine whether he had connected the dots correctly, he heard Harrison swallow before he spoke.

"Don't be ridiculous Steele, why would I want to do a thing like that?" Harrison sounded almost convincing, if it hadn't been for the hesitation at the start.

"Cut the crap Bruce, I know it was you. No way our little José had the kind of cash he gave me just lying around. Somebody provided it, and that somebody was you."

"Again." Harrison started, his voice a little stronger this time. "Why the fuck would I want to do that?"

"If I had to guess Bruce I'd say it had something to do with getting back at one Abigail Storm who not only sent me to prison but fucked up your little plan too."

"Don't be ridiculous Steele, revenge is so not my style. I have moved on and Miss Storm means nothing to me now." Harrison was ready to end the conversation, whatever Steele wanted was no concern of his now. His attempt to distract Sullivan had failed and now Bruce was busy with other things, he had no time for the lowlife who was Aaron Steele.

"FBI wouldn't think so." Aaron said quietly. "I'm only guessing but I'd think assisting a prison break is a federal offence?"

"What do you want Steele." Harrison hissed through his teeth, he was quite sure it was a federal offence although he was equally sure Steele was bluffing.

"Money and information."

"Then I never want to hear from you again, agreed?" Harrison knew it was easier this way, if necessary he could tell Burt Tomasino where to find Steele and be done with him once and for all. For now it was simpler just to give him what he wanted.

"Agreed."

"How much money and what information?"

"I need to know where to find Storm. I know she lives in Manchester, but I need an address. And a hundred thousand dollars." Aaron knew he was going to have to disappear for a while after he finished with Abigail and he had no intention of slumming it.

"Call me back in an hour." Harrison did not even hesitate, it was a small price to pay to get rid of this imbecile for good. "Although, considering you've fucked it up three times now I very much doubt you'll live to spend the money. Sullivan won't let you get away with it, even if you manage to get near her." He hung up abruptly leaving an incensed Aaron staring into the mouthpiece.

Exactly an hour later Steele placed the same collect call.

"There are at least a dozen western union offices in and around Manchester. I will wire ten thousand each to the following ten addresses." Harrison reeled of the ten sites as Aaron wrote them down. "All in the name of Michael Gresty, the first three will be there already, the others before 5pm local time. As for Storm's address, I doubt it'll be any use to you."

"I'll be the judge of that..." Aaron prepared to argue but was immediately silenced as Harrison went on.

"She's probably at Sullivan's house, he can protect her better there and after your little fuck up in Gabon I'm guessing he will definitely be protecting her."

"Give me his address then." Aaron barked, annoyed to be reminded of his failure in Gabon again.

"I've got three addresses for you Steele, Sullivan's, Storm's and Molloy's. You'll find all three of them probably at one or other address." He reeled off the three addresses. "Now we are through Steele, I never want to hear from you again. If I do I'll call the feds myself! It'll be your word against mine and I reckon my chances are pretty good given your status. Now fuck off." Harrison slammed the phone down so hard he cracked the plastic of the receiver. He despised the creepy man intensely but could not help being pleased that Aaron intended to try to cause Sullivan more grief, after his failure to unseat him in Gabon the previous week, anything which added to Sullivan's stress levels was good with Harrison.

Aaron folder the piece of paper and stuffed it in his pocket, finally escaping from the confines of the telephone box, back out into the more breathable cold March air, he hauled the collar of his coat up around his ears and set off in the direction of the first of the Western Union offices on his list. According to the map he had purchased earlier, all the addresses were in central Manchester so he knew he had something of a walk, he had left the car in a multi-story car park there and walked to try to find a telephone box somewhere quiet and out of the way, where nobody would notice if he had to wait around, just as he had done.

The walk helped to crystallize his thoughts, after he had dealt with Storm there seemed to be a growing list of people he had to pay visits to. Harrison was now definitely one of them, but before he could think about that he was going to have to plan how to get to Abigail. Much as he hated to admit it, Harrison was right in that Sullivan, whoever he was, presumably one of the Englishmen she had been travelling with, would be protecting her.

There was no way he was just going to be able to walk in and take her this time. He was going to have to work out how to deal with Sullivan and his sidekick before he was ever going to get to Abigail. He had heard that the supposedly anonymous witness who was to testify about getting Abigail out of her apartment in Boston was named Molloy. So it followed Sullivan had been involved in that too. As he also knew she had been in Africa with two Englishmen he reasoned these had to be Sullivan and Molloy.

By 5.30pm he was back in his car, driving along the M602 motorway out of central Manchester towards the east before turning left onto the M60 motorway now heading south and towards the Cheshire border towns of Altrincham and Hale. His plan so far was merely to get a good look at Sullivan's house, he hoped he might find inspiration for his ongoing plan from there.

Sullivan's house was an early Edwardian pile on South Downs Road in Hale. From the road Aaron could barely see the house, just catching a glimpse of the black and white façade through the trees which lined the property. There were large electric gates at the end of the sweeping drive and as he drove past Aaron spotted at least one security camera trained on the gates and the road outside. He had no doubt there would be others inside. Driving further up the road he found a right turn and then another and managed to get a look at the side and back of the property but again, all he could really see were trees, and no simple way in.

He headed back the way he had come and found there was also no real place for him to stake out the property. Ideally he needed to be able to see the gates, to see who came and went but there was not a spot on the road where he could park up without it being blatantly obvious to anybody who cared to look. Despite the properties along this and neighbouring roads being substantial and well-spaced, there was no shortage of passing traffic, from apparent residents in their very expensive cars to delivery vans and workmen of all types. It was far from a sleepy backwater.

Aaron had spotted a hotel just before he had turned off the main road so decided to head back there for the night, he needed food, he did not think well when he was hungry, and he needed to come up with a plan quickly. He was sure spending time around here would get him noticed before too long and that was something he was keen to avoid.

Sitting by the window in the hotel bar, after a very pleasant meal of beef wellington and a bottle of red wine, Aaron swirled brandy around a glass as he contemplated his next move.

Being so calm and calculated in his approach was of no special interest to him. Had he thought about it seriously he may have realised he had crossed a line somewhere, now he was no longer operating out of rage. He could no longer claim to be in the grip of a temper induced psychosis. Assuming he ever wanted to claim anything of course. At the moment he felt completely at ease, his motives for being here were as uninteresting to him as the thought of being caught and held to account. He had succeeded in shutting down his rational mind completely, his neuroses were now in complete control but far from sending him uncontrollably into a battle he was unable to win, he was calmly and carefully calculating the risks.

Perversely, this very calm calculating persona he had adopted could very well make him actually good at something, even if that *something* was planning to murder. All his life he had fought against the knowledge he was merely mediocre, he had wanted to be special, to be revered by others and adored for what he could achieve. He had so badly wanted this he had allowed the desire to cloud his every move, instead of striving to achieve he had mainly striven to ensure others did not achieve more than he did. To win at any cost meant obliterating the competition not beating it. Had he used his energies to try to better himself, he may well have found something he was exceptionally good at, he was far from a stupid man, however, having spent his life trying to manipulate others to make himself look good he had failed most spectacularly to shine in any field.

Unfortunately he had felt it was unwise to try to get the gun into the UK, he had taken it on-board the yacht and had got into Spain with it without any problem, but, when he had realised that the security checks at the Eurostar terminal in the Gare du Nord in Paris were akin to those at an international airport, with x-rays for both himself and his baggage, he had ditched the gun in Paris.

Sitting in the hotel bar in Hale he wondered just how difficult it would be to come by another one in the next twenty four hours. His chances of getting past both Sullivan and his monkey without some sort of serious weapon were next to zero he assumed, if prior encounters had in fact been with one or other of these two, they were not going to be pushovers.

It would have been so much simpler had he been in the States, where almost every household had a gun, he could simply have broken into any house on any street and found himself exactly what he needed. Here the guns laws were so archaic the only guns for miles around probably belonged to the police themselves. As he pondered the problem a thought suddenly occurred to him. He was in Cheshire, almost at least, not far from actual countryside. He wondered if somewhere near here there might be a gun club. He was aware from TV coverage he had seen back home UK gun clubs existed for those for whom shooting was a sport. He knew guns would be stored on these premises but had no idea just how secure these places might be.

He pulled out the smart phone he had acquired in Manchester earlier that day once Harrison's first ten thousand dollars had arrived. Pulling up the google app he typed in 'nearest gun club' and was rewarded with a list. Picking the website at the top of the list he scrolled through all the club rules and regulations before finding a page which offered members a forum to buy and sell guns to each other. For sale on this page was exactly what he was looking for, a handgun with plenty of ammunition.

All he had to do now was work out how to get round the rules, clearly stated on almost every page of the website, which said he couldn't buy the gun, at least not within any timeframe which was acceptable to him. By the time he retired to his room he had the makings of a plan. He would call the gun club and make an appointment in the morning siting his tourist status as a way to explain the urgency of his visit, until then he needed sleep. If he was going to have to be around for longer than twenty four hours he also needed to change hotel tomorrow. He was too close to Sullivan's house to stay here without the risk of being seen.

The next day when he walked into the gun club near Stockport, he had identified a new hotel much closer to the club and far enough from Hale to ensure he did not bump into any of his quarry before he was ready to confront them, he would check in there later after he had concluded his business.

"Good Morning, Mr Gresty I presume?" The bearded man behind the counter addressed Aaron as he entered the reception area.

"That's right." Aaron was careful to affect his best Texan drawl, hoping the range manager had heard of Texans and their love of guns and would therefore not think his request too abnormal.

"Very pleased to meet you." Malc, as his name plaque stated, held his hand out to shake Aaron's. "Glad we could accommodate you at such short notice, usually an appointment can take up to a week." He added with a friendly smile.

"Ah am grateful to y'all." Aaron drawled. "Ah'm only here until tomorrow but as Ah told you on the phone there's a gun on your site Ah just have to have in my collection."

"Yes Mr Gresty, you did tell me, repeatedly." Said Malc with a benevolent smile. "The gun is now here for your perusal." He gestured to an office just behind the counter, "If you'd like to step through here."

Aaron followed Malc through the office and out into a corridor on the other side. Some way along the corridor was another door and, after unlocking it with a key attached to his belt Malc showed Aaron inside.

On the table in the windowless room was a gun box, opened to display its contents. To Aaron's relief it was the handgun he had seen on the for sale page the night before, a large box of ammunition sat next to the gun box as did a great deal of paperwork.

"As I told you on the phone Mr Gresty, the gun laws in this country are somewhat different from in the US. You cannot simply purchase this gun and walk out of this building."

"But Ah can buy the gun?" Aaron drawled, looking directly at Malc for the first time.

"You can, Mr Gresty. Although I am still not sure what the attraction is. It is not a particularly rare gun. Nor is it offered at a particularly advantageous price."

"They are difficult to find in the States though." Aaron said with a conspiratorial wink which he hoped would divert any further questions. "And the price is fair I think?"

"As you say." Malc took the gun from its foam bed and handed it grip first to Aaron. "I assume you would like a closer look before you buy?"

Aaron turned the gun over in his hand, it was heavier than the one he had left in Paris, but the grip fit his palm beautifully and the thing looked mean, which was basically all he needed it for anyway. He was sure if he actually had to shoot it then it would make a hole in whatever he hit.

"So, once Ah've bought it and done the necessary paperwork you will send it to a secure shipping firm who will ship it to the States for me?" Aaron confirmed the gist of the conversation they had earlier on the telephone.

"That's correct Mr Gresty. Depending on how much shipping you wish to pay it can either go airfreight or sea freight but the gun and the ammunition have to be shipped separately and both will be sent to a licenced gun dealer in the US city of your choice. You can then collect both from there."

"Great. Where do Ah sign?" Aaron smiled at the range manager as he sat down in front of the pile of paperwork, placing the gun gently back in its box as he did so.

After what seemed like an age, Aaron had signed all the necessary documents, remembering every time to sign Michael Gresty, and he had noted from the paperwork, the name and address of the shipper to which the gun would be delivered for onward shipping to the States.

"And it will go today you say?"   Aaron said casually as he collected his passport from the table and stuffed it back in his jacket pocket.

"As you have paid for airfreight Mr Gresty, yes, the gun will leave today. There are a number of flights to Texas I am told so both packages should fly out tonight and be available from your dealer when you get there by tomorrow evening or the next day at the very latest." Malc extended his hand again.   "A pleasure doing business with you Mr Gresty."

"You too Malc, thanks pal."   Aaron affected his best drawl and slapped the unsuspecting man on the back as they headed back towards the reception area.

Once outside, Aaron drove his non-descript little car some way down the road and parked up. He could see the entrance to the gun club in his mirror and all he had to do now was wait. He had hoped to have the opportunity to steal the gun whilst inside the gun club but no suitable moment had arisen, so Aaron had reverted to plan B which was to get the gun before it was shipped to the States.

Sure enough, less than half an hour later the range manager himself came out of the front of the building and climbed into a car. Seconds later he drove past Aaron, his body language suggesting he barely noticed the parked car.

Whilst waiting Aaron had studied various routes from the gun club to the bonded warehouse near Manchester airport on the map on his phone and was very hopeful Malc would take the back roads to avoid the heavy daytime traffic. The way he saw it Aaron had two choices, he waited until the gun was in the warehouse and tried to steal it from there, or he grabbed it en route.

His knowledge of bonded warehouses was limited to what he had gleaned from the internet, but even this small insight had assured him they were not for the amateur burglar, so he was left with en route.

The back roads would provide plenty of opportunities for Aaron and fortunately for him, as the A6 through Stockport was a road to be avoided at all costs if you ever wanted to get anywhere, his hopes were realised as his quarry headed out of town, away from the mad traffic and into the countryside.

Aaron had identified a bridge passing over a waterway some mile or so onto the back roads. He had managed to get a road view from *Google Earth* and now knew if he could get Malc to swerve just before the bridge then the unsuspecting range manager would end up nose down in the river. If the impact did not render him unconscious Aaron had no doubt he could manage that himself, after all, it would hardly be the first time. The possibility of killing Malc in the accident had not crossed Aaron's mind and it would not have made a difference even if it had.

On the next available stretch of straight road Aaron accelerated round the little Ford Malc was driving very sedately along the picturesque country road and sped away into the distance. He had to get to the bridge and arrange his ambush. Turning sharply to the left just before the bridge Aaron hid his car in a concealed field entrance which he had also identified from *Google Earth*. As he leapt from the car he marvelled at how helpful such devices were now to the would-be criminal. Gone were the days of having to reconnoitre everything in person, just a couple of clicks of a mouse or taps of a touchscreen and there you were, standing in whatever street you chose.

Arron dug the spare wheel and tyre out of the recess in the boot of the car and crouched in the bushes at the side of the road. He could just see the penultimate turn before drivers hit the up ramp for the bridge and was gratified to see the little Ford was the only car to round this corner in the minutes Aaron was waiting, the road was quiet and no other cars had passed, Aaron could only hope this situation would continue as he carried out his mission.

As soon as he heard Malc begin to accelerate up the small hill of the bridge Aaron jumped up and threw the space-saving wheel into the path of the oncoming vehicle.

With absolute predictability Malc swerved to avoid the projectile entering his peripheral vision from his left. He threw the car into a right hand skid, through the flimsy barrier and, as expected, he nosedived into the river below.

The river, although almost eight meters wide at this point was a mere eighteen inches deep and both Malc and his car ended up at a forty-five degree angle with the nose of the car buried in the gravel riverbed, the body and rear end were wedged into the mud and foliage of the riverbank.

Aaron scrambled down the bank towards the rear of the stricken car, his eyes firmly fixed on the back of Malc's head, looking for movement. He saw none.

As he reached the driver's side door he realised instantly it was improbable Malc would ever move again. He head was against the steering wheel at an impossible angle, his eyes wide and staring while blood trickled from his open mouth, his ears and the large gash on his forehead.

Careful not to touch any part of the car with his bare hands Aaron swiftly retrieved what he had come for, collected all the paperwork with the package and retraced his steps up the slippery bank and back to his waiting hire car. He was about to drive away when he remembered the spare wheel, having no idea if these things could be traced back to a particular car he went in search of it. It took him many precious minutes to find it and he was sweating when he finally had it back in the boot and was on his way. Not a single car had passed the spot during the entire proceedings and he knew it was only a matter of time before somebody came, he wanted to be as far away as possible when that happened.

He had decided against the hotel near Stockport as soon as he had realised Malc was dead, it was too close to the gun club for comfort and he now headed back towards the airport, knowing there were plenty of hotels there if it became necessary to stay the night and it was only a short distance from there to Sullivan's home in Hale. He suspected the police might check whether Malc had been carrying anything significant given his job and assumed somebody else at the gun club would be able to tell them he was in possession of the handgun when he had left the club.

Aaron had to assume this would make the police take much more of an interest than they may otherwise have done for a simple car accident, so he needed to try to get the job done tonight and get out of here as soon as possible. He had already decided he would head up to Scotland after he had finished with Abigail, he could lay low up there for a week or two while he worked out how to get back into the States without having to present his fake passport to the authorities. He now had scores to settle there too.

Having twice driven past the gates to Sullivan's home he parked his car some distance away and walked back. He had identified a small wooded area just back from the road about fifty yards from Sullivan's gate, he figured he could hide in here for the time being while he perfected his plan to get into the house and deal with Abigail once and for all.

~CHAPTER FORTY~

"With respect Boss, it's not our problem." Frank stated again as he moped up the last of his gravy with another Yorkshire pudding.

"If that bastard is after uranium it might just be all of our problems Frank." Sean said grimly, trying to savour the delicious dinner he had just eaten whilst seriously discussing Harrison's antics.

"Yes Boss, but a couple of phone calls and it's somebody else's problem. As it should be." Frank said sitting back with a satisfied smile. "Miss, that was fantastic." He smiled in Abi's direction before looking back at Sean. "I should make the call Boss."

"Yes Frank, you're right. Make the call, oh, and don't forget to tell them that Koudjo reports heavy machinery moving to the north of the plateau at N'Goutou." He added as Frank rose to leave the room.

"Yes Boss."

"He's right Abi, that meal was fantastic." Sean beamed at her as Frank's bulk disappeared through the doorway. "And you are absolutely correct, Yorkshire puddings do go with everything!"

Abi giggled, "I'm glad you enjoyed it." She said "I'll go and put the coffee on." She rose and gathering the dirty plates she headed out to the kitchen to put the coffee machine on.

As she passed the open door to the living room she noticed Frank leaning against the side of the French windows. He had his phone in his hand but his head was back against the woodwork and his left hand was pressed hard against his abdomen. Abi was about to walk past when he rolled his head towards her and she noticed the expression on his face. His eyes were tightly closed but his jaw was clenched and she was in no doubt he was in a great deal of pain.

"Frank?" She said quietly entering the room. "Are you OK?"

"Yes Miss," Frank started, instantly dropping his hand and opening his eyes, he straightened up and added. "Just a touch of indigestion Miss, nothing to be worried about." With a smile he turned his concentration to his phone and began to tap purposefully at the screen.

"Tablets in the kitchen cupboard if you need them." Abi said a little dubiously as she left the room, receiving a sharp nod from Frank to indicate he had heard her.

Returning to the dining room with the coffee, Abi found Frank was back, his phone call apparently made.

"I'll get off home now Boss if that's OK?" He said quietly as Abi began to pour the coffee from the pot. "Not for me Miss. Thank you, and thank you again for dinner." He bowed slightly to her as he left. "See you both tomorrow."

"Night Frank." Sean called after his retreating form.

"Frank seemed to be in a lot of pain earlier, I spotted him in the living room just after dinner." Abi told Sean as she handed him his coffee. "He said it was just indigestion but I'm a little worried."

"Yes, he's had that for a while now. I noticed it first a few months back. I've asked him too but he insists it's just indigestion." Sean smiled his thanks to Abi as he sipped at his coffee, indicating they should move to the living room with their drinks.

"You believe him?" Abi said suspiciously, following him out of the room and across the hallway.

"No reason not to." Replied Sean, "Why would he be anything but truthful?"

"I don't mean he's lying, just that he may not actually know what it is and he's assuming it's indigestion. Just seems a bit severe to me." Abi said quickly, the mere suggestion Frank would lie as abhorrent to her as it was to Sean.

"Well, I have suggested he consults a doctor but he's not having any of it." Sean winked at Abi. "You know how us men are about doctors!"

"Maybe we can get Sam to talk to him next time he's over, just might be able to persuade him to get checked over. I mean, even if it is indigestion there's no need for him to be in such pain with it, there is medication he can take." Abi concluded, grateful to see Sean nodding his agreement, knowing she could not keep up this idle chatter for much longer, she was going to have to say what she needed to say.

"There's something we need to talk about." She took a deep breath as she started. "About who you think I am." There, she had said it, now she had to have the conversation she had wanted to avoid. Now she had to be honest with Sean and just accept whatever his reaction was to be.

"And who do I think you are?" Sean put down his coffee and turned, from his position at the opposite end of the sofa, to face her, his blue-grey eyes boring into hers as he spoke.

"I...well..." She stammered, unnerved by him more than usual. "You think I am someone who you could have some sort of life with." She began, knowing she wasn't really explaining herself very well.

"I do." He confirmed with a smile. "What else?"

"You think I am someone worth your time and feelings." She had started now and was going to have to get this out as fast as possible before her courage deserted her. "You think I'm nice, and caring and worthy of you and you think I am someone you might be proud to be with. But..." She swallowed hard. "I am none of those things, I am a coward, a nasty ungrateful girl who only uses people for what I can get out of them. I am dishonest and mean and I tell lies even when I don't know I'm doing it and I am hateful and disloyal and horrible and...and..." tears were running down Abi's face now as the words tumbled out in a torrent she could no longer stop. "You see, I'm not a nice person at all." She sobbed.

As she sobbed she eventually became aware of being wrapped securely in Sean's arms, he was kissing her hair gently as he stroked her cheek with his free hand. He waited patiently for her sobbing to subside before he spoke.

"Abi I know who you are." He began softly. "I fell in love with who you are the day you walked into my father's office four years ago." He held her tight as she tried to pull away. "No, just listen." He whispered. "I also know who you think you are, and given your background I am not surprised you think the way you do. But..." He paused to kiss her hair again. "I am determined to help you see yourself the way I do. You are a beautiful person, both inside and out. You are warm, kind, honest and loyal and you have the courage of a lioness." He turned her face up so she had to look at him. "I am so proud of you Abi, you have been to hell and back more than once but you are still a good person. Yes you have some issues to deal with, your lack of self-belief is your biggest burden right now, but it's a burden we will deal with together, if you'll let me of course."

"You think I don't know myself?" Abi whispered into his eyes.

"I think you believe what too many nasty people have told you to believe for too long. Tell me, Abi, who said you were an ungrateful or nasty girl?" He waited, smiling into her eyes all the time.

"My Dad first told me I think." She whispered, trying to remember a start to it all. "Mum agreed as far as I know..."

"And then Aaron used all the same words to get you to do his bidding?" It was something Sean had been secretly dying to get out in the open for months. He knew she needed to exorcize the demon which Aaron Steele now represented within her psyche, but he hoped he wasn't pushing her too hard or too far.

"Aaron just saw the same in me that they did." Abi confirmed, her tears starting to flow again.

Sean rolled her more tightly into his arms, pulling her legs up across his so he could hold her as close as possible, for the moment he just held her as she cried.

"Your parents are alcoholics, they should never have had a child, a life with them was no place for any child. As long as you had your grandmother you would have done OK, but losing her so early gave you no chance. Ironically, it was your grandmother's love which made them keep you around. I have no idea if you would have been better or worse off in care but regardless, the damage was done." He noticed she had stopped crying and was listening to him quietly, she made no attempt to extract herself from his embrace.

"As for Steele, he is a bully, and all bullies look for the person with the already damaged psyche so they can use that damage to further manipulate that person and gain whatever gratification it is they are looking for." He pulled her face up to look at him again. "With me so far?" He whispered and was rewarded with an almost imperceptible nod. He continued. "Bullies are exceptionally good at detecting who is already damaged and who isn't. They always attack those they can tell have been attacked before. That's because all bullies are cowards, they do not want to get anywhere near a person who may fight back. They want to dominate and instil fear, as it makes them feel important and big." He paused to kiss her on the nose, desperately resisting the urge to kiss her lips, her blue eyes were pools of pain and fear and all he wanted to do was cocoon her in his arms and protect her from the world. "None of this is your fault Abigail. None of it."

"But it is." She whispered. "It's all because I am such a bad person. They all said so. If I wasn't so bad they wouldn't have to treat me the way I deserved to be treated."

"Abi, I know that's what they told you. I'm guessing you heard that from being very young but it's not true." He whispered back, trying to work out how to get her to see it from a different perspective. "It was just what they told you to justify their own behaviour. They are the ones in the wrong Abi." Looking deep into her eyes Sean knew he was not getting anywhere. She needed a professional if she was ever going to unravel the damage of years of physical and mental abuse she had endured. "Do me a favour?" He asked quietly.

"What?" She replied, wondering what this amazing man could possibly need from a worthless piece of junk like her.

"Ask yourself why I would lie to you?"

"I don't think you would." She answered instantly, surprising herself at her conviction.

"I think...no...I know you are a beautiful, sensitive, sexy, honest, loyal, sincere and intelligent young woman." He put a finger over her lips to prevent her protest. "I know this." He asserted. "I want you to promise me something." Seeing her nod he continued. "I want you to promise to stick around long enough for me to make you know this too."

"But I'm not worth it." She began to sob again, this conversation was supposed to make him see her as she really was and she had failed miserably.

"Abi, I understand you believe that, and I am so grateful you felt the need to be honest with me, it means the world to me, however, I disagree and I want your promise you will allow me the time to prove which of us is right?"

Abi knew she was cornered, he had accepted her confession apparently, and still he wanted her around. There was nothing she could do to argue with that, after all, she really did not want to be without him. Had he walked away when she told him who she really was she would have accepted his decision, indeed, she had expected him to make that decision. So now he had made the opposite decision she almost had to accept that too. She still felt guilty though, but again he read her mind.

"My choice Abi, you have been honest and I have made a decision. You have no reason to feel guilty any more, you have done what you can, it's my problem now." He added with a smile, he knew she did not really want to leave.

"I promise." She whispered, grateful he seemed to understand her better than she understood herself but still apprehensive as to where this would lead.

Sean could not help himself, he bent his head and kissed her, full and hard on the lips. He felt more than heard her almost instant reaction. As she began to return his kiss he lost himself in the moment and began to push her back onto the sofa behind her. It was her almost stifled wince of pain which stopped him in his tracks. Opening his eyes he looked into hers.

"Your rib? I'm sorry." He began to pull her upright again. "And still fear." He added as he wrapped his arms round her again.

"I'm not afraid of you." She whispered into his chest. "And my rib doesn't hurt that much anymore." She added, surprised at her own boldness. Her rib did in fact still hurt intensely, especially if she twisted at all but right now she would have walked through fire to be close to this man, a broken rib was the least of her worries. She looked up into his face and saw the indecision there. "I am afraid of everything." She added. "I am afraid every minute of every day, people scare me, places scare me, conversations scare me." She stared into his eyes. "I am scared of life, I always have been, but I still want to live it." She stopped, hoping to see some understanding there. Slowly his indecision retreated, as he processed her words a slow smile spread across his face while his eyes filled with a fire Abi had never seen before.

"You will tell me if I hurt you?" He said thickly, the passion in his eyes boring through hers and setting fire to all her senses.

"Yes." She whispered thinking *"Not a fucking prayer!"* There was no way she was stopping him now, every inch of her ached for him, her broken rib was just going to have to get in line.

Pushing her back against the cushions Sean never took his eyes off hers, he began to peel her t-shirt up until he could lift it over her head. In one swift movement his shirt was off and he threw both garments across the room as he bent over her and began to kiss her again.

Starting at the side of her neck just below her ear he slowly and carefully kissed every inch of her exposed skin, expertly unhooking and removing her bra without breaking stride. By the time he reached the waistband of her jeans Abi was writhing beneath his touch. She had her hands in his hair and several times she had tried to pull his head backup to kiss her again but he would not be rushed.

Having unfastened her jeans he lifted her off the sofa and stood her before him, sliding both her jeans and her underwear off and letting them slip to the floor in one fluid movement. Now naked before him Abi shuddered with anticipation, her hands finding his belt buckle as his lips closed once again over hers.

No matter how hard she tried to concentrate on undoing his belt she failed, his kisses were so urgent, so passionate she almost forgot who she was never mind how to make her body do anything she bid it. Had it not been for the arms he had around her she would have buckled to the floor as she gave herself up to the incredible sensations he was causing in her.

Somehow, he managed to extract himself from his own pants whilst not allowing her to fall and the instant he was naked too she could feel his hot skin along the length of her body, the sensation was driving her wild. Seemingly it was having the same effect on him as he swept her up off the floor, wrapped her legs around his waist and lowered her bodily onto himself, momentarily breaking off from kissing her to look into her eyes as he delved deep within her. She moaned, and held his head against her pounding chest as he gently but firmly slid her slowly up and down, the strength in his arms and legs as sexy to Abi as the look in his eyes.

Abi's breath was coming in short sharp gasps now, her body was alive with a passion she had not known until now. She knew she was so close to orgasm her mouth had gone dry, when suddenly he stopped, he withdrew from her and slid her gently to the floor.

"Not so fast." He breathed into her ear as he changed his grip on her and swung her up into his arms again and carried her out of the room. She wrapped her arms round his neck and dragged his face round so she could kiss him again, drinking in the taste of him she could not get enough. She probed his lips with her tongue, insistent and sensual she forced his lips apart and licked the inside of his upper lip. He groaned, slid her feet to the floor, she found it was uneven, they were halfway up the stairs but now nothing could wait. Hooking his leg in behind hers he swept her feet out from under her and gently lowered her onto the stairs. Without pausing he was inside her again, this time he was less gentle, he was grinding his groin into hers, holding all his weight on his arms he thrust deep inside her, deeper with each stroke. Abi was beyond ecstasy, she could feel the explosion starting in her groin, she knew it was going to be a big one, bigger than she had ever experienced before. She bit her lip hard as she grabbed for the banister rail with both hands, something hard to hold onto as her body came apart. But even biting her lip could not stifle the scream building in her throat.

"Don't fight it, scream baby." Sean whispered, a throaty thick whisper full of need and desire. "Just let it come."

Abi did not need asking twice, the scream she emitted tore through her throat and out of her mouth before she had chance to register the necessity. Her body convulsed with a terrifying heat before the orgasm ripped through her sending wave after wave of pure rapture up and down the length of her body, lighting every nerve ending it passed.

When eventually it subsided, Abi opened her eyes to find Sean still suspended over her, sweat glistened on his forehead but the fire in his eyes still burned.

"Impressive, Miss Storm." He smiled as bent to kiss her again, his eyes never leaving hers. "More?"

Abi could barely move, every muscle in her body now basking in the afterglow of her orgasm, even the throbbing pain in her lower back could not dampen her delight, she smiled into his eyes. "More!"

~CHAPTER FORTY-ONE~

From his hiding place just across the road Aaron saw Frank Molloy leaving Sullivan's house. It was eight thirty at night and the road was dark as Frank drove his car out of the driveway and waited just outside until the gates had closed completely.

Seeing Frank gave Aaron an idea, and he hurried from the cover of the trees back to where he had left his car earlier. Luckily for Aaron, Frank's phone rang just as he was about to leave so he was stationery for several minutes while he answered the call, giving Aaron ample time to get back to his car and be ready to move by the time Frank passed him.

Hanging back well out of sight Aaron followed Frank home. He had no need to keep Frank in close view as he already had the address from Harrison, driving straight past the house where he saw Frank had pulled into the drive and parked in front of the garage, he pulled up further along the road.

Cursing himself for not having had the forethought to check Frank's house out in daylight he got out of the car and wandered back along the road.

It was a typical suburban street, houses along both sides, trees interrupting the pavements from time to time. All the houses were detached but nothing like the size of Sullivan's. They had between four and six large windows on the front so Aaron estimated they all had maybe five bedrooms or so.

"*Pretty big house for a sidekick.*" Aaron thought as he walked past Frank's gateposts and on up the street.

So far Aaron had no real plan but the idea which had formed when he saw Frank seemed to him to be the most likely way he could get into Sullivan's house.

Breaking and entering was a non-starter as far as Aaron was concerned, it was possible a professional burglar might manage to get in but Aaron knew he alone had no chance. So, the idea he had formed used Frank to get him in. So far he was not quite sure how, but he intended to sit here in Frank's street until a plan presented itself. He sauntered back to the car.

By dawn the following morning he had what he decided was the only viable plan. To try to get into Frank's house would be stupid he had reasoned, he would only have to make the slightest error for Frank to discover him and potentially turn the advantage against him. Then, not only would his plans to get to Abigail be ruined, but it was quite conceivable Frank would turn him in to the authorities who would waste no time in sending him back to the US where he would be put back in prison for a very long time.

So he had decided to wait until morning, lay low near Frank's car and jump him when he came out in the morning. He did have a gun and as long as he managed to surprise Frank he would hold the gun to his head and get him to do his bidding.

Having no way of knowing what time Frank might emerge, Aaron got himself into position in the trees behind Frank's car early. Not long after dawn broke he had seen a light come on in Frank's house and he hoped the man did not take hours with his morning ablutions, it was really quite cold outside and Aaron had only a thin coat on.

Less than an hour later Aaron heard the front door open and then close, he heard footsteps on the gravel drive and then he heard the distinctive chirp of a car alarm being deactivated.

As he heard the car door open he pounced, rushing out of the treeline and up behind Frank, the gun already in his extended hand.

Frank was fast, he heard the commotion and turned to face his attacker. Had Aaron not been armed he would not have had a chance, Frank's training, however long ago, was ingrained in his muscle memory, he would have taken Aaron out without pausing for breath. However, the sight of a gun barrel levelled at his head had exactly the effect Aaron had hoped it would. It stopped Frank dead in his tracks.

Aaron had no idea but the first thing Frank looked for on the gun was the position of the safety, determining it was off and the gun was live and therefore a real threat, Frank had no intention of causing Aaron any reason to fire. At this range even an amateur like Aaron couldn't miss.

"Steele, you get around." Frank stated in a deadpan, emotionless voice, nowhere near as panicked as Aaron would have liked.

"Get in the car, don't try anything stupid or I will shoot you." Aaron hissed, opening the rear door of the car with his free hand.

Frank did as he was bid and very soon the pair were driving back the way they had come the night before.   Aaron was in the back seat directly behind Frank, the gun pushed hard into Frank's neck.

"You and that boss of yours have got in my way for the last time."   Aaron asserted from the backseat. Frank declined to answer knowing now was not the time to wind the maniac up. He would bide his time, Aaron was just an amateur and he would make a mistake, when he did Frank would make the most of it and the world would be rid of a scumbag it really did not need.

~CHAPTER FORTY-TWO~

When Abi woke she was still wrapped in Sean's arms. She was curled on her side with her back to him, she could feel his naked body against her skin, his legs were tucked up against the backs of hers and she could hear the steady rhythm of his breathing.

As soon as she stirred he was awake, pulling her to him and kissing the hair on the side of her head just above her ear.

"Good morning." He mumbled into her hair. It had been several hours before they had finally slept the night before and now it was just after dawn, neither had slept for long. "I love you." He whispered, Abi wasn't sure if he was asleep or awake, she wriggled around in his arms until she was facing him. His eyes were open and he was smiling at her. "Do I frighten you now?" He asked with a grin.

"No." She giggled. "Are you trying to?"

"Never." He smiled, "If my loving you doesn't frighten you I guess we're making progress."

"Hmm." She murmured, bursting to utter those words to him too but too scared of her own feelings to allow it.

Suddenly she remembered a thought which had occurred to her at some point the previous evening, at the time she had felt it was not quite the moment to ask. She giggled again at the thought.

"What's funny?" He asked.

"I just remembered I wanted to ask you something last night but at the time it wasn't really appropriate."

"What was happening at the time?" He asked, sure he already knew why it had made her giggle.

"It was somewhere between my third and fourth orgasm I think." She said slightly coyly.

"Ah..." He raised an eyebrow. "Would that be before or after I came in your mouth?" He asked, the laughter in his eyes daring her to answer.

"After." She giggled again, blushing scarlet right up to her hair roots.

"Abigail Storm I believe I made you blush." He teased.

"Last night will make me blush for many weeks I should think." Abi replied, still giggling.

"My god you're adorable." He breathed taking her face in his hands and kissing her long and hard on the lips. "However, if I remember correctly that particular moment was all your doing, nothing to do with me. Not that I minded of course." He winked cheekily at her, feeling her start to squirm in his embrace. "Don't be embarrassed Abi, I am ecstatic that you felt so relaxed you were able to drop all your inhibitions, and anyway, it seems you have something of a talent." He concluded, planting a soft kiss on the end of her nose. "What did you want to ask?" He said, finally pulling away and allowing her to breathe.

"Well, you mentioned the day we first met." She began, looking at him carefully, hoping what she wanted to ask would not make him angry with her.

"Abi, ask me anything." He was reading her mind again. "If something matters enough to you to want to ask then it matters enough to me to want to answer."

"Well, I was just wondering..." She began hesitantly. "That day, what would you have done? I mean if I hadn't made you that offer?"

Sean smiled as he looked deep into her eyes. "I have thought the same thing many times since that day Abi and the honest answer is I don't know. As I told you before, I was only standing in while Father recovered so I was up against a wall really. Father would have demanded I carried out the threat, but I know I couldn't have done that, not to you anyway." He looked deep into her eyes again. "I think it's possible Mother and I might have been able to persuade Father to sell you to me, but honestly, I really don't know. It makes me shudder to think about it, and so grateful you gave me such a perfect way out." He kissed her again, his deep passion spilling over her in waves.

Somewhere in the back of her mind Abi wondered if she should be concerned by his answer, but as her body reacted to him she swiftly decided she did not care.

Their love making this morning was slow and gentle, he caressed her with kisses as he tantalisingly drove her again to orgasm. She marvelled at just how amazing her body could be made to feel, knowing instinctively it did not get any better than this.

Afterwards they must have slept again as they were woken by the sound of the buzzer from the front door.

Sean reached over to the control panel by the bed and pushed the intercom button.

"Yes?" He asked.

"Boss?"

"Two minutes Frank." Sean was out of bed in an instant, dragging on joggers and a t-shirt he found on the chair near the door.

"What is it? What's wrong?" Abi was instantly alarmed, the look on Sean's face told her she needed to be.

"Lock this door behind me Abigail." Sean said in the most commanding voice he had ever uttered in her presence. "Do not unlock it or come out until either me or Frank comes back for you, no matter what you hear. Do you understand?"

"But..." Abi began.

"Do you understand?" Sean repeated himself, glaring at Abi.

"Yes, I understand Sean but what's going on, wasn't that just Frank at the door?"

"Yes it was but..." He paused with his hand on the door handle and looked her hard in the eyes. "...Frank doesn't knock!"

~CHAPTER FORTY-THREE~

"Mr Harrison Sir, I must ask you to get those permits to me as soon as possible." Angus McBride was yelling into the telephone over the noise of whirling helicopter blades and much shouting.

"Oh don't worry about them Angus, they'll arrive when they arrive." Harrison tried to play down the urgency in his General Manager's voice. "The powers that be know they're in place so just get started and all will be well."

"You don't understand Sir." Angus started again. "I really need those permits today Sir."

"Why the urgency Angus? Surely the locals aren't asking for them." He added with a chuckle, knowing most of the locals couldn't read them if they saw a mining permit.

"No Sir, but the commandos who landed in the Apache gunships about ten minutes ago are demanding to see them, they're threatening to arrest us all if we don't comply Sir." Angus was trying very hard to remain calm.

"Don't sound so panicked Angus, Gabonese soldiers are just conscripts, they won't have any idea what they are doing."

"Maybe not Sir." Angus replied. "But these are Americans Sir."

"What the fuck? Why would they be American Angus?" Harrison was starting to wonder if his General Manager was under the influence of something other than caffeine.

"I don't know why Sir but they are definitely American. There are stars and stripes on their uniforms and on the gunships and half of them are white Sir!"

"Well, put like that Angus I would have to agree, they don't appear to be Gabonese. I guess you'd better just tell them I will be there with the permits as soon as I can, they better make camp, it'll take me a couple of days to get over there." Harrison was desperately trying to make sense of the situation when Felicity, his secretary, opened his office door. "I said no interruptions." He barked at her, waving her away with his free hand and trying to concentrate on the call he was on. He did not notice the three men who then entered his office directly behind her.

"FBI Mr Harrison, we'd like a word if you don't mind." The lead agent announced as he strode across the office and took the phone from Harrison's hand.

"Mr McBride?" The FBI agent said into the phone. "Please put the Captain of the marine platoon on the line.

"Ach, they're marines then are they?" Angus replied as he motioned to the man with the most shoulder stripes to come and take the phone from him. "That'll explain it then."

"Captain Shelton? This is FBI Agent Kent Sir, is everything under control there?"

"Yes Sir." Replied the Captain. "We'll just hold them all until the locals arrive Sir, our orders are to secure the equipment, hand over all the personnel to the Gabonese and get out of here as fast as we arrived."

"That's correct Captain, your orders haven't changed. I'll be in touch." FBI Agent Kent hung up the phone and turned back to Harrison.

"Mr Harrison, the police officer in your outer office will now come in and read you your rights, you are under arrest, charges to be determined at a later date but will definitely include something to do with terrorism."

~CHAPTER FORTY-FOUR~

Aaron waited until Sullivan clicked off the intercom before hitting Frank viciously with the gun across the side of his head. Frank went down without a murmur, slumped in a heap against the impressively large solid wood and steel front door. Positioning himself directly in the doorway, gun raised and held steady with both hands he waited. Seconds later the door opened and Aaron came face to face with a very angry looking Sullivan.

"Mr Sullivan?" Aaron smirked as he asked the obvious question, knowing the gun levelled at Sullivan's face would prevent him from doing anything rash or stupid.

"Steele. I might've guessed a scumbag like you wouldn't know when he'd run out of lives." Sean hissed through clenched teeth, his eyes rapidly taking in every detail from the scene he was confronted with.

He had checked the CCTV monitor just inside the doorway before he had opened it and witnessed Frank being unceremoniously clubbed on the side of the head with a gun. He was glad however, he had refused Frank's offer of acquiring a gun for him as he knew he would now happily shoot the deadbeat on his doorstep but he also knew he would do a long stretch in prison for the satisfaction, leaving Abi alone again, he was just going to have to do this the hard way.

He too looked first to see if the safety was engaged on the gun, he was dismayed to find it was not but encouraged slightly to see that Steele did not have his finger quite on the trigger but around the trigger guard.

"I think you'll find I'm the one with the gun Sullivan, so be careful what you say or I might have to use it!" Aaron spat back, his eyes now no more than angry slits. "Get this piece of shit indoors." He commanded, kicking Frank's inert body, now slumped half inside and half outside the doorway, as he spoke.

Sean did as he was told, he grabbed Frank by the lapels of his jacket and dragged him into the hallway, closely followed by Steele who then kicked the seemingly impenetrable door shut behind him.

As he laid Frank down Sean surreptitiously checked the pulse in his neck, gratified to feel his heart beating strongly, he rolled him slightly onto his side, whilst not taking his eyes off Steele and the gun for a second.

"Where is she?"

"Seriously? You think I'm going to tell you that?" Sean was not about to roll over for Aaron Steele, even if he was pointing a gun at him.

"I have a gun to your head, in case you hadn't noticed." Aaron spoke very slowly as if explaining something to a small child.

"So shoot me." Sean glared at Aaron. "Then I'll be dead and you still won't know where she is." Sean could see the indecision in Aaron's eyes, clearly he had thought this would be easier.

"Move." He commanded, indicating Sean should walk backwards further into the hallway. As they passed each doorway Aaron took a quick look inside to identify each room, unfortunately he was just too far away from Sean for him to take advantage of these moments of distraction. Sean did, however, manage to press the front door release button on the panel beside the kitchen door while Aaron was momentarily distracted inspecting the dining room.

On reaching the kitchen door Aaron seemed to like the look of this room and he motioned for Sean to enter.

"Sit on the floor over there by the range." He instructed while he pulled a small plastic bag out of his pocket. Tipping the bag upside down revealed a set of plastic cable ties which he kicked across the floor to the now seated Sean. "First, tie your ankles together, good and tight please. Then tie your right hand to the oven handle." He commanded, again the smirk had returned.

Sean did not like the turn things were taking, with his legs tied and his arm attached to the oven he would be virtually useless, he doubted Aaron was going to leave his left hand free either, just long enough to tie his own restraints he assumed.

Sure enough, as soon as his legs were secure and his right arm rendered useless, Aaron put the gun down on the centre island unit and walked over to where Sean now sat. After he had checked the ankle and right arm ties were as tight as they would go he dragged Sean's left arm over towards the centre island, it was obvious what he intended to do and Sean tried to fight back, pulling his arm away and managing to land a well-aimed but largely powerless punch, because of his sitting position and the fact he was right-handed, to Aaron's face.

Aaron reacted by elbowing Sean hard in the side of his head, hard enough for Sean to momentarily see stars. By the time he had shaken his head clear Aaron already had the cable tie round his wrist and was tightening the slipknot to secure Sean's left hand to the centre island leg.

Sean's kitchen was bespoke, sturdy and very well put together, the centre island was solid walnut and brushed steel and was bolted to the floor and the cooker was in fact an Aga made of cast iron and weighing just short of six hundred kilos, there was no way Sean was moving either of them. He could only wait for Frank to come round now, pray Abi stayed locked in his bedroom and hope Frank could overpower this maniac before he did any more serious damage.

"Well, you're not going anywhere for now." Aaron seemed childishly pleased with his handiwork. "Best go and make sure the sidekick won't be helping any time soon." He added as he collected the gun and the cable ties and wandered back out to the hallway where Frank as still unconscious on the floor.

He cable tied Frank's wrists together behind his back and when he reached down to tie his ankles together he felt a bulge in the side of Frank's trouser leg. Pulling up the fabric he uncovered a knife in an intricately decorated leather sheath, strapped upside-down to Frank's ankle.

"You won't be needing this." Aaron was apparently enjoying himself as he relieved Frank of the weapon before securely tying his ankles together. He stuffed the knife and its sheath into his back pocket and sauntered back into the kitchen.

Pulling a chair out from under the other side of the central island and dragging it round to the same side as Sean, Aaron sat down, still holding the gun loosely in his right hand.

"So, now I guess we just sit here." He said with a mock smile at Sean, "No doubt she'll turn up sometime. You banged her yet?" He grinned as he saw the murderous look cross Sean's face. "Of course you have." Aaron continued. "Whore that she is, that's probably the first thing you did."

It was plain to see he was enjoying himself and Sean decided it was best to stay quiet for the moment and just let him believe he was commanding the authority he so obviously craved. He did not however even try to hide the homicidal feelings he was having and he was sure were displayed openly on his face.

"Wanna compare notes?" Aaron's voice had taken on a singsong quality Sean associated with utter insanity. "No?" Aaron looked slightly disappointed when Sean failed to comment. "Maybe I should just tell you what I did to her then, just so you know what you could've had if you had the balls to take it."

Sean bit back the reply he was so sorely tempted to give, he needed Aaron far more riled before he challenged him in any way and the longer he allowed the madman to talk the longer Frank had to come round. The plan starting to form in Sean's mind required a very angry Aaron to hopefully force him to make a huge mistake. Sean bit his lip and bided his time, listening to the sickening litany of crimes Steele had committed against Abi.

"Obviously the best fuck ever would've been the time I had her tied to that hospital bed. Beggin' for it she was, all wide eyed and desperate until some bastard pulled me off. Just about to nail her then all of a sudden I'm on the floor and the world went black." Aaron paused in his soliloquy as he noticed the flash of triumph briefly flare in Sean's eyes. "You?" He breathed, daring Sean to deny it. "You were there?"

Before Sean had chance to say anything Aaron was off the chair and across the six feet of gap between them, the gun now gripped firmly and pointing directly at Sean's face.

"So it's all your fucking fault!" He declared, his face inches from Sean's, the barrel of the gun now against Sean's temple. Still Sean kept silent, staring into Aaron's lunatic eyes, daring him to make a move. "If you hadn't fucking interfered, she'd be fucking dead now and I wouldn't of had to drag my ass half way round the fucking world trying to finish the fucking job." He then hit Sean hard across the side of the head with the gun, just as he had done with Frank earlier. Sean again saw stars but as the second blow landed he too slumped into unconsciousness.

Aaron stared at the man before him, unable to work out what could possibly make such an apparently successful, and therefore presumably intelligent, man do something as stupid as pander to a woman who was such a waste of skin she didn't deserve to live. He leaned back against the kitchen cupboards, he was going to have to wait until Sean came round to ask him his motives, before he killed him too obviously.

~CHAPTER FORTY-FIVE~

She had locked the door behind him and curled up behind it, listening for any sounds to tell her what was going on. Sean's house was so big and so old however, sound did not carry well through it and once she heard Sean's footsteps walk away from the door she could hear nothing more.

After several minutes crouched on the floor Abi suddenly realised she was completely naked. Not only that, but the last time she had seen her clothes was, the previous evening in the living room. There was nothing in Sean's room belonging to her.

She dug around in his drawers until she found a t-shirt which she hurriedly pulled over her head, it was more like a dress but at least it covered her enough to give her the courage to run along the landing to her room and find something more suitable to wear.

Quietly unlocking the door she opened it just a crack and strained to hear what was happening downstairs. She could hear nothing so she hesitantly stepped out of the room. To get from Sean's room to hers she had to completely cross from one side of the house to the other, unfortunately the only way to do that was to go along the galleried landing which looked down over the hallway below.

On tiptoes she ran to the end of the corridor to the point where the wall ended and she would be seen by anybody in the hallway. She took several deep breaths to try to steady herself, it did not work but it made her feel as though she were doing something to combat the fear coursing through her.

She peeked round the corner, across the landing, the relative safety of the other corridor was a mere ten yards away but from where she was standing it felt like a hundred. She chanced a look down into the hallway and had to stifle a gasp.

Frank was lying motionless on the floor, his wrists and ankles were obviously tied together but she could not tell from this distance if he was dead or alive, in fact she could not even tell if he were conscious or not as he had his back to her.

As she could see nobody else in the hallway she forced her legs to carry her along the landing to her room. She would check on Frank just as soon as she had some clothes on. In the safety of her room, she locked the door and after a moment to catch her breath she began digging in her bag for some suitable clothes.

Her jeans were somewhere in a heap in the living room so she pulled on a pair of joggers, deciding to keep Sean's t-shirt on as it smelled of him and was remarkably comforting under the circumstances. She did however put a vest on underneath as one tug in the wrong direction and she would most certainly be out of the oversized t-shirt. A situation she was keen to avoid as despite her repeated assurances to herself that it was not possible, she had a sinking feeling the cause of this latest upset was again Aaron Steele.

Even the thought of him made her shudder but having seen Frank just lying there she knew there was no way she could just sit up here with the door locked and wait to see what happened. She was going to have to go down and try to help.

Quickly tying her trainers she put a hairband in her long hair and twisted it into a tight bun, there was no way she was leaving it loose for him to be able to get a hold of, she knew just how much he could hurt her by pulling her hair.

Taking several more deep breaths, attempting to give herself more courage than she knew she possessed she again unlocked the door and stepped out onto the landing, running back to the corner of the galleried area knowing if she did not keep moving she would lose her bottle completely and run back into her room to hide.

She peered around the corner, seeing Frank still inert on the floor in the hall she made her way swiftly and silently down the stairs, hugging the wall all the way as if it might protect her should Steele suddenly appear below her. Her heart rate was alarming and the sweat began to run down her back, she did not have the time to analyse it now but had she been able to she would have known this was her post traumatic stress disorder trying hard to dissuade her from going any further. Unfortunately Abi was unaware she was suffering from PTSD as she had so far refused to seek professional help to deal with the traumas she had already been through in her life. She still believed any normal person could and should master their own life, she made no allowance for the input of people hell bent on making her life impossible as she firmly believed that was all her doing too.

When she reached the bottom of the stairs she finally heard Aaron's voice filtering through from the kitchen, the sound made the hairs on the back of her neck stand on end but she could not make out the words at this distance and was more worried about Frank. Silently she crossed the hallway and knelt down next to his immobile body, feeling for the pulse in his neck but in her distressed state she was unsure if it was his or hers she could feel.

She put her cheek in front of his mouth and waited, breathing a sigh of relief when she felt him breathe out. A quick inspection of the cable ties binding both his wrists and ankles told her she could not undo them without some sort of sharp tool. Knowing Steele was in the kitchen she darted into what she knew to be Sean's office hoping to find a pair of scissors or some such with which to cut Frank's restraints. Eventually she found a letter opener in the drawer of Sean's desk, it was not especially sharp but it was the best she could do, she was about to head back out to the hallway when she spied a small silver object poking out from behind a book on the shelf behind the desk. Reaching up she pulled out what turned out to be a pair of nail clippers.

"Better." She whispered to herself. "Much better." And she hurried out of the room, back to Frank on the floor in the hallway. As quickly as her shaking fingers would let her she worked the clippers underneath one side of the cable tie, they were not big enough to cut through in one go so she had to clip and move several times before she managed to get through the whole plastic tie. She started again on the tie on Frank's ankles and soon he was free of his bonds, still unconscious but no longer tethered.

Grabbing him buy the shoulders she shook him as hard as she could, hoping to get him to come round, knowing he was not asleep so shaking him would have little effect but not knowing what else to do. Frank did not stir so she decided she would try to get him into the office where hopefully he would be out of harm's way, at least he would not be in such an exposed position as he was here in the hall.

Getting hold of his jacket she attempted to pull him across the floor, he did not move, not even an inch and Abi soon had to give up on that quest too. Frank was going to have to stay where he was and come round in his own time, she was on her own, she realised she was just going to have to get on with it and headed more than reluctantly towards the kitchen door glad when she noticed she still had the letter opener in her hand.

Standing with her back to the wall, the door to the kitchen on her right, Frank inert on the floor down the hall to her left Abi could finally hear what Steele was saying.

"...had to drag my ass half way round the fucking world trying to finish the fucking job."

Every hair on Abigail's body reacted to the sound of that voice, her mouth went dry and her heart rate went up another gear. Then she heard two sickening cracks followed by a thud and then nothing. She held her breath, unsure what to do, not hearing Sean's voice she could only assume it was him Aaron had been talking to. She wanted to run but her legs simply would not move, she could no more go into the kitchen to confront him than she could retreat to her bedroom and hide. In her panic she began to hyperventilate, her breaths coming in short gasps, audible now to all but the dead. The knowledge she was giving her position away did nothing to help her state as she tried desperately to regulate her breathing.

Too late she realised she had been heard, rapid footsteps approached and almost before her paralysed mind could process the new danger, she was face to face with her arch enemy.

Aaron just stood in front of her, watching as she gasped for air, her back to the wall, a wide eyed and terrified look on her face. He could not have been more delighted with the turn events had taken. Both her protectors were unconscious and she was hardly in any state to present him with any problem.

"Fun time." He whispered into her ear as he grabbed her by the upper arm and dragged her stumbling form into the kitchen. Sweeping away all the cooking utensils and other items from the top of the central island he forced her backwards over it, shoving her hard until she lay on her back on the cold surface with her legs from the knees down dangling over the side.

By this time Abi was almost catatonic, she could barely breathe and none of her limbs were responding to the panicked signals she was sure she was trying to send to them. The only tangible thing her mind seemed able to focus on was the sharp pain now throbbing in her lower back. She could do nothing but wait to see what he had planned.

"Abigail." He breathed into her ear as he circled her prone form, the central island could almost have been designed for just this occasion. "Oh how I've missed you Abigail." He continued, running his cold finger along the side of her cheek. Abi tried to roll her head away from his touch but her body refused to respond.

As she realised she was helpless she began to pray her galloping heart would stop, it would all be over, then whatever he was going to do he would do to a dead body, she would never have to remember it. Never have to wake up in the night after dreaming about it.

"Abigail." He began again, his singsong voice new to Abi, she had never before witnessed him in such a state of insanity. "Did you miss me Abigail?" He grabbed her face and forced her to look at him as he spoke. "Answer me bitch." He suddenly hissed, this was the Aaron Abi knew, this was the man she had virtually lived with all those months. This was the man she was programmed to deal with.

"Yes Aaron." She whispered dutifully, knowing there were tears running down the side of her face into her hair now but wholly unable to stop them. She could only hope he didn't notice, the punishment for crying was always severe. Her hopes were dashed in his next breath.

"Tears of joy Abigail?" He hissed, squeezing his thumb and forefinger hard into her cheeks, causing lacerations as the inside of her mouth was forced against her teeth.

Abi tasted the blood, a reminder of the many times he had done this before and she tried to muster what strength she could find to stem the flow of tears before worse punishment followed. She had no idea she was far beyond her own control now, her unresolved PTSD had taken over her mind and she was unable to protect herself even as much as she had previously been able to, minimal as that had been.

"Do you want to see how much I've missed you Abigail?" The sing song voice was back and to her horror she could hear him unzipping his fly. Suddenly the pressure on her cheeks was directional as he forced her head round onto its side, displaying right at eye level what he had released from his pants.

"Look how hard you make me Abigail." He stroked the length of his engorged penis, the tip almost touching her face. "I'm going to put this in every hole you've got you bitch. No denying me this time Abigail, you've been asking for this for months now." He slapped her hard on the cheek as she began to heave at the proximity of him, she screwed her eyes tight shut but she could smell him, she could feel him touching her with his revolting flesh.

Suddenly his hand moved, he now had hold of her bun at the back of her head, forcing her head nearer and nearer to his smell.

"Open your mouth you whore." He hissed. "Time for you to show me what you've missed."

She felt his penis pushing hard against her teeth, crushing her lips painfully, so painfully she had no option but to part them as she tried to avoid the torture. No sooner had he forced her lips apart he was inside her mouth, thrusting his entire erection to the back of her throat, she gagged and gagged but he refused to stop, plunging in and out of her mouth, holding her by the bun on the back of her head so she had nowhere to retreat.

His breathing became ragged and laboured, within moments he was ready and he came hard into her mouth, hot salty spurts hitting the back of her now very painful throat causing her to heave violently, this time the heaving was successful and vomit followed, but with his still engorged organ thrust deep into her mouth Abigail had no choice but to swallow it all, vomit and semen combined.

She sobbed silently when eventually he withdrew, still breathing hard he bent down until his face was level with hers.

"Just a little taster of things to come." He whispered, his mouth was smiling but his eyes were as evil and cold as she remembered them. "You remember this is what happens to wicked little girls who don't do as they are told don't you? You haven't forgotten how it's all your fault you have to be punished have you Abigail?"

Abi was unable to prevent the sob which now escaped from her mouth, she understood she deserved this, she was a wicked person, hadn't he told her that many times but she could not understand how her punishment was supposed to make her a better person, nor why, so far, it seemed it was not working.

A groan from somewhere below her alerted Abi to the presence of someone else. What was left of her mind told her it had to be Sean. She tried to speak but her damaged throat could only manage a faint croak.

"Sean?"

"Sean? So that's his name is it?" Aaron taunted her. "Well I don't think your new boyfriend is going to be much use to you today Abigail, he's a little out of sorts you see." Aaron sing-songed at her. "Oh, you can't see can you? Hang on I'll soon sort that out." He grabbed her by the ankles and pulled sharply, dragging her off the central island onto the tiled floor beneath, banging her head hard as she landed, the blow cushioned slightly by her bun but not enough to prevent causing her a great deal more pain, not to mention the searing pain it caused to her still unhealed rib.

When she managed to focus her eyes after the blow she saw Sean still slumped against his restraints.

He was sitting between the island and the Aga, his arms obviously tied one to each side, his ankles were tied together just as Frank's had been.

"Sean?" Abi managed again, seeing his head move and his hands twitch.

Slowly, painfully she saw him open his eyes, she saw him lift his head slightly as he began to look around, presumably reminding himself of how he had come to be sitting on the floor of his own kitchen. Eventually she saw recognition as he looked at her, recognition immediately followed by anger which flashed across his face as his head shot up and he now glared at Aaron who was just standing watching the two of them interact.

"Well hello again Sean." Aaron said chirpily. "Look what I've found." He grabbed Abi by the hair as he spoke, shaking her at Sean as if she were some kind of weapon.

"Leave her alone." Sean growled, his eyes never leaving Aaron's face.

"No, I don't think I will actually." Aaron replied with a grin, crouching down between his two prisoners. "You see, I have many things to punish this bitch for and you are not really in a positon to stop me are you, being tied up and all." Aaron continued, gesturing towards where Sean's wrists were tied. "I'll let you watch though." He added with a wink. "You missed the entrée but there's plenty more isn't there Abigail? You'll love the main course." He went on, warming to his tirade. "Abigail has never tried it before but I keep telling her she'll love it, don't I Abigail." He pulled her face up to within millimetres of his, forcing her to smell him again, as before she heaved violently but did not reply.

"I said, leave her alone!" Sean growled, louder this time, his body language threatening extreme violence as he strained at his restraints.

In reply Aaron heaved Abi round so she was lying with her feet towards Sean, then he grabbed the knife he had taken from Frank and he cut through her joggers from waistline to crotch, flinging the now separated fabric sideways and displaying her nakedness to a horrified Sean.

Aaron laid the flat of the knife against Abi's clitoris and slid it slowly forwards and backwards dangerously close to cutting her, all the time smiling wickedly at Sean.

"Wonder what fucking her with this would be like Sean? Wanna watch?" He laughed as Sean lunged against his restraints.

"You evil fucking pervert." Sean spat. "You cowardly little fucking excuse of a man."

"What you going to do about it then big man?" Aaron taunted, the knife still resting against Abi's skin. "You gonna stop me?"

"If you had any balls you'd fight me, not terrorise a helpless woman." Sean spat again. "You're just a wimp Steele, what was it? Mummy didn't love you enough? I'm not surprised, she must've been able to tell what a lowlife you would turn out to be." Sean's eyes were blazing, his whole body straining against the plastic ties now cutting into his wrists.

Suddenly Aaron grabbed the gun and lunged at Sean, screaming wildly as he pummelled the barrel repeatedly into Sean's chest. Sean had apparently struck a nerve and Steele had completely lost all sense of reality.

"You fucking bastard!" He screamed. "What the fuck do you   know about anything? That bitch ruined my fucking life, now it's my turn."

As he continued to rain blows against Sean's chest Abi's mind began to process some of her fears, suddenly she was angry, more angry than she ever recalled being before in her life. She watched, almost without registering it, as Aaron laid into Sean, but something was tugging at her, something about what she was seeing made her angry. It was at the moment she saw Aaron raise the gun and point it directly at Sean's face when her body snapped back into action, she launched herself off the floor towards the back of the form which was causing her so much anger. Almost in a trance she hit him hard on the back just under his shoulder blade, and was totally confused when she saw blood begin to appear from under her hand.

He spun round to face her, forcing her to remove her hand and fall back to the floor, as she saw him level the gun at her she heard an anguished voice cry out.

"Nooo..." Was the last thing she heard before the deafening bang as the gun went off. Something hit her hard in the chest and she was immediately pinned to the floor, a dead weight pressing heavily down on her.

Knowing she must be dying she tried to say some last word to Sean, she couldn't see anymore, all her world was black but she could still feel her body and hear a commotion around her.

"Sean..." She whispered. "Sean..."

There was the sound of a door opening and closing, then quiet, Abi wondered if this was when she died, if all went quiet then. But she could still feel her body and the immense pressure on her chest.

"Frank?" She heard a muffled voice say somewhere off to her right. "Frank?" The voice became more insistent.

"Boss?" The reply was fainter but Abi somehow sensed it was closer to her.

"Can you move Frank?" Finally Abi recognised the voice to be Sean.

"Yes Boss." The faint sound Frank made seemed almost to come from in her ear.

There was a movement close by her head and suddenly the pressure on her chest disappeared, she rolled her head round in time to see Frank haul himself off her and over to where Sean was still tied up.

"Frank, can you reach a knife, at least undo one of these ties for me?"

"Yes Boss." Frank, hauled himself up onto his knees and reached for a carving knife from the rack next to the Aga, he carefully slid it into the tie holding Sean's right wrist before yanking it upwards to cut through the plastic. It seemed this was as much as Frank could manage as he then slumped back to the floor.

Sean grabbed the knife with his now free hand and slit the binding holding the other wrist and his ankles. As soon as he was free he grabbed Frank by the lapels and set him upright against the kitchen cupboards. He hauled a towel off the rail beside the sink and bunched it into a ball, pressing it hard against Frank's side.

Frank winced but Sean did not move the towel.

"Hang in there Frank, I'm going to call an ambulance. Hold that towel on there as firmly as you can you hear me?"

"Yes Boss." Franks voice was weak but clear as he took over pressing the towel to his side. "And Boss?"

"Yes Frank?" Sean said as he pulled his mobile phone out of his pocket and began to dial 999.

"I think Miss might need you more than me." Frank said as he gestured over to where Abi now lay.

She had rolled herself into the foetal position and pushed herself as far into the corner of the room as she could get. Her eyes were staring at nothing and her entire body shook uncontrollably.

"Don't move that towel Frank, and tell them we need an ambulance!" Sean commanded as he put the phone in Frank's other hand and crawled across the kitchen floor to Abi.

She seemed to sense him coming and she shrank back as far into the wall as she could get.

"Sshh..." He whispered as he gently pulled her into his arms. "Sshh, it's all over now." Abi tried to fight him off but he held her tightly, rolling her into a ball on his lap and wrapping his strong arms around her protectively. "Sshh Abi, it's me, remember, you're not afraid of me?" He felt her start to relax into his arms. "You did good Abi, you fought back and saved my life. I love you Abi, sshh now, it's ok." He whispered constantly into her hair as she sobbed, slowly she managed to regain some composure. The sobbing subsided and she started to try to process what had happened.

"Where is he now?" She managed to whisper eventually, about the same time the paramedics arrived and started to treat Frank.

"I don't know." Sean replied truthfully, knowing there was no point lying to her. "He scarpered out the back door with my letter opener sticking out of his back." He added with a grin.

"The letter opener." Abi gasped. "I had it in my hand."

"You did baby, and you stuck it in that bastard's back, I'm so proud of you baby, if you hadn't moved when you did he would have shot me. You saved my life." He bent to kiss her gently on the forehead, his eyes smiling his genuine thanks.

"Shot." She exclaimed. "He shot me." She added with rising panic, her hands frantically exploring her body to find the hole.

"Sshh, it's ok, you didn't get shot." He said reassuringly, grabbing her frantic hands and holding her more tightly that ever.

"But I heard it go off." She said, sure she remembered hearing a gunshot. "And it was pointing directly at me."

"Yes you did, and it was, but Frank got there first." Sean said quietly stroking her cheek to try to calm her.

"Frank got shot?" She whispered. "And landed on me?" She looked up at Sean for confirmation.

"Frank threw himself between you and the gun, and yes he got shot, but he's still talking and the hole isn't bleeding too massively so hopefully he didn't get hit in anything vital. Paramedics are here now and they'll be taking him to hospital soon. I've no idea how he got out of the cable ties I'm sure Steele put on him but I'm seriously glad he did." He gave Abi a little squeeze, suddenly concerned as she began to cry again.

"It was me." She managed between sobs. "I cut the ties, it's my fault Frank got shot."

"Abi, Abi..." He soothed. "It's not your fault. You did good, especially by cutting those ties, if you hadn't we could well all be dead." He pulled her face up to make her look at him.   "You did brilliantly Abigail, without you we would quite possibly all have been shot or stabbed or both.   That manic was not going to stop with you, he was hell bent on murder and he didn't care how he did it."

"He's going to come back isn't he?" Abi said in a very small voice, tears stinging her eyes again.

"If he does he will be met by armed police Abi, they will be stationed all round this house until the day he is caught.   He will *never* get to you again, I promise. The police are out looking for him as we speak."   Sean had heard Frank relaying a description of Steele into the phone as he waited for the paramedics to arrive. "Abigail, look at me."   He commanded softly, waiting for her to raise her head and look into his eyes.   "I will never let him get near you again."

~CHAPTER FORTY-SIX~

The hospital waiting room was clinical and functional and smelled of disinfectant but to Abi it was strangely comforting. She had not let go of Sean's hand since leaving the house and she had no intention of doing so now.

The paramedics had loaded Frank into the ambulance and headed away to Wythenshawe hospital with lights flashing and sirens wailing. A detail which to Abi negated the fact that Sean said Frank was not badly hurt.

Sean had then carried her upstairs and held her tightly as he stood with her in the hot shower. The invigorating needles had served to revive her senses immensely, sufficient for her to manage to quietly gargle with Sean's mouthwash as he left her momentarily to get a towel. She had no wish to explain to Sean why she needed to clean her mouth, not yet anyway. After drying her in the biggest, fluffiest towel she had ever seen, he dressed her in his own warm sweats and a thick, fleecy jumper and lead her back down the stairs to the waiting police detective.

"Detective." Sean had begun. "At this point Abi and I will give you the best description of Aaron Steele we can, although, if you can get hold of somebody in Boston I'm sure they'll send you his mugshot, the man escaped from prison there a few weeks ago."

"I'm sensing you want to get to the hospital to check on your friend?" The gratifyingly perceptive detective commented.

"We would yes." Sean confirmed with a nod.

"That's not a problem Mr Sullivan, I can take statements from you later, right now the man hunt is our priority and nothing you can tell us about what happened here will help that. Please, go to the hospital. As you have requested already, armed police will be present here at all times, they'll let me know when you're back and I'll come and talk to you then. And Miss..." He turned his attention to Abi. "...My men will not let him get in here again, please try not to worry."

Abi had smiled her thanks, knowing she would worry, she would worry every day until either she or Aaron Steele died, but she could not say that to the kindly detective who was, after all, just trying to reassure her.

They had now been sitting in this waiting room for two hours. Frank, they had been told when they had arrived, was doing well but was in surgery and the nurses could say no more until he was out, a doctor would come to talk to them then, they had been assured.

Eventually the door opened and a young white man clad in blue scrubs with a blue paper hat tied around his head, presented himself to them.

"My name is Mr Temple, I have been working on Mr Frank Molloy."

"Is he OK?" Sean interrupted impatiently, the strain of the last few hours beginning to show.

"Yes, he will recover from the gunshot quite quickly I should think." The surgeon confirmed. "We had a good look round inside but the bullet doesn't appear to have hit anything important. He was very lucky, it passed through his entire body and missed everything that matters. Anyway, we have cleaned the wound and sutured the entry and exit wounds. He'll be sore for a while but you will be able to see him soon. He might be a little groggy, we have him on morphine for the pain, but don't let that worry you. If I can answer any questions please ask." He concluded with a smile.

"Thank you Mr Temple. We would very much like to see him as soon as possible. Thank you." Sean said, shaking the doctor by the hand.

"I'll get a nurse to come and tell you as soon as he's fit for visitors." The doctor replied as he turned and left the room.

Sean visibly relaxed, he folded Abi into a hug and she felt the tension slowly ebb from his body, she knew he had been worried for Frank, she was glad he was not seriously injured. Frank may act as though Sean was merely his employer but Abi knew Sean would be lost without him. Sean saw Frank as a good friend, someone who had been with him through most of his life, certainly much closer to him than his father had been.

"You're still shaking." He whispered, feeling remiss he had not noticed earlier.

"I'm Ok." She murmured into his chest. "It'll pass." She knew the shaking would eventually stop, it always had before.

"You're not OK Abi, you are a long way from OK. I think you have PTSD or something like it Abi, I confess I don't know much about it but the way you were this morning..." He caressed her hair as he spoke, kissing her softly on the top of her head. "You were almost catatonic while he was manhandling you, like you shut down completely. I was so scared for you baby…" He trailed off, unsure how she would react to his next suggestion but equally sure he had to make it. "If I swear to be by your side every step of the way will you go to see a professional counsellor?"

"I can manage." She insisted, still not lifting her head from his chest but he caught the disappointment in her voice nonetheless.

"Abi…" He lifted her chin to force her to look at him. "…it doesn't make you any of the things he said you are. Look, if he'd broken your leg you'd let the doctors treat it wouldn't you?" He asked with a smile and a raised eyebrow.

"Of course but…" Before she could defend her position he went on.

"It's exactly the same with your brain Abi, it's been broken, just like a bone, and you need a doctor to help fix it." He stopped and waited, seeing in her eyes she was far from convinced.

"I'll speak to Sam." She eventually relented. "I think Ginny has had him checking a few possible candidates." Her voice was heavy with defeat and Sean felt as though his heart could break for her.

"Sweetheart, it's not giving in, please don't think of it like that. It takes courage to face your demons, courage I know you have almost herculean reserves of." He smiled his conviction into her eyes, willing her to draw some comfort from it.

"We'll see." Was all the response she could give before the tears welled again and she crumpled into his arms.

Sean sensed it was going to be a long time and a lot of therapy before Abi even reached the level she had achieved before this morning's events. He knew he would have to push her into therapy and although he did not understand her reluctance, he sensed it was part of the problem. All he could really do was support her, and that he was determined to do for as long as it took.

"Mr Sullivan?" A voice from the doorway asked. Sean turned slightly to see who it was without releasing Abi for a second.

"Nurse?"

"Mr Molloy is settled in a side room now, I can take you to see him if you're ready."

"Thank you, we're ready." He confirmed as he turned Abi so she could walk without releasing his grip on her, she was still shaking but the sobbing had stopped for now.

Frank lay half propped on many pillows, a drip in his arm but otherwise no other signs of medical intervention. He was awake and surprisingly alert.

"Hey there Frank." Seann beamed as he saw how well his friend was looking under the circumstances. "Had us worried there for a while."

"Sorry Boss." Frank grinned back before looking at Abi's face when his grin disappeared. "Miss? You OK Miss?" He asked with obvious concern.

"Yes Frank, I'm OK." She replied, her voice small but her eyes showing the determination and strength she did not believe she possessed. "Thank you Frank." She added in a whisper. "Thank you for saving my life." She managed a small smile to try to convey her gratitude.

"Anytime Miss." Frank replied with absolute sincerity. "Anytime."

"Is there anything you need Frank? Anything we can get you?" Sean asked, trying to divert attention from Abi, who was struggling to hold it all together.

"Could do with some clothes Boss." Frank replied. "They cut the ones I had on off." He added indignantly. "I told them I could stand while I got my pants off but they wouldn't have it so all my clothes here are in bits."

"Not to worry Frank, I guess it was you they were more worried about at the time."

"They reckon just a couple of days here Boss, no serious damage in there so I won't have to stay here long." He looked up at Sean, the look on his face telling Sean far more than his words did.

"No rush Frank." Sean replied carefully.

"About that Boss, think I'm gonna need some time off Boss." Frank said, fiddling with the drip catheter in the back of his hand.

Sean looked hard at Frank who returned his stare without another word.

"Take all the time you need Frank, use the company credit card if there's anything you need." He said with a curt nod, careful to glance at Abi to see if she saw it.

"Looks like maybe you should take Miss home Boss." Frank said, his nod in reply almost imperceptible.

"You're right Frank, Abi needs some rest and so do you. It's been a rough day. Call me if you need anything Frank, I'll arrange to get those clothes brought in." Sean again turned Abi and began to head for the door.

"He took my knife Boss." Frank said very quietly as Sean reached the door, so quietly Abi did not hear

him but Sean did, he merely nodded as he walked
through the door.

~CHAPTER FORTY-SEVEN~

The burning in his back was becoming unbearable as Aaron finally managed to find a spot on the perimeter of Sullivan's property where he could scale the wall and drop over into the road beyond. He knew he was somewhere at the back of the property and had no intention of trying to get round the front and back to the main road. He was going to have to try to get across a few more gardens of the rich, which surrounded him on all sides.

First he had to get this damn thing out of his back, he had no idea what the bitch had stuck in him but it hurt like hell.

Climbing through a gap in the opposite fence he found himself at the back end of a garage wall. He sidled along it until he reached daylight at the end and peered round the corner. He found himself at the top of a long driveway, the house was away to his right and he could see washing hanging out on a line between the corner of the garage and the rear wall of the house.

It was mainly children's washing but he quickly grabbed a pair of tights and a couple of t-shirts, stuffed them inside the jacket he had over his arm and walked swiftly down the driveway towards the road, hoping nobody had seen him but prepared to throw his jacket over his shoulders and play the door-to-door salesman if challenged. People could generally not get rid of such nuisances quickly enough.

Ducking quickly across the road he squeezed through a gap in the opposite fence, unwilling to stay on the road in case he was seen, and into the back garden of yet another enormous house. Three gardens later he climbed a fence into an empty field, he could see a road running along the far edge of it and set off in that direction. When he reached the hedgerow on the far side he sat down, it was time to remove whatever it was sticking into his shoulder.

It was at an awkward angle to remove himself but he eventually managed to get a decent grip on it and he tugged it out, the pain the movement caused paralysing him on the ground for several moments.

When he got his breath back he could feel the trickle of blood now running down his back, he bunched up the t-shirts into a pad and used the tights like a strap to hold them in place over the wound. He tied the woollen tights as tightly as he could and shrugged back into his jacket. Apart from looking like he had a mild hunchback there was now no obvious signs of injury.

He left the letter opener where it lay and made his way onto the road. Pulling out his smart phone he activated the GPS app which told him exactly where he was and also, after tapping in a few more commands, how far it was back to his car, a couple of hundred yards down the road from Frank's house. Deciding it was way too far to walk he called a taxi, it arrived five minutes later and he was soon back in his car heading north on the M6.

He had no real plans regarding where he was headed but he knew Scotland was to the north so that is the way he went.

He had been driving for several hours, past Carlisle and well into Scotland when his vision became too blurred to drive further. He pulled into a rest stop, parked the car and wandered into the café, thinking some food and coffee would revive him and he could be on his way.

He awoke sometime the following day in a bed with crisp pale green sheets. The room was quiet and smelled faintly of disinfectant. He looked around and soon realised he was in a hospital. As he became more aware he felt a slight pressure on the back of his hand and looked down to see a drip catheter sticking out of the back of it, linked to a bag of fluid rhythmically dripping away over his left shoulder.

The pain in his back was reduced to a dull ache for which he was grateful but he had to get out of here, somewhere in the back of his mind he knew hospitals were supposed to report knife wounds and gunshot wounds and there was little chance they had not recognised his wound for just one of these.

Swinging his legs over the side of the bed he tried to raise himself up on his elbows, the resultant pain in his shoulder forced him to stop.

"Fuck!" He exclaimed laying back against the pillows and waiting for the pain to subside. He realised he was going to have to try to roll then slide off the bed, tensing any muscles in his back to try to rise was going to result in more pain.

Gingerly he rolled over onto his side, using just his arms and legs as leverage, it was still a painful process but much less so. Finally when he was lying on his left side he pushed his legs back again over the side of the bed, the momentum forcing his body over onto his front, then he simply slid backwards until his knees touched the floor and he straightened his torso by using just his arms. From his kneeling position it was much easier to rise to a stand without putting any strain on his upper back muscles and so keeping the pain to a minimum.

He turned and sat on the edge of the bed, his head was swimming and the effort of rising had worn him out. Whilst getting his breath back and waiting for the dizziness to subside he surveyed the rest of the room.

It was not much to look at. A bed, a TV suspended from a bracket on the wall, a chair and a small cupboard with wheels. There were two doors, one he assumed was to the corridor or whatever beyond and the other, according to the sign on it, led to the bathroom.

He reached out to open the door on the small cupboard and was delighted to find his clothes folded neatly inside, underneath the pile of garments he also found his rucksack which he pulled swiftly into his lap.

Delving into the contents he was relieved to find that his money and passport were still in it and he was thankful he had left the gun and the knife in the car, although quite where the car was now was anyone's guess, or rather, where he was now was anyone's guess, his car presumably would still be at the rest stop where he had left it.

Realising he did not even know how long he had been here he decided it was best to work these things out after he had put as much distance between himself and this hospital as possible, he had no way of knowing whether Sullivan would have involved the police but if he had or he hadn't *somebody* would be looking for him.

He carefully pulled the drip out of his arm, pressing hard on the resultant hole to try to stop it bleeding all over himself. Once satisfied he carefully, but as quickly as he could manage, pulled on his clothes.

When dressed he grabbed his chart from the end of the bed, opening it he turned to his admission page where a quick scan told him where the ambulance had collected him from. He stuffed the file into his backpack and slung it over his good shoulder.

Gingerly opening the door he peered out into the corridor. There were people milling about all over, in and out of rooms just like the one he was in but nobody appeared to be looking in his direction. Ensuring he had identified the exit first he confidently strolled out of the room and along the ward towards the door and out into the hospital's main corridor, where he turned left and followed the signs for the exit. He was not challenged once, anybody who did look at him merely presuming he was a visitor or a discharged patient going home.

Outside he found the taxi rank and instructed the driver to take him back to the rest stop where he hoped his car awaited. As it had been parked legitimately in a twenty-four hour carpark there was no reason for the police to have moved it, assuming they had identified it as his at all.

Half an hour later he was back in the car heading north again. The date and time on his smart phone which he had retrieved from the glove-box told him he had lost almost sixteen hours in the hospital so he needed to get as far away as possible now and find somewhere to lay low while he made some plans.

There was no way he was finished with Abigail Storm, not only was she still alive, which as far as he was concerned was a wholly unacceptable state, but the bitch had stabbed him in the back with a fucking letter opener. His previous plan to get back to the States was now on hold while he worked out how to get back at her, and eliminate the boyfriend.

The glance back he had just managed before he had barrelled out of the back door of Sullivan's house had told him that the sidekick was probably dead already, he had shot him at close range and seen the blood starting to spread.

"That bitch is not going to get away with this." He hissed to himself as he negotiated the now windy Scottish highland roads. "She's going to die, slowly and very, very painfully." He added through gritted teeth, the notion he was talking to himself was irrelevant to him, as was the insane bloodlust he held towards Abi. As far as he was concerned she was his enemy, she had made herself his enemy and if he was any kind of man he had to put a stop to her antics.

He drove on into the growing darkness, night fell early at this latitude at this time of year. He knew he was going to have to find himself somewhere to stay soon, he could not drive all night, not least because the pain in his shoulder was now throbbing badly and he was going to have to stop soon.

He saw the sign for a public house just a little further up on the left and swung the little car into the almost deserted carpark.

"Evening Sir." The barman greeted Aaron as he walked into the small, cosy pub. "What can I get you?"

Aaron ordered a large whiskey and dinner of Aberdeen Angus burger and chips. "I don't suppose you could tell me if there's a hotel or guest house around here anywhere?" He asked politely as he paid for his order.

"No' really." The barman replied scratching his head. "Were you looking ta stay long?"

"Well, possibly yes." Aaron replied, the lie already thought out and ready to deliver. "I'm a writer you see, just need somewhere quiet to hole up and finish my latest book." He added with a wry smile. "And no, unfortunately you won't have heard of me yet but I live in hope." He said, neatly deflecting the next question.

"Well, if it's peace and quiet you're after, I can probably help you there." The barman replied with a knowing wink. "Hang on there an' I'll go and telephone a friend, she's a cottage on the loch up the road, it's no' big but it's comfy and warm and you'll have more peace and quiet than you can imagine."

"Sounds   fantastic."   Aaron   replied enthusiastically as he wandered over towards the fire where he sat down to wait.

Two hours later he had eaten the most delicious burger he had ever had, met the barman's small, round, red faced friend Morag and having agreed to rent the cottage for two weeks was now happily ensconced in the little place, a fire was roaring in the hearth in the centre of the quaint living room and he was drinking brandy he was very glad he'd had the forethought to purchase a bottle of before leaving the pub.

Tomorrow he would work out where he was and how he was going to make Abigail Storm pay for completely ruining his life.

~CHAPTER FORTY-EIGHT~

"For now just try to treat her as normally as you can I think Sean." Sam said into the phone. "She will believe her current state proves how useless she believes she is, she certainly won't see it as a normal reaction to what she's been through. Therefore if you wrap her in cotton wool and treat her with kid gloves you are, to her mind at least, proving she's right."

"Really?" Sean was unconvinced. "Why would she not know she's quite normal to react to a terrifying situation?"

"Because she believes she is worthless. She's been told this from being very young, she believes it just as people who have religion instilled in them from birth believe in God. It's an absolute, and nothing she has been through so far has challenged that truth as far as she is concerned, the opposite in fact, Steele re-enforced the indoctrination tenfold I should imagine." Sam knew he probably was not explaining the situation very well but this really was not his field. "I've found two psychiatrists for her to try, a man and a woman, I wasn't sure which she'd prefer."

"She'd prefer neither I think Sam but she has agreed to talk to you about it so that's a start. Perhaps you and Ginny should come here for dinner tonight, that is, if you really think I should try to do normal things with her?"

"I think that's a great idea, maybe not to ask her to cook though. Take-away perhaps?" Sam suggested.

"OK, good idea, about 7.30pm then?"

"See you then, I know Ginny will desperately want to see Abi so I'll call her now and let her know. See you later." Sam hung up.

Sean wandered up to the bedroom where Abi was curled in a foetal position on his bed.

"I just spoke to Sam and he and Ginny are coming for dinner tonight." He said brightly, sitting down on the bed beside Abi and pulling her arm away from her face so he could see her.

"Really?" She whispered, the look on her face a cross between terror and disbelief.

"Really." Sean confirmed with a smile, resisting the urge to roll her into his arms and hug her, Sam's words still ringing in his ears. "So, we're either going to have to go to your place and get you some more clothes, gorgeous as you look in my sweats, they really are a bit big." He lifted the fabric as he spoke revealing the fact she hardly filled half of each leg.

He was rewarded with a tiny giggle, the sound made his heart soar and he ploughed on.

"Or we could go shopping, I feel the need to spend some money, I think you could probably help me with that don't you?"

"I can't go shopping dressed in these." She pointed out very quietly, unfurling herself from the ball she had been curled in. "We'd have to go home for me to get changed first, what happened to my jeans?"

"They're downstairs but I think they've had several police size 11's on them, they're very dirty." Sean replied apologetically. "I guess they were on the floor." He shrugged, gratified to hear Abi's second tiny giggle. "OK, we'll go to your house on the way then. Come on, let's go. Sam and I decided we'd get a takeaway tonight so no cooking required, we can just shop for nice stuff!" He added with a cheeky grin, thrilled that Sam's advice appeared to be working.

Several hours later they arrived back at Sean's house with many shopping bags. It had taken some persuasion but Abi had finally agreed to allow him to spoil her.

"Abi, I have more money than I know what to do with." He had explained to her after she had politely declined his offer of buying everything in which she had shown any interest in the first two shops they had visited. "Really Abi, the money is not relevant here, I just want to spoil you for a while, please let me?"

She had eventually agreed, although he could tell it was a completely alien situation for her and she was not altogether comfortable with it. But, in true Abigail style she had swallowed her fears and gone with it. Sean firmly believed she actually began to enjoy the freedom it represented after she had persuaded herself she was allowed to enjoy what apparently was making him happy.

"We have an hour before Ginny and Sam arrive." He announced as he followed her into his bedroom, walking past her he entered the bathroom and proceeded to start to run a bath, after adding some delicately scented foam bath he wandered back out to see her sitting pensively on the bed.

Buoyed by the knowledge that Sam had been right so far he pulled Abi up from the bed and wrapped his arms around her, he felt her stiffen but she did not pull away. Gently he bent his head to kiss her, tenderly on the lips. She kissed him back but he could feel her reticence even though she seemed to be acquiescing. Slowly but determinedly he peeled away her clothes, shedding his own as he went, when finally they were both naked he swung her up into his arms and carried her into the bathroom.

The entire time he had been holding her he had not taken his eyes off hers, the emotions he had seen flashing through hers almost made his head spin but he was determined to continue, unless she told him otherwise.

Still carrying her he climbed into the now filled bath and sank down into the bubbles and hot water beneath. He shuffled her round so she was sitting in his lap with her head resting on his chest and he leaned back into the welcome heat of the bathwater.

As he slowly poured handfuls of water over her exposed shoulder and down her back and arm he gently kissed her hair.

"I'm so proud of you Abi..." He began, the emotion catching in his throat made her look up at him. He kissed her on the nose before continuing. "...you have been amazing today."

She stopped him by leaning up and planting a kiss firmly on his lips, he could still feel her trembling all over but what she wanted now was evidently more urgent to her than the state of shock she was apparently still in.

Sean wondered whether he was doing the right thing here, the last thing he wanted to do was damage her further, but with Sam's advice still seeming to be working he decided if she could handle normal, he was going to give it to her.

By the time Sam and Ginny arrived Abi had an almost genuine smile on her face, her eyes still belied her true state, she still looked like a rabbit caught in the headlights of a passing car but she had a hold of her emotions.

"Wow, Abi, you look better than I thought you would." Ginny exclaimed as she wandered into the kitchen and smothered her friend in a big hug. "Love the new threads." She said admiring Abi's outfit.

"It's just jeans and a jumper Ginny, how the hell do you know they are new?" Abi asked, genuinely perplexed.

"Abi, your usual jeans and a jumper looks like, well, how can I put this? It looks like you spent about a tenner on the lot." Ginny said, raising her eyebrows at her friend, knowing perfectly well Abi probably had spent a tenner on the lot. "This however..." She indicated Abi's current attire. "Looks expensive, therefore, it must be new and I'm guessing you had to be dragged kicking and screaming to buy it." She concluded with another grin, this one in Sean's direction.

"Like you wouldn't believe." He confirmed laughing. "The first woman I have ever had to persuade to buy stuff!" He added, winking at Abi, his eyes conveying how much he thought of her.

"So, you've been shopping this afternoon Abi?" It was Sam this time, he nodded his approval at Sean before he went on. "You never cease to amaze me." He added with a smile.

At that moment the door buzzer announced a presence at the front door and Abi froze, dropping the glass she was holding which promptly smashed on the tiled floor. The sound seemed to snap her out of her momentary paralysis and she immediately dropped to her knees to clear up the mess she had made.

"I'm sorry, I'm sorry..." She repeated again and again as she attempted to pick up the broken glass with trembling hands.

Sam reacted fastest, pulling her up onto her feet and holding both her shaking hands in his.

"Abi, you have post-traumatic stress disorder. It is completely normal under the circumstances." He waited for her to focus on his face before he continued. "The slightest thing can and will do this to you until you get this under control, and to do that you need a professional." He waited to see his words had registered and as he saw the understanding in her eyes he added. "You *need* a professional. I know Sean has already mentioned it to you?"

Abi nodded, finally feeling her heart rate begin to slow back to something like normal. "I said I would talk to you." She squeaked, her voice seeming to belong to someone else.

Sean let out the breath he had been holding, for a moment he had been convinced the day had finally broken her but the knowledge she remembered their conversation earlier convinced him Sam was right, normal was good but she needed a psychiatrist.

"Good Abi, that's good. Now, we can talk about that a little later, have you eaten anything today?" Sam asked her, still holding both her hands and looking steadily into her eyes.

Abi thought about the question and realised she had not eaten anything since the roast dinner the night before, she shook her head.

"Then we should eat." Sam concluded, leading her out of the kitchen towards the dining room where Ginny was busy setting out the takeaway Chinese food she had collected from the man who had pressed the door buzzer which had so upset Abi.

Sam was right again, a decent meal inside her made Abi feel much better. She had picked at first but as the conversation began to flow and the first morsels she had eaten began to revive her flagging system she had felt better and better and had in the end eaten a good sized dinner.

By the time Sam and Ginny left she was feeling more optimistic. She had agreed to meet both Sam's recommended psychiatrists to see which she preferred. Sam had assured her neither would mind if she did not pick them as both merely wanted to help her and both understood the person she was most comfortable with would do her the most good.

Sam had promised to call the next day with appointment times and Sean had promised to be with her every step of the way.

When at last she and Sean made it to bed, she curled up in his arms again and although she would be hard pressed to define how she felt, she could honestly say she felt considerably better than she had about twelve hours earlier.

~CHAPTER FORTY-NINE~

When Frank finally persuaded the doctors to release him from the hospital, despite it being wholly against their advice, Aaron Steele had a four day head start. Add to that the time it took for Frank to acquire the provisions he needed for the job in hand and it was just short of a week after the incident when he could begin to track his quarry.

Calling in a few favours he had found out from the police investigation that there was a report of a man with a knife wound to the back having been admitted to a hospital near Dumfries in Scotland. Apparently the man had disappeared before police had chance to talk to him. His name was unconfirmed but as he had carried an American passport in the name of Michael Gresty, it was assumed to be this.

Frank's first stop on the hunt was to the Scottish hospital where, having shown Steele's photograph to several nurses, he now at least had a positive ID. Unfortunately nobody had seen him leave and his medical file was missing so no further information was available.

"He did arrive by ambulance though, I do remember that much." A petite nurse by the name of

Sarah had told Frank. "The ambulance service might be able to tell you where they found him if that helps?" She suggested before going back to her paperwork.

Sarah was correct in her assumption and the ambulance service, after much deliberation did confirm they had collected an unconscious male with a stab wound to the shoulder from a rest stop just off the A74. Frank headed for the rest stop.

"What can I get you?" The redhead behind the counter asked politely, her scots accent barely evident.

"Just coffee thanks." Frank replied then slid a photograph across the counter. "Recognise this man?" he added.

"Who's askin'?" Came the redhead's suspicious reply.

"He's a murdering, rapist bastard." Frank said evenly, his eyes never leaving the waitress' face. "And I need to catch him."

Redhead's eyes widened at Frank's direct words. "Really?"

"Really." Frank nodded curtly. "Seen him before?"

"Sure." She said hurriedly. "He arrived about a week ago now, evening it was, dark outside, collapsed right there where you're sitting, ambulance took him away."

"Seen him since?" Frank could only hope.

"Nope." She shook her head. "Mind you, somebody came back for his car next day." She added.

"How do you know it was his?"

"Keys were in his bag, I was looking for ID for the ambulance men. When I went home later it was the only car still outside with English plates, reckoned it had to be his. Anyway, when I came on shift next day it was gone." She said with a nod, confirming to herself she had remembered correctly.

"Wouldn't remember what sort of car it was would you?" Frank asked hopefully.

"Nah, but the garage next door have CCTV which covers that end of our carpark, if they keep it this long you might be able to get a look at it." She added helpfully, placing Frank's coffee in front of him. "I'll give them a call, the attendants got the hots for me anyway, sure I can get him to help if he can." She said with a wink as she headed over to the phone at the back of the serving area.

Two coffees later Frank was back in his car holding a grainy but clear enough video still of a pale gold Peugeot 308, the licence plate was only partially visible but had enough showing that Frank would be able to identify the car if he found it.

Unfortunately that was all he had. Steele had collected the car sometime before 5pm when redhead started her shift five days earlier. Where he had headed after that was a mystery but Frank decided that as he had been heading north before he would continue that way. He had put a call in to another friend in the police force asking for any traffic camera data showing this car to be forwarded to his mobile but he did not really expect much. This far north traffic cameras were much less well used and would get more and more sparse as he got further north still.

Frank had to assume Steele would have been looking for somewhere to hole up. Probably the more remote the better so north would definitely be the way to go for now. He decided to stop at any hotels or public houses he found on the road and show the photographs around, hopefully somebody would have seen something, even if it was only the car passing them on the road.

He was about to give up for the night and find somewhere to stay for himself when a short, round, red faced woman walked directly up to him as he stood at the bar of what he had decided was the final pub of the day.

"Word is you're looking for an American?" The short, round woman said as she eyed Frank through mildly bloodshot eyes. "Rumour you're spreading is he's a bad man?"

Her tone caused Frank to gather it was a question so he merely nodded his reply.

"You got a picture there?" She said indicating for him to show her.

He complied, pulling both photographs from his jacket and handing them over.

"Aye, that's' him." She confirmed, handing them back to Frank. "What's he done?"

"He's a murderer and a rapist." Frank replied evenly, his gaze not wavering from hers.

"Aye, I already heard that but Ah said what's he done?"

"He's murdered and raped." Frank was not sure he was willing to get into details with this slightly unnerving woman and there was not much else he could say.

She just looked at him and waited.

"He murdered a hotel receptionist who got in the way of him abducting, raping and murdering a good friend of mine. Unfortunately he had tried before and been partially successful." This was as much a Frank was prepared to say and hoped she would be satisfied.

Apparently it was not the details she was after but the truth in his eyes as he spoke, she was entirely satisfied he was being completely honest.

"He's staying at my cottage up on the loch, apparently he's been asking around about getting boat passage to America or Canada or thereabouts, seems he wants to go home." She said as she grabbed a paper napkin off the bar and began to write directions on it.

"You'll try not to damage my property I hope?" She said as she handed the napkin to Frank. "It's no much but it makes me a few bob when people want a quiet space to be."

"I can't promise no damage." Frank said with a grateful smile. "But I will make sure you receive whatever the repair or clean-up costs might be. Will that do?"

"Fair enough, ye can contact me through this place if ye need to." She nodded once at Frank and left.

Frank must have looked a little astonished at the turn of events as when he turned back to the now grinning barman he said.

"That's Morag. She knows everything happening in about a hundred mile radius. Can I get you anything else?"

"Thanks, but I'd best be on my way. Do you have a card or something with this place's number and address on, so I can contact Morag should I need to?"

"Aye sure." The barman pulled a business card from the holder next to the cash register and handed it to Frank. "Ye be careful now ye hear?" He said as Frank headed out the door.

Morag's instructions were surprisingly simple, once Frank had managed to decipher the spidery scrawl, and he was soon approaching the loch. He had doused his headlights and picked his way slowly up the road in the moonlight, aware that any light would be seen from miles away up here where the street lights were just a distant dream.

As the road opened up onto the shores of the loch Frank could clearly see the cottage about five hundred yards further round the glistening lake, the lights in the windows standing out against the background of black of the hills and forest beyond.

Frank parked his car in a thicket of trees just before they ran out, he did not want to drive the last distance for fear Steele might hear the engine and be alerted.

He climbed out, his body a bit stiff now, he had been driving on and off all day. The gunshot wound was throbbing but he had been in worse pain for several months now so could largely ignore this one. Reaching into the boot he hauled out the bag containing all the provisions he had brought for this mission, he slung it over his shoulder and set off into the trees. His intention was to get as close to the cottage as possible without breaking cover from the tree line.

When the cottage was directly between him and the loch shore, he dumped the bag on the ground and unzipped it.

He pulled out a long high powered rifle and laid it on the ground. Next he retrieved the tripod legs he had brought and set them up carefully, wedging them firmly into the soft vegetation which made up the forest floor.

When he was satisfied they were as steady as was possible he raised the rifle and clipped it into position on the top. Adding the sight to the top of the rifle when he was done. Pulling a sleeping bag from the still well stuffed bag he laid it on the ground behind the tripod and lay himself on his front on top of it. After looking through the scope and determining the rifle was at the right height for use he pulled a couple of pork pies and a flask out of the bag at his side and turning his coat collar up around his ears against the chill night air he ate his food before settling down to try to get some sleep.

He woke at first light, stiff, cold and in a lot of pain again. He rolled into a ball and willed himself to breathe deeply until the pain subsided. Eventually he could uncurl himself and drained the last of the contents of the flask of coffee into his mug. It was not exactly hot but the caffeine did its job anyway.

This time when he looked through the scope he could clearly see the outline of the cottage in the growing morning light, soon he would be able to make out the features. While he waited he wondered whether what he was doing was a bad thing or not.

He knew from the law's point of view he was planning to commit murder but the man he was stalking deserved nothing less, and would no doubt have killed Frank without a moment's hesitation. Not to mention the Boss and Miss Abigail. After some deliberation Frank decided he did not really care about the legalities or even the moralities of his actions. Thirty years ago he had vowed to Mr Sullivan Senior that he would protect his son with his life if necessary. Now he deemed it necessary.

The sudden startling of the birds in the tree above his head told him something had moved, he rolled over into position again and looked through the scope. Sure enough, Aaron Steele had wandered out of the cottage and down towards the shoreline, what looked like a hot cup of coffee or tea in his hand.

"Perfect." Frank whispered, took a breath and held it, this was a long shot even for the calibre of rifle he had. He centred the crosshairs on the small of Steele's back and pulled the trigger once.

Through the sight he saw the burst of blood which was blown out of the hole he had just made through Steele's torso. He had hit him exactly where he had aimed, hopefully severing the spinal column just above the kidneys. Steele hit the floor like a dead weight, Frank still watch through the scope and smiled when he saw Steele trying to drag himself back towards the cottage using only his arms.

Frank dismantled the gun and the tripod, placing all the pieces carefully back in the bag along with his now drained flask and his sleeping bag. He set off in the direction of the cottage.

Now out of the tree line he could see how little progress Aaron was making towards the cottage door and knew he would get there before Steele had any chance of getting inside, he was also aware Steele could now see him coming, he hoped the sight instilled terror in the craven bastard.

Frank was aware Steele probably still had the handgun and would no doubt use it if he could get to it but, in his current state it was the getting to it which would present the biggest problem.

By the time Frank had reached the cottage Steele was halfway through the doorway. Frank dumped his bag outside, stepped over the half useless body still being dragged by its owner and into the small interior of the quaint cottage.

"Morning Steele." Frank growled as Steele looked up and saw who his assailant was for the first time.

"You're dead, I shot you!" Steele hissed through his teeth, a mixture of exertion, pain and anger in his voice.

"Well, you shot me that's true." Frank agreed with mock seriousness. "But, as you are such a complete fuck up, even at that range you managed to miss everything important. I, on the other hand, have shot you and hit exactly what I aimed for."

Frank waited for the realisation to dawn on Steele, watching as the fear started to creep into his eyes.

"You thought I'd missed didn't you Steele, you thought I'd aimed to kill you and missed." Frank smiled as the dull implications of his words hit home to Steele.

"What are you going do with me?" Steele's voice waivered, gone was the cocky, self-possessed man, replaced with what he really was, a cowardly weasel without conscience or moral compass. "I didn't mean to shoot you..." He began, starting to snivel. "You got in the way that's all." His eyes were now pleading with Frank.

"Where's my knife?" Frank growled, making a sudden decision. When Steele's gaze moved to the table Frank spotted his knife in its sheath and retrieved it quickly. "I was going to torture you just like you did those poor women, stick things in places where things shouldn't be stuck, you get my meaning. You deserve to be strung up by the balls for what you've done. But looking at you snivelling there I realise you're not worth it. You're not worth my time and anyway, it would serve no purpose. The whole point would be so you had to live with it forever, just like Miss Abi and those others and you're not going to live past today."

Without further warning he grabbed Steele by the hair on the top of his head and swiped swiftly and smoothly across his throat with the knife. Blood shot out of both carotid arteries and Frank held onto Steele's hair until he was sure the life had ebbed out of him then he lowered him to the ground.

Taking out his mobile phone Frank took a photograph of the head and shoulders and surrounding pool of blood which was now all that was left of the once terrifying Aaron Steele.

He cleaned his knife on Aaron's shirt and put it back into its sheath, then tied it back onto his ankle where it had lived for the previous thirty years.

The pain in his gut had returned with a vengeance and he struggled to get back to his car parked some five hundred yards away along the shoreline of the loch. Once there he changed out of his blood soaked clothes, setting fire to them instead of taking them with him. He sat for a long time watching the surface of the water as it rippled in the breeze. It was now 8.15 am and it was a really long drive home, if the pain did not ease off soon he doubted he would manage to get back to the main road never mind to Manchester.

Reaching into the bag he carried he found the bottle of painkillers he had been given. So far he had managed without but today he decided he would have to try one, it was time.

As he waited for the drugs to do their job he pulled a business card out of his pocket and dialled the number.

~CHAPTER FIFTY~

"Mr Sullivan?"

"Speaking?"

"Good Morning Mr Sullivan, my name is Sister Michaels from Wythenshawe Hospital. We have a patient by the name of Frank Molloy who I believe is a friend of yours?" Sister Michaels' voice was soft and clear with a slight Irish lilt.

"Frank? What's Frank doing there?" Sean was alarmed, he had thought Frank had been discharged well over a week ago.

"He was readmitted three days ago, Mr Sullivan, apparently he was with us about a fortnight or so ago with a gun-shot wound?"

"Yes that's right." Sean confirmed. "Is that what the problem is? Has there been some complication?"

"No Mr Sullivan, perhaps you had better come in and the doctor can explain everything to you, Mr Molloy has expressed a wish for you to be fully informed now. He's in Ward F14." Sean could hear the sympathy in the nurse's voice but was nevertheless optimistic all would be well.

"We'll be there in twenty minutes." He said hurriedly and hung up the phone before the Sister had chance to comment further.

When Abi and Sean rounded the corner of the corridor leading to ward F14 neither of them had any idea what they were expecting. One thing they were definitely not expecting was to be met outside the door to Frank's room by Gerald Goldblaum.

"GG?" Abi stopped in her tracks. "What the hell are you doing here?"

"GG?" Sean's question was directed at Abigail. "The GG from Austin?"

"Yes. Sean Sullivan meet Gerald Goldblaum." Abi hurriedly introduced the two men then nodded turning back to GG, waiting for an answer to her question.

"Frank called me four days ago." GG began. "Said he had more information on the Harrison story and could I fly over. I met him at his house the following morning where he did indeed give me some great info about illegal mining and commando raids and arrests by the FBI." GG smiled at Abi. "Seems your story was only the tip of the iceberg Miss."

"It was indeed GG, but Frank could've told you that over the phone, why did he want you over here?" Abi asked again.

"Apparently he also wanted me to tape his confession, figured I could use this information as well as a side bar to the story, at the same time he ensured the police made sure to keep their facts straight."

"What confession?" Sean's eyes were dark now, he felt he already knew what was coming but hoped he was wrong. The thought of Frank spending the rest of his life in prison did not sit well with Sean.

GG pulled out his iPad, scrolled through a few pages and then opened up his photograph file.

"He sent me this." He said simply, turning the screen so Sean could see but Abi could not.

"Shit!" Sean exclaimed. "Shit, Shit, Shit!"

"Show me." Abi demanded, trying to crane her neck to get a view of the screen.

GG looked to Sean for permission. Sean, remembering what Sam had told him about lying to Abi knew that withholding the truth would be just as bad.

"It's not pretty Abi, it's a photograph of Steele." He said.

"Why would Frank have a photograph of Aaron?" Abi did not connect the dots.

"He's dead Abi." Sean added gently. "Frank has killed him."

"That's a photograph of Aaron Steele dead?" Abi whispered, wide eyed and suddenly aware her heart rate had jumped massively. She began to gasp for air, holding her chest, her palms sweaty and her head spinning.

Sean caught her and guided her to a chair over by the wall.

"Head down Abi, breathe as deeply as you can, you're having a panic attack." He squatted down in front of her and held her hands. "It's OK Abi, just breathe, it'll pass."

After a few minutes Abi's heartrate began to slow and her head spin decreased to mild dizziness although the nausea remained. She looked up with tears in her eyes.

"It's OK Abi, Sam told me to expect something like this, it's part of the PTSD, you need to tell Dr

Hargreaves next time you see him." Sean stroked her cheek gently, smiling reassuringly at her as he did.

Abi had decided on a psychiatrist named Dr Hargreaves, so far she had only seen him a few times and he had warned her it could be a long process.

"Can I see it now?" She asked eventually in a croaky but determined voice.

"Sure?" GG asked with concern.

"I'm sure GG, show me the picture please." Abi nodded and held out her had for GG to pass her the iPad.

GG turned the iPad to face her, displaying the head and shoulders shot of a very dead Aaron Steele, his throat obviously open from ear to ear and a vast pool of blood spread around his head.

"Oh My God!" Abi looked for the briefest of moments before covering her eyes in horror.

"I'm sorry Abi, I said it wasn't pretty." Sean pushed the iPad out of her line of sight and GG understood the hint and turned it off.

"Frank did that?" She looked up at Sean. "Really?" Suddenly her eyes widened as a thought obviously came to her. "Did you send him to do that?" She asked Sean, unsure whether she really wanted to know the answer but it seemed important to ask.

"No Abi I did not." Sean shook his head as he spoke, his eyes never leaving hers.

"Is this why Frank said he wanted some time off then? I thought he just wanted to take it easy for a while to let his wound heal." She was still whispering, as if saying this any louder would somehow make it worse.

"It would seem so." Sean agreed, deciding that to tell Abi he had suspected this was Frank's agenda all along would do nobody any good. "We should go in to talk to him. Has he seen the police yet Mr Goldblaum?"

"Er...yes Mr Sullivan, we've spent most of the past two days trying to tell the police what he had done, where the body was etc. It took a while as Frank's condition has worsened considerably since he was admitted so the police interviews have had to be short and spread out. It wasn't until the police detective called this morning to say Frank's story checked out and they would not be looking for anyone else in connection with the murder that Frank allowed the hospital staff to call you." GG nodded to Sean. "Said he had to make sure neither of you were ever a suspect." He added before Sean could speak again.

"Do you know what's wrong with him GG? The nurse on the phone said it wasn't to do with the gunshot wound." Abi had composed herself somewhat, feeling guilty at the relief she felt at Aaron Steele's death.

"I do Abi, but I think Frank wants the doctor to explain, he's inside, I'll go tell him you're here." GG slipped into Frank's room before either of them could quiz him further.

Seconds later a man in his mid-forties with curly short cropped greying hair, friendly brown eyes behind silver rimmed glasses came out of Frank's room, stuffing a pen back into the top pocket of his white coat, closely followed by GG who waved quietly as he walked away.

"Mr Sullivan?" He enquired extending his hand for Sean to shake. "Shall we sit down?" He indicated the chairs next to where Abi was still sitting. He began as soon as Sean had complied. "Mr Molloy has asked me to explain his condition to you. I think he would find it difficult, I gather you have known him a long time Mr Sullivan?"

"Almost thirty years." Sean said in a dull, flat voice, his intuition was in overdrive, he knew this was not going to be good news.

"There is no easy way to do this you understand, I find the direct approach to be the best." The doctor paused and took a deep breath. "Mr Molloy has advanced Pancreatic Cancer. We found it when we treated his gunshot wounds a few weeks ago. He must have been in some considerable pain for quite a while."

Abi gasped and held her hand to her mouth, tears instantly forming in her eyes. "Oh my God poor Frank." She said quietly reaching for Sean's hand.

"How advanced?" Sean demanded, his eyes never wavering from holding the doctor's gaze.

"I'm sorry Mr Sullivan but I do not expect Frank to last the day." The doctor was blunt but compassionate, his voice loaded with concern. "If he had consented to treatment when we found the cancer we may have bought him a little more time, but there's no way to know for sure and he was adamant that he had to leave as he had something more important to do." The doctor gave Sean a brief glance before continuing. "At the moment he is drifting in and out of consciousness. We have him on intravenous morphine for the pain. He has a PCA pump to administer pain relief as and when he needs it, I have just taken the limiters off it." He paused while he watched Sean digest this information. When he was satisfied Sean was keeping up he continued. "Morphine will supress his respiratory effort but will also considerably ease the pain."

"So you're saying the more morphine he gives himself the faster the end will come?" Sean's voice was hoarse with emotion, the thought of losing Frank was more than he was able to process.

"That's right Mr Sullivan, at this point it is all we can do. I do not agree with allowing my patients to be in serious pain to prolong their life by a mere few hours." The doctor smiled gently at Sean. "He is as comfortable as we can make him. Both myself and the nurses are on hand if you need anything, simply press the call button." He rested a reassuring hand on Sean's arm before stepping aside so both Sean and Abi could enter Frank's room.

Frank appeared to be sleeping as Abi and Sean entered the room, but as he heard the door close he opened his eyes.

"Boss?" His voice was weak and reedy but his eyes were clear as he looked at Sean standing at the end of his bed. "Sorry Boss." He added with a faint shrug.

"I guess it wasn't indigestion then Frank?" Sean said in the lightest voice he could muster, but the tears in his eyes belied his joviality.

"Miss Storm?" Frank whispered, noticing her standing by the door. "That scumbag won't bother you again Miss." By the time he had finished the sentence it was apparent a wave of pain had hit him and Abi rushed to his side, he depressed the button under this right thumb, the little machine whirred slightly and gradually Frank's whole body visibly relaxed again.

"Boss?" His voice was weaker still now and there was a distinct rasp to his breathing. "My knife...Ellie?" He could say no more, the effort was too much but he managed to nod towards the knife in its sheath which was sitting on the little table by his bed.

"I'll see to it Frank." Sean had to swallow hard before speaking, helplessly watching his friend die was almost unbearable, he was rooted to the spot, half of him wanting to hold Frank in his arms, the other half wanted to run.

Abi was staring at Sean, she could sense his dilemma even though she did not understand his reticence. After a moment when Sean had not moved she climbed onto the bed with Frank, rolled him gently into her arms and rested his head on her chest.

"There Frank, you just relax now, we'll take care of everything." She whispered, stroking his cheek and rocking him gently like she would a child. "Thank you for what you have done Frank." She whispered. "I can't tell you how scared I have been that he would come back."

"I...know...Miss." Frank managed, the rasping breathing causing him to have to gulp air in after every word. "Couldn't...die...without...sorting..." He broke off even this laboured talking as another wave of pain cause him to convulse in her arms.

"Press the button Frank." She whispered. "I've got hold of you, I won't let go."

As she saw Frank move his thumb to press the PCA button again, the control slipped from his hand. She quickly reached over for it and laid it gently back into his palm, placing his thumb once again on the button and closing her hand round his so he could not drop it again she said. "Go on Frank, don't be in pain."

But it seemed Frank no longer had the strength to depress the little button, and the pain was still convulsing his body. Abi looked up at Sean, seeing the distraught look in his eyes and sensing he was unable to speak she simply raised her eyebrows at him. He replied with an almost imperceptible nod.

Resting her thumb on top of Frank's Abi gently helped him depress the button again.

"Thank...you...Abi...look...after...Sean." Frank just managed to rasp out the words before the morphine coursed through his system again reducing his breathing to a shallow wheeze.

"Do it again Abi." Sean's voice seemed to come from somewhere off in the distance and Abi had to look up at him to make sure she had actually heard him speak. "Do it again." He whispered, tears coursing down his cheeks, his fists clenched by his sides.

Abi pressed the button under Frank's thumb again, knowing Frank's body was not able to take much more. This time the effect was absolute, Frank's body relaxed completely in her arms and after less than a minute his last breath slowly and peacefully left his body.

With tears running down her cheeks Abi kissed the top of Frank's head and laid him gently back against the pillows. She climbed carefully off the bed and walked round to stand in front of Sean. He was rigid as a pole, silent tears coursing down his cheeks, his arms still straight by his sides, his fists clenched. She reached up and gently but firmly took his face in her hands forcing him to look down at her.

"So, what do we do when I see fear in *your* eyes?"

~**Acknowledgements**~

Although I have personal knowledge of the psychological causes and effects of bullying and related unpleasantness I found the following website to be invaluable in assisting me when writing the more technical parts of this book.

Many thanks go to www.bullyonline.org and the Tim Field Foundation.

For the manuscript I must thank my proof-readers, Lisa Davis and Gordon Smith for picking up all my typos and mixed metaphors!

Also for the fabulous cover design I must thank www.lisadavisdesigns.co.uk - go check out this website where you'll find all sorts of great creative genius.

Cover   Photo   © Jk3291 | Dreamstime.com - Lightning In The Sky Photo

© Jeff Kinsey | Dreamstime.com

If you have enjoyed CROSSED STEELE, please consider putting a rating and a short review on the Amazon site from which you bought it. Reviews and rating make a huge difference to Independent Authors, it doesn't need to be a critique, no essays necessary, just a few words will do nicely.

Many thanks,
Claire.

Finally, for more from Claire Smith look for :-

NO MORE BUTTERFLIES on kindle and in paperback from Amazon.

http://smarturl.it/NoMoreButterflies

No More Butterflies is an emotional roller coaster of a ride, combining an enduring love story with heart-breaking reality. It is a gritty, fast paced tale of manipulation, rejection, abuse, love, honour and friendship. Having faced them all our heroine Emma learns to stand on her own two feet, damaged but determined and still capable of giving her all for what she believes to be right.

This surprisingly uplifting psychological drama, with dark moments and romantic overtones, deals with the subjects of domestic psychological, physical and sexual abuse and the lasting damage these do to their victims.

It covers twelve years in the lives of two initially unconnected girls, Emma and Helen, both the victims of some form of abuse and the very different consequences this abuse has to both their lives.

There are some dark and tragic moments as Emma stumbles from one emotional or physical disaster to the next from the ages of sixteen to twenty-eight. Ultimately it is the realisation of all her clichéd romantic dreams which provides her with the trigger she desperately needs to enable her to take control of her own life. It makes her realise the only way to no longer be a victim is to stop relying on others for emotional and physical stability and to stand on her own two feet. It gives her the courage to face her fears and to do what is right for her daughter.

Helen, on the other hand, uses abuse as a weapon with which to defend herself from a world she cannot understand. In reality the abuse she has suffered is difficult to define and the line between legitimate psychological damage and inbuilt character traits is blurred.

The two girls' lives come together with devastating effects.

And :-

A STORM RISING (Storm Series Book 1) on kindle and in paperback from Amazon.

☐ h ttp://smar turl.it/AS R.k

As the newly appointed wedding reporter for The Boston Globe, Abigail thought she had left her troubled past behind her. Life for Abi had always been tough but after meeting Aaron Steele it really ought to have carried a government health warning.

With the battle raging between her own damaged psyche and her need to do the right thing, is Abigail setting herself up for defeat or can she overcome her fears and let her true personality help her triumph. Her inbuilt self-loathing and distrust of others drags her inexorably downwards until she hits crisis point.

With her life, her sanity and her journalistic future on the line Abi must learn when to call for help and most importantly, who she can trust.